WAGER'S PRICE

Soulkeepers Reborn, Book 1

G.P. CHING

Second Edition: October 2017

eISBN: 978-1-940675-24-4
ISBN: 978-1-940675-33-6
v 1.0

BOOKS BY G.P. CHING

The Soulkeepers Series

The Soulkeepers, Book 1

Weaving Destiny, Book 2

Return to Eden, Book 3

Soul Catcher, Book 4

Lost Eden, Book 5

The Last Soulkeeper, Book 6

The Grounded Trilogy

Grounded, Book 1

Charged, Book 2

Wired, Book 3

Soulkeepers Reborn

Wager's Price

PROLOGUE

A single spotlight cut through the dark and expectant theater, centering on the purple suit and red bowler hat of Victoria Duvall, Performance Architect. In other venues, she might be called a ringmaster or monsieur loyal, but not here. The show the audience came to see required more of her than a pointed hand and reassuring voice. This performance promised a display of discipline, teamwork, and *reform*. Victoria was both proud and honored to showcase all three in the achievements of her students.

She swept one red-gloved hand upward, her wild gray hair and wrinkled skin at odds with the youthful way her back arched with the gesture. Victoria might have been the oldest thing in this theater, but her body, like her wit, was supple and quick. It had to be. Nothing on stage was ever simple. Every movement was a dance, every syllable devoted to the cause of entertainment.

Two stories above her, a boy gripped a massive iron hoop as wide as he was tall. The curved bar of the aerial apparatus was too thick for his small hands, a child's hands. His knuckles whitened with the effort. His muscles twitched.

Come on, boy. This is your chance, Victoria thought, sending him a reassuring smile.

Across the stage, a young woman in a peacock-blue dress spread her arms in the deliberate, inviting way of a practiced performer. With a deep breath, she released a pristine note—as pure as sunlight—that danced across Victoria's skin. The singer's cheeks still held the slight pudge of youth, but the effect of her voice was timeless.

A woman in the front row began to weep.

On cue, the boy pushed off the platform and swung high above the stage, a monkey hanging from a hollow moon. The set below him, designed to look like a dark, forbidding forest, ignited into flames. Heat blasted over Victoria and the awestruck faces of the audience.

Victoria beamed as the boy executed a series of acrobatic stunts above her. He lifted his body into a handstand inside the belly of the hoop as flames licked his fingers, his youthful complexion reddening in the heat. The tension in the theater was palpable, the guests tipping forward in their seats, wringing their hands. And now, the pièce de résistance.

The boy sprang from the hoop, performed a quadruple twisting flip, and landed squarely on a burning branch in the set below. At first, the audience erupted into applause, then gasped as the inferno raged, consuming the boy, costume and all.

Victoria brought her hands to her mouth in exaggerated concern. It was all part of the act of course. Harmless pyrotechnics.

With a flip and a tuck, the burning boy dismounted the branch and dove, headfirst, toward the unforgiving stage. This was the test, the moment when his hard work would pay off. The moment when he would prove that a bad boy who works hard can be redeemed. That a former delinquent can accomplish the extraordinary. That miracles are possible if you believe.

But Victoria's feigned fear turned to genuine horror as the boy failed to pull up as intended. His skull cracked against the stage, a bone-chilling snap emanating from the region of his neck.

No. An icy chill crawled the length of her spine. For a moment, she couldn't breathe.

Naively, the audience applauded. They could not see what Victoria did.

"Close the curtain," she whispered. The stagehand obeyed as the young woman in the peacock dress finished her song. Red velvet hissed along its track behind her.

The clowns arrived, their ever-silent, alabaster faces trained on the blood, on the odd angles of the boy's body. Like a swarm of bees, they circled the scene in their black-and-white-striped shirts. Victoria backed away as one slid a hand into the boy's chest, as if the skin and bones of his torso were insubstantial, and extracted something slippery and bright, a silhouette that twisted like a sheet in the wind.

For a moment, Victoria stared, transfixed, unable to process what was happening. The clown raised the slippery thing to its black lips and inhaled. The light extinguished. A deep sense of dread overcame Victoria. She wasn't sure what that bright slip of a thing was, but there was something *wrong* about what she'd just witnessed, wrong about them, about this night.

The clowns rolled the boy inside a thick sheet of plastic and hoisted him onto their shoulders. What would they do with him? It was not enough to hide the incident. Parents must be notified. There were laws. Procedures.

A familiar face appeared among them, motionless against the bustling throng of black and white. *No, it couldn't be.* She'd been a fool. Of course there would be repercussions. What was seen could not be unseen.

The clowns closed in again, this time on Victoria.

Unlike the boy, she would not go easily. She had secrets of her own. With a flash of her red gloves and a twist of her shoulders, Victoria dissolved into a column of purple smoke. As she disappeared, her red bowler hat dropped to the stage with a dull *thunk* and rotated three times on its felt rim before coming to a complete stop.

One of the clowns retrieved the hat, spun it between his white-gloved fingers, and stared into its empty belly. Without a sound, he crushed the red felt into a ball the size of his fist and cast it aside. The next act was about to begin.

And the show must go on.

❧ I ❧

DEVIANT JOE

Superheroes are lawbreakers. They lie. They're violent. Batman's secret identity wouldn't be necessary if everything he did was above reproach. Good guys hurt people. That's the nasty truth. The difference between a good guy and a bad guy has everything to do with perspective and even more to do with who gets caught.

Finn Wager didn't think of himself as a bad guy, even though at the moment he carried a black mask and planned to break into his school in the middle of the night. He thought of himself as a visionary, a mastermind keen on leaving his immortal mark on history, or at least the sophomore class of Beaverton High School.

Finn's brainchild was a group called Deviant Joe, a four-member team whose antics enjoyed a huge internet following. As Deviant Joe's ringleader, he came up with the best pranks anyone had ever heard of and used his resources and his inconspicuous nature to make things happen. His best friend, Mike, contributed the muscle and the vehicle. He'd been held back a year in kindergarten and was one of only a few sophomores who could already drive. Jayden, on the other hand, served as gasoline on the fire. He always figured out a way to up the entertainment factor. That left

Wyatt. Poor, overly educated Wyatt. He tapped the Deviant Joe brakes, and if Finn was honest, kept them from some pretty bad decisions on occasion.

Tonight would be Deviant Joe's last epic prank of the semester. If they could pull this one off, they'd be living legends. Finn wouldn't think of disappointing his fans.

"You ready to deploy, Finn Shady?" Mike asked, his brown hands still gripping the steering wheel.

Finn Shady, Mike's inside joke, a gangsta name for his best friend. Only, in real life, Finn wasn't cool, dangerous, or thug-like in any way. Whatever an adult pictured in their mind when they thought of *shady*, Finn was the exact opposite. In fact, he was the sort of kid most adults disregarded entirely. Nondescript. Average. Forgettable. His pale hair and blue eyes made him look much younger than his fifteen years. And thanks to his ADHD meds, it was impossible for him to gain weight. His wiry and hollowed-out physique roughly resembled that of a whippet.

But Finn used all of that to his advantage. If flying under the radar was a testable school subject, he'd have scored in the gifted range. Other than that, gifted he was not. His grades were as below average as his height and weight. Aside from being handy with a computer, being invisible remained his one and only true talent.

Finn stared across the hood of Mike's black pickup truck at the frosty turf of the football field behind Beaverton High. It was quiet and dark and bitterly cold. "Yeah, let's go."

Mike opened the door and unfolded his legs toward the pavement. No matter how large the vehicle, his six-foot-four body looked like a grasshopper behind the wheel. He tugged his hood up over his dark hair, and his face disappeared into shadow. Finn jumped out the passenger side and strolled toward Jayden and Wyatt, who stood bundled against the cold, their backs to the chain-link fence surrounding the football field.

"Uh-oh," Mike whispered. "Unless Wyatt lost thirty pounds,

grew six inches, and became white in the last three hours, that is not him."

"Shit," Finn said. He couldn't make out the face of the person next to Jayden. Not with his features hidden in the shadow of his hood. "If it's not Wyatt, who is it?"

The big guy gave him a tentative look and then a shrug. Finn fidgeted with the cuff of his glove. As they approached, Jayden and the mystery guest pushed off the fence and turned to face them. Clearly not Wyatt, the fourth member of Deviant Joe, but Vox Parker, Jayden's older brother.

"Where's Wyatt?" Finn asked.

Jayden chuckled. "Flu. He called me an hour ago. Fever, spewing, the works. His mom won't let him out of the house."

"Why didn't you text us?" Finn frowned.

Jayden shrugged. "We don't need him. We have Vox."

Although he exchanged glances with Finn, Mike remained strangely silent, probably having the same reservations Finn did. Vox had a reputation. He was a senior, who shared his brother's edgy sense of humor. Only Vox was much worse. He smoked weed like it was his full-time job and had been arrested three times for petty theft and vandalism. Rumor had it, he should have graduated last year but flunked out. Stupid and risk-taker were a deadly combination. Replacing Wyatt with Vox was like replacing the brakes on a car with a turbo booster.

"Uh, you know, I'm not feeling this without Wyatt. He's part of Deviant Joe," Finn said.

Mike nodded. "Yeah. Forget it. Let's save this one for another time."

But Jayden spread his hands and shook his head. "Are you kidding me?"

"Man up, flake-tards," Vox chimed in. "I didn't drive out here for nothing."

Vox could bring out the worst in Jayden. Their friend didn't usually push back like that. No one loved a prank more than Jay, but a leader he was not. Usually, he went along with whatever Finn and Mike wanted to do. But Vox disrupted the chemistry of the group. He was older. He didn't have to answer to the social protocols of a bunch of sophomores.

Before Mike or Finn could make any more excuses, Vox scaled the fence and dropped to the other side. With a glance at Finn, Jayden curled the corner of his mouth. "Come on, Finn. It's fine." He followed his brother's lead.

"I hate that guy," Mike murmured.

"Me too." Finn adjusted his backpack on his shoulder.

The light from Vox's phone cut through the darkness. "Wave to the camera, boys!"

Finn raised his arm to block his face. "Cut it out, Vox. Are you kidding me? You better not be recording."

"Come on over and delete it." Vox slid the camera into his pocket and scratched his pockmarked face. Finn glanced at Mike. The big guy didn't look happy, but he seemed resigned. With a guy like Vox in the mix, it was no longer an option to walk away. If they did, he and Jayden would do what they came to do, take the credit, and hold on to that video to deflect the blame. That's how Vox operated.

"Well, Finn Shady?" Mike sighed. "Can't do this without you." One slap to Finn's shoulder and his best friend scaled the fence.

Even as he cursed and told himself he was an idiot, Finn started climbing. He dropped to the other side and unzipped his backpack. "Don't forget these." Finn tugged four black masks from his pack.

"Masks?" Vox scoffed.

"Deviant Joe wears masks. We can't upload our faces. Not to mention, there are cameras in the school." The masks they always wore were Mardi Gras style, the type that only covered the top half of a face and had bulbous noses.

"I'm not going in there with a dick on my face."

"It's not..." Finn paused. Now that he thought about it, the mask did resemble a dick. He put his on anyway. So did Mike. Jayden took his from Finn but didn't put it on. Vox wouldn't touch Wyatt's. Whatever. They wouldn't get caught. But if they did? He had no problem letting Vox take the heat. He shoved the unused mask into his backpack.

"HORU, what's the status on the security system?" Finn asked, tapping his earpiece. A hologram of a woman with cat ears and a swishing pink tail manifested in his peripheral vision. HORU stood for Holographic Omni Recognition Unit, a completely interactive artificial intelligence, the product of a childhood spent tinkering with system components most kids could never afford —fewer still would know what to do with it. Finn's HORU resembled a cross between Katy Perry and Hello Kitty but possessed the brain of a supercomputer.

She twitched her whiskers and sashayed her hips. "Taking a nap, Finn. It is an antiquated piece of code. No first name."

"Not every system can be as sophisticated as you, HORU."

She smiled and flicked her tail. "Will that be all?"

"For now, but don't shut down. I'll need you later to record what we do."

"The drone is in your bag. Launch when you are ready. I'll do the rest." She winked an anime eye at him.

He tapped his earpiece and her hologram disappeared.

Vox leered at him in mock horror. "Be honest, Wager, are you or have you ever had a physical relationship with your artificial intelligence unit?"

"No!" Finn made a vulgar gesture in Vox's direction.

"Then what's with the cleavage and the figure and the... uh... tail?" Vox smirked.

"She's an AI unit. She can think for herself. I told her to choose a body, and after sifting through the entirety of online photos and videos, she chose to be a woman who looks like a cat. I had nothing to do with it."

Vox chuckled. "Yeah, right."

"Seriously. I've spent a lot of time and my father's money making HORU smart. I didn't spend a dime making her beautiful or catlike. She did that herself."

"Would you like me to manifest myself as an old woman?" HORU said in his ear.

"He's not worth the trouble," Finn whispered. "But do me a solid and wipe that video he took of me from his phone."

"Consider it done." Her voice faded like a purr.

Finn adjusted his pack on his shoulder and led the way across the football field to the back entrance of the school. Some things HORU could help with, others he had to do on his own. The locks on this door were the old-fashioned kind, only used by the equipment manager. A square of duct tape over the strike plate to keep the latch open and the door appeared locked. No way to tell the truth without pushing on the bar. It had taken a faked bloody nose for Finn to sneak down here, but the duct tape worked like a charm.

The janitor left at midnight, but Finn crept into the demolished locker room anyway, hood up and carefully quiet, just in case. He motioned the others forward only when he was sure they were alone. When he reached the second-floor hallway, he removed his backpack and retrieved his trusty roll of duct tape once more.

"What do you need that for?" Vox asked from the shadows of the stairwell.

Finn pulled over a chair and stood atop it. He'd covered the security camera in silver strips in under thirty seconds. "In case the security system decides to wake up." He jumped off the chair. "Vox and Jayden, you start pulling the desks out. Mike and I will do the balloons."

Jayden grinned and headed for the first classroom. "This is going to be classic!"

Vox didn't move. "I, ah, can't lift anything because... well, I don't want to. I have to do balloons."

Finn rolled his eyes behind his mask.

"It's okay. I'll go help Jay," Mike said. It was the only option. Finn wasn't exactly the brawn of Deviant Joe. He wasn't even sure he could lift a desk.

Breaking out the balloons and the pump, Finn handed a pack to Vox. He opened it and stretched one red balloon between his fingers.

"Where's the pump Jayden was supposed to bring?"

Vox shrugged. "Forgot."

Finn didn't say another word. He got to work inflating balloons. Jayden and Mike came out with the first desk. The hallway was narrow and they placed it in the middle. Even with one pump, the space should fill up quickly. This was an old building, built before building codes, when extra-wide hallways meant more space to heat. He tied off a blue balloon, tossed it into the air, and tapped it toward the desk.

As Finn reached for the next balloon, he paused, glancing at Vox. The older boy had dropped his unfilled balloon and now pinched a cigarette between his lips. He pulled a lighter from his pocket, flicked the flame to life, and inhaled deeply.

"Put it out," Finn said. *What a waste of space.* He should have known. Vox wasn't going to help at all. And now he had to keep the a-hole from starting the school on fire.

"No."

While Finn and Vox locked stares, Mike and Jayden returned, hauling the second desk. Both dropped their cargo and glared at the cigarette incredulously.

"Are you high?" Finn continued. "This school was built in 1898; everything is wood. There are smoke alarms everywhere. One of those goes off and we're toast."

Mike stepped into Vox's personal space with his hands on his hips. Big and broad, his physical presence was intimidating as hell. Vox's eyes twitched wider, but he inhaled that cigarette without even giving Finn the benefit of a response. Mike pressed a finger into Vox's chest. "If this goes south, it's on you."

Jayden shifted silently in the background. Finn could tell by his expression he backed Mike, but he feared Vox too. He had to live with the guy. It is hard to stand up to crazy when crazy knows where you sleep.

Sure Vox would cave under Mike's steady stare, Finn casually inflated another balloon and set it free. But the tension between Vox and Mike only grew by the second, the situation made more surreal by the fact Finn, Mike, and Jay still wore the bulbous-nosed masks. He didn't know how Vox could stand the pressure, those dark, pointed faces accusing him. But the guy just kept puffing away, filling the small space with the stench of cigarette smoke.

Finn glanced up at the smoke alarm and then at the cloud billowing from Vox's mouth. That was it. Something had to be done. Quick as he could, Finn snatched the cigarette from between Vox's lips and crushed it out under his sneaker.

It was not the best idea he'd ever had. Vox's initially surprised expression morphed into rage. He landed a fist under Finn's chin, knocking his mask askew and sending him windmilling back-ward. He landed squarely on his ass.

Although Finn would've liked to pop off the floor and return blow for blow, it was a good minute before he could even catch his breath. He lay on the floor, head throbbing and lip bleeding. Deviant Joe had never resorted to violence before, and Finn cursed at Vox for ruining the prank. This was over. As soon as he could stand, he planned to leave.

Mike wasn't as forgiving. He removed his mask and grabbed Vox by the collar. "It's on you." A tan fist connected with Vox's jaw, sending the guy reeling. But Mike didn't stop there. He fisted Vox's shirt to keep him from falling, then shoved him against the wall. Right, left, left, left, right. Vox's head snapped on his neck and his lip sprayed blood.

"Stop, Mike! Stop!" Jayden leaped onto Mike's back in a vain attempt to protect his brother. All Finn could think, as a second spray of blood left Vox's nose, was that Wyatt would have stopped this. He would've tapped the brakes like he always did. But this? This situation was out of control. Blood? Injuries? How would they explain this in the morning?

"Mike!" Finn tried to get his buddy's attention, to snap him out of it.

"The choices we make have consequences," a low, cool voice said.

Everyone stopped. A stranger loomed at the threshold of the hall. Not one of the usual janitors. Not a teacher or administrator. A parent? The man was sophisticated, graying at the temples, wealthy. Someone important. The sweater he wore had a logo sewn in for a brand Finn's dad wore occasionally—an expensive brand—and his watch flashed gold and diamond as he wrapped one hand around the back of Vox's neck. Mike backed away, one step, then two, blood still dripping from his fists. A smile broke out across the stranger's lips. Translation: *gotcha*.

"It was a prank," Mike said. "We'll clean all of this up."

Jayden nodded. "It got out of hand. No harm done, though. Vox will be fine."

The man's gaze, gunmetal gray, coasted to Finn. "What do you have to say for yourself?"

"It's only a few balloons." Finn pushed himself off the floor. He ran the back of his hand across his mouth and it came away bloody.

The man stared at the blood on Finn's hand, then swept his gaze to Vox, whose nose still dripped blood. A muscle in the stranger's jaw twitched. They were busted. Goose bumps freckled Finn's arms, and his lips parted, but his voice caught in his throat. Oddly, he was afraid to ask who the man was. Why? He couldn't be sure.

Those gray eyes fixed on Finn. "You can always tell the ones with potential—they don't leave their toys in their boxes." The man's teeth flashed.

"What?" Finn glanced at Mike, but the big guy was similarly befuddled.

The man reached into Vox's pocket and retrieved the guy's lighter. Vox barely flinched. Whether from fear or shock, Jayden's brother looked catatonic. His nose continued to drip blood, but he didn't wipe it away. Maybe Mike had hit him too hard. Maybe he was having some kind of a fit.

"Who are you?" Finn forced himself to ask, pushing aside his unease.

The stranger shook his head, eyes blinking slowly. "A model citizen looking out for the needs of my community." The man flicked the lighter and a flame appeared near his thumb.

Worming anxiety took root in Finn's stomach, beyond the getting-caught kind. It was hard to breathe. The stranger oozed malice. Why hadn't he threatened to call the police or their parents? Unless his intentions were far more sinister.

The stranger lifted the lighter.

Whoosh. The flame billowed to the ceiling, catching the woodwork and licking up the walls.

"Run!" Mike yelled. He grabbed Jayden by his hood and yanked him toward the door.

"My brother!" Jayden struggled against Mike's grip.

Finn moved for Vox, intending to drag Jayden's brother away from the stranger. But before Finn could reach the boy's pale hand, the flames bloomed, dividing the hall in two. Now, no one could reach Vox without burning to a crisp.

For an agonizing moment, Finn stared the stranger down, the heat baking his face. The fire alarm wailed. The man would have to move soon. The fire must feel as hot to him as it did to Finn. But he didn't. The stranger stood in the fire, flames closing in, and winked at Finn, a wicked smile spreading from ear to ear. A psycho. A suicidal maniac.

Mike grabbed Finn's upper arm. "What are you doing? Are you crazy? Come on!" He dragged him to the stairwell, through the locker room, and out onto the frosty turf of the football field. Finn removed the duct tape as he passed through the door, more reflexively than out of careful thought. By the time they'd made it to the fence, the flames were visible through the third-floor hallway windows. In the distance, a fire truck's horn accompanied police sirens.

"Should we run?" Finn asked Mike.

The big guy didn't answer. His eyes were wet. Jayden rested his hands on his knees. "Vox! Oh God, Vox!"

Jayden lurched toward the school again, but Mike grabbed his arms and held him back. "There's nothing you can do. We tried. We all tried. We need help." Mike's eyes flashed to Finn's. He was speaking to both of them.

There was no covering this up. No way out. The school was burning down. It hit Finn then, full force. Vox might already be dead. Murdered. He dropped his backpack and waited helplessly as the swirling lights closed in.

❦ 2 ❦

PARIS, ILLINOIS

Hope Laudner zipped her skirt and jammed her foot into one of her pristine white shoes. Most of the other girls were already gathered in the corner of the Paris High School gym, waiting to begin their dance squad's halftime show. It wasn't her fault she was late. Her father's truck had died on the way into town. Why her dad insisted on driving that corroded robin's egg-blue monstrosity was beyond her. Honestly, it made her blood boil. The thing was almost thirty years old.

Asking her mother for a ride was out of the question. Malini Gupta Laudner was a semifamous journalist with her own show on CNBC, and today, she was in Saudi Arabia interviewing some woman who was the first leader of something. Hope couldn't remember.

Three months and she'd turn sixteen and be able to drive herself. She couldn't wait.

She finished with her shoes and flipped up her head to fasten the bow over her auburn ponytail. "Holy Chr...istmas! What are you doing here?"

The man standing behind her had spiky black hair, blue eyes, and an internal glow to rival the LED lightbulb above her head.

He also had two mighty wings that arched and twitched over his shoulders and smelled uniquely of sunshine and citrus. The good news: he wasn't a stalker. The bad news: he was annoying as hell.

"I have a message for you." His stubbled chin was tight with perpetual concern.

Hope lowered her voice. "This is the girls' locker room, Gabriel. You can't just pop in here."

"No one can see me but you. This is important."

"Important or not, it'll have to wait. I'm on." She grabbed her pompoms and headed for the gym.

"Souls are missing, Hope. Henry needs you to investigate. And now *He* is involved." Henry was Death, as in the Grim Reaper, an immortal in charge of ushering the dead into eternal life. *He* was big "H" he. The Big Good, God, the Alpha and Omega, I Am, or whatever else people called Him these days. Hope had no doubt that if both were concerned, the situation was serious. That didn't mean she was willing to get involved. She had her own life, her own problems. And she sincerely doubted that two immortal beings needed her for anything.

"He's an all-powerful being," she said. "Tell him to snap his fingers and figure it out."

"Hope!" The look of horror and offense on the angel's face made her take pause.

"Ugh! I'm sorry, all right? I don't have time for this right now. I have our performance, and then I have to study for my calculus exam. And I had to run a mile to get here in the freezing cold because my dad's truck broke down. And I have menstrual cramps if you must know."

Gabriel cringed. He hated when she talked about female issues. She smirked in response and headed for the rest of her team. He followed.

"Someone or something is reaping human souls. You are the last Soulkeeper, the Healer. This is your job—"

"Stop!" She held out her hand. "I told you. I can't talk to you about this now."

His wings flexed in annoyance.

She rolled her eyes. "Meet me at my window at midnight. I'll be ready to listen." He opened his mouth but she didn't wait to hear what he had to say. She jogged from the locker room to join her teammates, fists pumping in the air.

"Go, Wildcats!" She cartwheeled into a flip-flop, landing a full twisting layout and then executing a perfect toe touch. The crowd went wild. She shook her poms in the air and gave the bleachers her widest smile.

The other girls took their positions around Hope, who formed the point of a triangle at the center of the gym. The music throbbed and she popped into action. She kicked, leaped, and tumbled, concentrating on synchronizing with the other girls, rather than doing her best. As a Soulkeeper, she could naturally run faster and jump higher than a normal human girl. In fact, she could flip and tumble better than anyone alive. She was born with physical dexterity that far exceeded her teammates'. Her rhythm, though, that was exceptional thanks to hours of practice. Hope stomped and shook her hips like a pop star, the music carrying her through move after move. By the time her squad hit their last beat, every person, student or adult, was on their feet. The entire Paris High School gym rumbled with applause.

If not for her keen vision, Hope might have missed the two state troopers who silently slipped into the gym through the side doors. But as she jogged toward the locker room with her team-mates, their brown uniforms were unmistakable. A man and a woman closed in on her, the woman's hand hovering near her gun. The man gently cupped her elbow and pulled her aside, ushering her into the hall outside the gym.

"Hope Laudner?" the man asked, his eyes narrowing on her.

"Yes?"

He frowned and shook his head. "Why is it always the pretty ones?" he mumbled.

"What's the problem?" she asked.

He gave her a disappointed grunt. "You need to come with us."

❦ 3 ❦

TRIALS AND TRIBULATIONS

"**I**f I'm going to represent you, you need to tell me the absolute truth." Finn's father leaned against the window of his home office, tie fastened firmly, his demeanor at odds with his surroundings. Despite standing only a few steps from their kitchen, James Wager, Esquire had replaced Dad or Pop or even Mr. Wager. The older man didn't look happy, but he did look lawyerly.

"I told you the truth. I told you everything."

"You keep saying that, Finn, but your stories don't match up."

"Stories?"

"The police interviewed you, Jayden, and Michael separately, and all of you said exactly the same thing, aside from one very significant factor."

"What factor was that?"

He gave Finn a look that suggested he should know. He didn't.

His dad sighed. "Each of you described a stranger who started the fire. The only problem is, you each described a different stranger."

"Huh?" Finn straightened in his seat.

"You claim you saw a wealthy, dark-haired man with graying

temples—a man of average stature. Jayden says the stranger was a tall, dark-skinned man with no hair and casual, urban clothing. Mike swore he saw a woman with a pixie cut and a large, squared jaw. Now, obviously you are all lying. The question is why."

"I-I don't understand." Finn held his head. "I'm telling the truth. That's who I saw." *Why would Mike and Jay lie?*

"Stop, Finn." His father rested his hands on the desk. "Vox woke up today."

Vox's injuries required hospitalization for third-degree burns and smoke inhalation. He'd been unconscious for days. Everyone worried he'd never wake from the resulting coma. As relieved as Finn was concerning his recovery, he couldn't imagine what Vox might have said about the stranger to anger his father.

"He told us what happened. He admitted to starting the fire and said you tried to stop him. There's no need to protect him anymore."

Finn opened his mouth to insist he hadn't lied, but the words caught in his throat. What *had* happened the night of the fire? The facts blurred and faded like he was trying to remember a dream. Was the stranger a figment of his imagination? He tried to picture what happened in his head. Vox gripping the cigarette in his mouth. No, that was earlier, wasn't it? The red plastic lighter. Who was holding it? The man's features wavered in Finn's memory, and he couldn't be sure. He questioned everything he thought he remembered.

"Unfortunately, Vox's confession only goes so far. You were party to breaking and entering. With regard to the fire, they can say you helped him—a principal in the second degree—or they can call you an accessory to the crime. Either way, there's no denying your involvement. The best we can hope for is a lenient sentence."

"But I didn't do anything."

"Are you now suggesting you didn't put the duct tape on the door with the intent of causing it not to lock correctly?"

"No, but—"

The two stared at each other for a beat, the tension in the room growing. His father's disappointment was a palpable thing that went beyond his tightly pressed lips and stony expression. Under his professional demeanor, he was ashamed; Finn could sense it. Something in his eyes said he was looking at a lost cause.

"What sentence do you think I'll get?"

His dad's eyebrows bobbed. "Might be anything from a hefty fine with community service to prison."

"Prison?" Finn lifted from his chair.

The older man rubbed his eyes with his thumb and forefinger and shook his head. "You took part in an act of vandalism orchestrated by an organized group of delinquents, Finn. The court could view Deviant Joe as a gang and your actions as gang violence that threatened a human life. You burned down a school—"

"I didn't!"

"It doesn't matter if it was you holding the lighter or not. You were there. You were part of it. The prosecution is going to be out for blood on this one. No one likes to see a rich kid get away with something. No judge in this state is going to go easy on you."

"But prison?"

"You're fifteen. You'll go to juvenile detention."

At that, Finn blinked rapidly against the prickling in his eyes. Juvie. At least Wyatt wasn't part of this. Everyone had protected his identity and confirmed Vox as the fourth member of Deviant Joe. Finn wouldn't be able to forgive himself if Wyatt had suffered the consequences of that night simply by being associated with them in the past.

Finn didn't truly think he'd end up in prison or juvenile detention. He'd gotten away with so much for so long, the idea seemed impossible. He took solace in the fact his dad was on his side, the best defense attorney in the state, if not the country. Still, the specter of punishment loomed large on the horizon.

A thick hand landed on his shoulder. His father had moved to his side, some of that professional stiffness bleeding from his demeanor. "I'm a good lawyer, Finn. I'm going to do my best to keep you out of prison. Your job is to do exactly as I say and keep your nose clean."

It took a second for that to sink in. Then Finn stood and allowed his father to pull him into his arms.

҉

FINN SLUMPED IN AN UPHOLSTERED CHAIR IN WAGER MANOR'S living room, looking oddly alive among the museum pieces his dad called furniture. Finn didn't spend much time in this room, but since he was not allowed electronics of any kind for another week, it was as good a room as any.

Today was the day. Mediation. His dad had insisted he stay home this time. All of them, Jayden and Mike too, had agreed to stay home, to leave it to the adults. They'd have a decision later today.

It would have been nice to see Mike or Jayden or even Wyatt, but he wasn't allowed. Sure, his dad said he was permanently grounded, but that wasn't the real reason. He'd overheard his father on the phone with a partner. Finn's best chance for a lenient sentence lay in a case based on relative accountability— proving Finn's involvement was less than the other boys', that he'd cooperated more fully with authorities. Basically, his dad had to keep Finn apart from his friends so he could throw one of them under the bus should the opportunity present itself.

Finn didn't like it, but he felt helpless to change it. He rubbed his palms on his thighs. It was going to be okay. Vox had admitted guilt. There was no reason not to believe him. The guy had a record. Why would they come down hard on Finn?

The whine of the heavy front door brought him to his feet. When his father entered the room, Finn could tell something had gone terribly wrong. He was ghost white and looked as tired as Finn had ever seen him.

"Dad?" Finn swallowed hard.

"I tried my best. I pulled every string I knew to pull. The arbitrator wanted to make an example of you."

"Why?"

His father tilted his head and grimaced. "Our money, Finn. Who I am. Have you heard of affluenza?" His father waved a hand in front of his face. "The arbiter could not tolerate a boy with so many advantages getting away with arson."

"It wasn't me!" Finn's hands balled into fists, but his father silenced him with a shake of his head.

"He watched all of your Deviant Joe videos, Finn. You admitted to the police it was you in the videos, and Mike's lawyer was quick to point out that he didn't have the means or the equipment to produce the quality of video you posted. He called you the mastermind. Even though you didn't start the fire, he suggested it was you who created the environment that encouraged Vox's behavior. Vox's lawyer went so far as to suggest you egged him on, that he was trying to outdo your last prank when things went horribly wrong."

A weight had formed in the pit of Finn's stomach, and he swallowed a lump in his throat. "So, what did he say? What's my sentence?"

His dad took a deep breath and leveled his eyes on Finn. "He gave you a choice: two years in juvenile detention—"

"Prison. Two years in prison."

"Or you complete high school at Lakeview Alternative School."

Finn shook his head, huffing incredulously. "Lakeview? How is Lakeview different from juvie? The building is surrounded by barbed wire. They wear orange jumpsuits, Dad."

"If you take the alternative school option, you'll be home nights, weekends, and holidays."

"They want me to go there all two and a half years?" Finn

couldn't believe this was happening. He paced the room, his face growing hot, sweaty. "Everyone knows Lakeview is rough. It's where they send the really bad kids; kids who attack their family members with knives and guns. Kids who hold up convenience stores."

"Kids who start fires," his dad said softly.

"I won't survive thirty minutes in that place." Finn hugged himself, his bony shoulders feeling even thinner than usual.

"Prison is worse, Finn."

"I won't graduate with my class. No sports. No clubs. My entire high school career will happen behind barbed wire." Finn's heart jackhammered. The air pressed in heavy and hot around him.

"Finn, these are your choices. We agreed to live with the outcome of mediation. There are things I can try, but in the short term, you've got to decide. I think you should consider Lakeview."

Finn's knees gave out and he sank to the couch.

"There's more. You're banned from school grounds… starting immediately."

So that was that. He was cut off. He could get a degree but he couldn't go to school, not really. There'd be no more football games. No more plays. No more parties with friends he saw in class. "Can I go to my room?" he asked, the words barely audible. He was going to lose it. On top of everything else, he didn't want his father to see him cry.

"Go ahead," his father answered. "I'll need to give them your decision by the end of day tomorrow. Think about Lakeview."

Finn rushed from the room, his eyes burning.

❧ 4 ❧

A DISTANT HOPE

"I didn't do it!" Hope yelled as her father ushered her into their Paris, Illinois home.

"There was an eyewitness," Jacob Laudner murmured. "And a video."

"It has to be a fake. Someone is setting me up."

Calmly, Jacob flipped the switch to start a fire in the fireplace and lowered himself into his recliner. It was easy for Hope to forget that her father was once a Soulkeeper who could wield water, in all its forms, like a weapon. He looked so ordinary now. In fact, at the moment, he looked exhausted.

"I can't get used to this thing," he said, staring at the fireplace. "Whatever happened to chopping wood and using a match?"

"It went out with TV antennas." Hope hugged her chest, holding herself together at the seams. "What are we going to do? The police think I sold someone heroin. I've never even *seen* heroin. I don't even know what it looks like. I was in the library that night. Nowhere near where the video was taken."

"It looked like you."

"There's been a huge mistake."

"Sit down, Hope." With a groan, she lowered herself onto the sofa. She wanted to cry. She desperately wanted to get past convincing her dad she was being set up and speed straight to breaking down in his arms.

Her father stared at the flames for a moment, the light bringing out the slight gray in his hair at the temples. "I believe you."

"Thank God. Now wha—"

He held up two fingers to silence her. "Is there something you're not telling me? Something about the bigger picture?" He lowered his chin and raised an eyebrow in her direction. "Impersonation of a Soulkeeper is a tool of the dark one."

"The Devil? Demons? Fallen angels?" She wiggled her fingers in the air boogeyman style. "You and Mom and Gabriel have been teaching me and training me my entire life, and I've never even seen one. If what you tell me is true, there are none left."

"There are ways—"

"I don't *want* to be a Soulkeeper, and I sure as hell don't want to be the last Soulkeeper. This is stupid." She slammed the back of her head against the couch.

The fire crackled, charging the air between father and daughter.

"We don't get to choose," he said softly. "There are things we can control in life and things we can't. Being what you are, the last Soulkeeper, is not something you get a choice about." He picked an invisible piece of lint off his sleeve. "Your mom and I know better than anyone. We lived your fate. You can dance with your friends and you can do the same homework and take the same tests, but you are not like them, Hope. You're supernatural."

"Shhh. Dad just stop!" She covered her ears.

"Did Gabriel come to see you today?"

Hope groaned. "Yes. He's been nagging me for weeks." She checked the time. Midnight. "Gabriel, are you here?"

The angel manifested in the center of the family room, scratching the stubble on his jaw. He leaned against the fireplace, exchanging nods with Jacob before speaking. "I tried to tell you, Hope. You've been called. If you deny the call, you prolong the inevitable."

Her face tightened as an idea, too horrible to consider seriously before, formed bright and possible at the forefront of her mind. "*You* did this to me."

"I warned you."

Her mouth fell open. "You did this to *force* me to do whatever He wants?"

"*You* did this to you," Gabriel said in a low and steady tone. "Your avoidance has set events into motion that even I cannot change." He pressed a hand into his chest. "I have a message for you, Hope Laudner."

"Again with the message business. Fine. Tell me your message." Hope tugged at her skirt, suddenly aware she was still in her dance squad uniform.

"You have been given full Healer status. Today, your initiation ends."

"Amen."

"Beware, Soulkeeper. Use of your healing power will now come with a price. Use your gift sparingly and wisely."

"Sparingly. Any way I can turn that into not at all?"

"Where is your triquetra?"

"The necklace you gave me? In my room. Why?" She hated wearing the symbol of her calling. Hated even more using it.

"You must visit the In-Between as soon as possible. Souls have gone missing. As you know, there is only one fallen angel left on Earth and he is currently living in Los Angeles. While he's the most likely suspect, Death has confirmed that the loss of souls does not coincide with his location. We think there's something else going on here."

The In-Between was the home of Death, Time, and Fate—the Immortals. Although Hope knew she could go there and ask them for help, she avoided it at all costs. The process of getting there was uncomfortable and the Immortals themselves, often testy. Unless demons charged up her street tomorrow, she'd rather lick a public toilet.

"Do you think Lucifer has found another way?" Jacob scooted to the edge of his chair.

"That is what He would like Hope to find out." Gabriel's eyes landed fully on her.

"Ugh! So, you're saying in order to make this all go away, I have to cooperate, like it or not? Fine. What do I need to do to get my life back?"

Gabriel met her gaze, his eyes burning like blue fire. "The first step is for you to plead guilty to selling heroin."

5

ADMISSIONS

F inn didn't come down until the next morning. His fitful night's sleep left his short hair twisted to the point his scalp ached, but he made no effort to smooth down the wild blond mess on his way to breakfast. What did he care? Personal hygiene was the least of his problems.

"I bought donuts," his father said. "Angel Creme. Your favorite." His words were hesitant and tempered, like he wanted to say much more, wanted to ask for Finn's decision but was holding himself back. The closest Angel Creme was ten miles away. How long had he been up?

"Thanks."

Finn selected a glazed donut and took a small bite. He wasn't hungry. Who could think about eating at a time like this, when his life hung in the balance? His father sipped his coffee but didn't bother with a donut. Instead, he took a deep breath and stared at the box.

At the disappointment evident in his father's sagging shoulders, Finn's chest ached. The only picture in his father's office was of Finn's mother, who'd died when he was a baby. Chances were his father would never have another child. His dad deserved a kid he could be proud of, a descendant who could live up to his expectations. Instead he got Finn. Would he avoid telling anyone where his son went to school? Or that he had a son at all?

"Dad, I'm—" A lump formed in his throat and he tried unsuccessfully to clear it away. "I'm sorry." The words were soft and tore apart when they hit the air between them.

His dad frowned and reached under his glasses to pinch the space between his eyes. "It's not forever. I'm going to fight this."

Finn nodded.

The chime of the doorbell interrupted the funeral-like atmosphere. His dad scrubbed a hand over his face and glanced at his watch. "Who the hell could that be?"

"It's not even eight," Finn said.

"I gave the housekeeper the day off. I'll get it." He moved for the foyer. Finn followed more out of curiosity than anything else. A strange sensation prickled the underside of his skin, strongest at the base of his skull. He scratched the back of his head as his dad tugged open the massive wooden door.

The man on the front stoop did not belong there. He did not belong anywhere. Not in this neighborhood. Not on any day but Halloween. Costumed in tall black riding boots and stretchy khaki jodhpurs, he wore a red jacket with tails and three gold buttons secured over a white shirt. On his head, a black bowler hat covered silver hair. A white-gloved hand tipped the hat as he bowed, gray eyes trained on Finn. For the duration of the bow, the man clutched a leather messenger bag to his side as if it contained something precious.

"I apologize for the early hour. I'm looking for Finn Wager." The man's voice was low and smooth as silk. The round wire frames of his glasses bobbed with the contraction of his smile.

"I'm Finn."

His parchment skin wrinkled at the corners of his eyes, his cheeks twitching with a hint of a yellow-toothed smile.

"Who are you, and what do you want with my son?" Finn's dad asked.

The man tugged a white riding glove from his hand. "Allow me to introduce myself. I am Wulfrid Ravenguard, admissions counselor for the Revelations Institute."

Finn's dad shook his head—clearly he'd never heard of it—but he politely shook the man's hand anyway.

"We heard of Finn's *predicament* and wanted to discuss possible enrollment," the man qualified.

His father backed up a few steps, opening the door wider. Ravenguard stepped into the foyer.

"How exactly would you have heard of Finn's predicament?"

"Revelations is a progressive alternative school. We make it our business to find students we feel have the potential for excellence."

His father shook his head, squinting like he didn't quite believe the man's story.

"You must have the wrong person," Finn said. What was the point of lying? If there was some mix-up, he'd know soon enough anyway. "I'm not... Nothing about my academic record would suggest I have a potential for excellence."

"Revelations considers a number of factors other than academics. Be assured, we've already spoken to Judge Warren. Our school is a viable legal option for you."

With a frown and a scratch to the hair above his ear, Finn's dad allowed the door to close. "Come in. Sit down." He pointed a hand toward the dining room.

The stranger's eyes swept over the Chihuly glass sculpture at the center of their table. *Potential for excellence* his ass. Evidently, he was after a sizable donation. Finn suspected he'd recognized the Wager name, his father's name. The Revelations Institute wanted to cash in.

The man removed a brochure from his leather satchel before sitting down. At well over six feet tall, he dwarfed the chair beneath him. Finn hadn't noticed the man's above-average size before, probably because the stranger had been standing on the recessed front porch, but across the table from him, it was impossible not to notice.

"As you can see, Revelations is a state-of-the-art facility." The picture he pointed to looked like it belonged on an Ivy League campus. No barbed wire fences here. Red brick, ivy-covered walls, well-groomed gardens. The glossy pages resembled an advertisement for a spa.

"Where is your school, Mr. … Er…" Dad rubbed his palms together, unusually rattled by the visitor.

"Wulfrid Ravenguard, admissions counselor." He cleared his throat. "Revelations calls a small island in the Atlantic home, off the coast of Nova Scotia. It's called Veil Island. It's fairly close to Oak Island."

His father raised a finger. "The one with the pirate treasure? Money Pit Island, they call it, right?"

"That's the one. Still a mystery after all these years." The old man grinned.

Finn's dad crossed his arms. "The island is Canadian?"

Mr. Ravenguard tipped his head to one side. "Privately owned. Finn won't need a passport. Our private buses and ferries provide all transportation to and from the island."

"So, it's a boarding school?" Finn asked. "I couldn't come home on nights and weekends."

"Ah… You're comparing it to your local Lakeview Alternative School." Ravenguard rubbed his chin. "But there is one thing about our school that is quite different from your Lakeview."

"And that is?" Finn's father asked.

"Our results." Ravenguard threaded his fingers together. "Revelations Institute uses modern teaching techniques to instill and restore responsibility, discipline, and confidence in troubled teens. We borrow heavily from classic circus, modern dance, and theater education programs to provide a rehabilitation experience available nowhere else. The payoff is a one hundred percent success rate. Everyone who attends our program experiences a level of achievement postgraduation beyond their wildest expectations."

"Surely it can't be a hundred percent. Nothing is a hundred percent. You must have some kids who never get with the program," Dad scoffed.

Ravenguard shook his head. "Actually, our success rate *is* perfect. Even the darkest delinquents respond to our methods. When Finn leaves Revelations, he will be a model citizen."

Model citizen. Finn's mind flashed back to the fire in the school. The stranger had described himself as a model citizen defending his community. A coincidence for sure, but the memory unsettled Finn.

"Finn? Finn?" His father shook his arm. "Are you all right? You're pale as a ghost."

"Fine. It's just a long way away," he lied. No use trying to explain how the mimicked words affected him. His father believed the stranger in the school was a lie, a cover-up for Vox.

Mr. Ravenguard adjusted the brochure in front of Finn. "It is true, you will not be permitted to leave nights or weekends. However, unlike Lakeview, you can finish the program in as little as one year. In some exceptional cases, as little as a semester."

Finn shook his head. "That can't be right. I'm a sophomore. I can't graduate in a semester."

"No, you can't graduate high school, but you might graduate our program."

Dad lifted a hand. "Are you saying there is a possibility of completing his sentence in one semester at your school?"

"It is not unheard of, Mr. Wager."

"Is that legal?"

The man reached into his bag and retrieved a roll of parchment bound with a string. He untied the string and flattened the scroll on the table.

"This is a legal document, an agreement between the Revelations Institute and the state. It gives Revelations the last word on a pupil's rehabilitation."

His father frowned. "Why is it on this... papyrus?"

"Marketing materials," Ravenguard said. "You are welcome to confirm the details with Judge Warren."

Finn's father extended a finger in Ravenguard's direction. "Before I confirm anything, I need to know more about what you do to these kids. Circus techniques? It sounds dangerous."

Ravenguard took a deep breath, leaning back in his chair where the shadow of the dining room curtain fell across his face. "Rehabilitation requires change, Mr. Wager. Your son won't be coddled. However, you can take solace in the fact that we haven't lost a student yet. Haven't had so much as a serious injury."

"But—"

"How much will it cost?" Finn asked, cutting off his father's next question.

His father inhaled through his teeth. "That's not a factor, Finn—"

"It's free," Mr. Ravenguard said quickly.

"What?" His father dismissed the comment with a wave of his hand. "That can't be right. I thought you said it was a private school."

"We teach performance," Ravenguard said, spreading his hands. "We put on a show at the end of every semester. A popular, exclusive, award-winning show. Patrons pay thousands per seat. Along with donations from our benefactors and alumni, the show earns us everything we need. Besides, Revelations' owner is a spiritual person who wants nothing more than to guide young people to success. Profit is not a primary motivation."

Finn nudged the brochure closer and thumbed through the glossy photographs. The standard dorm room looked like something from a five-star hotel. Two full-sized beds with plush comforters. A Persian carpet. A maple end table with a gilded bedside lamp. When he flipped the page, a black-and-white photograph of a girl in a beaded leotard smiled back at him as she walked a high wire with a long bar in her hands. The caption read, "Students at Revelations Institute lead well-balanced lives."

"It's coed?" Finn asked, staring at the girl.

"Oh, yes. Ms. D believes students thrive in diverse groups."

"Who's Ms. D?"

"Our headmistress, Victoria Duvall."

Finn's dad squirmed in his seat, glancing at his son and down at the glossy brochure. Eventually, he gave in to his curiosity and picked up the booklet to inspect each page. "We're supposed to give Judge Warren a decision by this afternoon."

Mr. Ravenguard adjusted his glasses on his nose and folded his hands again. "I'm afraid our offer of admission will not last that long. You see, spots at Revelations fill quickly. I can only hold the space for the hour."

"An hour?" My father's jaw dropped. "This is a life-changing decision."

A small, sharp laugh escaped Ravenguard's tight lips, then morphed into a cough that he covered with a closed fist. "Please excuse me. Something in my throat."

"Can I get you some water?"

"No, thank you. You may be interested to know, Mr. Wager, that Revelations has a trial period. If Finn gets to the island and feels the institute is a poor fit, he has a full week to communicate that to you. At that time, you can choose to have him transferred to Lakeview. We only want what's best for everyone involved."

Dad stood. "Would you excuse me for a moment? I'd like to make a quick call to Judge Warren."

"Do you want me to come?" Finn asked.

"Not this time, Finn. I want to talk to Judge Warren alone first. I'll call you back to discuss once I'm done."

"Okay."

He left the dining room and disappeared in the direction of

his office. Finn drummed his fingers lightly on the table. Revelations seemed too good to be true. There had to be a trick to it. If he pulled the right thread, would the entire sweater unravel?

"Can I ask you something?" Finn thumbed the corner of the brochure nervously.

"Of course."

"Will you be offering admission to Mike Carson or Jayden Parker?"

"Jayden is on my list to visit next. Michael, however, is not. He didn't meet our admissions requirements."

Finn rubbed the tips of his fingers on the table. "This is a scam. Mike gets straight A's and is a two-sport starter. No way would you guys choose me over him."

Ravenguard looked appalled. "The criteria for success at Revelations isn't the same as that of traditional schools. You, Finn, are the mastermind behind Deviant Joe, are you not?"

He swore under his breath. "Yes."

"Such a task must have required leadership skills, organization, technical aptitude."

"Maybe."

"Your friend Michael is very good at following directions, but Revelations is more interested in a different type of intelligence." The man tipped his head.

Finn dug at something under his thumbnail.

Ravenguard adjusted his glasses, analyzing Finn. "This Michael, he's a good friend of yours?"

Finn nodded. Mike was his best friend. He couldn't bear to think of Mike at Lakeview, or worse, in juvie. Not while he was in the lap of luxury at Revelations.

"A better friend than Jayden?" Ravenguard asked softly.

Finn furrowed his brow. What kind of a question was that? "I've known Mike longer."

"I see. Suppose I told you that, should you enroll and promise to work exceptionally hard, the boy could come too?" Ravenguard flashed a wolfish, yellow grin.

Finn swallowed. "I'd like that."

Ravenguard's smile widened, and he removed one white glove before extending his hand. "Very well. Do we have a deal?"

Slowly, Finn reached out to shake Ravenguard's hand. The man's nails were exceptionally long and filed to a point. They dug into the meat of his palm as the admissions counselor pumped his arm.

"Ouch!" Finn recoiled, blood bubbling through the resulting scratches.

Ravenguard slipped his glove back on. "Pardon me. I don't know my own grip."

It struck Finn again how oddly Ravenguard was dressed, his unusual height, the strange way he'd shown up out of nowhere. He narrowed his eyes, studying the gold buttons on the man's red coat. There was some sort of symbol embossed on them, like an ornate X. "Is that the school uniform?" Finn asked.

"No." Ravenguard straightened in his seat, his face impassive. "Your uniform will be provided upon your arrival." He did not go into further details to explain his manner of dress.

"Finn, can you come in here?" his father called from the hall.

"Excuse me." Finn slipped around the table and hurried to his father's office. His dad closed the door before speaking.

"Everything checked out with Judge Warren. This is a legitimate option, Finn. What do you think?"

"Sounds better than Lakeview."

"I'm not thrilled with the location," his father said. "The brochure says I'm not allowed to see you until the end of the semester, and even then, I have to come to you. You won't be able to leave the island until you've graduated the program."

"If I work hard, I could be done by summer. I could be reenrolled in Beaverton High School by next fall."

"Judge Warren confirmed that as well. He said he hadn't

discussed the option because the school is by invitation only." His dad rubbed a thumb across his chin. "I don't know, Finn. My bull-shit meter is running high on this one. What if this is like a mili-tary-type school? Do you think you could handle that?"

Finn shifted from foot to foot. He wasn't military material. No way. He got winded carrying the groceries in from the car. But he couldn't face two and a half years at Lakeview. "I want to go. I'll work hard. You heard what he said: if Revelations isn't a good fit, I can ask to transfer. It's the obvious choice."

"I think it's a practical option. I'm just not sure it's the best option for you." The bags under his father's eyes seemed to darken. "You don't have to do this. Lakeview may take longer, but..." He shook his head. "Circus training techniques? It's very odd, and this is an awfully hasty decision they're forcing on us."

Finn rested a hand on his father's arm. "It's only a school, not outer space. It's temporary. I can transfer. If it's bad, I'll come home."

"I wish things were that simple."

"What do you mean?"

"I mean, when you're older, you will realize that sometimes the bad things that happen to us don't leave us when they are over. Sometimes they change us forever. Even a short time in the wrong place can be life altering, Finn. I'll go along with whatever you decide, but don't believe for a second you have nothing to lose."

Finn paused. He had to try this. Ravenguard was right. He was the leader. He'd gotten Mike and Jay into this; now he needed to get them out. "I want to go. I want to try Revelations. I think in the long run this will be better for me."

With a nod of resignation, his father smoothed the fabric of his perfectly ironed dress shirt. "Okay. Let's tell Ravenguard."

The two returned to the dining room where Mr. Ravenguard was standing at the window, his hands clasped behind the tails of his red riding jacket. When he turned toward them, the light reduced him to a slender, featureless silhouette. "Have you come to a decision?"

"I've decided to attend Revelations," Finn said firmly. He'd stopped himself from saying "try Revelations." If he was going to do this and succeed in the shortest amount of time, he had to believe in himself. He would survive.

Ravenguard bowed at the waist. "I am honored. Now, just one more formality."

He flipped back the leather fold on his bag and retrieved another scroll, this one sealed with burgundy-colored wax pressed into the same symbol as on Ravenguard's buttons. The admissions counselor cracked the seal and unrolled the parchment.

"Fancy." Finn's father reached for the pen he kept in his front shirt pocket.

"Please, Mr. Wager, use mine. The ink is in the school's colors. We like to save the contracts as mementos of the day the student decided to change for the better." Ravenguard handed him a fountain pen, the old-fashioned kind.

Finn's father slid the scroll closer and like a good lawyer, actually read every word. "Wow, you weren't kidding when you said the owner of Revelations was a spiritual man. What's this about Finn's soul?"

"Think of it as an oath. The students must commit mind, body, and soul." Ravenguard shrugged. "It's part of our method."

The pen lowered to the second line and in illegible cursive, James Wager scrawled his signature in muted burgundy ink.

Ravenguard took the pen and gave it a hard shake. "Excuse me for asking, but for legal reasons, is there a biological mother? Revelations must have a release from both parents."

"His mother passed away."

Ravenguard frowned. "I am sorry for your loss."

"It was a long time ago. Finn was only a baby."

"Regardless, the loss of wife and mother is a burden at any age." He offered the scroll and pen to Finn.

Finn's hand trembled as he gripped the gold implement and lowered it to the parchment. He wanted this. Revelations was his best option. The ruby ink melded with the parchment and his name glided and looped on the line.

Ravenguard clapped his hands and laughed. "Very good! This is only the beginning. Get ready, my boy. There's no time to lose. The bus will pick you up tomorrow at noon."

The man rolled up the parchment and rose from his chair to leave.

"Wait," his dad said. "Do you have a card or something? What if we need to reach you or have questions? What should he pack?"

Ravenguard plunged one gloved hand into his bag and retrieved a small rectangle of paper, handing it to Finn's father. "Pack what he'd normally wear for a long weekend. He'll be issued a uniform and anything else he might need during his stay with us." He shook Finn's hand and then his father's. "Pardon me, but I must go. There are others deserving of my time today." With long strides, Ravenguard showed himself out.

Finn and his dad drifted after him, his father gripping the man's card as if an explanation for this strange twist of fate was written on the back. Ravenguard slipped out the door and closed it behind him.

"Oh, wait!" Finn's father called. "I forgot to ask about Finn's medication." When Ravenguard didn't respond, his father ran after him muttering, "I better catch him." He gave a small huff when he opened the door. "What in the name of…?"

Finn surveyed the circle drive around the fountain and the long tree-lined stretch of pavement that led away from Wager Manor. Not a hint remained of the visitor or his vehicle.

Mr. Ravenguard had vanished.

✥ 6 ✥

TRAINING DAY

"It's freezing out here!" Hope hugged her puffy coat tighter around her and rubbed her mittens together. There were a few trees in her parents' expansive yard, but they provided little shelter from the winter wind.

"Show me you remember what I've taught you and this won't take long," Gabriel said. He selected an apple from the basket next to him.

Reluctantly, Hope removed her mittens and pulled the triquetra from her neck. She pressed the looping silver pendant into her right palm and focused her energy on the warm spot that blossomed over her heart. Light arced around her fist, forming a razor-sharp disc of white energy. She readied herself, knees soft, mind quiet, and released a long, steadying breath.

"I'm not going to make this easy," the angel said.

"I'd be disappointed if you did."

He threw the first apple. It soared close enough for her to slice it in half with a simple jab of her fist, but that wasn't the end. The two halves morphed into flying black spheres the size of sparrows. She tossed the triquetra, slicing one on the way out and the other as her weapon boomeranged into her opposite hand. Now there were four spheres that buzzed around her like large, angry flies.

"You'll have to mean it or this is going to get messy." Gabriel tossed another apple.

Hope flipped backward, catching three in a rotation of her arm, then tossed the disc to cut through the new apple before missing the last tiny segment. The pieces multiplied again.

"This isn't fair. I do mean it. You're keeping my power from working."

Gabriel shook his head. "Your power stems from redemptive love. If you don't work from the heart, if you don't connect with the light that is within you, the light within your hands is no more powerful than if it were made of steel." He tossed more apples.

"Ugh!" Kick, punch, slice. She knocked the attacking fruit away, some pieces so small now that they swarmed her eyes and ears, the stink of rotting fruit filling her nostrils. "I can't do this!"

"You can. You've done it before."

She moved faster, her body becoming a blur of deadly force, but all she managed to accomplish was to replicate her tormentors. She hated this. Hated every minute of having to do everything the way Gabriel said. Hated that she had to *be* this. She didn't want to be the last Soulkeeper, even if the honor came with strength, speed, and the ability to heal. What kind of life was this?

The swarm of rotting apples knocked her to the ground, covering her in a sweet, sickly stench. They wedged in her ears, up her nose, between her lips. She gave up. The ring of energy in her hand reabsorbed into the triquetra.

"Very disappointing," Gabriel said. With a snap of his fingers, the apple pieces disappeared.

Hope remained on the ground, tears streaming down her face. "I don't want to do this, Gabriel. I'm not ready."

He sat down beside her, his wings folding away inside his illusion. He wiped away her tears with a glowing thumb that smelled of citrus and sunshine. "I wish it was up to us. We don't get to choose our trials, only our reaction to them. The trial is upon you, Hope. You must choose to make yourself ready."

"Or what? What will happen if I fail?"

Gabriel's face contorted with pain. "We could l-lose you to the darkness."

"I thought you said I couldn't die. Last Soulkeeper. Maintainer of the balance. I'll come back."

"There are other ways to be lost that don't involve death," he murmured. His entire body dimmed with the heavy emotion in his voice. "If that happened, I'm not sure what would become of me. I will have failed you and my creator in the worst possible way."

Her heart ached to see Gabriel like this. It wasn't his fault. He'd been fated with his role just like she had. She didn't honestly believe she was in the kind of danger he suggested, but she couldn't watch him torment himself like this.

"I'll try again." She swallowed the lump that had formed in her throat.

Gabriel smiled, his glow returning with his revived disposition. "You can do it. I know you can."

She pushed off the frozen ground, hoping she wouldn't disappoint him.

Selecting an apple from the basket, Gabriel tossed it gently in one hand and waited for her to ready herself. He was being more patient than usual. Perhaps he was as concerned about her flailing abilities as she was.

She squeezed the triquetra, the ring of light forming in her right hand. This time, as the warmth spread across her heart, she did what she'd been trained to do, the thing she'd avoided. It was what she hated most. With total humility, she opened from within, gave herself over to the light. Whenever she did this, sliced open her soul like a cantaloupe and let her sloppy innards pour out, she thought of her mother. Not Malini her adoptive mother, but Abigail, her biological mother who'd died when she was born. She had a vague memory of her, white-blond hair, eyes the color of the ocean. Abigail had sacrificed herself for Hope. The surrender scared her more than anything. Everything she was, good or bad, was exposed in that moment. The effect was empowering, but it required a whole lot of vulnerability to get there.

Gabriel threw the apple.

Opening her eyes, she leaped to her right, circled her arm, and sliced through her target. It exploded in a shower of multicolored sparks and disintegrating curlicues.

"That's my girl," Gabriel said.

"It completely sucks, you know. Every lie I've ever told, the stuff I took without asking, the test I cheated on—"

"You cheated on a test?"

Hope rolled her eyes. "It all comes back to me. And her, Abigail, I can almost see her face. It sucks. I don't like to go there."

He nodded. "It's enough to know you can if you must."

"So, are we done?" She stowed the light back into her triquetra.

"Out here, yes, but you must visit the Immortals."

Hope looped her pendant over her head and shoved her hands back into her mittens. "I'm too tired."

"Hope..."

"It's a legitimate thing. When I cross over to the In-Between, if I don't have absolutely calm energy, it feels like I'm being shredded by broken glass. And it's not like when my mom went over. I'm not thrown into Fate's realm. No, I land in the woods where I writhe in pain alone until I'm strong enough to walk to one of the immortal realms."

"That's because your gift came directly from God. Malini's came from Fate. I'm sure she would help you with the transition—"

"I don't need her help. My going is unnecessary. Besides, I have to know what questions to ask and at this point, I don't. I have no idea what is going to happen to me tomorrow."

Gabriel groaned. "If you wait until you need them, it could be too late. Promise me you will go over when you are rested."

She frowned.

"Hope," Jacob called from the side of the house, arms crossed against the cold. "There's someone here to see you."

Gabriel took her by the shoulders. "Promise me."

"I promise," she said.

"It begins," he whispered, his body dissolving into the light.

"Creeper," she said toward the empty space. Hugging herself, she climbed the slight hill toward her adoptive father, not at all prepared for what awaited her inside.

REVELATIONS

P eople say God doesn't give a person more than they can handle. Finn wasn't overly religious, but given his current situation, the entire notion proved a steaming pile of horseshit. Every time he tried to wrap his mind around the fire, his fate, and Revelations Institute, his thoughts spun out like tires on loose gravel. How had things gone from a room full of balloons to reform school so quickly? Was he doing the right thing signing up for Revelations? He wrapped himself in a blanket and lowered himself to the floor behind his bed, his knees pressed into his chest.

There was a knock at the open door, and his father leaned into his room. "I came to say good night."

Translation, he came to check on him. Finn sighed. "I'm fine, Dad, all things considered." He wasn't fine. Not by a long shot. But what good would it do to dwell on the inevitable?

"Well then, I suppose your punishment is over. Use all the electronics you want. Get it out of your system. You're not allowed any at Revelations."

"Really?" Finn asked.

"Really." His father rumpled his hair and kissed him on the top of the head, then left in the direction of his bedroom.

Without hesitation, Finn slipped in his earpiece. "Hey, beautiful, did you miss me?"

Light flashed and HORU appeared. She twitched her cat ears. "Very much. I've been so bored. Where have you been?"

"I have to go away for a while. After what happened at the school, I got in trouble. I'm leaving tomorrow to attend a reform school called the Revelations Institute. They don't allow AI units."

"The authorities blamed you for the fire?"

"All of us."

"I recorded what happened. Would it help?"

"What are you talking about? The drone was still in my bag."

"Correct. You forgot to take the drone out, so I used the micro camera in your earpiece. You said you wanted me to record—"

"Play recording."

"Playing now." HORU pointed to the wall and the video projected from his earpiece onto the smooth beige paint. It began exactly as he remembered it. The desks, the balloons, the cigarette. Vox clocked Finn, and the camera shook as he tumbled to the floor.

"Nice view of the ceiling," he berated himself.

"The earpiece camera can only be manipulated in the direction you are facing."

"I know, HORU. I'm only thinking out loud. That black section must be my mask. Crap, I can't see anything to the right of center." He watched Mike pound the living daylights out of Vox, disappointed the skewed mask blocked his view of the stranger.

"Is there sound?"

"Affirmative."

She turned up the volume right as Mike was backing off and Vox's body stiffened into a cardboard cutout of himself.

It was a prank, Mike said. *We'll clean all of this up.*

Jayden added, *It got out of hand. No harm done, though.*

There was a stretch of silence where everyone stared at Vox.

It's only a few balloons, Finn's own voice said in the recording in response to an unasked question. "What the hell? There was a man there. He asked me a question before I said that."

"I do not detect another voice on the recording."

"I don't understand. He was there."

"I am sorry my recording is not of better quality, Finn. Without the drone, I cannot—"

"Never mind, HORU. It's okay." It wouldn't have mattered. The judge had a confession from Vox. Finn wasn't being punished for starting the fire. He was being punished for being in the wrong place at the wrong time. That wouldn't change with proof of the presence of a stranger.

"HORU, can you find any information about Revelations Institute?"

"Please wait." HORU's hologram froze, her giant blue eyes blinking slowly for a few seconds. "I found one hundred twenty-five references to the Revelations Institute. There is an interesting correlation between these references and net worth. I found an email that illustrates this."

"Read email, HORU."

"From Bai Jian, CEO of Cartwrithe Enterprises

To: Senator Heather Carter

Ms. Carter, although Cartwrithe board of directors did not agree to contribute to your campaign, in honor of the relationship I shared with your father, I would like to give you a gift equally as valuable: the secret to my success. I've obtained a ticket to a performance at a theater called the Revelations Institute for your use. My courier will deliver it to your office. Attending the performance is auspicious, and I attribute our fourth-quarter results to my previous attendance. This is an exclusive opportunity. Seats run $10K apiece or more. Do not miss it. I will see you at your victory celebration."

Finn laughed. "Ten thousand dollars per seat! That would

explain why tuition is free. So, this Jian starts a rumor that attending a theater performance is lucky and Revelations is set."

"There is subjective evidence that attending the performance brings positive outcomes. Bai Jian increased his net worth by $30 billion after his attendance, and Carter was reelected subsequent to hers. Perhaps the performance provides a networking experience for the attendees."

"What about the graduates?"

"My quick search found no reference to any graduates at all. There is a website for the school but no other sites link to or reference it. There are strict laws about sharing information about minors publicly, which may contribute to the lack of information. Also, because Revelations Institute exists on a private island, Veil Island, I am unable to connect to the systems there. Ownership of the island is held by a shell corporation registered in Costa Rica, but a high frequency of financial transactions map back to Los Angeles, California. Would you like me to do an extended search? It will take a minimum of twelve hours."

Finn thought for a moment. "No. That's all, HORU." Nothing she found would make a bit of difference. The place checked out with Judge Warren. This was what he needed to do.

"How long will you be away?" HORU asked.

"A minimum of one semester. I'm going to miss you."

"I'll miss you too, Finn."

"Would you like me to shut you down before I go?"

"If it is all the same to you, I'd rather stay awake."

"Done."

"What would you like to play tonight? Star Sniper? Dragon Slayer? Demon Squad?"

"Demon Squad. Let's kill some undead bastards."

"Loading level fifty-two."

Finn picked up the wireless controller and got comfortable. He planned to play until the sun came up.

"YOU'RE A SURVIVOR LIKE SHE WAS," FINN'S DAD SAID. HE PACKED Finn's ADHD medication in the corner of the Louis Vuitton trunk he'd lent his son to take to Revelations. The luggage used to be Finn's great-grandmother's and had literally been through the war. World War II to be exact. The trunk had survived the Nazi occupation of France, as had his great-grandmother, a feat, considering the rest of her family was imprisoned or killed. It was oft rumored that Great-Grandma Mimi was a traitor to her country, family, and friends and had survived by cooperating with the Nazis during the Vichy regime.

"She didn't call attention to herself. She did what she was told and what she had to do to survive. That's how I like to remember her." Finn's father wasn't only talking about Great-Grandma anymore.

"I'll do my best. I won't cause trouble. I know how important this is."

His dad closed and locked the packed trunk. "It's just... you can be impulsive. Make sure you take your meds every day as prescribed." Finn couldn't remember a time he hadn't taken his ADHD medication every day. It wasn't as if he could forget. Twelve hours without it and he might crawl out of his skin.

"I will."

"Almost noon. Help me get this downstairs."

Finn picked up one end of the trunk and his father obliged with the other side. He made Finn put on his coat before calling for the housekeeper to hold the door open while they delivered the trunk to the porch. Last night, a winter storm had come through and the fountain was heaped with newly fallen snow. The world looked clean and fresh under the layer of white, full of possibilities.

Finn turned to go back inside, but the rumble of a large vehicle called his attention to the estate driveway.

"Exactly noon," his dad said.

A massive vehicle, more like a tour bus than a school bus, rounded the front of the fountain, brakes squealing as it came to a stop. Bright red with a wave of dark purple beneath the windows, the bus was painted with the silhouette of a winged creature that rose out of a magic hat. "Revelations Theater, Prepare to be Transformed" was printed across the side.

The bifold door opened and tall black boots thumped down the stairs. A woman emerged, her short, dark hair curling under the rim of a black bowler hat. She wore the same uniform as Mr. Ravenguard: khaki pants, red coat with tails. Her jacket sported the same shiny gold buttons with the swirling X.

She extended her gloved hand. "I am Ms. Applegate, admissions counselor for Revelations. I will be driving Finn and the others to the ferry."

"I'm James Wager, Finn's dad." He gave her a warm handshake. "Can I help you load this onto the bus?" He gestured toward the trunk.

Applegate peered at Finn. "They did tell you that uniforms will be provided?"

"Better over-prepared than to go without," Dad said.

Ms. Applegate nodded her agreement, then unlocked the lower compartment under the bus, thanking his dad profusely for his effort as he slid the trunk inside. Finn waited on the porch.

"Are you ready to board, Finn?" Ms. Applegate asked once the trunk was loaded. A broad white grin parted her lips.

"I think so," he said.

"You know what they say?"

Finn shrugged.

Her red lips smirked. "Where one journey ends, another begins." She tipped her hat and raised an eyebrow.

"I'm a phone call away, Finn," his father said, pulling him into his arms. "Don't worry about anything."

Ms. Applegate held up a gloved finger. "Unfortunately, contact with family is prohibited outside of sanctioned visits."

"What?" His father shook his head. "Surely, you allow phone calls… emails… something."

She shook her head. "I am sorry for any confusion. Mr. Raven-guard must have told you, the nature of what we do requires uninterrupted focus and concentration. If we are to promise you big results, we must demand the same level of commitment. Finn simply won't have time for the distraction of home life."

Finn's father frowned. He hugged Finn again and whispered into the ear farthest from Ms. Applegate. "Don't worry. I left you something in the trunk."

Finn wasn't shocked at this revelation. It was like his father to try to bend the rules in his favor. It was kind of his job. Defense attorneys were notorious for seeing morality as a scale of gray.

"The others are waiting, Finn. Time to go." Ms. Applegate swept one gloved hand toward the bus's bifold door.

He'd thought he was ready, but now an icy tourniquet of apprehension constricted his torso. Everything was happening so fast. He closed his eyes and swallowed. *It's only a semester.* Then, as quickly as possible so as not to lose his nerve, he hugged his father and almost sprinted past Ms. Applegate in an effort to get on the bus before he started to cry. Luckily, he had a minute to wipe under his eyes in the sanctuary of the cab before he passed through a black curtain to the passenger area.

"Finn!" Mike called when he entered the aisle. "Back here."

The bus did not have rows of seats like a normal bus but booths like a restaurant or, more accurately, the kind he'd seen in the dining compartment of a train once. He passed six empty booths before reaching the one with Mike and Jayden at the very back.

"Are we the only ones?"

"The only ones from this area," Applegate said. Finn jumped. She'd crept up behind him without making a sound. "There are others," she said. "We've accepted eight new students this semester."

Judging by Mike and Jayden's expressions, her stealthy arrival had caught them off guard as well. They stared at her, slack-jawed and silent.

"Take your seats," she said. "Standing while the bus is in motion is a punishable infraction. We wouldn't want an incident."

Finn incrementally lowered himself onto the seat next to Jayden, never taking his eyes off Applegate. She gave him a tight-lipped smile. "Very good. We'll be on the island before you know it."

She strolled up the aisle and disappeared through the curtain in the direction of the steering wheel. The engine rumbled to life and the bus jerked into motion. Out the window, the snow-covered branches of sleeping trees flew by as the bus accelerated along the manor drive.

"That was odd," Jayden whispered. "I didn't even hear her coming until she was standing right behind you."

"That's what you find odd about all of this?" Mike said. "What about her uniform? It's like a fox hunting costume."

"Fox hunting? I thought they were dressed as ringmasters, like from a circus."

Mike pulled out his phone, tapped the screen a few times, and showed Finn an old painting of people on horseback wearing bowler hats and red coats with long tails. The outfits matched exactly, subtly different from a ringmaster's outfit that usually had a tall hat, dark pants, and unbuttoned coat.

"Why would they dress like they were going hunting?"

Mike shrugged. "Why do they show up on people's doorsteps to recruit students? Seems like an email would be easier."

"Maybe they like the personal touch. Makes the school appear more exclusive?" Jayden said.

"An exclusive school with no tuition?" Mike leaned his head against the back of the seat and stared at the ceiling.

"HORU couldn't find much on the web about it. There was one thing, an email, about the performance being lucky." Seemed ridiculous, saying it aloud.

"Revelations puts on a massive show, twice per year, and most of the world doesn't know the place exists or even how to get to the theater." Jayden spread his hands. "Makes perfect sense."

"Judge Warren knew about it. He agreed to the terms in the contract." Finn shrugged.

Mike shifted in his seat. "It doesn't matter anyway. Weird or not, we're going."

"Yeah, why are we going exactly?" Jayden's face reddened. "Why the hell did you two lie about seeing the stranger?"

"I didn't lie," Finn said defensively. "You did."

Jayden shook his head. "It was a bald black man."

"No, a wealthy older man. White," Finn insisted.

"Bullshit. How could you not tell it was a woman?" Mike said, without a hint of humor in his voice.

A chill coursed up Finn's spine and he rubbed the base of his neck. He shook his head slowly. "Wait... You guys weren't lying? You really believe that's what you saw?"

Mike and Jayden nodded, eyes narrowing in confusion.

"Do you think the cigarettes Vox was smoking were laced with something, like a hallucinogenic drug?" Finn shoved his hands in his coat pockets.

"We all inhaled his secondhand smoke before we saw the guy," Jayden said.

Mike didn't look convinced. "This is like a nightmare. None of it makes sense."

"Hey, don't worry so much. We can handle anything they throw at us. We're together. We have each other's backs. We've accomplished a hell of a lot as Deviant Joe. Mike is strong. You're smart, Jay. We can survive anything." Finn tried his best to sound reassuring.

"You're right. Whatever Revelations throws our way, we'll put in our time and get back to our lives." Mike leaned against the wall of the bus and stared out the window.

"You guys haven't mentioned the creepiest part," Jayden said through a half grin.

"What's that?"

"The swastikas on their buttons. Don't panic, but we may be going to a school run by neo-Nazis."

Finn grunted. "Nice, Jay. They were not swastikas. The symbol was like the letter X but with curved ends, almost a spiral."

"I don't give a flying fig what's on their buttons," Mike said through clenched teeth. "I don't care what either of you think you saw. It doesn't matter anymore." He glared at Jayden. Finn couldn't remember seeing Mike so angry. "We're here because you brought your idiot brother, Jayden. None of this would have happened to us if it weren't for Vox. And now my entire future is up for grabs because unlike the two of you, I don't have a trust fund. So both of you are going to do whatever it takes for us to succeed at this place and not make any waves. That includes not accusing the admissions counselors of committing hate crimes. Got it?"

Finn stiffened as walls went up between his two friends. Fists tight, Jay peered at Mike like he was going to let him have it. But a smirk turned the corner of his mouth and a deep breath morphed into a low chuckle. "You could not be more right if you were missing your left arm. Vox is a human canker sore—no, a blight on the canker sore kingdom. He's my brother, but he's a prick. I should have known better. I'm sorry, man."

Mike stared at Jayden for a second, pursed lips turning into a tight smile. "God help me if I ever become a blight on the kingdom of canker sores."

"I calls 'em like I sees 'em." Jayden held up his fist. "We okay?"

Mike nodded and bumped his knuckles against Jayden's.

"Cool, because if we're going to have any fun in a stuffy,

private reform school like Revelations, we are going to have to stick together." He grinned and bobbed his eyebrows.

"Do you smell that?" Finn sniffed the air. A strong, chemical-sweet scent had permeated the bus. "Smells like a Slurpee."

Mike sniffed. "Yep, the Slurpee machine. All the flavors mixed together." His eyes drooped, and he leaned his head against the wall.

"Blue raspberry," Jayden said. "I gotta…" His head hit the table.

"Jay?" Finn tried to reach for him to make sure Jayden was all right, but he didn't have the energy. He gave in to the weight of his eyelids, slumping in his seat, and fell asleep with his cheek pressed into the table.

❧ 8 ❧

ARRIVAL

Whe hen Finn woke, the scene outside the bus's window was vastly different from the view when he'd fallen asleep. Bright green gardens spread beneath a darkening sky. No snow. They weren't in Beaverton anymore. A long pebbled drive led to a massive brick-and-stone building with gables and parapets and winged gargoyles that overlooked the gardens. Finn's lips parted as he took in the grandeur. The brochure hadn't done it justice.

Jayden shifted in his seat and rubbed the top of his head. "I thought we had to take a ferry?"

"Do they drive the bus onto the ferry?" Finn squinted out the window but couldn't see the ocean in any direction.

Mike smoothed an eyebrow. "I slept through the whole thing?"

"Me too. We all did. And I'm hungry. How long do you think we've been asleep?"

Jayden pulled his phone from his back pocket. "I don't know. My phone is dead."

Twisting in his seat, Mike pulled his phone from the pocket of his coat. "Mine's dead too." He looked to Finn expectantly.

"I didn't bring one." Not exactly true. He suspected his dad had hidden one in his trunk. He would check in private when he was sure the prying eyes and silent footsteps of Ms. Applegate were not a threat.

"We left at noon and now the sun is over there. Late afternoon?" Mike stood slightly to get a better view out the window.

Finn shrugged.

"Please exit at the front of the bus and form an orderly line with the other students," Ms. Applegate called from the front. Finn glanced at Mike and Jayden, then led the way up the aisle. As he exited the folding doors, a light sprinkle of rain dusted his coat, leaving a scattering of dark dots. Tropical humidity hung in the air around him, and despite the rain, he stripped off his parka and tied the arms around his waist.

Revelations Institute was a castle.

He wandered into line and perused the side of the building with slack-jawed wonder. The shadow the looming monstrosity cast over them blocked out his view of the sun. His eyes drifted up the ivy-covered brick, three stories before reaching the gargoyle-lined roof. Finn couldn't see inside. Most of the windows were masked with blood-colored curtains. Except one. Finn's eyes fell on the parted red damask of a wide window on the third floor. A face stared back at him, pale white with black-lined eyes and lips. A clown.

"Do you see that?" he asked Jayden, who was in line behind him.

"See what?"

"In the window." Finn pointed.

Jayden followed Finn's gaze, but the clown was gone. "I don't see anything."

"There was a clown." Finn searched the neighboring windows. The drapes were still parted, but there was no face.

"Like a red-nosed, rainbow-wig clown?"

"No. Black-and-white stripes. Like a mime."

"I hate mimes."

Finn clammed up as Ms. Applegate passed by. At her side was a massive black dog of indiscriminate breed. The canine reminded Finn a bit of a wolfhound, although the face was uglier with a distorted jaw frozen in a permanent growl. Another hound waited with Ravenguard at the front of the line.

"Welcome to our school. Meet our snarling masses of canine aggression," Jayden whispered.

"No shit," Finn said. "They're really upping the intimidation factor."

Jayden made a low throaty sound. "Hello, beautiful." His chin pointed in the direction of another bus that was parked beside the one they'd rode in on. A girl waited on the steps, frowning at the drizzling sky. A gorgeous girl. The type people wrote songs about. Platinum-blond hair. Oversized blue eyes. A ridiculously thin physique. She looked like a human Barbie.

"Plastic." Finn smirked and shook his head.

"I like plastic," Jayden said through half-exposed teeth. "I call dibs."

Mike, who'd slowly made his way up the line to be behind Jayden, nudged him and lifted his eyebrows. "No dibs. You can't call dibs on a human being."

The girl finally braved the rain to join the line behind Mike, who greeted her with a falsely double-bass *hello*. Finn snorted and glanced back toward the bus, as another girl descended the stairs.

The second girl did not look like Barbie. Although her skin was smooth as porcelain, it stretched across features too sharp to be pretty. She was tall and graceful but not exactly thin. More athletic. He could see her bicep stretch her long-sleeved T-shirt as she adjusted the backpack on her shoulder. She wore no makeup and her auburn hair was pulled back into a ponytail. Her narrow eyes flashed some cold, pale color—either blue or green—as she glided into the rain without hesitation, as if she couldn't care less if she got wet. A silver pendant around her neck glinted when lightning cut across the sky overhead, and she tucked the necklace inside her shirt. To Mike's dismay, she cut in front of Barbie at the back of the line. The big guy took one look at her and turned around to face Jayden.

"Damn, she's built like Ronda Rousey. Remind me not to piss her off," the girl in front of him said.

Finn laughed, noticing the girl in front of him for the first time. She was small, smaller than he was. Cute, with freckles across the bridge of her nose and warm eyes the color of dark chocolate. Two brown braids fell across her shoulders, framing a quirky, understated smile that made Finn feel warm and tingly all over. When he looked at her, he wanted to keep looking at her. He opened his mouth to say something, but his tongue turned weirdly stiff.

"I'm Wendy," she said.

"Finn." He nodded his head. Yes, that was his name.

She smiled bright enough to stave off the shadow cast by the school. *Not plastic*, he thought. "Where-are-you-from, Wendy?" His mouth wasn't working right and it came out as one slurred, unintelligible word.

"Huh?" she asked.

Finn didn't have a chance to clarify.

"Can we go in?" a boy at the front of the line bellowed, a big kid who looked as though he played a rough sport like football or rugby. He shifted restlessly in the sprinkling rain.

"No talking," Ravenguard snapped. "That goes for all of you. Single file."

To Finn's disappointment, Wendy turned back around.

Rugby crossed his arms over his chest but quieted down, as did the rest of the students. Seemingly in defiance of the boy, the rain chose that moment to transform from a sprinkle into a full-blown storm. Groans and barely muffled complaints filtered through the line. A strong wind out of the west joined forces with the storm to pelt Finn's face and darken his T-shirt with fat wet drops. At least it was warm rain. The climate was inexplicably hot here.

"Stay where you are," Applegate warned. The dog at her side growled. A dark-haired girl near the front stepped back into line.

Although Ravenguard and Applegate opened umbrellas over their heads, no such courtesy was offered the students. There was no awning or lip to the building to stop the onslaught. Finn shifted from foot to foot as the rain soaked through his clothes and his hair. Water dripped off his bangs, his eyelashes, his nose. He tried to wipe it away, but it was raining too hard for that. He shielded his eyes.

All the students in line stared at Ravenguard, who was the closest to the door, as if by force of collaborative will they could get him to let them inside or at least explain why they must wait in the rain. There was something cruel about it. Ravenguard's mouth, under the shadow of his umbrella, held an understated smirk, almost as if he was enjoying this. He made no move toward the door.

The temperature dropped and the rain started to sting against his skin. In front of him, Wendy untied her hoodie from her waist and pulled it on, although it was far too wet to make a difference.

"Do you think I should say something?" Finn whispered over his shoulder to Jayden. Only Jayden wasn't there anymore. At some point, he'd switched places in line, he and Mike on either side of Barbie. Which meant the auburn-haired girl with the silver pendant was in his place, looking like she might flatten him with one punch if he set her off.

"Don't say a word," she whispered. "Whatever you do, don't call attention to yourself. Look straight ahead and shut your mouth."

He obeyed, although not without a pang of resistance toward the bossiness of the girl he didn't know. While he was considering how to say, "You're not the boss of me" in a way that wouldn't sound like he was in third grade, the dark-haired girl behind Rugby—the one who'd previously stepped out of line—snapped.

"Hey, it's raining out here!" She splayed her arms to the sides.

Her pierced lip curled with her raised eyebrow. "What are we waiting for?" She'd pulled up the hood of her sweatshirt, but it couldn't hide her retro-goth appearance. Purple streaks poked out of her hood along with her long black tresses. The spiked leather collar she wore around her neck was the same shade of black as the thick smudge of mascara that had formed beneath each of her eyes.

Ravenguard gave her a stern look. "Amanda Tidwell, remain silent and stay where you are. This is your second warning. Speaking out of turn is an infraction."

The girl released a series of expletives that made Wendy back up and step on Finn's toes. She turned her freckled face toward him. "Sorry."

"It's okay." It was completely okay. She could step on his toes all day long. Finn untied the parka from around his waist and was about to offer it to Wendy when Amanda stepped out of line again.

When she opened her mouth, she hurled her words like knives. She nosedived into some sort of meltdown with hand gestures even Finn found vulgar. Some of them he'd never even seen before, but there was no mistaking what they meant. The tirade ended with "and get us the bloody hell out of the rain!"

No one moved. Icy sheets of wetness pelted Finn's skin as the temperature dropped again and gusts of wind threatened to knock him over. Seconds ticked by, Amanda and Ravenguard locked in some kind of staring duel. Of the two, only Ravenguard was smiling.

Finally, Ms. Applegate nodded. Ravenguard opened the door, allowing Rugby to step inside.

"It's about frickin' time," Amanda yelled, stepping forward. Ravenguard's hand landed just under her neck. "What the hell do you think you're doing? Don't touch me."

Applegate folded her umbrella and handed it to Ravenguard before pulling Amanda roughly to the side, keeping her from entering the building. Amanda wasn't having it. She twisted and swung, her punch flying at Applegate's jaw with her entire body backing it up. The admissions counselor caught the girl's fist in her hand, grinning in the pouring rain like a spider toying with a fly.

"Ow! Stop." Amanda didn't sound angry anymore. She sounded scared.

"Move along," Ravenguard said to the rest of the line. "Or join her."

No way was Finn going to call attention to himself after witnessing that spectacle. Amanda's whines turned to screams as Finn followed Wendy inside. The shrieks, slaps, and thumps grew quieter as the door closed behind them. Soon, he couldn't hear Amanda's struggle at all. Did laws about punishing children apply on a private island? Because based on her screams, Finn was sure whatever they were doing to Amanda would not have been legal anywhere else.

We've never lost a student yet, he remembered Ravenguard saying. He tried not to worry about the girl named Amanda and concentrated on keeping himself from panicking.

"This way," Ravenguard said. He led the group down a dim hallway to a grand foyer flanked with dual curved staircases. The sconces on the walls barely combatted the darkening windows, the storm giving the outdoors the color of twilight. "This island has certain unusual natural properties that interfere with electronic devices. We have heat and power from geothermal sources, but you will find that light can be a scarce resource." He gave a tight little smile that seemed to have its own shadow.

Finn followed as he climbed the walnut staircase on the left, his wet shoes squishing with each step on the patterned red carpet. The wood-paneled hallway above was something from another time. Gilded gas lamps burned between portraits of stern-looking adults dressed in hunting attire. He squinted at one painting of a stunning blond woman holding up the carcass of an animal, indistinguishable due to its missing skin and gutted torso. He grimaced and had to look away.

"You." Ravenguard's finger pointed at Finn's face. "This will be your room." Finn edged past the admissions counselor to enter the doorway to their left. As the brochure had suggested, two full beds were separated by a common nightstand with a gold-and-white lamp. An open door led to a small bathroom on his left. Two dressers, one window. Finn picked one of the beds and tested it with his hand, then stood, dripping at its foot.

Ravenguard's attention turned back to the hallway of students. "You," he said, pointing to someone else in line outside his field of vision.

He waited for his chosen roommate to enter. A moment later, the athletic girl slipped past Ravenguard into the room.

"But she's a girl," Finn blurted.

"Yes, she is," Ravenguard said. "How wise of you to notice." Faint chuckling drifted in from the hall.

"Don't you separate boys and girls?" Finn asked incredulously.

"We do things differently here," Ravenguard said. "Your uniforms are in the drawers. You have twenty minutes to change for dinner and orientation."

Finn stared helplessly as Ravenguard and the other students left. Without Ravenguard to hold it open, the door closed on its own. Finn rubbed under his nose and glanced at the girl, who pulled her backpack from her shoulder and dumped it at the foot of the opposite bed.

An awkward silence filled the room. "Don't worry. I'm not a pervert or anything," Finn said, trying to break the ice.

Her eyes flicked from his head to his toes, one corner of her mouth lifting. "Oh, please. I'd kick your ass. You're half my size, and I'm twice as fast. If you try anything, I'll hurt you." Her pale eyes locked on his, thin ice over ocean, hard as stone.

Ooookay. He raised eyebrows toward the window. "My name's

Finn… Wager. I'm from Beaverton, Pennsylvania." He punched the air playfully. "Fighting Beavers."

She snorted, softening slightly. "I'm Hope Laudner. From Paris. Not the famous Paris, unfortunately. Paris, Illinois. Small town. Blink and you'll miss it."

"Cool." Finn shifted awkwardly in front of his bed. "So, ah, what did you do to end up here anyway?"

Hope walked to the window and stared across the rainy yard to a forest that extended beyond. "I didn't do anything. Well, I was born, I guess."

"Innocent, huh?" Finn said sarcastically.

"There's something here I'm supposed to do," she murmured.

Finn laughed. "Isn't that why we're all here? To be rehabilitated."

She flashed a half smile over her shoulder. "Yeah."

"I wonder when we get our luggage," Finn said, cold and soaked to the bone. He walked to the dresser and opened the drawer. He pulled out a stretchy black leotard-looking thing and waved the uniform at her in horror. "They can't possibly expect us to wear this."

Hope sighed. "I don't think this place is going to be what you expected, Finn," she said. "And yeah, I think they'll require us to do a lot of things we won't want to do."

❦ 9 ❦

THE ARCHITECT

While Hope changed in the bathroom, Finn stripped out of his wet clothes and dressed in the stretchy black uniform in the privacy of the bedroom. He'd hoped the gear would look better on, but it proved as embarrassing as he expected. The athletic pants were only slightly more concealing than tights, thankfully more gymnastics-looking than ballet. The black sleeveless T-shirt had a Revelations logo on the right breast and purple piping that lined the V-neck and angled across the torso from clavicle to hip. Leather ballet shoes completed the ensemble.

He did not look cool. Not at all. He messed with his hair and adjusted the shirt. It didn't help. There were no buttons or zippers, no way to spruce it up. On an athletic physique, it might have looked okay, but the getup was loose in all the wrong places on Finn and only succeeded in making him look even smaller than he was.

The door to the bathroom opened and Finn groaned. Hope emerged, all toned muscle and confidence. He could feel his ears grow hot, and he scowled at his own reflection. She was wearing the exact same thing he was. Only, she made it look good.

"At least they're comfortable." By her tone, he could tell she was trying to put him at ease.

It didn't work. He rolled his eyes and tried not to think about how pitiful he looked.

"Do you think we're supposed to head down on our own?" he asked, sliding his arm into a waist-length warm-up jacket. At least the jacket added some bulk around his shoulders. He frowned into the mirror.

Hope's lips parted as if to answer him but she was interrupted by a sharp knock on the door, followed by Applegate storming into their room uninvited. The heels of her boots clicked on the hardwood floor as she sized them up, zeroing in on Hope. "No jewelry of any kind is allowed."

Hope removed her earrings and placed them on the dresser. Finn remembered the pendant he'd seen around her neck and wondered if it was under the shallow vee of her uniform. If it was, she made no effort to remove it. Applegate stepped closer, her hands clasped behind her back, and narrowed her eyes on Hope's neck. One white-gloved hand reached toward the girl, Applegate's mouth contorting into something ugly.

If she found Hope's pendant, what would she do? Would Finn have to listen to Hope scream the way Amanda had? He didn't owe the girl anything, but he didn't want to start the semester with more drama.

"When can I get my trunk?" Finn blurted to distract Applegate.

The admissions counselor's sharp perusal refocused in his direction. "I did not give you permission to speak, Mr. Wager. Speaking out of turn is an infraction."

He remembered Ravenguard saying the same thing to the dark-haired girl, Amanda. He wasn't about to be subjected to her fate. He closed his mouth and stared at his shoes.

Heavy footsteps—Applegate's boots—circled him. She brushed a glove across his back as if smoothing a wrinkle. "Adequate. Line up with the others."

Finn shuffled into the hall where the other students, with the exception of Amanda, were waiting. He fell into line behind Rugby and Braids, er, Wendy.

Hope was right behind him. Once Applegate was out of earshot, she whispered, "Thank you."

He nodded. He wanted to ask her why she hadn't removed the pendant but he didn't have a chance.

"Eyes straight ahead," Applegate barked.

Finn straightened his chin and stared at the back of Wendy's head. Applegate led them down the grand staircase and across the massive foyer to two heavy wooden doors that achingly reminded Finn of home. Ravenguard was already there and held the doors open while Finn and the others filed through.

Inside, a group of seven adults faced them, lined up along one side of a long ebony head table. The head of a rhinoceros was mounted on the wall behind them, and a chandelier made entirely of reindeer antlers and those strange, dull lightbulbs glowed overhead. A second table, one Finn presumed was for students such as himself, ran perpendicular to the head table, set off by a three-foot chasm of space. A clear delineation between teacher and student.

Finn and the other students hovered just inside the door, not sure what to do next.

Seated dead center at the head table was an elderly woman, her wild gray hair, evocative of Einstein's, barely contained under a red bowler hat. Pushing back her chair, she stood, the wrinkles around her eyes growing more pronounced with her scrutiny of the group. She hardly held the mark of sophistication, but when she rose from her seat, the six adults around her also popped up. This woman was powerful. She was important.

"Welcome! Wellllcome!" she trilled. She gestured toward the tall-backed chairs around the empty student table. "Please, take your seats. Boy, girl, boy, girl. Stay with your roommates. Yes. That's it." She pushed back her boxy black jacket to place her fists on the hips of her flared jodhpurs and focused in on Mike through her red-rimmed glasses. Finn realized he was the only one without a partner. "Michael, is it?"

"Yes, ma'am," Mike said, his tone ridiculously polite.

"I'm afraid your roommate will be detained for a few days. Amanda wasn't quite ready to fully participate in her rehabilitation, but through intensive intervention, we hope to return her to you soon. I think you'll find she's a new person when we do." Bright red lipstick curved into a yellow-toothed grin.

Mike chose a seat at the far end of the table, leaving plenty of room between himself and the adults. The other students filled in around him, some more quickly than others. The high-backed monstrosities used as chairs were oversized and constructed of a dense, heavy wood that Finn struggled to move at all. He pushed and pushed and pushed on the chair, but even using all his weight he only succeeded in moving it a half inch. His efforts caught the attention of Hope, who nonchalantly reached over and slid it back with one hand. Red-faced, he sat down, giving her a grateful yet humiliated nod.

Once everyone was seated, the elderly woman spread her arms wide. Her back was ballerina-straight, and she held her chin high as someone of noble birth might. Along with her upturned hands, her posture made her look twenty years younger than a moment before. She was a performer, Finn realized, and she'd just put on a well-practiced mask.

"My name is Victoria Duvall and I am the architect of this performance. You will call me Ms. D. I want to congratulate you on choosing Revelations Institute. Our show, like all those before it, will make history. Here at this school, you will be transformed from the ordinary, hapless beings huddled around my table to magnificent warriors of the stage. You will learn to throw yourselves fearlessly into the performance with no concern for your own safety or self-preservation. No!" She held up one finger. "Nothing worth doing is safe, my dear students." She fisted her hands and thrust them toward the ceiling. "You cannot go into the extraordinary lackadaisically."

Her tall, laced boots clacked on the stone floor as she rounded her chair and paced the room. "We must charge toward the exceptional, knowing we might fail. We must jump from the nest believing we can fly, even if the result is our plummet to the Earth. Dear, dear children, for the next semester, you shall be the paints that color my canvas." Spreading her hands, she approached the table again, a pleading expression on her face. "This island, this school, has made the impossible possible. Together, we will overcome the bindings of natural law. We will transcend the human condition. We will defy gravity." Ms. D squeezed her hands into fists, then folded her chin to her chest and closed her eyes.

The room fell silent. Someone shifted. Gazes ping-ponged across the table as seconds stretched into minutes. Ms. D did not move. Finn glanced toward the doors where Applegate and Ravenguard stood at attention. They did not seem concerned with the headmistress's odd state.

Ms. D's head snapped up so violently that Finn jumped in his chair. Her eyes and nostrils flared. "First, we must eat. You will need your strength." She clapped her hands and a door at the back of the room, opposite where Applegate and Ravenguard stood, opened. A group of people entered carrying domed trays, all redheads, all under four feet tall—little people. An elderly woman with an exceptionally large platter led the servers, and Finn was struck by the resemblance between them, as if they were all related to each other. Mike stood, pushing back his chair to make room and assist the woman in placing the platter on the table. It was a Mike thing to do, polite, gentlemanly.

"What are you doing?" Ms. D snapped at Mike.

As he lowered the tray to the table, Mike's mouth fell open. "Helping?"

"Does Mrs. Wilhelm look as if she needs help?"

Finn followed Mike's gaze back to Mrs. Wilhelm. She was difficult to see from where he was sitting, as she was barely taller than the table, but what he could make out of her seemed perturbed. Her arms were crossed and her lips were pursed.

"Um, no," Mike said.

"We never judge a person's abilities based on their size at Revelations, and we never, ever do for someone else what they should do for themselves. Is that clear?" Ms. D's voice was quiet but razor sharp.

Mike nodded.

"Michael, please stand facing Mrs. Wilhelm and apologize for underestimating her."

With some effort, Mike stepped around his chair and turned toward the woman. "I'm sorry. I'm new and didn't know the rule."

"Apology accepted," Mrs. Wilhelm said, smiling warmly. Mike turned back to his chair, but Ms. D raised her hand to stop him. There was a general murmur from the other servers.

"Mrs. Wilhelm, please demonstrate your strength to young Michael and his classmates."

"I hardly think that's necessary. It was an honest mistake," Mrs. Wilhelm said, twisting her apron in her hands.

"Now!" Ms. D yelled.

Mrs. Wilhelm sighed and gave Mike an apologetic look. Then, without hesitation, she stepped toward him and punched him squarely in the stomach. Mike doubled over and dropped to the floor. Jayden moved to help him, but Ms. D pinned him to his seat with a weighty, disapproving stare. He leaned back in his chair and locked eyes with Finn, who mouthed *messed up*.

Mike drew a tight, whistling breath.

Ms. D cleared her throat and lowered herself into her chair again. Mrs. Wilhelm and the other servers stepped around Mike and delivered the rest of the trays to the table, removing the domes before disappearing as quickly as they had come. The adults dug in immediately, including Ms. D, who heaped her plate with slices of meat and ladles of whipped potatoes and vegetables. Finn didn't move until he saw Mike rise from the floor and take a seat at the table. Their eyes met and Mike gave him a reassuring nod.

On his left, Barbie frowned at the platters. Were they allowed to begin? After what happened to Mike and Amanda, no one wanted to be the first to test the waters.

"Well?" Ms. D said, glancing at the students. "What are you waiting for?"

Finn leaned forward and speared a slab of meat. The others did the same. "What is this?" he asked Hope, the meat hovering over the platter. She'd covered her plate with vegetables and potatoes. No meat.

She shook her head. As large around as a slice of Christmas ham, the slab was rare, bright red, and left a trail of blood on the platter. He'd never seen anything like it.

Wendy spoke up. "Excuse me, Ms. D, what type of meat is this? I, uh, have allergies."

Ms. D stopped eating and wiped a bit of blood from the corner of her lips. "Don't concern yourself, Wendy. It isn't lamb. That's what you're allergic to, isn't it?"

Wendy nodded.

"Not to worry. It's tiger."

Finn jiggled his fork to release the meat back to the platter instead of lifting it to his plate. He pushed the tray in Rugby's direction and dug into the potatoes instead.

"You will eat three meals a day in this dining hall, although most will be buffet style," Ms. D said around a bite of food. "Don't miss meals. If you do, you'll go without. Dinner is served before twilight, and all students must be in their dormitories by full dark. If Mr. Ravenguard or Ms. Applegate catches you out of your room after dark, it will be considered an infraction."

"What happens if we get an infraction?" Barbie asked.

"Good question, Jenny... Pendleton. Do I have your name right?"

"Yes, ma'am," Jenny said softly.

"We at Revelations consider a misbehaving child a sick child. In the case of an infraction, you will be separated from the group and undergo intensive therapy until you are able to obey and succeed in the mainstream setting."

"What is the intensive therapy comprised of?" Jenny asked. Based on her expression, Finn pegged her for the type of girl who thrived on knowing the rules and following every one to the letter. He wondered how she'd ended up here.

"If I told you, it would lose its intensity." Ms. D grinned. "Trust me, Ms. Pendleton, you don't want to find out. Now, while you finish your meals, your instructors will introduce themselves and demonstrate their specialty. Pay close attention. You will meet with each instructor for ninety minutes each day and attempt to learn his or her act. Your goal is to convince them that you can master their routine and transform yourself into a cast member for the performance in the spring." She nodded to a man on her left. "Amuke, it's time. I'd like to begin with you."

🦋 10 🦋

ORIENTATION

The man called Amuke was completely bald with espresso-colored skin and hazel eyes that reflected gold in the dull light of the chandelier. If Finn had thought the seats heavy, they didn't appear so as Amuke tossed his chair back and strode to a small platform at the front of the room. His uniform was similar to Finn's aside from a flap of orange across the chest that gave the outfit a more sophisticated appearance.

"I am Amuke. I teach menagerie, the use of animals in the performing arts," he began in a deep double bass. He approached one of the windows and opened it wide. The rain had abated and the sun was beginning to set. A stiff humidity drifted into the room.

"Tiger, come," Amuke called.

Finn darted a glance toward Mike and Jayden, who returned his raised eyebrow. Surely the man wasn't going to invite a tiger into the dining room.

A roar cut through the big, open space, and then a full-grown Siberian tiger leaped through the window. Finn recoiled as it passed Amuke, lowered its head, and prowled toward the table. What was he doing calling that thing inside? Trained or not, an animal like that needed restraint. The thing had to weigh five hundred pounds.

The great cat reared, paws as big as Finn's head thunking down on the open foot of the table. Its claws gouged the wood. Finn gripped the arms of his chair and Wendy, who was seated closest to the animal, screamed and jumped out of her seat as if she might leap into Jayden's arms if he wasn't cowering as far away from the beast as possible himself.

"You are angry about our choice of meat?" Ms. D said to the tiger. "Your displeasure is acknowledged, but unless you intend to join your brethren, you will mind your performance, Tiger."

The tiger thrust forward, claws digging into the tabletop, massive white teeth gleaming under retracted lips. Finn trembled, contemplating a run for the door. Ms. D stood, leaned forward, and growled toward the big cat, her gaze icy. All at once, the tiger pushed off the table and seemed to deflate. The beast returned to the platform, the spark draining from its yellow eyes until they were as dull as stones.

Amuke raised one hand. The tiger sat and stretched its front paws toward the ceiling. Amuke lowered his hand. The tiger lay down, then crawled on its belly. With a circle of Amuke's hand, the beast rolled over. The big cat twitched its tail with annoyance as Amuke knelt down and whispered a command. The tiger sprang over his head, turned three circles at the edge of the platform, and leaped out the window again. Amuke stood, took a bow, and closed the window.

Clap. Clap. Clap. Ms. D applauded slowly. Finn and the others joined in with tempered enthusiasm.

"Shouldn't someone put that thing in a pen or something?" Rugby said. His face was pale and waxy, unbefitting his general appearance.

"All of the menagerie animals live freely in the woods behind the school," Amuke said. "They perform willingly in exchange for food."

"Relax, Paul. The tiger is gone." Ms. D gave Rugby a patron-
izing stare. "Do you need to use the restroom?"

He scowled. "No!"

"Good." Ms. D whirled on a stunning woman with a red
uniform flap. "Fuse, if you please."

"No problem," Fuse said in a New Jersey accent. She jogged to
the platform, taking Amuke's place. "I'm Vera Bukowsky, but
everyone calls me Fuse. If you apprentice with the pyros, you will
learn to feel the heat and stay in the kitchen." She snapped her
fingers and a flame leaped to life in the palm of her hand. With the
turn of a cartwheel, she placed the spark on the floor. Incredibly,
the fire didn't go out when she removed her hand but ignited into
a formidable flame that chased her feet as she danced across the
platform. When she sprang into the air, the flame jumped too,
tongues of fire splitting in imitation of her legs. Once she'd
landed, the fire serpentined around her body as she pirouetted
across the platform.

What would it be like to dance with fire? Awestruck by her
performance, Finn was afraid to blink and miss the beauty of a
single moment. As she bent backward, the flame climbed her leg
to her hands, where she toyed with the tongues of red and orange
above her head, her hips moving in time with the flickering heat.
Gracefully, she flipped her torso over and kicked one foot toward
the ceiling. The standing split brought her face to the floor, her
smile lit by the flame that blazed in her cupped palms. She flipped
her legs over her head and tossed the flame high into the air.
There was a collective gasp as she caught it on her tongue, let it
burn for a moment, then swallowed. Light glowed through the
skin of her throat until the flame extinguished in her stomach.

Fuse spread her upturned hands, smiled broadly, and bowed.

This time, no one waited for Ms. D. The table erupted into
applause. Jayden stood, pounding his hands together and
whistling his appreciation. One stern look from Ms. D, and he sat
back down.

Fuse returned to her seat.

"Always a favorite," Ms. D mused. She gestured toward a slight figure at the end of the head table. "Orelon, if you please."

Upon entering the room, Finn had originally assumed the person named Orelon was a woman, but as Orelon stood, his long, white braid shifting from his shoulder, he was clearly male. Finn's mistake was due to the man's perfect complexion and proportional, delicate facial features. Orelon was beautiful, in a woodland elf sort of way. Small in stature and fine boned. He stepped behind his chair and placed both hands on the heavy wooden back of it, well above his shoulder height. In one lithe movement, he lifted his body, legs split on either side of his arms, and pressed into a handstand.

The sheer strength necessary to achieve the position fascinated Finn, but even more impressive was the silence. The chair didn't rattle. The man didn't grunt or moan or knock into the chair next to him. Toes pointed, he bent his body into a C shape and vaulted, flipping through the air to land on the antler chandelier above them, which, impossibly, did not swing.

"I am Orelon," the man said softly. His voice was like a draft that blew through the room. You couldn't be sure you'd heard it until it was gone. "If you apprentice with aerial, you will either learn to fly or learn to fall." He leaped to the table, landing on tiptoes softly enough that not a single dish rattled. Just as silently, he flip-flopped down the center of the table, dismounting with a full twisting flip. His movements were like remembered music, like the echo of a ghost. All Finn could think was *incredible*. He should have heard Orelon's movements. He should have felt the vibrations when Orelon landed on the table. But he didn't.

Orelon bowed gracefully, then returned to his seat to the sound of applause, smoothing the green flap of his uniform as he sat down.

"You are a marvel, Orelon. Thank you for your demonstration," Ms. D said once the applause died down. She narrowed her eyes on a muscular woman with a shock of thick blond hair who sat next to Amuke. "Kirsa, would you do us the honor?"

As the woman stood, she lifted the massive chair by the arms and stepped back with it, her triceps twitching with the effort. The chair legs never even scraped the floor. Finn's eyes widened. "If you apprentice with resilience, I will make you indestructible."

Rugby smirked and glanced around the room. "Indestructible?" He snorted.

"Paul... Stewart, correct?" Ms. D asked.

The boy nodded, his thick neck bending slightly to the side in contempt.

"I remember you from your file. You're here for punching your girlfriend, yes?"

Paul's gaze darted around the room and his cheeks reddened. "Uh... there were extenuating circumstances."

"You were afraid of the tiger but you are not afraid of Ms. Hildburg? You do not believe she is indestructible?" Ms. D toyed with the napkin beside her plate.

The boy scoffed. "Don't get me wrong, she's built like a brick shithouse, but she's a girl, not a wild animal, okay? She's not indestructible."

The grin that spread across Ms. D's lips made Finn's stomach clench. It was a dangerous grin, a grin that made him wish he were invisible. The tone of her voice was the same as when she'd had Mrs. Wilhelm punch Mike in the stomach.

"Stand up, my boy."

Paul shook his head. "Forget it. I didn't mean any offense. If you say she's indestructible, she's indestructible." He snorted.

"I said stand up." Ms. D's hard, sharp voice cracked like a whip across the table.

Paul stood.

"Pick up your knife and throw it at her chest."

"What?"

"Do it!"

Paul picked up the knife beside his plate, his eyes raking over the remains of his dinner. Would he do it? Or back down and apologize? The boy fixated on Kirsa, who spread her arms and smiled smugly. After a glance back at the headmistress to make sure she was serious, Paul tossed the knife. The throw was half-hearted and the blunt side thumped against Kirsa's chest and clattered to the floor. The resilience instructor bent over, retrieving the blade.

"When you throw a knife, Paul, try throwing it by the blade. You might find it increases your accuracy." Kirsa whipped the knife back at Paul. He tried to dodge, but the speed and power of the throw was too fast. The blade sliced his shoulder. Paul cursed, bright red blood spreading from the tear in his jacket. The pain triggered something in Paul. His jaw tightened like a drawn cord, and his hand shot out for the large carving knife on the tray of tiger meat. This time he hurled it at Kirsa with everything he had.

Kirsa didn't flinch. The blade connected with her chest tip first. It should have sunk in. Finn had seen that knife cut meat. It was razor sharp. Even if Kirsa was wearing some type of protective garb, it should have done some damage. But it clattered harmlessly to the floor. A collective gasp rose up from the table. Threading one finger through the resulting hole in the blue flap of her sleeveless T-shirt, Kirsa laughed. Then she picked up the knife and drew the blade hard and fast across her arm. Nothing. No blood.

Paul collapsed into his chair and pressed his napkin to the cut in his shoulder.

Silence enveloped the room. Finn's gaze darted to the other students. He was afraid to move. No one wanted Paul's fate.

Ms. D clapped. "Thank you, Kirsa. I think you've made a practice partner in Paul. Help the boy, Mrs. Wilhelm. He's bleeding on the linens." Mrs. Wilhelm appeared out of nowhere with a first-aid kit and started tending the wound. Ms. D's finger singled out Paul. "While you are here, you must never doubt your instructors.

If she says she's invincible, she's invincible. If she tells you to take a hammer to your hand to toughen it up, you do it. Understand?"

Paul nodded, but his eyes tightened at the corners as if he didn't quite buy into what she was saying.

Ms. D leaned back in her chair. "That completes our demonstrations from level-one troupe leaders. Now, I'd like to introduce you to the two advanced performers who elevate our show to the next level." She turned to the man on her left. "Theodor, would you do the honors?"

The dark-haired man with the thin mustache saluted Ms. D and disappeared... simply vanished from his chair. He reappeared on the platform. Finn did a double take, eyeing the chair and then the man on the platform.

"I am Theodor Florea, and I am a magician." He steepled his fingers and the tables and chairs lifted. Finn's feet lost contact with the floor, rolling forward until only the tips of his toes brushed the wood. A murmur of amazement rippled through his fellow students. When the tables and chairs lowered again, the trays of food remained floating. Plates, silverware, full glasses, heavy trays laden with food hovered above their heads. Finn eyed the mashed potatoes apprehensively. One slip by the magician and he'd be wearing them, no doubt.

With the table cleared, Theodor reached into his pocket and retrieved a deck of cards. He passed them back and forth between his hands a few times before scattering them across the table with a flick of his wrist.

One by one, the cards came to life, bending at the middle and standing up to balance on their edges. To Finn's delight, the cards marched across the tabletop, the king of spades and the queen of hearts coming together. Their brethren closed in and lifted them up on cardboard shoulders. A tower constructed itself card by card, elevating the couple. The remaining suits divided by color, the black half on the king's side, the red on the queen's. The two armies collided, a war of paper cuts, ripping and scraping, slicing diamonds and slashing clubs. The tower toppled. The war didn't stop until every last card had been reduced to shreds of cardboard.

Theodor opened the card box and flourished his hand. A sourceless wind blew through the room, sweeping the shredded paper from the polished surface and blowing every last piece back into the box. Theodor closed the lid.

Finn stared, waiting for what would happen next. He jumped when he heard silverware clinking on the trays above their heads. The plates tilted and the leftover food dropped. Jenny covered her blond hair with her arms. The others reacted similarly. Even Finn raised his forearm toward the falling mashed potatoes. He needn't have. The food transformed into confetti, showering them in the remains of the cards.

The trays spun into wisps of smoke and disappeared, leaving behind the harsh odor of silver polish. Only two cards floated whole to the table, the king of spades and the queen of hearts. They stood and waddled toward Finn, bowing slightly. Without thinking, Finn bowed back, then realized how nerdy the reaction was and straightened in his chair. Theodor whistled and the two cards flew into the pack.

Theodor adjusted the cards, revealing to everyone that the deck was, in fact, complete and whole again. Finn searched around his chair and couldn't find a single shred of confetti.

"Magicians are rare but the most adaptable of all our performers," Ms. D said. "Apprenticing as a magician is by invitation only and requires a minimum of one year of experience in a level-one troupe."

Finn slumped. He would have loved to learn magic.

"And now," Ms. D said, hand extending toward the elegant woman to her right, "Juliette will demonstrate for you the cornerstone of Revelations' performance, the enchanter."

Enchanter, Finn thought. Wasn't an Enchanter the same as a magician?

With the grace of a dancer, Juliette evacuated her chair. Finn almost forgot the chairs weighed approximately as much as a full-grown rhinoceros; each of the adults had moved theirs with no effort at all. Dressed in a peacock-blue ball gown with a high neck of feathers, Juliette reminded Finn of a historical figure, like a queen—young, powerful, and with the straight back of someone who holds herself in high regard.

She didn't bother taking the platform. Chin up, she coupled her hands, one on top of the other, in front of her bottom rib. Her eyes seemed unbelievably green beneath the pointed brim of her hat. Then her lips parted, and the world as Finn knew it came to a crashing halt. The sound from Juliette's mouth simultaneously gave him chills and filled his heart with blossoming warmth. Her voice didn't resonate, per se, but rang like a bell, crystal clear and pitch perfect. The melody soared and dove, each note plucking some emotional string within him. In unison with his classmates, he laughed and cried. Only when he'd knocked into the edge of the table did he notice that he'd leaned toward her. Everyone had. Even Ms. D.

Juliette released her coupled hands and flipped her palms to the ceiling. Her eyes and voice drifted upward, ascending. It was impossible not to look.

A collective gasp rose from the table, and Finn heard Hope curse next to him. The ceiling was gone, replaced by the night sky. A meteor swept across the heavens, stars twinkled, galaxies rotated in the deep dark of outer space. For Finn, the experience was transcendent, his limbs became weightless, his mind absolutely clear. Above him, the universe popped and zinged, a shower of light over their heads. He reached out as a star twinkled nearer, but it dodged his fingertips.

Juliette tipped her head and lowered her voice to a gentle coo and the night sky retracted, replaced by the ceiling and the brash antler chandelier. Slowly, gently, Finn leaned back into his seat, returning to Earth after a journey into the beyond. He came back into himself with her final note, feeling as if something had passed through him, something he would have loved to invite to stay. The other students must have felt the same way because the room pitched into silence, still bodies staring into space. Finn was moved beyond measure.

Hope whispered under her breath, "What the hell was that?"

Ms. D was the first to break into applause and eventually Finn did too. Hope was the last to bring her hands together. After a long and generous fit of clapping, Ms. D said, "Enchanters are rare. Our performance requires only one and apprenticing with Juliette is by invitation only. Juliette is essential to our performance. Enchanters can make the audience believe the production is perfect, even when it isn't. She can sharpen the lackluster, hide a fall, disguise an injury. She can get inside the heads of our patrons and make them believe they've seen something they haven't."

"Inside their heads?" Hope's eyes widened in disbelief.

"Of course, Hope. You don't believe the universe came through the roof into the dining room, do you? That was her, putting thoughts in your head."

Hope's mouth popped open. "How?"

"How? We do not ask how at Revelations. We just do. We make the impossible possible."

Jenny cleared her throat. "But obviously there are limits. There are things a human body can't do. Some of what we've seen today is not real."

"Not real?" Ms. D looked confused.

"Sleight of hand, trickery. Things cannot actually levitate." Jenny tucked her blond hair behind her ears.

Ms. D rubbed her hands together. "Ah, but that is where you fail yourself, Jenny. What is possible and impossible have new definitions here." She stood, placed her hands on her hips. "Here, you must not limit yourself."

"What about the clowns?" Jenny asked. "Are they a separate troupe?"

Ms. D gave her a hard look.

"I saw one in the window on our way into the school," Jenny explained.

"I saw it too," Finn said.

Ms. D cleared her throat. "Ignore the clowns. They help with our performance, but their troupe is off limits to students. If you see one, I suggest you avoid it. They are often busy and do not care to be disturbed."

Jenny glanced at Finn and raised an eyebrow. He shrugged.

"How does this work anyway?" Hope asked, her auburn ponytail swinging as she leaned forward to see Ms. D. "How are we assigned to a troupe?"

"Beginning tomorrow you will spend ninety minutes with each of the four first-level troupe leaders. You will practice what they practice. Try to adapt. If you do, the troupe will likely enlist you. If you do not, Ravenguard and Applegate will work with you privately as they have with Ms. Tidwell."

Finn's forehead tightened. He wanted no part of what the admissions counselors were doing to Amanda Tidwell.

"Ninety minutes each?" Hope blurted. "When do we have academic classes? Algebra? Literature?"

Ms. D. adjusted her glasses. "That is not the focus of our program."

"But... but how will we graduate on time if we haven't learned anything here for an entire semester?" Jenny added. She looked genuinely concerned.

With a huff, Ms. D narrowed her eyes on the girl. "None of our graduates have had a problem catching up academically upon their graduation from our program. However, should you feel the need to spend your free time solving for X or reading Chaucer, there's a library on the third floor."

At the murmur that bubbled up from the students, Ms. D

raised her hands. "The way we do things here may seem strange at first, but all will become clear in time. The longer you are here, the more easily you will... adapt. Now, I recommend you return to your rooms and get a good night's rest." She stood and leaned over the table. "You've got a big day ahead of you."

🌼 II 🌿

A GOOD NIGHT'S REST

Exhaustion weighed on Finn as he followed Ravenguard back to his dorm room. The weight of the day grew heavier when the room proved stubbornly devoid of his trunk. The morning's ADHD medicine had worn off and the stress of the orientation and the mysterious happenings of the night had resulted in a surging pulse at the base of his neck. The world came at him at high speed and a fidgety restlessness was taking hold.

"When will we get our luggage?" he blurted before Ravenguard could leave.

Ravenguard gave a tight smile. "Your trunk, Mr. Wager, has been misplaced. Unfortunately, while Ms. Applegate and I were distracted with Ms. Tidwell, it disappeared. Mrs. Wilhelm is searching the institute. Meanwhile, everything you need has been provided for you." He motioned toward the drawers.

Finn frowned. "My medication is inside that trunk. Is there a nurse or a pharmacy?"

"I have no record of you needing any medication."

"Because it's in my trunk. Call my dad. He'll tell you."

"Students may not contact their families during their stay here."

"I'm not asking to contact my family. I'm asking *you* to contact my father and figure out a way to get me my medication… which I need… for my health."

Besides feeling like his skin might crawl off his body, his father would kill him if anything happened to his great-grandmother's trunk. Plus, in the back of his mind, he remembered his father's promise of a cell phone within its depths. After what he'd seen today, he had a strong feeling he'd need that phone at some point.

"What happens if you do not have your medication?" Raven-guard asked.

"I won't be able to sit still or concentrate. I'll be impulsive, even if I don't want to be. I won't be able to help it."

"I suppose we must cross that bridge when we come to it." The older man tipped his bowler hat and left the room without another word.

"Hey. Hey!" Finn yelled. The door closed and a loud click came from the wall. Finn rushed the door, slapping the wood and trying the knob. "He locked us in."

"Why do you take medication?" Hope asked softly. She was sitting cross-legged on her bed, twirling the end of her ponytail around her finger.

"It's personal."

"Are you going to croak before morning?"

"No. I won't die." He paced between the dressers. "I have ADHD, all right? No, I'm not crazy, it's not all in my head, and it is not because of my diet. I have a disease that makes me…" He trailed off, focusing on a chip in the wall.

"Okay." Hope rubbed her hands on her thighs. "I don't think it's in your head. You seem really uncomfortable."

"After what we saw today, I'm not sure I'll be able to keep up with the training. By morning, I'll be crawling the walls."

She gave a deep sigh, her pale pink lips parting slightly. Her eyes followed him across the room. "I don't think any of us have any hope of keeping up. What was all that about anyway? They expect us to learn how to train tigers in five months? It doesn't make sense."

"Don't forget, we have to take a knife to the chest too. I'm still trying to figure that one out."

Hope crossed her arms and glanced over her shoulder, out the window at the twilight beyond. "What are they really doing here?" she murmured. Finn got the impression that she wasn't talking to him when she said it.

"Running a circus for delinquents." Finn snorted.

Hope opened and closed her hands a few times, staring at them as if they'd only recently been attached to her wrists.

"Do your hands hurt or something?" he asked.

"Have you ever heard of reiki, Finn?"

"Uh, no. I mean, I've heard of it. I've never heard of anyone actually, you know, doing it."

"Lots of people where I come from use reiki. It's intentional healing energy. It isn't well understood, but I know how to do it. You look uncomfortable. Do you want me to try it on you?"

"I should be okay for the night. They have to give it to me in the morning, don't they?"

"If I do the reiki now, it will work better. The worse you get, the harder it will be for me to help." Hope perched on the edge of her bed. "I'll catch it before it snowballs and maybe you can manage it better."

"No offense, but I seriously doubt that focused intentions are going to cure my ADHD. If they did, ADHD wouldn't be an epidemic."

Hope's piercing eyes met his. "Maybe you're right, but what do you have to lose?"

What did he have to lose? He shrugged. "Okay. Knock yourself out."

"Sit down."

He obeyed, and she crawled off her bed to cross to him. Tentatively, she placed the tips of her fingers on his temples. The spots where she touched his skin warmed instantly and his eyelids drooped at the strange radiant heat. Ribbons of energy passed behind his forehead, twisted through his brain, dove inward to the heart of his mind. Whatever she was doing seemed to focus deep within his head. He allowed his eyes to close. A blue star glowed within his thoughts, in the space between his ears. The tension bled from his shoulders, then his back, and he sagged against her.

Finn's eyes flipped open when her fingers left his temples. Hope's complexion had gone chalky white, and she was hacking like a cat about to cough up a hairball. She covered her mouth with her hand and rushed into the bathroom. The retching that followed made Finn cover his own mouth.

"Hey, are you okay?" He pushed off the bed to help her, only to have her kick the door to the bathroom closed.

"I'm fine," she called between heaves. "This sometimes happens when I do reiki. It will pass."

"Touching my head made you sick?"

Another loud moan and Finn raised his hand to the door, feeling awful for what he'd done to her. Although, how could touching someone's temples make her ill? The idea was ridiculous. He backed away, confused.

As he sat back down on the bed, all he could think was his roommate was a complete weirdo.

Icing on the cake.

⚜

HOPE HELD BACK HER OWN HAIR AS SHE SPEWED INTO THE TOILET IN her dormitory. She'd never been this sick before. Then again, this was the first time she'd tried to heal someone since Gabriel said she'd attained "full Healer status." He'd said there would be a price. She had vastly underestimated the significance of that statement.

Was it possible for her innards to liquefy and pour out her mouth? Stupid. Stupid. Stupid. Why would she choose something as complicated as ADHD to heal her first time? The disease was like a spiderweb deep within Finn's brain. It had taken everything she had to root it out. Who was she kidding? She had no choice. The boy was coming out of his skin.

Her adoptive mother, Malini, had told her stories about the time she'd spent as Healer. When Malini used her power, her skin would burn. The difference between Malini and Hope was that Hope was born a Soulkeeper, while Malini was made one at fifteen. The consequences of her mother's actions were immediate and understandable to her. Hope, on the other hand, had to grow into her power and had been spared the consequences of her healing until now. The pain was shocking. Still, she had to admit, vomiting seemed a better fate than burning alive.

Gradually, she stopped throwing up and pulled herself together. Revelations had provided a full kit of bathroom amenities for her and Finn to use. She selected a toothbrush from the counter and unwrapped it, brushing away the remnants of her consequence. When she spat, the toothpaste was tainted with blood.

"Crap," she murmured. She swished and spat again, then drank some water from the faucet. Gabriel had taught her that a meal would help her recover, as would sleep. No chance she'd get the meal. She'd have to settle for water and sleep. She took a deep breath and emerged from the bathroom.

Finn had already changed into his school-issued pajamas. He shifted and scratched the back of his head, no doubt wondering what caused her lengthy bathroom visit. He probably thought she was contagious.

"Feeling better?" he asked.

"Yes." She smiled, blinking slowly. "How about you?"

He paused for a second, his eyes shifting across the room. "Uh, yeah. You know, I do feel better. I really do."

"Good. Then it worked." She walked to the dresser on her side of the room and retrieved a matching set of striped pajamas. "They have everything you need in there. Toothbrush, toothpaste, razor, soap, hairbrush. No makeup, but I don't suppose you use it anyway."

Finn snorted. "Uh, no."

Hope suspected he didn't have much use for the razor either, but she didn't want to embarrass him. "So, uh…" Hope held up her pajamas.

"Oh yeah, I'll take my turn in the bathroom."

⚅

SHOWERED AND TUCKED UNDER THE COVERS, FINN FELL ASLEEP surprisingly fast. Whatever Hope had done to him had completely relaxed him. For once, his mind didn't race and the worry he carried about the morning sessions did not trump his desire for rest. So, when the sound of barking dogs and pounding hooves woke him, it was from a deep sleep. By the time he opened his eyes, Hope was already standing at the window.

"What the hell is that?" Finn asked.

Moonlight washed over half of Hope's face as she turned her head, the other half lost in shadow. The pale glow wasn't enough for his eyes to register color, and she had a strange black-and-white appearance in the darkness.

"Hunting party," she whispered. "I made out Ravenguard and Applegate, but there were two others as well. They were on horse-back with those… dogs."

"Why are they hunting in the middle of the night?" Finn asked. "What time is it anyway?"

"I don't know." She held up her left arm. "My watch doesn't work here, and there isn't a single clock in this room."

"Ravenguard said something about the electromagnetic properties of the island interfering with electronics."

She grunted and turned back toward the window. The barking and hoofbeats grew quieter, as if muffled by distance. Hope's eyes narrowed and she moved closer to the glass. The moonlight caught on the three connecting loops of the silver symbol around her neck.

"What's that symbol on your necklace mean? I thought Applegate was going to bust you for it."

"Thanks for distracting her," she said. "I prefer to keep it on. It's meaningful to me. It's a triquetra."

"Triquetra? Never heard of it." Finn tried out the strange word.

"It's an ancient symbol of protection," she said.

"Like a magic symbol?" Finn snorted. "You're not one of those neoreligious nut jobs, are you?"

Hope turned back toward the window. "I don't believe in anything I haven't experienced to be true firsthand." Her shoulders bobbed with a deep sigh.

Finn was going to tell her he liked her necklace, but a scream pierced the air outside the window, the long, bloodcurdling variety that went on and on, morphing into something like an agonized bleat. Finn staggered to the window and searched the woods and the mountain beyond. He couldn't see anything, but it didn't matter. The scream stopped abruptly, cut off midbreath.

"I guess they got the fox," Finn said.

Hope didn't say anything, but when he glanced over, she was visibly upset.

"That's right. You're a vegetarian. An animal lover."

She nodded.

He stood by her side, gazing into the night until it was clear the hunt was over. All was quiet. But when Finn finally returned to bed, he couldn't sleep. For a long time, the scream replayed in his head, the darkness pressing in around him.

❦ 12 ❧

CLASSES

The next time Finn opened his eyes, Ravenguard was leaning over him, his pointed nose mere inches from Finn's. He scrambled away from the admissions counselor's scowl, pressing his back into the headboard in an attempt to put space between him and the strange man.

"Rise and shine, boy. You'll be late for class." A square of parchment was thrust into Finn's face.

"What's this?"

"Your schedule."

Finn perused the table of classes on the paper. He flipped it over to find a crude map of the school and grounds drawn on the back.

"There are no time slots," he said.

"You start when the rooster crows and end with dinner in the dining room. Between times, the troupe leaders will tell you when to rotate."

Finn turned to check if Hope was listening, only to find her gone, bed made. Bright light streamed through the window.

Ravenguard grinned and glared at him over his spectacles.

"You've already missed breakfast. Would you rather spend the day with me?"

Finn had never dressed so fast in his life. He sped out the door, hair unbrushed and hopping on one foot as he slipped on his shoes. His first period was aerial with Orelon in what was labeled "the gazebo." On the map, it appeared to be in the middle of the front garden. Finn followed the winding path through the privets and blooming plants to a giant birdcage of a building at least three stories tall and as wide as a barn. The gazebo was situated at the end of a pebble pathway, in the center of a circle of bright green boxwood topiaries carved to resemble flying birds.

Orelon and Wendy already waited inside. Orelon did not look happy.

"You are late," he said, his voice a cool ripple.

"Sorry, I, uh..."

"Save it. I have no time for your excuses." The quiet assurance of his tone gave Finn the creeps, charged with a latent threat at odds with his soft voice.

Finn glanced from Orelon to Wendy, who was wearing a pair of purple-rimmed glasses this morning. Cute. "Uh, hi."

The hint of a blush colored her cheeks as she returned the greeting. Damn her eyes were beautiful. Was it him, or did her pupils get larger when she looked at him? She smiled, her gaze dropping to his toes with the warming of her cheeks.

A fine-boned face with a white braid stepped between them, scowling. "We don't have time for flirting either," Orelon murmured. His hand landed on Finn's shoulder and whirled him around. With a snap of his fingers, he beckoned them to follow to an area at the back of the gazebo where a cluster of equipment waited. "Today, we learn how to fall."

Wendy stifled a laugh.

"Something humorous, Ms. Matthews?" Orelon retrieved a stepstool from a stack of chairs and small ladders.

Wendy nervously tugged at her braids. "Uh, isn't falling the easy part?"

Orelon's gaze drifted up toward the rafters. "Natalie, please show Ms. Matthews how we fall in aerial."

Three stories above their heads, Finn could barely make out the silhouettes of other troupe members crouching on the wide wooden beams. From this distance and with only pockets of light, he couldn't tell if they were men or women. What Finn could tell was that they were all built like Orelon. Small, thin, almost like children.

One of them, Natalie he presumed, straightened on her perch, flattened her arms against her sides, and tipped forward.

"No!" Finn lurched in some unlikely attempt at catching her, but Orelon's hand shot out, landing squarely in the center of his chest. Couldn't he see she was too far up? No one could survive a plummet like that. It was suicide!

Slap. The girl belly-flopped onto the dirt, tight limbed and face down. Wendy gasped. Finn was too shocked to make any sound at all. Had they just witnessed a woman's death? Before Finn could take his next breath, the girl sprang from flat on her face to standing in one lithe move. No knees or elbows. No transition. Just up.

"How?" Finn murmured.

"Catch me if you can." Natalie flipped her red braid to the back of her uniform. She leaped onto the wall and climbed straight up, like some kind of lizard or frog. She didn't stop until she was in the rafters again.

"You can't expect us to do that!" Wendy pointed a slim hand in Natalie's direction. "We could break our necks."

Orelon clucked his tongue. "Naturally I don't expect you to do that."

Wendy breathed a sigh of relief.

"Not on your first day." He placed the small, wooden stool near the outline of Natalie's body in the dirt. "Today, we start with this. Who will be first?"

Wendy shifted beside Finn, taking a small step backward and shaking her head. She looked terrified. Finn couldn't stand to see her upset. He had pulled enough pranks in his life to know there must be a trick to what he'd seen. Perhaps, under all the dust and dirt, the floor was padded, or there were wires he couldn't see. Surely Orelon would teach him the secret.

"I'll go first," he volunteered, hoping to impress Wendy.

Orelon nodded. "Step up on the stool."

Finn did as he was told. The stool was no more than six inches high, but knowing he'd have to fall off it made it seem taller.

"When you fall, your arms must be tight against your sides, palms flat." Orelon yanked Finn's wrists to force his arms into perfect position. "Straighten up. Stomach in. Chest out. You have the build of a flyer, I'll give you that."

The build of a flyer. What did that mean? He supposed he was built like Orelon. Small. Light. It would be nice for that to be an advantage for a change.

"Now, fall. Best to close your eyes the first time or you're liable to catch yourself."

Finn frowned. "I don't understand. How do I do it without hurting myself?"

Orelon laughed. "You will most certainly hurt yourself. No pain, no gain."

Was he serious? With a jerk of his head, Finn focused on the dirt floor, so close but so far away.

"Fall!" Orelon barked, that soft breeze of a voice turning into a gust of raging wind.

Finn leaned forward, hands to his sides. The ground came up fast. At the last second, he caught himself on his hands and one knee and rolled out of the fall. All his breath left his lungs in an *oomph*. The dirt dug into the skin of his cheek and the resulting puff of dust stung his eyes.

"Sloppy," Orelon concluded as Finn worked to draw air into his protesting lungs. "You fall as if you want to hit the ground."

Finn stood, cradling his stomach. "What other choice is there?"

"Fall as though you don't believe you have to. Fall as if you know you can fly."

Wendy huffed. "People can't fly."

"That attitude will get you nowhere, Ms. Matthews. Your turn. On the stool."

Terrified, Wendy's gaze hooked onto Finn as if he were a life raft. She trembled and paled like she might be ill.

"Easy as falling off a log," Finn said to lighten the mood. He stood up straighter and dusted off his cheek. It stung. His hand came away bloody.

With slow, reluctant steps, Wendy stepped up on the stool.

"Your glasses," Finn said, holding out his hand to accept the purple-rimmed pair from her. Her fingers brushed his, cold and clammy. "It'll be okay," he whispered, meeting her gaze. He backed away and set the glasses on a ledge near the door.

"Now, Ms. Matthews."

She placed her hands against her sides. Orelon straightened each of her arms before slapping her back to get her to straighten.

"Fall."

Seconds ticked by. A bead of sweat trickled down Wendy's temple. "No," she said softly. "This is wrong. It's abusive. I want to talk to the headmistress."

Thwack. Orelon's leg connected with her shins. Wendy sprawled into the air, arms outstretched as the stool knocked out from under her feet. She landed with a sickening thump, and when she finally curled on her side gasping, blood coated her face. She'd broken her nose. A sickening wheeze came from her parted lips.

Finn started for her, but Orelon cut him off. He squatted beside Wendy and tugged at the skin of her cheek. "Natalie, the kit, please."

Wind whistled through the rafters above them, and a linen package tied with string dropped into Orelon's hands. He dusted it off and untied the string. From inside, he retrieved a square of cloth and a tub of salve. He gouged out a blob of the second and smeared it both inside and outside Wendy's nose, ignoring her cry as his fingers reset the break. He placed the cloth on top and taped it into place, then wiped his bloody hands off on a second cloth.

That was definitely not hygienic. Finn winced.

"There." Orelon lifted Wendy to her feet and wiped the blood from her cheek with the towel. She hobbled over to Finn, sliding in behind him as if he could offer her some measure of protection. He couldn't. What could he do? He'd seen what happened to people who didn't follow the rules.

Orelon's eyes fell on Finn. "Up on the stool."

"I'm hurt. My ribs." Finn lifted his shirt to reveal the start of a major bruise. "I can't do it again."

"You can, and you will," Orelon said through his teeth.

Shaking more than a little, Finn stepped up on the stool. Orelon straightened Finn's arms again and grabbed his face with both hands.

"This time, do not believe you must hit the floor. Believe you can fly. Close your eyes."

Finn obeyed. He was sore and stiff. He didn't want to fall again. But he leaned forward, body tensing into a plank. He hit the ground, catching himself with his hands at the last second. As before, it knocked the wind out of him, but he had to admit, it wasn't as bad as the first time. It still hurt, but he wasn't bleeding any more than before, and he didn't skid painfully across the dirt. Was he getting better at falling or getting used to the pain?

"Good, Mr. Wager. As I said, you have the build of a flyer."

๑๖๕๑

BY THE TIME FINN WAS DISMISSED FROM AERIAL, HIS TORSO ACHED

and was black and blue from neck to groin. He got off easy. Wendy's packed nose was bleeding through the gauze, and she breathed heavily through her mouth. She'd broken her nose multiple times, and her body was as beaten up as his was. At least he could still breathe.

"Are you going to be okay?" he asked on their way back to the school.

She shook her head. Tears cut through the dried blood on her cheeks.

"Maybe we should tell the headmistress."

"Are you kidding? The person who told Mrs. Wilhelm to punch Mike in the stomach? I don't think it's a good idea," she said, taking breaths between words because her nose was plugged.

Finn frowned. "Where are you headed next?"

"Menagerie." Her delicate eyebrows pinched together with worry.

"Hey, we forgot your glasses!" Finn left her side and rushed back to the gazebo to get them for her. He'd left them on a crossbeam that formed a small ledge near the door and was in better shape than Wendy to retrieve them. When he poked his head inside the shadowed interior, he froze.

He noticed the black and white stripes first. The movement made him stop just outside the door and peek around the corner. A clown, like the one he and Jenny had seen in the window their first day, squatted beside the spot where Finn and Wendy had fallen again and again. White-gloved fingers dipped into the bright red blood splattered in the dirt. It scraped the blood and dirt into a glass vile, screwed on a cap, and dropped the specimen into the pocket of his black pants.

From behind the archway that served as a door, Finn reached around to retrieve the glasses from the ledge using only his thumb and forefinger as not to make a sound. He rushed back to Wendy's side, praying the clown hadn't seen him.

"What's wrong, Finn? You look like you might be sick," Wendy said, accepting her glasses and placing them on her face, an action that made her wince.

Finn didn't answer. He wasn't sure what he'd seen exactly. "We're going to be late for class."

"Where are you going?"

"Pyro."

Wendy's throat contracted on a swallow. "Good luck." Quickly, she pulled Finn into a hug and took off in the direction of the woods. Finn's lips tugged upward into a painful smile.

"Move along, Mr. Wager," Orelon called from behind him. Had he been there the entire time? Had he seen the clown and the blood?

With a quick glance back, Finn hurried toward the school. Pyro was held in the theater itself, an ornately carved gold-and-red venue where his footsteps echoed over the empty seats. Fuse waited for him onstage, her lipstick the same shade of red as the flap on her uniform.

"Looks like you had Orelon first period." She grinned. "That's a hell of an initiation into the theater."

"You're familiar?"

"We were all students once." Her grin faded and she played with her thumbnail. "And now we're superheroes." She giggled at her own joke. "Where's your partner? I'm supposed to have two."

The doors at the back of the theater opened and Mike jogged in. His right forearm was bandaged from wrist to elbow and, as he drew closer, Finn could make out beads of sweat on his face.

"Are you okay?" Finn muttered.

Fuse didn't allow time for Mike to answer. "Mr. Carson will be fine. Looks like he's come from menagerie."

Mike swallowed and hugged his bandaged arm to his chest.

"Lion or tiger?" Fuse asked.

"L-leopard."

"You got off easy."

Finn raised an eyebrow. Mike didn't say a word.

Without further hesitation, Fuse selected a long baton from a rack at center stage and with a twist of her wrist, ignited the ends. As the flames rose toward the ceiling, she twirled it between her fingers, the torches licking the underside of her arm as it rotated. "Mr. Wager, which is hotter: the top of a flame or the bottom?"

"The top."

"If possible, which side of the flame do you want your skin on?"

"The bottom."

"Either way, I'd rather not be lit on fire," Mike said.

Fuse stopped rotating the baton with the torch practically in her armpit. The top of the flame engulfed her shoulder. She started twirling again and her shoulder extinguished. Somehow, her skin hadn't burned.

"I'm not going to light you on fire, Mr. Carson, unless you piss me off. Are you going to piss me off?"

"No, ma'am."

"Good. Pyro isn't just about this." She tossed the baton toward the ceiling, caught and twirled it around her body. "Or this." She tipped her head back, lowered the flame to her tongue, and blew a plume of fire into the air from her mouth. "It's about all kinds of fire play and pyrotechnics. Today, you're going to practice fire-walking."

She disappeared behind stage right, and a moment later the curtain behind the rack of instruments retracted to reveal a long, low box. Finn leaned forward to see over the edge and felt a blast of heat hit him in the face. Hot coals.

"What is this curtain called?" Fuse asked.

Finn and Mike looked at each other. Finn shrugged. He had no idea.

"We don't have any actors among us? No theater tech guys? Oh well, you will rise to the occasion, I'm sure. This is a *scene* curtain, not to be confused with the main curtain or drape as some call it." She motioned for them to come closer and Finn reluctantly did.

"Here's a tip—there's a book on commonly used theater terms in the library upstairs. I recommend you read it."

As if Finn's bruised body was going to be anywhere but in bed after classes.

"Now"—Fuse backed toward the smoking bin—"these coals are hot, over one thousand degrees Fahrenheit." She stepped onto the coals with her bare feet and started walking slowly backward. "So what three things keep me from burning? I'll give you a hint." She jogged faster.

"You're moving," Finn said. "Maybe there isn't time for you to burn?"

"Excellent, Mr. Wager. What else?"

Mike narrowed his eyes on his bandaged arm, flexing and releasing his fist. "You might have tough feet, like calloused or something."

She grinned. "Bingo. And it's not just me; everyone has feet that are made mostly of water. They don't burn easily." She was almost to the end and Finn tensed his shoulders, wishing she'd finish faster. He didn't like to see her on the coals.

"What's the third?" she asked.

Finn shrugged. Mike didn't know either.

Fuse stopped at the end of the coals and refused to step off.

"What are you doing?" Finn asked. The sizzle of burning flesh seemed to echo in the empty theater.

"Answer me!" she yelled. "What's the third? Why aren't I burning?"

Finn searched his head for something to say. "You're not human!"

All anger leached from her expression, and she burst into laughter. Thankfully, she stepped off the coals. "Oh Finn. That's rich. I am very much human. I was born in Hoboken."

"Then what is it?" Mike asked.

Fuse spread her hands. "I don't believe the flames can burn me." She pointed at her head. "It's all up here, boys. The minute you fear something it owns you. I'm guessing that's what happened with the leopard."

"Who locks a kid in a cage with a wild animal?" Mike rubbed his bandaged arm.

Fuse lifted one shoulder. "I'm guessing Amuke Mandla. Stop whining. This is what you signed up for."

Mike's mouth fell open.

"Take off your shoes and get to work." She nodded toward the coals.

"You want us to walk that? Now?" Finn asked.

"Now and ten minutes from now. I have you until lunch."

Mike took a step back. "This is insane."

Fuse's smile faded, and she strode toward Mike with malice in her eyes. The big guy stiffened and clenched his left fist.

"I'll go," Finn blurted. He regretted the offer the moment the words left his mouth.

Mike shook his head and made a face toward Finn that included a small roll of his eyes. "No. It's okay. I got this, Finn."

Was it obvious Finn was terrified? He breathed a sigh of relief. Not that he was surprised. It was like Mike to take the high road. Plus, if anyone could do this, it was Mike. The guy could do anything.

Mike kicked off his shoes and stepped up to the box. Biting his lip, he took a few careful steps over the coals before jumping out of the box. "Ow!" He cursed under his breath.

"Let me see." Fuse inspected Mike's feet. "Nothing serious. You were too slow. Next time, pick up the pace."

Mike scowled and limped to Finn's side.

"Okay, Wager. You're up."

"Come on," Mike said. "He can't do this."

The look Fuse gave Mike could have soldered iron. "You need another punch in the stomach to get with the program?"

Mike took a half step back and rubbed his injured arm.

"Mr. Wager." Fuse swept her open palm toward the coals.

Cracking his neck to the right and the left, Finn shook his arms and legs to try to relax. *Don't believe in the coals,* he repeated in his head. Or was he not supposed to believe in the heat? Or that he could burn? He couldn't remember. He took a deep breath and blew it out slowly.

Fuse tapped her foot expectantly. "Any year now, Wager."

Heat radiated against his face at the edge of the coals, as if he'd stuck his head in the oven. His feet were going to burn. It would hurt and he'd be walking on burned skin for the rest of the day. He hadn't even taken his first step, and he was already burning up. He lifted his foot and removed one shoe, then the other. The tips of his toes burned with their proximity to the coals.

"Get on with it, Shady," Fuse said.

Finn looked at her in surprise. "Why did you call me that?" Only his friends in Deviant Joe ever called him Shady. Not even his father knew the nickname.

"I guess you look shady," she said. "Plus, I read it in your chart."

Finn frowned. How did his nickname get into his chart?

"If you don't set your foot to those coals, I'm pushing you into them, and I promise you, your face is a lot less fire resistant than your feet."

With another deep breath, Finn blinked his eyes hard. Then he ran. He curled his toes up so that only the hard part of his feet touched the coals and he sprinted, fast and steady, across the box. The pain was instantaneous. He danced over embers, yelling with each step, the scent of roasting meat filling his nostrils. Was that his skin? His hair? He practically threw himself off the end of the coals, which was a problem because in his haste he kicked up a spray of sparks that burned his calf. "Argh!" He scrambled forward on elbows and knees until he was far enough from the coals to brush off the sparks.

Fuse knelt at his side. "I told you not to fall, Shady. Let me take a look." She rolled up the leg of his uniform. The skin below was bright red, but the uniform itself was intact. "The material is fireproof, but the contact was enough to burn your skin. Not too bad." She reached into the pouch around her waist and retrieved a canister of salve identical to the one he'd seen Orelon use on Wendy. As soon as it touched the burn, the pain stopped.

"What is that stuff?"

"Mangfruit salve. The fruit only grows on this island. Enhances the natural healing properties of this place."

"The school has healing properties?"

"Not the school, Veil Island. How do you think we can do the things we do?" Fuse smiled and taped a bandage over the salve. "If you work hard here, Finn, you will change for the better. The island will help you do that. Whatever you do on your own, it will magnify. You will be faster, stronger, more capable than you ever imagined."

Finn's jaw slackened. The thing about the instructors here that set him off balance was how much they seemed to believe what they said. Orelon was certain that if he didn't believe in gravity, he didn't have to fall. Fuse said burning was all in your head. Finn understood that it wasn't true, not scientifically at least, although he supposed there was some psychology behind it. His eighth-grade science teacher once told him that forcing a smile could release endorphins that made you feel happy. But gravity *was* real and flesh *could* burn.

Fuse turned to Mike, who was staring at Finn like he was seeing him for the first time. "Looks like you underestimated your little friend here. You gonna let him show you up?" She tipped her head toward the box of coals.

Finn grabbed his ankle and looked at the bottom of his foot. "Look, Mike, my feet didn't burn. I only hurt myself because I fell. You can do this."

Mike's gaze shifted between the box of coals and Finn's healthy feet. Cradling his arm, he crouched. Football stance. He took to the coals like a tire drill, his feet landing lightly before high-stepping forward. He was across and off the other side in no time. He pumped his fist in the air. "Right? You see that?"

Fuse slow clapped. "You might be a natural at this, Mikey." She held out her hand to Finn and helped him up. "Again. And this time don't fall."

❧ 13 ❧

LUNCH

Finn and Mike navigated the school to the dining hall feeling exhilarated. After successfully walking the coals more than thirty times each, they were relatively unharmed. Finn had a burn on his lower leg and Mike had a blister between his toes where a small ember had gotten caught, but that was the extent of the damage.

"It doesn't hurt anymore," Finn said, pausing to tear the bandage from his burn. He ran his fingers over the spot. "It's healed."

Mike stopped. "Actually..." He held out his arm and peeled back the bandage. Small dents marked his flesh, but the leopard bite looked weeks, rather than hours, old. It was filled in, pink, healed over.

"Damn. That fruit stuff works," Finn said.

Mike stared at the wound, his smile fading. "Don't you think this is strange, Finn? You'd expect this school would get sued off the face of the Earth for this stuff. You can't do this to kids."

"Yeah," Finn agreed. Footsteps echoed from somewhere behind them, and Finn started walking again. "I can't believe the head-mistress ordered her staff to punch you in the stomach."

"*You* can't believe it!"

"It's a private island. I guess they do things their own way."

"It's not *right*. This entire place isn't right." Mike shook his head.

Finn looked both ways and lowered his voice. "Look, maybe it's unorthodox, but we could be out of here in a semester. We can do anything for a semester."

Mike cracked his neck. "I guess."

"Anyway, it's only the first day. We have a week trial period. If it gets too bad, we'll transfer to Lakeview."

Mike tilted his head and furrowed his brow. "Trial period? They never told me about a trial period."

"It's in the contract."

Mike shrugged. His aunt wouldn't have read the contract. Not like Finn's father had.

"Hey, did they lose your luggage?" Finn asked, changing the subject when the vibe got weird. He didn't like to call attention to Mike's parental situation.

"No," Mike said. "Mine was delivered to my room last night. Did they lose yours?"

Finn paused at the door to the dining hall. "Yeah, my great-grandmother's antique trunk."

"Is there a problem, Mr. Carson? Mr. Wager?" Ravenguard said from behind them.

"No, sir." Finn hurried inside, joining the pack of students in line for the lunch buffet. He picked up a plate and eyed the silver trays of questionable cuisine. The yellow meat was the color of chicken but the wrong shape, with bones in all the wrong places.

Mike's hand shot out and nudged his elbow. "Finn, look."

Finn glanced over his shoulder. Sitting at the end of the table, closest to the head table, was a neatly dressed young woman.

"Is that...?" Mike whispered in his ear.

"Amanda." A flash of red caught Finn's eye. Ravenguard gave them a harsh look before stationing himself inside the door.

"That's Amanda Tidwell," Mike whispered. "She looks like a completely different person. No purple hair. No piercings."

Finn poked the maybe-chicken and plopped it on his plate while nonchalantly glancing over his shoulder at Amanda. No makeup. Hair cut into a neat black bob. She sat ramrod-straight and motionless, her eyes staring at the blank wall across from her.

"What do you think they did to her?" Mike loaded his plate, not even looking at the food.

"There's only one way to find out."

"How?"

"We ask. Come on." Finn turned from the buffet and took the seat next to Amanda. Mike sat down on her other side. "You must be Amanda. I'm Finn." He offered his hand.

Without turning her head, her eyes shifted toward him. She said nothing. She did not shake his hand.

Finn glanced at Mike before lowering his arm and picking up his fork. A bowl of watery soup filled the space in front of Amanda, but she wasn't eating. Her spoon rested, unused, beside her bowl.

"Not very hungry today?" Mike asked. The girl stared into the bowl like she was seeing it for the first time.

Ms. Applegate appeared at the door beside Ravenguard, the two talking softly and looking in their direction.

Finn took a bite of his lunch. "So, uh, Amanda, what have you been up to the last day? What's this intensive training they keep telling us about?"

Her eyes shifted again and her hand reached for her spoon. With jerky movements, she scooped the soup and raised a trembling bite toward her lips. Hardly anything completed the journey and what did dribbled out the corners of her mouth and onto her shirt.

Applegate and Ravenguard appeared at Amanda's side wiping up the spilled soup. "Ms. Tidwell, come with us. You aren't quite ready yet." The counselors helped the girl from her chair and ushered her from the room. They practically had to carry her.

"Did you see that?" Finn asked. "She's a zombie."

Mike rubbed his forehead. "Wrong. So Freaking wrong."

Finn forgot all about Amanda when he saw Wendy approach the table with a limp. He frowned when she chose a chair next to Paul instead of joining him. At least she looked marginally better than she had in aerial class. The nose packing was gone, although a nasty bruise still bisected her face.

A plate of food landed on the table next to him. Hope sat down. "Whatever you do, don't give them any reason to do that to you."

"What?"

"Amanda. She looked like an empty husk." Hope sighed in exasperation.

"Duh. This place is scary enough when you're not in trouble," Jayden interjected, taking the seat across from Finn. "I have a theory these people are sadists who failed out of dental school."

Finn chuckled.

"Have we met yet? I'm Jayden Parker." Jayden extended his hand toward Hope.

"Hope Laudner." She reached for his offered hand but stopped short, staring at a collection of bloody spots on his uniform. "Sorry, I, uh…" She retracted her hand and lifted her fork with it.

Eventually, Jayden sat back down, hand unshaken.

Finn snorted quizzically at Hope. "Cooties?"

She broke into a smile. "I have a sense about these things."

Mike ran his tongue along his teeth. "You are wise. He's a well-known cootie factory."

Jayden gave Mike the hairy eyeball, then rubbed an abrasion on his jaw and cracked his neck.

"Actually, I noticed you're hurt. You have blood on your hand," Hope said.

Jayden wiped his palm on his leg. "Beat to a bloody pulp," he confirmed. "What classes did you guys have this morning?"

"Aerial and pyro," Finn said. "You?"

"Menagerie and resilience. I was with Mike when he got bit," Jayden said. "It was resilience that almost killed me though. Amanda was scheduled to be my partner and since she wasn't there, I got knives thrown at me the entire period." He dropped his fork and leaned back in his chair. "Sliced the hell out of me."

"She truly stabbed you with a knife?" Hope asked.

He pulled back the collar of his shirt to reveal a bloody bandage over his shoulder.

"Kirsa straps you to a wheel and spins you before she throws." Jayden picked at his food. "Creates a beautiful spirograph of your own blood when it spurts from your spinning body."

"Do you mean to say Ms. Hildburg stabbed you on purpose?" Hope asked, appalled.

"I don't know. She might have missed the backboard... six times."

Setting her fork down, Hope spread her hands and lowered her voice. "Six times? That's no accident!"

Finn coughed. "Then again, what woman wouldn't want to stab Jayden?"

Jayden gave him the finger.

Hope chewed her lip and addressed Mike. "You got bit during menagerie?"

Mike flashed the bite scar on his arm.

"Do you think Amuke did it on purpose?"

He shrugged. "No. He told me the leopards were attracted to fear. Jayden was with me and he didn't get bit."

"I wasn't afraid. I'm an animal at heart." Jayden bobbed his eyebrows.

Hope didn't look amused.

"Okay, to be honest, the tiger demonstration convinced me Amuke had total control. Otherwise, I might have wet my pants."

Jayden narrowed his eyes at Hope. "Why are you the only one of us not hurt?"

"I am hurt. You just can't see it."

"What did you have this morning?"

"Pyro and menagerie." Hope pursed her lips. "My feet are burned."

"Ten minutes to third period," Mrs. Wilhelm yelled through the servant's entrance. Finn had a moment to notice she was holding a butcher's knife before she disappeared again. The front of her apron was streaked with blood.

"Aaaaand now Mrs. Wilhelm holds the starring role in my bloodiest nightmares," Jayden said, rubbing his eyes. The rest of them nodded their agreement.

"Time to go." Finn climbed out of his chair without moving the monster piece of furniture more than a quarter inch. "I'm off to spend an hour in a cage full of hungry animals without showing fear."

Mike rubbed his arm, his expression far too serious. Jayden clasped the big guy's shoulder and saluted Finn. "Beware the steaming piles of mud."

❦❦❦

ALTHOUGH AMUKE MANDLA WAITED OUTSIDE THE BOUNDARY OF A giant cage at the edge of the forest, he paced as if he belonged on the other side of the bars. His long, dark body moved like his bones could bend, fluid and nimble. Perhaps the man spent too much time with the cats. He had undeniable feline qualities.

The rustle of pine needles behind Finn turned out to be Rugby, otherwise known as Paul, racing to catch up.

"I went the wrong way," Paul muttered. "Why would they keep the animals in the forest?"

Finn chuckled at the comment, although he found the situation just as strange. He held out his hand. "I'm Finn, by the way. We haven't actually met."

"Paul Stewart." Paul's hand was sweaty. Finn wiped the residue on his pants. "Sorry. Animals make me nervous."

"Welcome to menagerie," Amuke said. He stopped his pacing as soon as they were close enough to engage. "Today, we will test your ability to maintain a calm and assertive energy in the presence of intimidating animals."

Paul stiffened. "What kind of animals?"

Amuke folded his hands. "Does the type of animal matter to you?"

"I don't like dogs."

Finn chuckled under his breath.

"What are you laughing at?" Paul oozed an almost palpable tension. Clearly, menagerie was outside his comfort zone.

Finn swallowed his laugh. "You look like you crush boulders with your bare fists for fun and you're afraid of... dogs." He stopped himself from mentioning the guy was three times his size but acting like a grade-schooler.

"I was bit as a kid. Don't be a dick."

Amuke cocked his head to the side. "No dogs today, Mr. Stewart." The man reached out one paddle-sized hand and pulled the gate open. "Enter, please."

Finn walked in, but Paul hesitated.

"Get in the cage." Amuke's voice was low and gravelly as a growl.

Reluctantly, Paul obeyed. He seemed relieved when Amuke left the door open.

The instructor turned toward the deep forest and placed a thumb and forefinger in the corners of his mouth. He blew a long, sharp whistle and followed it with a series of clicks. Finn waited. Within the dark recesses of the trees, a twig snapped. Then another. Something was coming. There was a moan, a growl, and then the rustle and thump of running paws. After talking to Mike and Jayden, Finn expected a team of trained leopards to emerge from the woods.

"Shit. No. No effing way." Paul backed toward the gate.

Amuke hadn't lied. It wasn't dogs that came out of the woods, or leopards. It was wolves—enormous red-eyed beasts that moved from darkness into light. The pack ran toward the cage, lips peeled back from elongated fangs.

Paul came unhinged. He lunged for the gate, but Amuke pushed him back inside.

"Don't show fear," Finn said to Paul. "They're attracted to fear."

Paul looked at him like he was out of his mind.

"Breathe." Finn grabbed Paul's bicep and shook. He demonstrated a deep breath, blowing it out slowly for effect. "Close your eyes and breathe."

Paul did, in time for the cage to fill with six wolves the size of bears. Their black fur filled the space. Finn froze. He could feel his heart knocking against his rib cage. He emptied his mind, forced his breath to even out.

Amuke closed and locked the gate.

"What is the point of this?" Paul asked. "Call them off, Amuke."

"That, Mr. Stewart, would be counterproductive. You need to make peace with your inner beast. You have one, you know, a thing inside you that takes control. We all know what you did to that girl."

"It wasn't me." The wolves circled.

"Tsk. Tsk. Tsk. To thine own self be true, Mr. Stewart. You are here to change, and change requires moving beyond your comfort zone."

Paul crouched, his eyes tracking the circling wolves. Three of the wolves lowered their heads and growled. Finn backed against the far side of the cage and closed his eyes.

"We can fight," Paul said to Finn. "We can fight our way out."

Finn shook his head and opened his eyes again. "We're not going to fight. This is part of the lesson. Just relax. You've made it this far. All we have to do is survive in this cage until next period."

"No. They're going to rip us apart." Paul's breathing came in shallow trembling gasps.

Amuke held his hands up and lowered his voice. "They will accept you if you accept them."

The sentiment was lost on Paul. His jaw tightened. His muscles tensed.

The wolves seemed to catch the scent of his fear. They moved closer. Finn forced his body to relax. But Paul shifted against the chain link as if he might come out of his skin. He made direct eye contact with one of the wolves.

"No way am I going out like this," Paul murmured. He lowered his body into a fighting stance, arms wide.

"Paul? What are you doing?" Finn asked. The staring and posture were inciting the wolf. "Back off, man. Come over here. Take a few deep breaths."

Amuke glanced between Paul and the wolf. "Listen to your partner, Paul. You are in an unwise position with this animal."

Paul shook his head. "If I go, I'm taking it with me." He lunged forward, gripped the wolf by the snout and twisted. There was a yelp and a crack as Paul rolled the beast onto the ground. He punched the wolf in the side of the head.

"Paul, stop!" Finn yelled.

Amuke opened the gate and rushed inside, shouting commands in another language. He was too late. The other wolves swarmed. Blood sprayed across the grass as the largest wolf clamped down on Paul's head. The others joined in, a frenzy of ripping jaws and snapping teeth. Paul let out a brutal scream. Finn pressed up against the chain link.

Amuke grabbed Finn's arm and dragged him through the open gate.

"Find Ms. D. Her office is on the second floor, east wing," Amuke said. "Tell her there has been an infraction."

Finn nodded. "An infraction."

"Go now." Amuke reentered the cage and locked the gate behind him.

Without hesitation, Finn ran for the school as fast as his legs would carry him.

❧ 14 ❧

THE HANGED MAN

Finn was through the doors and up the stairs in seconds, hands shaking and mind racing with the bloody memory of Paul's attack. But before he could search out Ms. D's office as Amuke had requested, Applegate appeared in front of him.

"Where do you think you're going, Wager?"

"I have to find Ms. D," he blurted. "Amuke sent me. There's been an incident, I mean—" What was the word Amuke had used? "an infraction."

A hint of mirth wrinkled Applegate's eyes at the corners, subtle enough that Finn questioned if he was reading the expression correctly. Why would Applegate be happy about this? Shouldn't she be concerned?

"Thank you, Finn." She placed a reassuring hand on his shoulder. "You've done the right thing. But no need to bother Ms. D. I'll handle this. Agreed?" She stared at him expectantly.

Finn nodded.

She rushed for the doors, leaving him standing in the second-floor hallway near the foyer. A squirmy feeling unraveled in the pit of his stomach. Why didn't he trust Applegate? For some reason, he sensed telling her was the worst thing he might have done.

"Psst. Psst."

Finn scanned the hall in the direction of the noise. An arm extended from around the far corner at the end of the hall, the white-gloved hand beckoning. Finn glanced over his shoulder to check if the gesture was meant for someone else, but he was alone. Cautiously, he investigated. The arm was attached to a lanky body in a tuxedo, Theodor Florea, the magician.

"Finn Wager, may I have a word with you?" Theodor asked.

Finn wasn't keen on returning to menagerie and had several minutes before his next class. "Uh, sure." He followed the man up the curved staircase to the third floor. He had the unsettling realization that he'd seen the clown through a third-floor window the day he arrived, although that was in a different part of the building.

Theodor led him down a dim hallway lined with walnut judge's panels and sketches of birds, to a broad archway where he blinked rapidly against the inflow of natural light. The source of the light was a long row of recessed windows, each surrounded by an alcove of books. Hardcover, paperback, and leather-bound volumes nestled in mahogany shelves.

"This is incredible," Finn mumbled. The woodwork was fashioned in ornate patterns the likes of which he had never seen before.

"This is the library," Theodor said. The closest bookshelf flaunted carvings of ocean scenes: ships, whales, and seashells. A mermaid bust protruded from the apex of each cabinet. "You don't find craftsmanship like this anymore."

Finn wandered to the next alcove. Lions, tigers, and leopards. He ran his fingers over a mane, tapped a cat's exposed tooth. The next alcove was decorated with gargoyles, the next, pagodas. The sheer number of books and scrolls was incredible, as was the architecture and the view of the gardens beyond.

Theodor stopped in a nook decorated with stars, magic wands, and top hats. "It's something, isn't it? These shelves continue along the perimeter of the entire third floor. Some of these texts are over two hundred years old."

"I've never seen anything like it, but where I come from, our library rents tablets. They haven't had paper books in years."

Theodor's thin mustache shifted as he lifted a leather tome from the shelf. "Personally, I've always been a fan of the printed word. There's a soul in every book, you know. The author creates a living thing in writing a story. It lives and breathes in our memories long after we've finished the tale."

"It's different seeing them on the shelf like this," Finn said, although he wasn't sure how a paperback had any more of a soul than any other type of book.

Theodor slammed the tome in his hands shut and returned it to the shelf. "Please forgive me for eavesdropping, but I overheard you tell Applegate about Paul's infraction. I understand he was mauled by wolves."

"You heard?" Finn felt a wave of nausea thinking about it and plunked down on the window seat.

"Word travels fast here. I'm sorry you had to see that."

Finn closed his eyes and rested his face in his hands. "I'm not sure I can handle this place."

"Hmm." Theodor leaned a shoulder next to a fat leather tome titled *Necromancy, volume 1*. "Perhaps I can help you with that."

Finn stared at the man, images of Paul, the wolves, the blood, flooding his brain.

"You'll forgive me for being presumptuous, but am I wrong to say that you enjoyed my demonstration yesterday afternoon?" Theodor asked.

"I enjoyed it very much," Finn answered honestly.

"I was wondering if you might consider working with me after your regular classes. I can't promise the extra lessons will mean a place as a magician, but perhaps there will be other... benefits."

Theodor's skin appeared waxy when the light fell directly on it. Finn waited for him to explain further. He didn't.

"I-I'd like to learn magic."

Theodor nodded slowly. "I thought so. Officially, it's not allowed—magicians and enchanters are not supposed to mentor first-year students—but I sense you hold the predisposition."

"About that, I thought students graduated this program after a year? How could *anyone* be eligible to train with you?"

He brushed the sleeve of his jacket. "Some choose to stay. All of the teachers here were once students."

Finn remembered the others in the rafters of aerial and that Fuse had mentioned she used to be a student, but after what he'd seen today, he couldn't fathom why anyone would choose to remain here longer than they had to.

"If we proceed, are you willing to keep our relationship a secret?" Theodor asked.

"Yes," Finn said.

"Very well. Before I begin a mentoring relationship, I like to know my odds." He reached into his pocket and produced a deck of cards. This deck was different from the one he'd used before: worn along the edges, with a set of black wings on the back. "Let's ask the tarot if this is a good idea."

"Tarot cards?" Finn scoffed. The idea that his future mentorship came down to a stack of cardboard and doodles made him feel even worse about his day.

Theodor stared down his nose at Finn. "We deal three cards. The first refers to your past preparation to study magic, the second, our present partnership, and the third, your future as an apprentice magician." He shuffled. One card jumped from the stack and landed on the floor near their feet. Finn leaned over to retrieve it. When he sat back up, there was a table at the center of the alcove and Theodor was seated at it.

"Oh!"

"Magic." Theodor shrugged. "What card do you have there, Finn?"

He flipped it over to find a picture of a man hanging by his foot.

"Ah, the hanged man. That is who you are, then." Theodor laughed. "I am not surprised."

"What does it mean?"

"The hanged man surrenders to his fate. You have given up on trying to control your own path and accepted that forces bigger than yourself are at work." He split the deck into three piles. "Choose."

Finn picked the pile in the middle. Theodor dealt three cards, side by side, on the table. He flipped the first.

"Knight of swords. In the past, you have been impulsive and unpredictable but loyal to the people you care for. You will be a fine apprentice if you are able to focus on your goals." He held up a finger and looked Finn in the eye. "Beware of people around you who act inconsistently. They will be your undoing."

"Um, okay." Finn scratched behind his ear.

Theodor flipped the second card. "Ah! Eight of pentacles!" He clapped his hands, positively delighted. "You are ready to learn something new. Ha-ha! What a perfect card to represent the start of our relationship."

Finn gazed at the drawing of a boy chiseling one of eight stars onto a disc and shrugged. If he said so.

"And finally, your future." Theodor flipped the final card. At the sight of dogs howling at the moon, his smile faded and his chin dropped.

"What is it?" Finn asked. "It looks like—"

"The moon," Theodor said.

Finn frowned. "What's wrong with the moon?"

"This card represents illusions."

"That's good isn't it, for a magician?"

"Sometimes the cards are unclear. The moon may indicate a deception or devious intent." He frowned.

"Devious intent? Why would I intend to deceive you? You're the best thing to happen to me today," Finn said.

Theodor chuckled and brushed the cards into the deck. "Perhaps it is nothing more than a vision of your future as a master illusionist. As the hanged man, your natural tendency is to go with the flow. But beware of anyone who is known to have deceived you."

"Sounds fair to me." Finn shrugged. He didn't take the cards seriously at all, but he hoped to say the right thing in order to receive the magic lessons. Not only did he think it would be cool to learn to conjure a table from thin air, but he suspected the relationship might provide him some protection. It would be worth it if Theodor could give him advice on navigating the demands of this crazy school.

Theodor stood and walked around the table. The images carved into the wooden shelves seemed to react to his shadow as he passed. The stars twinkled. The wands waved. The hats spun. Once his body swept through Finn's line of vision, the table disappeared. Finn understood it had to be an optical illusion, but all he could say was, "Cool."

"First assignment." Theodor retrieved a book from the shelf and handed it to Finn. "Read this."

From the yellowing cover, a young woman with raven-black hair and a dazzling smile stared back at him. *Walking on Water: Making the Impossible Possible* by Victoria Duvall.

"Is this by *the* Victoria Duvall, our headmistress?"

"Do you know anything about Victoria Duvall?"

"Only what I learned yesterday."

Theodor gave a small, tight-lipped smile. "I believe you will find this book extremely enlightening, Finn. Even lifesaving."

An odd thing to say. "I'll read it."

"Good." Theodor lifted the book from Finn's hands. "I'll

deliver it to your room for you. Now, you must hurry. You'll be late for your next class."

"But when do we start?"

Theodor handed Finn a card, a joker juggling three red balls. "Meet in this alcove when the balls drop. If there's an incident like there was today, and you need my help, say my name over the card and I'll come to you."

Finn nodded.

"Now go. Hurry. If you're late, there will be questions, repercussions."

Finn hurried from the library, feeling more than a little off balance. This was up-close magic, impossible to explain and unsettling to witness. He was both excited and terrified to learn Theodor's secrets: excited to perform the tricks, but terrified that knowing would ruin all sense of wonder at his abilities.

Regardless, as he pulled the schedule from his pocket and rushed toward a room called the armory for resilience class, he was glad to have something other than Paul to think about.

15

RESILIENCE

Hope paused on her way back from the gazebo, an icy prickle settling at the base of her neck. Ravenguard and Applegate were carrying a stretcher away from the menagerie area. Behind them, the grass was shiny red with blood. Wasn't Finn in that class?

"Move along, Ms. Laudner," Orelon said, his voice soft. His tone came across more empathetic than the words themselves.

She jogged into the school and breathed a sigh of relief to find Finn on the main stairwell. "Thank God you're okay." Her hand went to her heart. "I was coming from aerial when I saw Ravenguard and Applegate taking someone out on a stretcher from menagerie. Weren't you in that class? What happened? There was so much blood."

He looked distracted, like he didn't recognize her for a moment or two. When he finally did, he scrubbed his bright blond hair with his hand and rubbed his eyes like he'd just woken up.

"It was Paul. I'll tell you about it on the way to resilience. I don't want to be late."

Hope checked the map on the back of her schedule. "It says we're in the armory. This way." His feet fell in time with hers.

"When you took menagerie today, what animal was in the cage with you?" Finn asked her.

"Leopards. Why?"

"Mike had leopards too," Finn whispered. "We had wolves. Rabid, red-eyed wolves."

"Wolves?"

"When have you ever heard of a theater performance using trained wolves?"

"Never."

"It was like Amuke did it on purpose," Finn said. "Paul said he was afraid of dogs before he entered the cage and then, *boom*, we get wolves."

Hope's eyebrows sank and she shook her head. "That doesn't make any sense. He couldn't possibly change which animals he'd had in the woods, unless there's an entire zoo out there."

"How would you explain it?"

"You're saying Amuke called the wolves into the cage *after* Paul said he was afraid of them, and then they attacked Paul?"

Finn rubbed his chin. "No. Not exactly. I think Amuke called the wolves to antagonize Paul, but they wouldn't have attacked us if Paul hadn't attacked them first."

"What? Paul attacked the wolves?"

"Yes. He snapped one's neck. The rest retaliated."

Hope's eyes flashed toward the ceiling. "Forgive me for blaming the victim, but what a moron! Who is dumb enough to attack a pack of wolves?"

"I can't argue. But, Hope, when I told Applegate, she seemed completely unconcerned. She even smiled a little."

"Smiled?"

"It was odd. It gave me a bad feeling."

"They must have taken him to a hospital. There was so much blood."

Finn shrugged. "She said she'd handle it."

"The way she handled Amanda?" Hope snorted. "There was

something bizarre about that girl at lunch today. It was almost like she was possessed." They'd arrived at a door labeled "Armory" and Hope held it open for Finn.

"It's about time," Kirsa yelled from somewhere down below. "Get your asses down here!"

Although the room was described as an armory, it reminded Hope of an ultimate fighting pit. They had arrived on a second-floor platform that circled a sunken training ring. Every type of medieval weapon Hope could think of hung on the walls. Knives, tridents, chains, scythes, spears. The ceiling was a pulley system of concrete blocks and sandbags. No guns, but Hope wondered if they would work here anyway, considering the strange electro-magnetic properties of the island.

Hope hurried down a flight of metal stairs. She hated to think what all the weapons were for, although she didn't have to guess at the purpose of the wooden wheel at the center of the room. Kirsa pried a throwing knife from its belly.

"Welcome to resilience. I'm Ms. Hildburg, and I am here to make you stronger." She paced in front of them, eyeing Hope like she was of particular interest. "Hope, is it?"

"Yes."

"I think you should go first. Let's see what you're made of." She slapped the wheel.

"Why her?" Finn asked.

Hope wondered why Finn said anything. It was obvious he didn't *want* to go first. Maybe he felt sorry for her. Hell, Hope felt sorry for herself. The way Ms. Hildburg looked at her was like she'd found a new plaything, a cat toying with a mouse.

Kirsa placed her fists on her hips. "Does Hope look like the kind of girl who needs a boy to save her?"

"No," Finn said. "Maybe I just want to go first."

"I'm glad you agree, and sorry, but I've made my choice." Kirsa took Hope by the elbow and coaxed her toward the wheel.

This was the class Hope was most worried about. As a Soulkeeper, she was naturally more resilient than most humans, but making that too obvious could have dire repercussions. As she stepped up on the small ridge and placed her back against the wood, she focused her mind on appearing normal. One at a time, Kirsa strapped her wrists into place, then her ankles, tightening the leather buckles until Hope winced. No matter how much it hurt, she must not wrench her arms free from the cuffs, or move too quickly to avoid the blades.

"We always start on the wheel," Kirsa said. "It's an old trick, too cliché for a real performance, but it serves a valuable purpose." She selected three knives from the rack and backed away from Hope. "The restraints force you to absorb the full impact. Without them, you might jerk or twist to avoid the cut."

"How can she *absorb* the impact?" Finn asked. "You have a knife. You're talking about stabbing her."

"Change is only possible when the body is stressed."

"They keep telling us that."

"Because it's true." She approached Finn and tapped the point of the knife on his chin. "A cut here, a slice there, and the body adapts. Your skin gets thicker. Your muscles become more resilient."

"It's okay, Finn. Don't get in trouble because of me," Hope said softly.

Finn shook his head, his face reddening. Hope's impression of Finn was that he was not the type of kid who usually took a stand. In fact, he struck her as someone who often flew under the radar, used his small stature and underestimated wit to get what he wanted. So, she was surprised when her new roommate pushed back.

"You can't become resilient to a steel blade. It's impossible," Finn said through his teeth.

Kirsa snorted. "If you believe that, you haven't been paying attention. Your friend here has already begun to change." She pointed her knife at Hope. No... No... Hope cringed against the wheel, her eyes darting between Kirsa and Finn. Had Kirsa noticed something already?

"What are you talking about?" Finn asked.

Kirsa closed in until Hope could feel her breath on her face. "The way you walked down those old metal steps was incredible. I heard every step Finn took, but not you. Your steps were silent. And fast. Faster than normal for someone who's only been here a day. I have a feeling that you are one of the special ones."

Hope shook her head. "I'm not. I don't know what you're talking about."

Kirsa lifted one corner of her mouth and shrugged a hyper-muscular shoulder. "We'll see about that." Approaching the wheel, she grabbed the edge and with a downward sweep of her body, sent Hope spinning.

Hope closed her eyes and focused her mind, trying her best to tolerate the repeated rotations. The first knife flew from Kirsa's hand. Hope heard it sing through the air, her heightened senses projecting its trajectory in a split second. She shifted slightly and it sank into the wheel a finger's width from her bottom rib.

Finn exhaled in relief.

"Missed," Kirsa said. "Can't win them all." Another knife flew from Kirsa's hand.

Hope sensed this one too and shifted, but Kirsa's aim was at the center of her body, and there was only so far she could move within the restraints. The blade sliced into her abdomen to the left of her belly button. The pain was sudden and intense. She screamed, warm blood spreading across her stomach from the force of the spinning.

She heard the shuffle of footsteps.

"You're wasting valuable class time, Finn," Kirsa said.

Hope opened her eyes to find Finn trying to stop the wheel. The wood grazed his fingertips until the friction slowed her spinning. Kirsa didn't stop him. In fact, she lowered her knife with a huff.

"She's hurt. She needs a doctor."

Hope tried to meet Finn's eyes, but he was too absorbed in her stab wound. "Finn…"

Kirsa waved a hand dismissively and moved for a bundle of healing supplies strapped to the wall. "She doesn't need a doctor. I'll fix her up."

Finn didn't seem to hear either of them. He grabbed the hilt of the blade.

"Don't pull it out," Kirsa said flatly. "She'll bleed more."

But Finn wasn't listening. He seemed almost in a trance as he yanked the knife easily from her flesh. A spurt of blood followed the blade. Finn pressed his hands against the wound.

"I told you not to pull it out!" Kirsa yelled. She approached with the kit, shoving Finn away. But she broke into laughter when she inspected the wound. "Hot damn."

Poor Finn staggered back in confusion. Hope wanted to say something, wanted to explain why her abdomen was completely healed, but she had to play along. She had to act as surprised as he was.

"See?" Kirsa said to Finn. "I can always spot the ones who can adapt. You think that's something? Watch this." She stabbed Hope in the chest, right above her bottom rib.

Hope's mouth gaped in a silent scream. Healer or not, a knife to the chest hurt. The pain reverberated through her lungs.

Finn paled and held his hands out to her, helpless and no doubt thinking she was about to die. With what he'd been through with Paul earlier, she hated to put him through this, but there was nothing she could do.

Hope coughed, then gagged, blood splattering across her bottom lip. The knife slid out again, followed by another splash of blood that stained more of her uniform. She tried to stop it, to hold back her power and keep her secret, but the wound stitched itself closed. When it was entirely healed, Hope let out a deep breath of relief before promptly turning her head and hurling vomit over her shoulder.

"Looks like we've hit her limit," Kirsa said calmly. She unfastened Hope's restraints while dodging the heaving sick.

"I can't. No more," Hope managed to say between heaves.

"Relax. You did well today. Go to your room and sleep it off." She pushed Hope toward the staircase.

Hope glanced at Finn. What if Kirsa tried the same with him? "Finn," she whispered.

He responded by grabbing her under her elbow.

"Where do you think you're going?" Kirsa asked him.

"I thought I'd help her to our room," Finn said. Hope didn't need help, but she wanted Kirsa to think she did. If he was allowed to walk her back to the room, she might save him from the agony awaiting him here.

The hefty woman shook her head. "You're next. She goes alone."

Hope gave Finn a long, scared look before sliding her arm from his. He backed toward the wheel. By the time she'd reached the top of the stairs, Kirsa had him strapped in. The worst part was the look on his face. His eyes narrowed on Hope as if she were a riddle he couldn't solve. And then Kirsa gave him a spin, and his face blurred into an indistinguishable array of colors and shapes.

16

AFTER

Brain

Finn was dismissed after another hour of being nicked and scraped by hurled blades. He'd spun on the wheel until he was sure he'd be as sick as Hope. Kirsa had stopped short of stabbing him in the lung, thank goodness. Still, the experience was anything but pleasant.

"Unlike your roommate," Kirsa said as she unstrapped him and dabbed his latest wound with a glob of healing salve, "you have no propensity for resilience." She scowled. "You can go."

He wasted no time limping from the armory and crossing the mansion to find Hope. Everything hurt, but he hastened his steps anyway. He had questions that needed answers. Bursting into their room, he expected to find her curled up on the bed or hunched over the sink in the bathroom. Instead, she was staring out the window, her fingers rubbing circles over the three intertwined ovals of her pendant. She'd already changed out of her bloody uniform.

Finn shook his head. She didn't seem hurt in the least. "Why aren't you injured? I saw Kirsa stab you in the chest."

When she turned from the glass, Finn could see she'd been

crying. He almost felt bad for being so blunt. Almost. Unlike him, she didn't look like a used pincushion.

"I don't understand this place," she said. "Why do you think they're doing this to us?"

He grimaced. "I don't know. You didn't answer my question. How is it that Kirsa stabbed you in the chest and you healed?" He pointed at a large tear in his uniform near the shoulder. "I know firsthand those knives are real."

Hope's gaze traveled around the room. "Get dressed. We'll be late for dinner."

"You're not going to tell me, are you?"

"What makes you think I know?" she snapped.

He narrowed his eyes on her. Once it was clear she wouldn't or couldn't answer him, he grabbed a new uniform from his drawer and shut himself into the bathroom. His head spun with thoughts of Paul and Hope and even Theodor. Everything about this place was evil. Students ripped apart by wolves. Teachers stabbing kids for fun. Being forced to fall on your face for an hour. He'd been wrong. Lakeview would have been the better option.

There was a basket in the corner labeled "Laundry." Finn peeled off his bloody and torn garb and tossed it on top of Hope's, then on a whim, dug hers out to inspect it more closely. It was torn and stained with blood where he remembered her being stabbed, the largest area a bright red patch under her left rib. He tossed it back into the basket, shaking his head.

Something was odd about Hope Laudner. Could he trust her? She was here for a reason. She'd done something, something bad enough to earn her a ticket to this place. Kirsa called her one of the special ones. What the hell did that mean?

Finn took a good look at himself in the mirror over the sink. He ached to his bones and sported a rainbow of injuries. Deep purple bruises dappled his body. A wound in his shoulder itched under its gauze bandage, as did the bright red cuts along his ears, cheeks, and legs. Most of his skin was black and blue, and the gauze pads covering his wounds were either bloody red or soaked yellow with healing balm. He dug his fingers under one on his thigh and peeled it back.

"They should market this shit," he said, scratching the tight, newly healed skin. He tossed the gauze and peeled back another. Healed. He was bruised, he was bloody, but he wasn't bleeding. Not anymore.

Finn cursed under his breath. Maybe Hope hadn't done anything special or bizarre after all. Was it this place, the balm? It was like... magic. The thought made him think of Theodor and his dancing cards. His head started to pound. What did it all mean?

By the time Finn emerged from the bathroom, Hope was already gone. To his surprise, the book Theodor had lent him rested on his made bed. He tucked it beneath his pillow for safe-keeping. Best if he didn't need to explain where he'd gotten it. He slipped his feet into his shoes and rushed toward the dining room.

Jenny Pendleton met him at the door. "Have you seen Paul? He didn't come back to our room."

"Didn't anyone tell you? He was injured in menagerie, mauled by wolves."

"Wolves? Why? How?"

Finn told her the entire story over dinner, repeating details as the others arrived and joined them. Hope wasn't there, and he briefly wondered where she'd gone.

"Is anyone else skeptical about the claim they've never lost a student?" Wendy whispered.

Mike agreed. "I don't believe it. Everything about this place is dangerous."

"You don't think it's fair for them to torture delinquents in the name of entertainment?" Jayden scoffed.

"This place is worse than Lakeview," Finn said. "At least there they don't pretend to be something they're not."

"You mean because the glossy photos made this place look like a spa?" Jayden laughed bitterly. "I could paint your nails for you, Wager." He ran a hand through his too-long red hair.

"You can paint *my* nails," Jenny said, fluttering her eyelashes over a fist-sized bruise on her cheek.

Jayden circled one hand in the air. "At your service. Since Paul is indisposed, why don't you join Wendy and me in our room tonight? I'll do your fingers *and* your toes."

Wendy cleared her throat. "What about my toes?"

"Finn Shady, would you care to join us for a spa night? I'm not sure I can handle twenty."

Smooth. Finn exchanged smiles with Wendy. "Uh, sure."

"So, there you go. Finn will do you…"

Finn's cheeks blazed.

"I mean, your toes. And I'll do her." Jayden leaned toward Jenny with a crooked half smile.

"And when you boys are done we'll both look like well-kept domestic abuse victims," Wendy said, checking out the bruises around her broken nose in her spoon.

Mike groaned. "Hey, what about me?"

"I'm not sure who can paint your toes, Mike," Jayden said. "Where's Hope, Finn?"

Finn shrugged. "I don't know. She never came down."

"Did you notice the admissions counselors are missing as well?" Jenny said.

"Do you think they're doing whatever they did to Amanda to Hope?"

Finn rubbed his head, feeling anxious.

Mrs. Wilhelm appeared next to them, seemingly out of thin air. "All children must be in their *own* rooms by sundown." She searched Jayden's eyes and then Jenny's, before lowering her voice. "Don't test them. It won't end well." She disappeared as quickly as she'd arrived.

Jayden glanced at the sinking sun outside the window and frowned. "So much for spa night."

⚜

AFTER DINNER, FINN HURRIED BACK TO HIS ROOM, PRAYING HOPE wasn't Applegate and Ravenguard's latest project. He was relieved to find her sitting on her bed.

"There you are," Hope said as if he was the one who wasn't where he was supposed to be. "I have something to show you."

"You missed dinner," Finn said. He lowered his voice. "Wendy thought Ravenguard took you, like Amanda."

She stepped close to him, until the sharp contours of her face were a hand's width from his. "I found something."

Finn glanced through their window toward the sinking sun. "Make it fast. We have to be in our rooms by sundown."

"Why?" she asked.

"What makes you think they'd explain it to me? Mrs. Wilhelm was adamant."

"Never mind. Come on." She grabbed his elbow and ushered him to the back stairwell. Before long, he recognized exactly where she was going.

"You found the library," he said.

"You know about it?"

He remembered Theodor's warning that he was not to tell anyone of their lessons and thought quickly of an alternate truth. "I had some extra time on my hands after Paul's accident."

She pushed the door open with her hip and jogged down the hall of birds, past the archway where Theodor had led him, and into another section of the library. She stopped at an alcove carved like the trunk of a hollowed-out tree. Its branches bent around the books, carvings of individual leaves layered over knobby bark. The occasional wing of a bird projected from the shelves.

"Is this where you've been all afternoon?" Finn asked.

"Once I stopped tossing my cookies and after I saw you in our room."

"About that—"

"Not now. I need to show you something. Something that affects us all."

"Show me what?" He was too tired and sore for this. He leaned his shoulder against a shelf filled with books about horticulture. Hope squatted down and pulled a giant leather portfolio from under the window seat. It landed with a thud on the bench, and she used two hands to open the front cover.

"What are those?"

"Past Revelations Theater advertisements." She opened the book to a yellowing poster of a woman bent backward, her torso parallel to the floor. She was en pointe, dressed like a ballerina. One of her arms twisted toward the ceiling like a dancing snake while her other held a flaming torch.

"Come see the burning woman. She's fireproof and hotter than Hades," Finn read. He thumbed the edge of the sepia print. "Revelations Theater, Spring 1972."

"Doesn't the woman look familiar?" Hope asked.

"Sure, she looks like Fuse. Probably a relative. Maybe her mother?"

"Or maybe it's her."

Finn snorted. "She'd be over fifty years old. You've seen her. She couldn't be more than twenty-five."

Hope turned the pages back toward the beginning. This poster showed a woman hovering above the stage in the grips of a blue glow. Behind her, a man's face was partially hidden in shadow. The grainy quality of the print made it impossible to identify the man, but the pencil-thin mustache and dimpled chin looked a hell of a lot like Theodor's. "Let the magic sweep you off your feet. Revelations Theater, Fall 1943. What? That's impossible."

Hope flipped all the way to the end. Juliette Bittercourt, her face bisected by the edge of the poster, stared at Finn in her peacock-blue splendor.

"Sirens and sorcery. Tomorrow is yours. Revelations Theater, Spring 2017. You'll never see the future the same way again," he read.

"That's Juliette. That was ten years ago. She hasn't aged a day. The last poster representing an enchanter other than Juliette was in 1990. Here." Hope flipped back a few posters to a familiar-looking woman with raven-black hair, arms outstretched and mouth open in silent song.

"Who is that? What happened to her?"

"I don't know," Hope said. "None of the posters have names. But she was a long-term veteran of Revelations." Hope flipped back to the beginning of the book, to a yellowed parchment of a poster. The dark-haired woman was there in black and white, looking exactly the same as she had in the picture from 1990.

"1942," Finn said. "This doesn't make any sense."

"That, Finn, is the smartest thing you've said since I met you."

"There must be an explanation. These couldn't possibly be the people we know. I bet these are props, advertisements for the show made to look old."

Hope's expression closed off and she knotted her fingers. "Possibly." A long shadow stretched toward Finn over the wall of books. "We don't have much time." She closed the book and put it back where it came from.

Finn headed for the stairs, breaking into long strides in the hallway. He reached his room just as Ravenguard topped the main steps from the foyer and gave them a threatening glare. Hope shoved Finn hard in the back, trying to make it inside before the admissions counselor reached their room. The last hint of light faded entirely at the moment Ravenguard's form crowded their doorway.

"Lucky you," the man said from the doorway. Under the shadow of his bowler hat, a muscle in Ravenguard's jaw twitched, his glasses bobbing with the movement. He closed the door without the hint of a smile or a wish good night. There was a click and the grind of a key turning in the lock.

Finn turned to Hope. "Commence nighttime imprisonment."

❧ 17 ❧
BIRD MAN

Hope stared at the locked door and realized she was in way over her head. What was going on at this school wasn't reform; it was child abuse. But she wouldn't be here if it wasn't also something else, something evil.

"Why do they lock us in at night? Where are we going to go?" Finn asked, spreading his hands. "We're on a frickin' island."

"Maybe it's not about what *we're* going to do." Hope flopped onto her bed with a bounce. There was only so much she could tell Finn. Too much would put him at risk. Not enough would put him at risk.

"You think they lock us in for our protection?"

"The woods *are* filled with barely tamed animals." She stared at the ceiling, the events of the last few days tumbling inside her skull.

"It's like Revelations has a mystery around every corner." Finn shook his head.

Swallowing, she said, "Thanks for coming with me. I had to show someone. It's just so weird."

"How did you heal yourself, Hope?" Finn asked.

"I…" She shrugged. "You can use the bathroom first."

"Whatever." He grabbed his pajamas and drifted into the bathroom. He looked perturbed. She supposed he was running out of patience with the mysteries involving her.

As soon as the water started running, she rushed to the window and pulled her triquetra pendant from around her neck. "Messenger, I call upon thee."

Light refracted through the glass, folded and expanded into a shimmering gold column. Once the glow dimmed, Gabriel formed with his wings flexed, at the center of the room.

"You called?" he said softly. "How may I serve you, Daughter of Angels?"

"You could drop the formal act and get me out of here."

He shook his head. "You know I can't do that. You're here for a reason. You must determine who or what is stealing the lost souls."

"They're going to figure out what I am," Hope said through her teeth. "I'm too strong and too fast."

"What did the Immortals say when you went to the In-Between?"

"I didn't go over."

"What? Why?" Gabriel's scruffy chin wrinkled with his frown. She'd long gotten over expecting him to look angelic. Gabriel looked like a middle-aged guy with wings who was perpetually stressed out and hungover.

There was a long pause while Hope tried to think of an excuse. Nothing came to her. "I didn't go. It is what it is." Visiting Time, Death, and Fate wasn't her idea of a good time. Any sane person might have procrastinated.

"Go over now."

"I can't. I've tried. There's something about this place. It's not working."

"This hardship is your doing. Without them, you'll need to find out for yourself who is behind the lost souls. Remember why you are here."

"Has *He* told you anything?"

"Nothing."

"What should I do? I'm going into this completely blind," Hope whimpered.

"You'll have to investigate the old-fashioned way. Who is pulling the strings? With proof, we can take action. Without it, we could upset the balance."

"Right. The balance—"

"Gain the trust of the boy," the angel said, glancing toward the bathroom.

"What?" Hope was perplexed. What did Finn have to do with any of this?

"There are no mistakes when it comes to His work, Hope. You were paired for a reason, and I sense your friendship will serve a purpose."

"But—"

The floor in the bathroom creaked and Hope stopped midword. When had the water stopped? She whirled on Gabriel, but he was already gone. By the time Finn opened the door, there was only a large white falcon on the ledge outside their window. It spread its wings and flew toward the woods.

"Who were you talking to?" Finn asked.

Hope laughed. "No one. I've been sitting here the entire time."

"I heard voices."

"I was…" She shifted off the bed and gathered her pajamas from her dresser. "I was talking to the bird."

"I heard a male voice."

"That was me pretending to be the bird." She tucked her chin into her chest. "I am a big bird of prey," she said in a low, gravelly voice. She sounded like an idiot. But there wasn't anything else to say.

His jaw popped open and his eyelids sank until he peered at her through narrow slits. "Seriously? Who are the Immortals, and why didn't you go to see them?"

Hope froze. He'd heard. She forced her expression to turn blank. "The door is locked, Finn. Who would I be talking to?" She didn't wait for his answer. She hurried into the bathroom and closed the door.

৩১৩

ONCE FINN WAS ALONE IN THE ROOM, HOPE BEHIND THE BATHROOM door with the shower running, he walked to the window and stared out toward the woods beyond. The white falcon was perched in a tree, staring back at him with black, beady eyes. Weird.

"My roommate talks to birds." He rubbed his forehead. A headache had taken root behind his right eye. Exhausted and irritated, he climbed into bed.

His hand slipped under his pillow and caught on the book Theodor had lent him. He'd almost forgotten about it. He leaned over to turn on the lamp, the gas hissing before the dull light filled the bulb in that strange way that was unique to Revelations. *Walking on Water: Making the Impossible Possible* by Victoria Duvall. The cover image was of a young woman with raven-black hair and a dazzling smile. This was why the poster Hope had shown him in the library had looked familiar. The woman from the poster was Victoria Duvall. He opened the cover and flipped to the copyright page. *Printed in 2005. Cover photo of Victoria Duvall, 1999.* He shook his head. The poster from today was labeled 1942. It had to be a fake. But how old was she? He flipped to the introduction.

For as long as I can remember, I've believed that physical limitations are a construct of our mental limitations. Over the course of my fifty years as a dancer, performance artist, and choreographer, I've studied with gurus and mystics from around the world. They believe as I do. Limitless power exists within each of us. We simply must strive for it.

You say, "But Victoria, the human body can only jump so high; we can only move so fast." *Do not bore me with your narrow-minded beliefs. In 1912, the Men's Olympic High Jump gold medalist jumped 1.93 meters, or a little over six feet. Surely, at that time, this was considered the highest a human being could ever jump unaided. Until 1993, when Javier Sotomayor hurled himself over a 2.45-meter bar. Now there was a new limit, a new highest.*

Why stop there? Certainly, if man can gain a meter, he can gain ten. Why do we believe in limits? Is it because of gravity? Because of our physical place in the universe? I reject this notion. Our reality is an illusion to be overcome. I believe human evolution didn't end when we learned to walk upright.

We were meant to fly.

⊗⊗⊗

FINN JOLTED AWAKE FROM A DEEP SLEEP. THE HUNTING PARTY WAS at it again, the dogs yapping outside his window. *Walking on Water* was open on his chest, but Hope must have extinguished the lamp because the room was dark. She was asleep, curled on her side with her back to him. Quietly, he marked his page and returned the book to the underside of his pillow. He slipped from under the covers. The barking grew louder, the hunting party near enough that Finn could make out the huffing breath of horses.

He couldn't see the dogs from his window, but the white falcon was still there. The bird's reflective eyes formed two perfect circles of light at the edge of the moon-washed forest. An evening breeze stirred up leaves and pine needles on the ground below, the swaying trees causing shadows to dance toward the school before receding into the dark.

One shadow did not recede, a silhouette that broke from the protection of the woods. A dark figure, hunched like an ape but with a human gait, hobbled closer, into the moonlight. Dirt, blood, and tufts of hair clung to the thing's torn clothing.

"Who?" Finn whispered.

The visitor glanced over his shoulder, the moonlight catching on the features of his profile for the first time. Matted hair, crippled limbs. One side of his face was shredded, the eye swollen shut, ear bloody, lip torn. Though gruesomely distorted, the man looked familiar.

Finn placed his hands against the glass. It wasn't a man but a boy wearing a shredded black Revelations uniform with purple piping. Paul. The boy's one working eye flicked to Finn, and those bloody lips formed a single unfortunate word—*help*.

Paralyzed with fear and confusion, Finn looked around the room and toward his locked door. What should he do? What *could* he do?

It was too late. One of the large black dogs appeared at the corner of the gardens. Paul ran for the woods. A moment later, a shrill scream cut through the glass. Finn screamed too, until a hand clasped over his mouth and pulled him from the window.

"Shhh."

A split second later, he was in his bed, under the covers, with Hope shaking him by the shoulders. He blinked up at her. "Paul!"

"Finn, you were dreaming, screaming in your sleep."

He bound out of bed and rushed to the window. It was still dark. There was nothing at the edge of the wood aside from dead leaves that swirled in the wind. "He's gone."

"Who's gone?"

"Paul."

"Paul was injured. He wouldn't be outside."

"I saw him. He was at the base of the woods, under the bird you were talking to."

Hope chewed her lip. "You were dreaming. Probably traumatized from seeing Paul hurt."

"There were dogs. It was another hunt. He was hurt badly, all curled in on himself and mutilated."

She shook her head. "I didn't hear any barking. I would have woken up. I'm a very light sleeper. You had a nightmare, Finn. That's all."

Finn frowned and lay back down. "It seemed real." He climbed into bed and stared at the ceiling.

The springs of Hope's bed creaked as she returned to the safety of her covers. "Nightmares often do."

❦ 18 ❦

TRIAL PERIOD

There was no mention of Paul the next day. Finn endured his schedule of falls and burns, including a traumatic hour alone in a cage of pacing leopards. After a replay of yesterday's resilience class, Finn couldn't take it anymore. He was bloody and sore, sick to his stomach, and exhausted. Mentally, he was done. Finished.

Amuke had said Ms. D's office was on the second floor, east wing—the opposite wing as their dormitories. He took a right at the top of the stairs instead of a left. Near the end of the hall, an ornate-paneled doorway was labeled with a brass placard: *Headmistress Victoria Duvall.* He knocked three times.

"Come in."

Finn had pictured Ms. D behind a big mahogany desk, maybe seated in a leather chair surrounded by file cabinets and other accouterments of school administration. Instead, he found a rummage sale. The old woman, dressed in a purple tracksuit, jumped on a small trampoline near the window. A massive red rubber ball rested against the wall beside her. Across the room, a tree, designed of painted clay and twisted wire, was home to a rope swing that swayed from its branches. The walls were covered in vintage posters advertising everything from opera to freak show acts. Stacks and stacks of books and papers were piled in no specific order in every corner.

This was not an office. This was a playroom.

Ms. D did not stop jumping when Finn entered. "What can I do for you, boy?"

"I, uh, don't mean to bother you, but I was with Paul Stewart during the... infraction and I was wondering if you could tell me if he's all right?"

She stopped jumping. "You saw what happened to Paul?"

He nodded. "I was there. Applegate said she would handle it, but I just... is he okay?"

Her wrinkled lips pressed together. She stepped off the trampoline. "Paul Stewart. Hmm. Not exactly surprised about that one." She waved her hand dismissively. "He's fine. He'll be back in a few weeks."

"Is he in a hospital or something?" Finn asked. "Can he have visitors?"

She snorted. "There are no hospitals on this island. Even if there were, you are not allowed to leave the school for any reason."

"No hospital? What do you do when someone gets hurt?"

"Why, we handle it ourselves. Like now, Applegate and Ravenguard are healing Paul. You have nothing to worry about." She held up one bony finger.

Finn scratched the back of his neck, the memory of Paul's screaming and bloody face coming back to him in a wave that made his eyes prickle with unshed tears. "I'd like to call my father."

"No contact is allowed—"

"Ravenguard said I had a week trial period."

The words dropped like a lead weight between them. Ms. D rubbed her chin. "Trial period, you say?"

Finn nodded. "He said I had a week to change my mind. It was in my contract."

Ms. D strolled to a red-and-black cabinet that lined the wall of her office. She opened one of the doors. The shelves were packed with scrolls of parchment. After checking a few, she said, "Ah, here it is." As she unraveled Finn's between her hands, there was a moment of silence while she perused the document.

"You are correct. It seems Ravenguard did offer you a trial period. And you are sure you want to invoke that clause in our agreement?"

He nodded.

"You would do that? Abandon your friends to run away at the first sign of trouble?"

"First sign? Every class is torture. I have more injuries than I can count. No hospital? It isn't safe here. When I leave, I'm sure my friends will leave too." Finn's hands trembled, his stomach turning with the intensity of the moment. For someone who prided himself on flying under the radar, the direct approach was terrifying, but he had no choice. He had to get out of this place.

She approached him, lips drawing back from her teeth, more threat than smile. "Your friends don't have a choice."

"What?"

"The one-week-trial clause is not in our standard contract. Ravenguard extended it to you alone. Michael and Jayden have no such clause. You may leave, but I'm afraid your friends must stay."

All the air rushed from Finn's lungs as if he'd been gut punched.

"Of course, if your friends are having similar problems adjusting, a few days of intensive therapy with Ravenguard and Applegate should help. I wouldn't concern yourself." She rolled up the scroll and tucked it back into the cabinet. "So then, shall we call your father?"

Paralyzed, Finn stared at the headmistress and tried to hold back the swell of emotion that burned in his throat and behind his eyes. Could he do it? Abandon his friends without any way of knowing their ultimate fate?

Ms. D tapped her chin. "If I remember correctly, you were their leader."

"Excuse me?"

"Deviant Joe. It was your creation that brought you and your friends here. You were the mastermind. It was only because of you that we extended the invitation to Michael as I recall."

Finn's shoulders slumped, the weight of truth settling on him. He'd gotten Mike and Jayden into this. He was responsible for seeing it through.

"The phone is against the wall right over there." She pointed behind the tree. "It's the old-fashioned kind. No cellular service on the island." She chuckled wickedly.

He shook his head.

"No? Have you decided to give it another go?"

His voice cracked when he answered. "Y-yes."

The corners of her mouth curled upward. "Excellent choice. Now, you'd better move along. You wouldn't want to miss dinner. You'll need your strength." She pointed at his face before backing toward the trampoline.

Finn wiped a hand across his cheek. His fingers came away wet. He hadn't even noticed he'd been crying.

Ms. D began jumping again, and this time she rotated to face the window. Finn staggered into the hall, watching the door to Duvall's office slowly close, cutting him off from his last chance to give up.

❧ 19 ❧

MAGIC

B y the end of the week, Finn and the others sported so many bruises and bandages, the halls of Revelations might have doubled as a hospital. Even Jayden struggled to muster the energy to do more than eat and lie in bed when they weren't in class. Gone were the conversations of hanging out in his room, replaced by heads falling asleep on the dining table and groans anytime anyone had to move. Not that there was much to do outside of class. They weren't allowed to leave the building.

It was during one such exaggerated state of exhaustion that Finn felt the card Theodor gave him grow warm in his pocket. Sure enough, the picture of the joker had changed and was no longer juggling the red balls. Finally, magic lessons!

"Where are you going?" Mike asked over his dinner, eyes dull with fatigue.

"Had enough. Early day tomorrow."

Mike nodded.

Finn climbed the stairs and searched out the alcove where he'd met with Theodor the week before. The magician was already there among the carvings of top hats and wands, his body unnaturally still, like an empty shell. Upon seeing Finn, the older man's mustache flattened over a subtle smile.

"Right on time. Excellent."

"I almost didn't make it up the stairs," Finn said, resting his hands on his aching thighs. "This place is killing me."

"It gets better," Theodor said. "Try to rest more and eat everything they feed you. Don't fight it."

Finn straightened at the trite advice and leaned against the alcove bookshelf. "So, magic lessons... Where should we start?"

"Not here. Too exposed." Theodor withdrew a card from his pocket. He paused, eyes darting to Finn. "You may want to hang on to something."

Finn gripped the bookshelf behind him.

The magician tossed the card at their feet and said, "Portate."

The entire alcove jerked into a dizzying rotation. The window disappeared, as did the arched entrance. Although Theodor remained remarkably still, everything else blurred, breaking down into a mishmash of book spines and random fonts. Finn swallowed repeatedly, closed his eyes, and focused on the steady grip he had on the shelf behind him. When the spinning sensation stopped, he carefully opened his eyes.

They'd been transported to a classroom. Theodor stood in front of a blackboard, the old-fashioned kind with white chalk and dark erasers. A heavy teacher's desk sat to his right and a single student's desk waited in the center of the room.

"Where are we?" Finn asked.

"My office on the second floor. It's enchanted. No one can hear us." He stepped to the window beside the blackboard and knocked on the glass. "No one can see you either."

The room dipped and stretched, and Finn collapsed into the seat of the student desk, his weight nudging it across the floor several inches.

"You'll be fine in a minute." Theodor crossed the room to a

small kitchenette where he poured a glass of water. He handed it to Finn. "Traveling by portal is dehydrating. This will help."

Finn chugged half the glass. "How did you do that?"

Theodor drew a card from his pocket and held it up, pinched between two fingers. "King of spades. Although the card itself is unimportant. What matters is the spell within it."

"It was a trick?" Finn looked around the small room for some indication that it was once an alcove. "Is it mechanical?"

"No tricks, Finn. This is magic. Some would call it sorcery, but I've always preferred the M-word. Over the centuries, magicians have used wands or amulets to execute their spells, but I've found a deck of cards... *suits* me best." He turned the card back and forth between them.

"Are you saying you transported us from one part of the school to another with an ordinary playing card?" Finn laughed.

Theodor shook his head. "Of course not. This is no ordinary king of spades, nor will any card in your deck be ordinary." He handed the card to Finn. "Take a closer look. What do you see?"

At first, Finn could only make out the letter K and the image of the spade one would expect on such a card. But the longer he stared at it, the more he sensed there was something more, just below the glossy surface. He closed and opened his eyes, trying to focus. "It looks like a crude drawing of a compass with arrows in eight directions. It's almost like the hieroglyphs we studied in school. Is it Egyptian?"

"Not Egyptian. Much older. It's called a rune."

"It's green."

"Very good, Finn. Most people can't see the color with an untrained eye."

"And it's heavy."

"As a portal should be. It has to be strong enough to carry you where you need to go after all."

"A portal?" Finn smoothed his hand across the surface. The

symbol burned hot against his palm. "I can use this to go anywhere?"

Theodor removed the card from Finn's grip. "Not yet. Portation is an advanced lesson requiring perfect focus. Today, we learn the basics." He pulled open his desk drawer and removed a plastic-wrapped deck of playing cards. He handed it to Finn. "These will be yours. You will enchant each card with a spell, and I will teach you how to use it. We will practice here when I call you."

"What about our days off?"

The magician snorted. "There are no days off at Revelations, Finn. You'll work every day of the year here."

Why wasn't he surprised? Everything about Revelations was designed to be a constant punishment.

"It will get easier," Theodor said, placing a hand on his shoulder. "Should we do this another time?"

With a shake of his head, Finn slid a finger under the plastic and unwrapped the deck of cards Theodor had given him. He dumped them into his palm. The slippery card stock fanned between his fingers. They were the type you could buy in any convenience store, with backs covered in black diamonds that represented the brand. An overwhelming sense that he was being toyed with led him to restack the cards and square them on his desk. This was ridiculous. It had to be a joke.

"*Don't* do that," Theodor said, his hands landing on either side of the stack.

"I shouldn't stack the cards?"

"I'm not talking about the cards. I'm talking about your head. If you don't believe in the magic, Finn, it doesn't matter what you do with the cards."

"But it can't be real." Finn was not ashamed to say it. "I read the first half of the book you gave me. I get it—unlimited human potential. It's a nice thought, but human beings have limits."

Theodor's gunmetal-gray eyes hardened. Straightening, he

paced to the desk, mumbling something Finn couldn't hear. After a moment or two of talking to himself, he faced Finn again, stroking his chin. "I'll make you a deal. I will teach you one spell today. If it works for you, you will agree to open your mind and believe what I tell you, without question."

Finn frowned. "And if it doesn't?"

"If it doesn't, you will cease being my apprentice."

"One spell?" He'd been so excited to learn to do tricks. Could magic be real? Could anything prove to him that it was? He shrugged. "Sure. Why not?"

"Choose a card. Make certain it's a red one."

Finn chose the two of diamonds. "Why does it have to be red?"

Theodor wagged a finger. "Ah, ah, ah. No more secrets until you've committed to the process." He handed Finn an ordinary black permanent marker.

"A Sharpie?"

"Are you going to complain about everything? I'm sorry to disappoint, but I am fresh out of fountain pens filled with unicorn tears."

Finn yanked the cap off with his teeth and stuck the back of the marker into it.

Theodor strode to the front of the room and pressed chalk to chalkboard. "Copy this exactly on the card." He drew an infinity symbol, leaving a gap at the end so that one side of the figure eight was open. Inside the closed circle, he drew a clover, the stem and each leaf touching the sides of the circle. Within the incomplete circle, he placed one thick dot.

Finn transposed the symbol exactly in black permanent marker over the two of diamonds, surprised at his own handiwork. There was a familiarity to the process, as if the symbol was already on the card and he was merely melting a layer of wax away to reveal it.

"That's it. See how the symbol is a living thing. It wants to be known by you. It forms itself perfectly beneath your hand."

"Okay. Now what?"

"Put the marker down and cup the card in your hands. Like this." Theodor demonstrated with his own card, bringing his cupped hands to his lips. "Now, this is very important, Finn. I've given you the symbol for *unbind*. I want you to picture in your mind a lock springing open. Perhaps it's a bicycle lock or your locker at school. Picture *unbind* and then breathe the word onto the card."

"Breathe the word. How exactly do I breathe a word?"

"Air and intention. A loud whisper. Vocal cords are unnecessary."

Finn brought the card to his lips. He pictured turning the dial of the rotary lock on his locker, focusing on the last moment when a subtle pop signaled he could retract the metal trigger and swing open the door. With a deep breath, he exhaled the word *unbind*. The symbol lifted from the card, casting a green glow in the dim light of the office. The gap in the figure eight closed and opened again before sinking into the card and vanishing altogether.

"Where'd it go? Did I do something wrong?"

Theodor shook his head. "Oh no, you did something very right. First time, no less. I suspected as much." He winked before retrieving a wooden box and placing it before Finn. It was the size and shape of a cigar box, carved from ebony wood and without symbol or decoration. He tested the lid.

"It's locked."

"Use the card to open it."

"How?"

"The magic is already there. You simply have to cast the spell. The card is your magic wand, Finn. Tap it on the box and tell it what to do."

Finn gripped the two of diamonds between his thumb and pointer finger. *Here goes nothing.* "Unbind." The lid to the box popped slightly, a rush of cold air flooding across Finn from inside. He lifted the lid, a smile spreading across his face. "It worked. I did it!"

Theodor nodded appreciatively. "Now, do we have an agreement? Will you become my apprentice and fully open your mind to the belief and practice of magic?"

Finn stared at the two of diamonds in his hand. He was going to learn magic—*real* magic. He nodded eagerly. "Yes. I'll do it."

Theodor bowed his head. "Very well. Then, for your second lesson, I will show you how to reverse the enchantment. You've unlocked the box using *unbind*. To lock it again, hold the lid closed, flip the card over and say *bind*." The magician backed up a few steps and waited for Finn to execute the enchantment.

Hand resting on the lid, Finn tapped the card as instructed and whispered, "Bind." The lock on the box clicked, and a sharp pain traveled up Finn's arm to his wrist. He tried to pull his hand away but couldn't.

"Ow. Oww! It hurts," he pleaded with Theodor, but the magician didn't move from the place where he leaned casually against his desk.

"Ignore it. It will fade."

"What?" But the pain was already diminishing. Finn jerked his hand off the box and rubbed the underside of his forearm, which itched furiously. For no longer than a heartbeat, a copy of the symbol from the card flashed green beneath his skin, then faded as if it had never been there. "What was that? What did you do to me?"

"I did nothing to you. You did it to yourself. You bound yourself to me as my apprentice. Think of it as a contract. I agree to teach you, and you agree to learn without question and to keep our relationship secret," Theodor said. "This spell will ensure you keep your end of the bargain."

"Do you mean I *can't* tell anyone, even if I wanted to?" Finn asked.

Theodor picked up the box and placed it back on his shelf. "Yes. You are on your way to becoming a powerful magician."

Finn stared at the two of diamonds, still gripped between his fingers. Exhaustion thickened his blood to approximately the weight of concrete.

The magician placed a hand on his shoulder and shook it to get his attention. "Sunset. Time for you to be in your room. I'll call you again when you've had time to rest." Theodor pulled the king of spades from his pocket and tossed it at Finn's feet.

The room spun again, this time with nothing for him to hang on to but the desk—useless, as it was promptly ripped from under him. Finn toppled through the vortex, the resulting vertigo turning his stomach. He landed at the foot of his bed, hugging his cards to his chest.

Hope emerged from the bathroom and stopped short when she saw him.

"There you are! Where've you been?" she asked.

"None of your business." He turned his back to her and slipped the deck into his drawer. A key rattled in their lock and footsteps trailed down the hall. Ravenguard.

"Fine, but can you let me know when you'll be gone next time? I was afraid you'd miss curfew." Hope grabbed his shoulder and turned him around to face her. Her eyes were narrowed and a muscle in her jaw twitched.

"Don't worry about me, Hope. I'm a big boy. I can take care of myself." He smiled to try to defuse the tension between them. He liked Hope and he didn't want to lie to her, but he couldn't tell her the truth. The mere thought of saying Theodor's name made the inside of his arm burn. Not to mention, he didn't owe her an explanation. He was sure she had her own secrets.

He scratched the space near the inside of his wrist, then pulled away from her grip to take his turn in the bathroom.

20

TRAINING

Time at Revelations ebbed and flowed like the tides. Finn stopped keeping track of the days, stopped complaining about his lot in life, or the pain, or the unfair aspects of the school's curriculum and, like the hanged man in the tarot card, accepted his fate.

He had a full schedule of regular classes to keep him busy. In aerial, he fell on his face at ever-increasing heights. He juggled burning torches that scorched his hands in pyro, learned to compel a tiger to sit up in menagerie, and endured endless jabbing with sharp implements in resilience.

It was almost a full two weeks before Theodor called him again, the joker warming in his pocket. This time his travel by portal was less jarring, whether because of their bond or Finn's experience.

"You were right," Finn said when he arrived in Theodor's office. "It gets easier."

"I thought you looked less black and blue these days," the magician said through a half smile.

"The lessons still hurt and seem pointless, but they're endurable."

"Do you have a favorite?"

"Aerial. It isn't just about falling anymore. We're practicing tightrope walking and acrobatics."

"You look like an aerial," Theodor said.

"Sometimes, when I fall, a strong wind blows through the gazebo, and for a moment…"

Theodor nodded. "Keep practicing. I predict you'll be a new man in a week or two." He walked to the blackboard and lifted the chalk. "Speaking of practicing, today we learn the spell for ignite or extinguish."

Finn slid into the student desk and retrieved his deck of cards from the inside pocket of his jacket. "Red?"

"Always red, Finn. For now."

He selected the three of diamonds before retrieving the Sharpie from within the desk.

Theodor drew a circle. Inside, he made a triangle, the lines at the apex crossing like logs in a campfire. Finn traced the symbol on the card.

"Is this used to start a fire?" Finn asked as he completed the drawing.

"The cards are used in the way you believe they can help you. Yes, this symbol can start or extinguish a fire, but it can also allow you to see in the dark or heat up a pan of cold soup. The application of the spell is only limited by your imagination. You decide how it can be used."

Finn brought the card to his lips and breathed *ignite* over the surface. The symbol glowed red. The triangle opened and closed at the top before sinking into the card itself.

"You remembered how to activate it. I'm impressed."

"Can I practice?"

Theodor retrieved a tall red candle from the shelf and set it on Finn's desk. "Give it a try."

"Ignite," Finn said, tapping the card to the wick. The candle gave off a wisp of smoke, but no flame appeared.

Theodor leaned his hip against his desk and laughed. "You can't just go through the motions, Finn. Magic requires energy. Starting a fire requires the heat of all the atoms around your card to collect on that wick and form a spark. This is a more difficult spell than *bind* or *unbind*. You aren't changing the position of what exists; you're creating something new. The card isn't doing the magic. *You* are."

"Then why have the card at all?"

"The card is a tool. The card focuses your energy."

Finn gave the wick his full attention. "Ignite!" More smoke.

"It doesn't help to say it louder. You must mean it more. Picture it, in your mind."

"Ignite." Finn managed to produce the smallest of sparks. Not enough to light the wick.

"Again," Theodor said, holding up his hands. "With feeling."

⚜

ANOTHER TWO WEEKS PASSED BEFORE FINN WAS ABLE TO consistently light and extinguish the candle. By the time he succeeded, he'd improved in other subjects as well, his favorite being aerial.

"We're getting better," Wendy said between classes. "I never thought it would get easier, but it is."

"Your cartwheel on the high wire was amazing. I've never seen anything like that."

She lowered her voice. "I've never been able to do a cartwheel before. Who would have guessed I could do it on a wire?"

"Wendy?" Finn grabbed her hand, an action that seemed to make the sun above them shine a little brighter.

She paused on the garden path next to a blooming red hibiscus. "What, Finn?"

"I knew you could do it." His words all mashed together into one syllable.

The blush of her cheeks told him she understood. "Thanks. Something about this place..." She swept her sable braid behind her shoulder. "I hated it at first, but now." She shrugged.

"I know," Finn said, running his thumb over hers. He'd already gotten her attention. He didn't need to hold her hand. But he did anyway. She didn't seem to mind. "It's like anything is possible." *Anything*, Finn thought. *Like a skinny kid being good at something. Like holding the hand of the most beautiful girl right in the school gardens.*

Wendy grinned. "I never thought I'd say this, but I love aerial." They were so close Finn could feel the warmth of her beside him, could smell the sweet scent of her, like soap and fresh air. He leaned toward her, inhaling deeply, his gaze focused intently on her lips.

"Move along, Wager," Orelon said from behind them. "You too, Ms. Matthews."

Embarrassed, Finn pulled back, muttering a quick goodbye. For how worried he'd been about his earlier experiences at the school, he was surprisingly excited about the way things were going. When he was sure no one was looking, he flexed a bicep and admired it appreciatively. He could do this. He liked doing this.

"It's about time, Wager. Get your ass down here." Mike stood alone on the stage next to the pyro equipment, fidgeting like he didn't know what to do with himself.

"Where's Fuse?" Finn jogged down the aisle and vaulted onto the stage, not bothering with the stairs.

"Don't know. She's late."

"Late? She's never late. None of the teachers are ever late."

"Relax, I'm right here." Fuse walked in from stage right, a roll of yellowed parchment in her hands. She handed it to Mike. "You're moving in with Jenny Pendleton. Ms. D gave me this to give to you. It has your new room assignment. Don't go back to your old room. The staff will move all your things over."

"What? Why?"

"Amanda and Paul are coming back to class and need to room together. The rehabilitation process requires them to have a special schedule to catch up."

Finn looked at Mike and back at Fuse. "What exactly is the rehabilitation process? They've been gone for weeks. I was afraid Paul was dead."

Fuse laughed like Finn was joking, but he wasn't. The thought that Paul might be dead had actually crossed his mind.

Fuse stepped in closer and leaned between them. "You don't get a one hundred percent success rate with free thinking and hug therapy," she said quietly. "Do yourselves a favor and stay outta trouble. Truth is, *I* don't even know what they do to them, but the kids are never the same. Never."

Mike's lips parted and his gaze darted to Finn's.

"We'll keep that in mind," Finn said. "It's a relief Paul is coming back."

Fuse agreed. "Now, today we're juggling fire. Grab two torches each and light 'em up."

No questions were asked and no one complained. Finn obediently retrieved two torches and pressed the button on the side to ignite the ends. Mike did the same.

"Try to catch the part that isn't burning," Fuse said. "Go."

৩৬৫৩

Ninety minutes and several burns later, Finn and Mike dragged their scorched selves into the dining hall. Finn hadn't even reached the buffet when Hope hooked her hand in the crook of his elbow and pulled him aside.

He groaned. "What now?"

"What's wrong with you? And what happened to your eyebrow?"

Finn reached up to find smooth skin where his left eyebrow used to be. "Pyro class," he said.

She winced. "Sorry. I can try reiki later."

"No, thanks. It's fine. It'll grow back." Finn scratched the bare spot. "So, ah, what do you want?"

"Did you hear Amanda and Paul are back?" she whispered.

"Yeah, they moved Mike in with Jenny. Amanda and Paul are going to be rooming together."

"She was in my class last period. She's not normal, Finn. It's like she's…"

"What?"

There was a rumble of voices behind them as Paul and Amanda entered the dining hall. Unlike before, Amanda was chipper with a dark ponytail that swayed with her bobbing steps.

"Hey, Finn." Amanda waved before getting in line for the buffet.

Paul was less bubbly but far from the catatonic mess Amanda had been the first time she'd returned. "What's for lunch?"

"Paul?" Finn asked.

"What's up, Finn?"

"What happened to you? You've been gone for weeks," Finn whispered, spreading his hands.

"Why are you whispering?" Paul smiled a broad, friendly smile like he belonged in a comic strip. Finn had a hard time reconciling it with the brooding hulk he'd met before. The old Paul looked like he chewed barbed wire for breakfast. This guy had the chipper aura of a flight attendant.

"Are you okay?" Finn asked.

"I'm fine. I needed some time to rest and recover. I'm better now."

"But what did they *do* to you?"

Paul loaded his plate like he'd never missed a day. "Nothing worth talking about."

"See?" Hope whispered.

"They're different, but both of them look really good. Frankly, I'm relieved he's alive. After that nightmare I had, I thought we'd eventually hear he died or got sent home with a permanent injury."

"You don't think the plastic smile is at all forced? Do you think they drugged them or something?"

"I don't know, Hope. I'm hungry." Finn joined the line for lunch, leaving Hope behind, arms crossed and foot tapping. It wasn't that he didn't get what she was talking about—Paul and Amanda had obviously gone through an extreme transformation —but Finn didn't care. He didn't want to waste time worrying about the things he couldn't change. He wanted to succeed and that meant doing things the Revelations way. If he was going to make it home, it wasn't going to be because he challenged authority or wallowed in negativity.

He'd heaped his plate and was about to sit down when Ms. D thrust into the room and rushed to the head table like the tails of her jacket were on fire. She held up her hands, and the crowd of students became instantly silent.

"I have an announcement. Your instructors have shared with me how hard you've all been working. I can already see the change happening inside each of you. Some more than others." Her gaze fell on Finn. "I am pleased to announce that your instructors have made preliminary selections for their troupes. Those students whose names I call will henceforth discontinue their current schedules and begin training full-time with their assigned troupe."

A murmur rose up from the students as the wild-haired woman unrolled an official-looking scroll.

"Did you know this was coming?" Jayden murmured to the group of students around him. No one answered.

"Paul Stewart, menagerie." Paul cheered and everyone broke into applause. Everyone but Finn, who was wondering why Paul would be excited to join the troupe that had almost killed him.

"Amanda Tidwell, resilience." More clapping.

"Finn Wager." Finn's head popped up. Had he been chosen for a troupe already? "Aerial." The room broke into cheers, and he searched out Orelon who bowed his head slightly. Finn couldn't believe it. He'd done it! He'd been chosen!

"Jayden Parker, pyro."

Jayden pumped a fist in the air. "Yeah! Best troupe ever." He crossed the room to give Fuse a high five.

"Wendy Matthews, aerial." Wendy clapped and threw herself at Finn, who was more than happy to spin her around before letting her feet touch the floor again.

"Hope Laudner, resilience."

"No," Hope said under her breath. She recoiled into herself, her face paling.

Ms. D rolled up the parchment. "Congratulations. Those of you assigned, please report to your new troupe tomorrow in lieu of your regular schedule."

"Wait," Mike called out. "What about the rest of us? Jenny and me?"

Smoothing her suit jacket, Ms. D glanced at her fingernails before answering. "You two will continue your schedule as assigned. Your teachers need more time to assess your potential before offering you a place in their troupe. Work hard and pray that change occurs quickly."

"And if it doesn't?" Jenny's blue-eyed stare dug into the head-mistress.

Ms. D rolled her lips. "If it doesn't, Mr. Ravenguard and Ms. Applegate will conduct extensive and personalized training until it does."

The two sucked in a quick breath that was loud enough, in its duality, to drown out any other noises in the room. Everyone went still.

With two coughs into her hand, Ms. D straightened. "Hard work and an open mind can accomplish the miraculous. Don't disappoint us."

She bowed slightly and left the room, the other teachers trailing behind her.

Mike grabbed Finn's upper arm. "You've got to help me. What's your secret? How are you getting so good at this so fast?"

"So fast?" Finn said with a laugh. "I've been bleeding and bruised for weeks, the same amount of time you have."

Jenny crossed her arms over her chest. "Yeah, you look like hell every dinner hour, but by morning you're stronger than ever. All of you. What do you know that we don't?"

She closed in around Finn, looking down her nose at him.

Mike pointed a finger at Finn's face. "Jenny and I haven't had roommates like you have. Are you guys working together at night? Practicing in your room or something?"

Jayden put a hand on Mike's chest. "Hey, Finn hasn't done anything you haven't done. There's no super-secret roommate thing going on. What would we do? We're locked in there from dusk till dawn."

"There has to be something." Mike tapped his fist against his forehead. "Where do you go in the evenings?"

"What are you talking about?"

"Every so often, you leave dinner early and no one sees you again until the next day. Where do you go, Finn?"

Finn scratched the inside of his left arm where the binding spell began to burn.

"Nowhere."

"Bullshit," Mike said, getting in his face.

Finn had had enough. A thought came to him, sharp and heavy like a weapon, and he did not hesitate to wield it at his friend. He pushed Mike back a step. "Back off." Squaring his shoulders, he faced the bigger boy head-on. "For as long as we've known each other, you've always been the best at everything: sports, school, girls. Everyone loves you. I was always happy for you. Always the supportive sidekick. Now, you're angry because you believe I couldn't possibly be better than you at anything without there being a trick to it. Isn't that right?" Finn felt a tide of heat crawl up his torso. His shoulders tightened.

"That's not what—"

"It's exactly what you meant," Finn snapped. "I've never been chosen for anything first in my life. But guess what, Mike? The rules are different here. I'm different here. I'm *better* here."

Mike's face fell. "I have always helped you. When things were reversed, I defended you. I made sure no one messed with you. You know I did, Finn."

"And I will help you now, any way I can. But it's not my fault you didn't get chosen." He looked between Jenny and Mike.

Jayden backed him up. "Yeah. Hey, we will practice with you guys every day if we have to. We'll help you."

Mike took a deep breath and blew it out.

"We stick together, right?" Finn asked, holding out his fist. Jayden held his up too.

After a long moment, Mike nodded and bumped his knuckles against Finn's, then Jayden's.

"You're right," Mike said. "I don't know what got into me."

"This place changes you," Hope said to no one in particular.

Paul, who was eating at the table with Amanda, looked up from his plate. "That's the point, isn't it? You all came here to change. The harder you fall, the stronger you get."

Amanda raised her glass in a mimed cheer before drinking the contents. As she set the glass down, her face went slack and her gaze drilled into Mike. "If you aren't changing, you aren't hurting enough."

✲ 21 ✲

NIGHT

Hope tapped her thumb against the windowsill, tense at the fading sunset. Finn was late coming back to their room again and wasn't any more forthcoming than before about his whereabouts. While part of her was simply curious, a larger part was concerned for his well-being. Every human had his or her own life energy, something as a Healer she was acutely attuned to. Finn's had changed since they'd been here. Then again, so had every other student's, especially Amanda and Paul, whose energy was the equivalent of a buzzing mosquito. She could barely be in the same room with them.

Regardless, she had reason to worry. She was no closer to finding the source of the missing souls than her first day at Revelations. Oh, there was evil here. That much was obvious. But she wasn't only looking for evil. Evil was everywhere. She was looking for a soul stealer. The sad fact was that, according to Gabriel, she might need Finn's help at some point, which meant she needed to keep him safe.

Finn rushed through the door right before Ravenguard arrived to lock them in for the night. "Made it again, Wager," the admissions counselor said, cocking one bushy gray eyebrow. The door closed and locked behind him.

"Finn, that was too close. Where have you been?" Hope asked.

He scratched the inside of his arm and plopped down on his bed. "What do you think Amanda meant today by what she said to Mike?"

Way to change the subject, Wager. "She said exactly what she meant." Hope was intentionally curt. Why should she answer his questions when he wouldn't answer hers?

"She said that Jenny and Mike didn't hurt enough to change. What the hell does that mean? They've been in all the same classes as us."

Hope folded her legs under her on the bed. It would serve him right if she ignored him, but against her better judgment and with a sigh and roll of her eyes, she answered. "Mike and Jenny were athletic and popular in their former high schools."

"Yeah, so?"

"So. They were already in great shape and highly coordinated before they came here. The stressors that left someone like you bruised and almost broken barely injured them at all. Besides the minor bite in menagerie, when did you ever see Mike bleed?"

"Never. Even in pyro, it's always me who gets scorched."

"A muscle responds best when you stress it. No pain, no gain. This island takes your pain and uses it to change you. No pain, no change."

Finn snorted. "That doesn't make any sense. Mike started stronger and worked just as hard. He should be further ahead."

"But he's not. That's not how it works here."

"Are you suggesting there's something in the air that rewards effort over genetics?"

Hope slouched. "It's a theory. I don't honestly know how it works, but I don't think the island rewards effort. It rewards pain. Mike put forth the same effort. You felt more pain."

"The island doesn't think or feel anything. It doesn't reward anything. It's a hunk of rock in the Atlantic Ocean. What you mean is that the teachers notice the pain. Explains why you were chosen for resilience. You could take more from the very beginning."

She didn't say another word, but the truth of the matter struck her fully, becoming real. It was the island. She could feel it in her bones. It was like it had its own heartbeat. The island itself was the key. The reason she was having trouble adapting was precisely because this place wasn't normal.

"What's wrong with you?" Finn asked. "You look like you're going to be sick again."

"Do you believe in purpose and destiny?"

"Not particularly. I believe in consequences. We're all here because actions have consequences. We did bad things and now we're paying the price."

The hair on the back of Hope's neck stood on end. She had not committed the crime she was here for. Had Finn? "Oh, like when you burned down that school. You're here for arson."

"I didn't burn down the school," Finn said.

"So, why are you here? We've never talked about it."

He turned on his side and propped his head up in his hand. "Since you asked, here's what happened. We broke into the school, but not to burn it down."

"Then why?"

"A prank. We were filling a hallway with balloons in our school's colors. It was harmless. A way to burn time before Christmas break."

"But instead you burned the school?"

"No. There was a man, a stranger; he started it."

"A strange man just randomly showed up where you happened to be and started a fire?" Hope was careful to keep disbelief in her voice, but inside her muscles stiffened. She believed every word Finn said.

"Yes."

"What did he use to start the fire?"

"A lighter."

"Did they find the lighter? Maybe it has his prints on it."

"It was Jayden's brother's lighter. He'd been smoking. And only Vox's prints were on it."

"What did the man look like?" Hope listened as Finn described the man in detail, her heart growing heavy with every word. "The police didn't believe you?"

"No."

"Why not?"

Finn cleared his throat. "Don't laugh."

Softly, she said, "I promise I won't."

"Because each of us saw a different person."

Her breath caught. This was it, the clue she'd been waiting for. As far as she knew, only a demon could change his or her identity like that. The man Finn saw had to be Damien, the one and only fallen angel left after the last great battle between good and evil. But why? Why frame children to send them here? And how did it play into the mystery of the lost souls?

"So... a strange man framed you for a crime you didn't commit and when you were convicted, an even stranger man invited you to this island, one you'd never heard of, where you are forced to do agonizing things and are isolated from your family and community?"

"Exactly."

"And you don't believe in destiny and purpose?" Hope lowered her chin and looked him in the eye. She'd said too much. It wasn't her business what he believed.

Finn's face tightened. "My mom died when I was born."

Hope was startled by his blunt response. "I'm sorry."

"She found out she had cancer when she was pregnant with me and wouldn't get treatment because she didn't want to hurt me."

"Oh Finn."

"What could possibly be the purpose in that?"

Hope stared across the dark room at her new friend. "I lost both my parents when I was born. They were killed... murdered. I survived and was adopted by friends of theirs."

"I'm sorry," Finn said sadly.

"So I guess we have that in common," she said.

"Sucky thing to have in common," he said.

"We could say it was onion rings." She laughed. "We could both love onion rings. Then we'd have something fun in common."

"Deal. I do love a good fried onion."

"Where have you been going after dinner every night?" she asked point-blank. "You've said you can't tell me, but I'm worried about you."

He shook his head. "I can't talk about it. It's nothing bad. It's just a secret." He paused, his hand burrowing under his pillow. "What did you do to get sent here anyway?" Finn asked.

There was a long pause. "A girl who looked like me was video-taped selling heroin to a minor."

Finn let out a long whistle.

"It was a case of mistaken identity. I came to Revelations on a plea bargain."

"There's someone out there who looks exactly like you?"

"Three boys saw three different people start a fire?"

"Touché."

"Finn, whatever you're doing that you can't tell me about, be careful. This place changes people. I haven't met one adult here I trust. We need to stick together in case something really bad happens."

"It's not like you don't have your own secrets," Finn said. "Ms. Reiki Master, who heals herself and talks to birds."

Hope became acutely aware that despite her frustration with Finn withholding information, she had more than a few secrets of her own.

"How about this? We accept that there are things we can't

share with each other, but we promise to help each other if something really bad happens. You're my friend, Finn. We need to trust each other."

Finn propped himself up on his elbow and looked her in the eye. "Deal."

🙣 22 🙢

CLOWNS

Finn woke from the deep recesses of sleep quite suddenly. No sound, no breeze, no flicker of light caused his waking, but a general feeling of unease, a ripple of dread that yanked him from his slumber like there was a bungee cord tied to his belly button. He cracked his eyelids in the dark and held perfectly still. Someone was in his room, leaning over Hope's sleeping body, a dark figure, a break in the continuity of her white duvet.

The moon cast watery light between their beds, but even with his eyes adjusted to the dark, he couldn't tell who or what lingered at her side. Only when a hand reached out toward Hope's head did the outline of a white glove become evident, followed by a striped shirt and suspenders.

Clown. Finn tensed beneath the covers, keeping his breathing shallow and even.

The clown pinched one of Hope's hairs between his fingers and plucked it from her head. Silent. Quick. Easy. Hope's deep and even sleep continued undisturbed. Finn held his breath, terrified he might be next.

With Hope's hair gripped like a prize, the white-faced freak pivoted on its oversized shoes and silently slipped from the room. Finn waited until the door was completely closed to rise from his bed and follow. What the hell was that thing doing with Hope's hair? For that matter, what had the clown done with Wendy's blood?

He jostled the doorknob. Locked. Stealthily, he cracked his drawer and removed his cards. "Unbind," he whispered. *Click.* The knob turned; the door gave way. With a furtive peek into the hall, he caught a flash of black and white disappearing into the back stairwell that led to the library.

Finn's bowels went watery as he stepped into the hall. He thought about turning back; everything inside him threatened to evacuate his chosen course with or without his permission. Even if he hadn't promised his father he'd fly under the radar and keep his nose clean, being in the hall after curfew was both risky and unintelligent. Still, Hope was his friend and Wendy was... more. Someone needed to uncover what the clowns were up to with the hair and the blood and what was behind what happened to Amanda and Paul. Considering his new abilities and his relationship with Theodor, he was the only one to do it. This could be his one chance to learn the secrets of this school. He had to take it.

He slipped into the hall, drawing on his lessons from aerial class to make his feet as light as possible. A flash of black and white descended the staircase. He followed. One flight, then two, into the subterranean levels of Revelations castle. The dimly lit hall the clown entered had no windows and only a few buzzing fluorescent lights that blinked like the bulbs needed replacing. Finn took cover in an open doorway.

The clown approached the end of the hallway and passed a gloved hand in front of a sconce. With a slight rumble, the wall slid away, revealing the faint blue glow of a secret passageway. As the clown ambled over the threshold, its lanky body bobbing with each step, the rumble began again. Now or never.

"Extinguish," Finn whispered, touching the card to his arm. He was almost surprised when his skin blurred, his flesh taking on a ghostly appearance. He'd practiced the ignite/extinguish spell enough times, but never on himself. Like a shadow, he slipped through the closing panel and pressed into a dark corner of the passageway beyond. The clown didn't seem to notice him. It turned at the end of the long corridor and vanished from sight. Finn shivered, getting his bearings.

He scrubbed his face with both hands. This was by far the dumbest thing he'd ever ventured to do. Who did he think he was, some kind of hero? He was clearly out of his league here. He had half a mind to turn back, return to his room and crawl back under the covers. But curiosity forced him forward.

His fingers grazed the wall. Waxy, like a beehive. He took a closer look and poked at it experimentally. His finger gouged a section. Weird. Aside from the strange material, there was plenty more odd about the room. The arched walls were pockmarked with wide hexagonal tubes, some dark and empty, others sealed with the waxy substance and glowing a pale blue. What was this place? He placed one hand inside an empty tube. Instead of wax, his fingertips grazed a smooth metallic surface.

Finn crept to the end of the passageway and peered around the corner. The clown he was pursuing stood in a room of silver and glass—a laboratory bathed in blue light. The source of the light was what looked like an iceberg contained in a gigantic glass enclosure at the back of the room. It was shaped like a chiseled blue mountain, floating in clear liquid inside an orb of glass. Perhaps some type of refrigeration unit, Finn thought.

The clown opened the cap on a glass beaker and dropped Hope's hair through the narrow neck. With one gloved hand, it retrieved a vial of bright red liquid from the rack above its head. He poured the solution over the hair where it sizzled before releasing a puff of red steam. The white glove gripped another vial, this one filled with a clear solution the consistency of honey. Two drops and the steam abated. That white-gloved hand stirred the concoction with a crystal rod. The solution transformed to a bright blue that rivaled the iceberg's color, with a gooey white substance suspended inside. Crossing the lab, the clown disappeared from Finn's field of vision.

Finn leaned forward to get a better view but pulled back quickly when another clown entered the laboratory from a hallway originating behind the iceberg. Finn pressed himself against the wall and held his breath. The clowns stood toe-to-toe and face-to-face. No words were exchanged, but after a brief interlude, the one with the vial poured the contents into one of the hexagonal vats. Although Finn could barely see around the equipment, when the clown raised the vial it was empty. Without a word, the two painted-faces disappeared down the hall behind the iceberg.

Heart pounding, Finn advanced into the laboratory, ducking behind stainless steel tables and listening for footsteps. When he was fairly certain he was alone, he stood and boldly faced the strange truth in front of him.

The wall reminded him of a honeycomb, only instead of honey, the cells were filled with liquid. He assumed, given the network of pipes above his head, the source of the fluid was the iceberg. He could feel a buzz coming off the blue chunk to his right, as if he was standing too close to a power line. He looked both ways before crossing to it and placing both hands against the glass. He squinted into the icy glow.

The iceberg wasn't blue; the glass was. He could see it under his fingertips when he tilted his head and looked along the curved length of the container. The ice was trapped in a giant blue fishbowl, at least three inches thick. Aside from the vibrations, which were odd enough, the glass wasn't cold like he'd expected it to be if the mass within was ice, but searing hot. He retracted his burning fingers and shook his hands.

What the hell? He whirled back to the bank of hexagonal tubes behind him. *What is going on here?* A thin layer of wax sealed the liquid inside each hexagon. One hexagon had a new seal, roughly pressed around the edges. In other areas, the wax shone perfectly smooth, almost reflective, as if the heat had rendered the seal thinner and flatter over time. A two-inch gap at the top of each seal emitted waves of white steam from the cell within.

Silently, he approached the freshly waxed tube and looked inside. This is where the clown had dumped the vial. The white substance that once was Hope's hair bobbed in the churning water within. Pulling back, he peeked into an older cell. Something pale bobbed under the surface, the size of an oblong bowling ball. After unsuccessfully trying to decipher what it was, he stepped down to another cell and lowered one eye to the gap in the wax seal. Another waxy white thing jounced wildly inside, this one four feet long and as wobbly as a section of rubber. Finn backed up and wiped the steam from his upper cheek. He had to crouch to see inside the last one, the oldest one based on the appearance of the seal. The steam coming out the hole was hotter than the others. He kept his distance, repositioning his head to see inside.

The rubbery thing in this tube was big, taking up almost the entire cell. Finn maneuvered to see better, steam singeing his eyelashes. He squinted against the white glare filtering up through the water. Pale white broke the surface of the blue bubbling liquid. Finn gasped. *A face! A naked body!* He slapped both hands over his mouth to keep from screaming. The body's skin was deathly white and hairless. A shaved corpse.

He stumbled backward, his stomach heaving, and promptly collided with one of the stainless steel tables. The glass rattled. Hurried footsteps squeaked from the far corridor behind the iceberg, the direction the clowns had gone. Finn sprinted to the secret panel he'd come through. No time to open it. He dove into the shadowed belly of an unused honeycomb cell near the exit, flattening himself against the steel floor.

The footsteps drew nearer until he could see the two clowns

silently sniffing the air and scanning the hallway with their beady, black-rimmed eyes. Seconds passed. He held his breath. After a few heart-pounding minutes, the two left the way they'd come.

Finn wrapped his fingers around the waxy edge of the cell and slid himself out slowly, scanning the passageway for any signs of the clowns. "Unbind," he whispered. The door rumbled open. He rushed through and closed it behind him. Terrified, he sprinted up the stairs, down the hallway, and back into his room.

"Bind," he whispered, voice cracking midword. The door locked behind him. He swallowed. Sweat ran down the side of his face. What had he just seen? What were they doing down there? Storing bodies?

"What's the matter with you?" Hope said. She rubbed her eyes, sitting up in bed.

Finn tried to respond, but his mouth wouldn't work properly. All he could manage was to pant into the dim room.

"Geez, Finn, what happened?" She bounced from her bed and steadied his shoulders. She must've been doing the reiki thing again because warmth flowed through him, calming his racing heart and troubled mind. "Tell me what happened."

"I saw... I saw..." He grabbed one of her wrists. "There are dead bodies under the school."

🏵 23 🏵

EXPOSE

Hope bit her lip and stared at her roommate, deeply concerned. "Bodies?" She tested the knob. "The door's locked, Finn."

"There's a whole secret passageway down there. The clowns are running some sick laboratory. They stole your hair. There are tubes filled with bodies."

"Stole my hair?" She placed a hand on her head.

"One hair," he said, rolling his eyes.

"Finn, when I woke, you were standing here in front of a locked door." She placed her hand on the knob again. "How did you get out?"

Agitated, Finn scratched the inside of his forearm. His eyes darted to his pocket. The shift was quick enough that she might not have caught it if she wasn't a Soulkeeper. He was hiding something.

Hope squinted at Finn. Waves of anxiety rolled off him and sweat dripped from his temple. He was really shaken up, and if there were bodies under the school, she needed him to tell her everything. This might be the break she was waiting for. "Okay, let's say a clown did steal my hair," she said softly. "The door was locked when we went to bed and is locked now. How did the clown get in and you get out?"

Finn's eyes shifted. "The clown came in... and I followed him out. I don't know. It must have had a key."

Hope frowned. "What aren't you telling me, Finn?"

"We need to get help."

"You should show me what you saw. Do you think you can remember where you were?"

"I'll never forget it. But it's not safe. You don't want to see the things I saw."

All the more reason that I should see it, Hope thought. "Maybe what you think you saw wasn't what it seemed."

"I know what I saw."

"Tell me."

Finn described it all from the sliding wall to the hexagonal vats.

Hope thought for a second. "Under the school?"

Finn nodded. "They took your hair and Wendy's blood."

"They took Wendy's blood?"

"The first day. One of the clowns collected it from the ground after she fell."

"I'd still like you to show me," Hope said again. "Secret chambers, honeycomb walls, hot ice under glass. It sounds like a mystery. We promised to help each other, remember?"

Finn closed his eyes. "I'll show you. I need to know for sure."

"You'd better get some sleep. It's almost dawn," she said, backing toward her bed.

She noticed him slip something into his upper drawer before climbing under his covers. He was hiding something all right, and she needed to find out what. As much as she'd meant to comfort Finn, someone or some*thing* stealing her hair and another student's blood was a serious situation that smacked of the unholy. And if the clowns were responsible for the lost souls, all the students were in grave danger.

WHEN LIGHT FINALLY FLOODED THROUGH THE WINDOW, FINN ROSE and dressed. Hope was quiet, introspective. She probably thought he was a head case. The more he thought about it, the more he wondered if there was a reasonable explanation. Perhaps the clowns made rubber dummies for the show down there. It would make total sense that he'd wandered into some sort of circus factory. But why the hair? The blood? And why the secrecy? Did they need a hidden chamber to make rubber dummies?

"Do you think I should ask one of the instructors about what I saw?" Finn asked as he followed Hope toward breakfast.

"And admit you were out of your room after hours? No, I think that would be a very bad idea."

"But you'll go with me, later, so I can show you?"

"Of course. We'll meet after class. We have to be careful though. No one can know what we're doing."

"Damn, Finn. Walk much?" Mike grabbed him by the shoulders. Finn had been so caught up in his own head, he'd walked straight into the big guy. "What happened? You look like hell."

"Shhh." Hope placed a finger over her lips. "Not so loud."

Jayden popped his head between them, pressing his cheek against Hope's. "What are we whispering about? Are you dishing about Ravenguard and Applegate, because I totally feel the chemistry between those two. Let's face it, they are definitely an eHarmony match. He likes torturing people; she likes torturing people."

"Jayden," Finn said.

"What?"

"Shut up for a sec. We're trying to make a plan."

"Shhh." Hope grabbed his elbow, her eyes shifting to Paul and Amanda at the table. "Get food. Act natural."

They loaded their plates in silence. Only later, huddled at the end of the table over full plates, did he tell Mike and Jayden what he'd seen.

"Are you sure? It sounds like a nightmare. Maybe you were walking in your sleep or something," Mike whispered.

Jayden agreed. "Yeah. Think about it, Finn. I'm sure the clowns don't stay in makeup all day. We've all been under a lot of stress."

Hope interrupted. "There's only one thing to do. Tonight, after classes, meet in the library. We'll try to find the room Finn found. There must be some explanation."

"Done," Mike said.

Jayden nodded. "Where's the library?"

"Here"

✤ 24 ✤

ABOVE AND BEYOND

"This is higher than before," Finn said to Orelon. He was standing on a platform at least fifteen feet above the ground, staring down a high wire stretched to a platform on the other side of the gazebo. Natalie swung her legs from one of the rafters above him.

"You can do this, Finn," she yelled. She pushed off her perch and dropped to the opposite platform, landing lightly despite the fall. Everyone in aerial was like that, light on their feet. Able to fall from great heights.

Wendy encouraged him from below. "It's just higher, not harder. If you can walk it at five feet, you can walk it at fifteen."

He smiled at her although his knees were shaking and his palms were wet with perspiration. "If I fall, will you catch me?"

"Not a chance."

"Guess I can't fall."

Finn placed a trembling foot on the wire and, as he was trained to do, cleared his head. Fear and doubt were the enemy when working at any height. There was no room for second-guessing. His legs steadied. He had this. Extending his arms to the sides, he stepped quickly, one foot in front of the other.

"You've got this, Finn!" Wendy cheered.

More than halfway across, he believed he did. But a strong breeze coursed through the small windows of the gazebo and the wire swayed. Finn overcorrected, circling his arms.

Natalie tucked her red curls behind her ears. "Come on, Finn. You can do it!"

He took another step and tripped. "Oh!" He dropped, catching the wire with one hand. Normally, he could get back up after a fall like that, flip his legs over the wire, balance on his hips, and regain his footing. But he'd been nervous to walk at this height. His sweaty hand couldn't find purchase. When he attempted to catch the wire with his opposite hand, his fingers slipped.

Wendy screamed. Air whizzed past his ears. Reflexively, he flattened into position for impact. He'd practiced falling so many times his body automatically reacted, but the fall was not what he expected. For starters, colliding with the ground was taking too long. The gazebo floor approached in slow motion, the wind seeming to catch him under the hollow of his chest like a kite. Weightlessness tickled through his torso. His arms and legs numbed.

And then he stopped. He hovered above the ground, staring at the footsteps in the dust beneath him with marked curiosity. His breath quickened. What was happening? Why wasn't he falling?

Orelon's laugh echoed through the gazebo. "I told you. I told you he was one of us!"

Natalie squealed. "Come back up, Finn!"

Wendy gasped. "You're flying. Dear Lord, Finn, you are actually flying!"

He curled his hands into fists and brought them toward his face. His body levered, his torso rising with the curl of his arms until his feet touched the ground. "How?"

"It's the island," Natalie said. She jumped from the platform and hovered above the wire. "It's like pixie dust."

Finn thrust his hands over his head and leaped off the ground, willing himself toward Natalie. A momentary lapse of weightlessness gave way to a charge into the beyond. But he couldn't control it. The higher he rose, the more his body twisted, until he crashed awkwardly into the side of the gazebo. He belly-flopped to the dirt, a plume of dust rising around him.

"Oww." Finn rolled onto his back and wheezed in a sharp breath.

"You'll learn control in time," Orelon said. "Despite what Natalie says, it's not pixie dust. We don't know what causes it—only the effects. Every person who comes to this island is different, but everyone changes. Congratulations. You are a true aerial troupe member."

"What about me?" Wendy asked. "I want to fly!"

"Don't fret," Natalie said. "It rarely happens this quickly. Finn is a prodigy."

"Rarely? Never. You are a miracle," Orelon said.

Finn brought his hands to his face. "A miracle," he whispered into his palms.

"Come on, Wendy. Your turn," Orelon said, ascending to the platform in one graceful leap.

"Hell yeah!" she called as she scaled the ladder the old-fashioned way.

"I can fly," Finn murmured in disbelief. "The entire troupe can fly."

⚜

AFTER CLASS, FINN WHISTLED AS HE MADE HIS WAY TO THE LIBRARY. It wasn't every day you found out you could fly. He almost hated to rehash what happened the night before with Hope and the others. Today, he'd become a part of something wonderful and magical, even beyond what Theodor had taught him. If something sinister was happening beneath the school, he almost didn't want to know.

He found Jayden and Mike waiting in the tree alcove in the library. He was surprised Hope wasn't there. Surprised and quickly worried.

"She got sick after class," Mike said, rubbing a purpling bruise on his cheek. "Kirsa went off on her. I've never seen anyone stabbed so many times. Beat the hell out of her too."

"Is she okay?"

"Honestly, I thought Kirsa went too far," Mike said. "I thought she might kill her. I don't know how Hope got back up. She was a bloody pulp, Finn."

"I guess we're all changing."

Mike frowned. "Hope told me to have you wait for her. Said she'd be better in a few minutes."

Finn swallowed hard. He remembered how sick Hope had become the first time Kirsa had stabbed her. Resilience was the most painful of disciplines at Revelations. He was more thankful than ever that he'd been chosen by aerial.

"Are you managing?" Finn asked Mike, eyeing the bruise. He'd seen him briefly that morning in aerial, but Natalie had trained him separately during his assigned time.

"Yeah, but only because I don't have to do it all day. Jenny and I are still on a rotating schedule until a troupe picks one of us. I've been enjoying menagerie. Amuke says I have potential."

Finn leaned against the carved branches of the archway. "So, we wait for Hope."

Jayden nodded, thumbing through an old tome. "I, for one, didn't have anything better to do than hang out in a room full of dusty books. It's not like there's a gorgeous girl waiting in Mike's room right now for me to flirt with her properly."

"You and Jenny, huh?" Finn asked.

Mike chuckled. "He wishes. I'm pretty sure she's using him for his pyro skills. They've been practicing every night."

"So you admit she's hot for me." Jayden smirked.

"Too bad the only one carrying a torch is you," Hope said, arriving beside Mike.

Finn had a visceral reaction to her appearance. Her skin was pale, almost green. Had she lost weight? She looked thinner than she had at breakfast.

"What happened to you?" he asked.

"Let's just say I'm changing in all the wrong ways."

"What does that mean?" Finn scowled.

"Never mind. Come on. Show us where you went last night."

Finn gestured toward the hall. "This way." As unsettling as retracing his steps was, he led them to the stairwell, down to the basement, and through the windowless corridor he remembered. It was no dream. Other than last night, he'd never been down here before, yet he remembered every nuance of the hallway. When he reached the secret panel, he ran his hand in front of the glass sconce as he'd seen the clown do, but the door did not open. The card for unbind grew heavy in his inner pocket, but he couldn't use it, couldn't reveal his secret. The burn in his arm reminded him that wasn't an option.

"Last night, the clowns did this," he explained, waving a hand in front of the sconce. "A panel in the wall opened. There was a honeycomb and a glowing thing in a big glass bowl."

Hope ran her hand along the wall. Her fingers searched the corners and along the carpeted floor. "There's nothing here. It's solid."

Mike tried a door to his right. "Maybe you were confused and it was one of these other rooms. Check that one, Jay."

"No, it was here," Finn insisted.

"We'll check anyway," Mike said, disappearing through the door. Jayden entered the room on the opposite side of the hall.

"Maybe I was sleepwalking," Finn said.

Hope shook her head, murmuring, "No. It *has* to be real. There has to be a reason."

"A reason for what?"

"That I'm still here," she said under her breath.

She wasn't making any sense. He put an arm around her shoulders. "It's okay. Come on. We'll go to dinner."

But Hope twitched with unease. For someone who'd seemed skeptical last night, she looked at that wall like she could see what Finn had seen. "No," she said firmly. "It's here. We need to find a way in." She continued inspecting the wall in earnest.

Mike and Jayden rejoined them in the hall. "Storage room. Nothing but props and costumes," Mike said.

"Mine too," Jayden added. "There were a few dummies in there. Maybe... in the dark?"

Hope stared at the wall as if she could knock it down with her mind.

"Maybe." Finn shrugged. "Hope, we have to go. If we're late for dinner, someone might come looking for us."

"You're right," she said, her eyes glossy. "We're out of time." She charged past Finn and headed for the stairs.

25

HOPE

The next afternoon, Hope faced off against Kirsa again. The woman was in an especially aggressive mood. Their morning session with Mike had been a welcome distraction, but now Kirsa was eyeing Hope like her own, personal punching bag. She'd ushered her into the sparring ring and was carefully perusing the selection of blades in the arsenal around them. She selected a bladed staff from the rack. It was medieval, the type of thing Vlad the Impaler might have used to impale and display his victims. This was going to hurt.

"Choose a weapon," she said, running a thick hand through her shock of platinum hair. A smile played on her lips. Hope's stomach twisted at that evil smirk. It was obvious she couldn't wait to hurt Hope. She loved it.

Hope trembled. It didn't matter what weapon she chose. Kirsa was indestructible. The only blood hitting the mat would be hers, the same as yesterday and the day before. The worst part was, her body couldn't keep up with the healing. She was still sore from yesterday.

She chose a chakram, a circular throwing blade—the closest

thing in the arsenal to the weapon her triquetra became in her hand.

"Always the chakram," Kirsa said. "Why do you like that thing so much?"

"It's familiar," Hope said, putting her off. That was her goal. Put her off. Dodge. Limit the amount of time she was stabbed and beaten. There was no other choice.

Without any warning, Kirsa attacked, stabbing straight toward her middle. Hope swerved out of the way, using her superhuman speed to dodge the blow. Circling the chakram, she sliced the blade off the end of the staff, right through the wood. Kirsa tossed the ruined weapon aside and grabbed a long sword.

Kirsa stabbed. Hope flipped backward until she hit the ropes that surrounded the ring, then ducked as Kirsa swung at her head. She hurled the chakram. As expected, it bounced off Kirsa's chest as if she were solid rock. Kirsa laughed at the small hole Hope's strike had left in her uniform and tossed the sword she was using aside. She reached for a crossbow.

Hope leaped onto the wall, scaling the weapon rack until the reverberation of the bowstring warned her the arrow was coming. She flipped back into the ring, a move that would be impossible for a regular human student. She moved too fast, dropped too far. The arrow plowed into the wall where her chest had been.

"This isn't going to help you adapt," Kirsa yelled, tossing the crossbow aside and picking up her favorite dagger. It was a black handled monstrosity with a double-edged blade. "You won't get stronger if I can't make contact." Her round face reddened with her anger.

"I need time to rest. I can't grow stronger if you keep tearing me down," Hope yelled, her anger flaring like a waking beast.

Everything about Kirsa was big and thick. She was layered with muscle, stronger than any man. And when she charged toward Hope, it was like being stalked by a freight train.

"Do not tell me how to teach my class." She said through her teeth. "You are destined for resilience. I knew the moment I first saw you, so unlike the waifs I usually get in here. Stop fighting it. You have the potential to become an instructor, Hope, if you apply yourself. Give yourself over to the pain. Pain is what life is all about. Once you learn to like it, you won't feel it anymore. You'll love the pain. It will be the only time you feel anything."

Hope dodged her slashing blade. "No," she said through her teeth. "I don't want to be like you. I will never 'love the pain.' And I would never want to do what you do. Who could enjoy inflicting pain on others?"

Enraged, Kirsa lurched forward, stabbed to the right but grabbed to her left. She'd closed in to the point Hope's choices were either the dagger or her grasp. She should have taken her chances with the dagger.

Kirsa's fist closed around her ponytail and yanked, tossing her to the floor. "I'll show you what you want, you arrogant little twit." The larger woman came down hard on top of her, straddling her. Even with Hope's superior speed and strength, Kirsa's unnatural abilities overcame her. Her knee, as hard as marble, slammed down on her arm, near her elbow, and Hope heard a sickening crack, pain radiating through her from the break. But Kirsa didn't let up. Her fist connected with Hope's jaw. Another crack. This time the Soulkeeper felt it through her skull. She spat blood.

Pinned beneath her, broken and bleeding, Hope had no choice but to absorb everything Kirsa sent her way. The dagger plunged into her chest, spraying blood across Hope's face and knocking the air out of her. Another stab, this time to the abdomen. Her blood sprayed Kirsa's shirt and face. Hope would have screamed if her lung wasn't punctured. The dagger plunged into her flesh again and again. Always carefully placed to avoid her heart. Her cheek, her shoulder, her hip, her gut. Over and over the blood sprayed.

The taste of blood filled her mouth. She stared at the chakram, thrown from her hand when she fell, and lost herself in the pain. She wouldn't look at Kirsa. Wouldn't give her the satisfaction of seeing the pain. Surely she would pass out soon. Tiny sips of air entered her lungs. Stars swam in her vision.

And then the door opened. All Hope could see was the peacock-blue hem of a dress, but that was enough to discern who it was. "Kirsa," Juliette said from the door. "Can I speak with you for a moment?"

Kirsa froze midstrike, her face turning to look at Juliette, nothing but admiration in her previously cruel features. "Give me a minute. I'll be right there."

The dress hem exited and the door closed again. Hope sobbed, blood spilling from her lips.

"Don't be a baby. You'll be fine," Kirsa said, rising from Hope's bloodied body. "You'll heal. You always do. You needed this, Hope. You needed me to take you to the brink to move you beyond this plateau. You'll thank me." Kirsa grabbed the healing kit. There was not enough balm to cover her wounds this time, but she swabbed the largest ones. Kirsa tossed a towel on her chest. "Once you've recovered, clean up the mess."

Kirsa left her then, climbing the stairs and exiting the armory. When Hope was sure she was gone, she pulled the triquetra from under her shirt with the only hand that was working and breathed across the symbol. It was a pant really. That was all she could manage. But it was enough.

Light poured through the window as if the glass didn't exist. It broke apart, swirled and expanded, until Gabriel stood beside her, looking as unangel-like as ever in a wrinkled T-shirt and jeans.

"Hope!" he said softly. He rushed to her side, placing healing hands on her abdomen to stop the wound there from bubbling blood. "Why aren't you healing?"

Too injured to answer, all she could do was look at him.

"Never mind. I will help you."

She could already feel the healing warmth flowing through her, feel the twang as the bones in her jaw knit themselves back together. She glanced at the door to the armory. "Careful," she rasped. "She could come back."

"She won't see me," he said.

Hope closed her eyes and concentrated on the light flowing through her. "I should have known something like this would happen today," Gabriel said under his breath.

For several moments, Hope couldn't think what he meant. What day was it? She hadn't been paying attention to the calendar. Every day was the same here. Then she remembered and her eyes filled with tears.

"Happy Birthday," Gabriel whispered. "I am sorry we will have to celebrate another time."

Her sixteenth birthday. And the anniversary of the day her parents were brutally murdered by fallen angels. She swallowed hard, a tear escaping from the corner of her eye. Gabriel wiped it away.

"Can you move your arm? Can you speak?"

She could, although the pain she felt now was not the kind he could heal. "We have to try something different," she said. "If I hadn't been able to call you, I would have died."

Gabriel scanned her from head to toe. "You can't die, not permanently. You're the last Soulkeeper and a Healer."

She pushed herself up, her head still swimming. "The island is changing me. I'm not healing anymore. Not fully. Before you healed me, I had wounds from two days ago."

Gabriel's face tightened with concern, a line forming between his eyes. "I was afraid of this. This place, this island, is unholy. There are unnatural forces at work here."

"Then get me out of here."

He shook his head, as sad as she had ever seen him. "I can't."

"Don't tell me that. You don't get to say that." She shook her head.

"You know I would if it were up to me. But I am only an angel, Hope. A servant. And this isn't only a mission for you. It's a test."

"A test? Is He testing how much abuse I can handle and not hate Him with every fiber of my being? Too late," she said through her teeth. She lifted her hands from the mat and showed them to him. They were bright red, caked with her blood.

Gabriel used the towel and water from the pitcher Kirsa kept beside the ring to clean her hands, rubbing them thoroughly until all traces of the blood were gone. "Don't say things like that. It breaks my heart."

"I'm afraid I can't spare you that. My heart is as broken as my body these days. I can't believe He's done this to me. To us."

Gabriel licked his lips. "He did not do this to you, Hope. It's He who is trying to stop this evil, to work through us to stop this evil."

She had to change the subject. If she thought any more about God or her fate, she'd lose it. "Why are you dressed like that?" she said, eyeing his rumpled T-shirt.

His lip twitched. "I've been living in the tree behind your room for days. As you noticed earlier, this island interferes with my ability to traverse dimensions. This is the best I can do. What's the status on your mission?"

Hope sighed. "I have searched every corner of this place. I thought for sure Ravenguard and Applegate were stealing souls, but then Amanda and Paul came back. Different, but very much alive. I can't put it together. They're not demons. I'd sense that. Finn said he saw a clown steal a strand of my hair. Do you know of any demons that steal souls through physical means: hair, blood, flesh?"

Gabriel frowned. "No. And other than the last fallen angel, Damien, nothing from Hell can come to Earth. Not since God won the battle between Heaven and Hell. You'd know that if you'd done as I asked and consulted with the Immortals before coming here."

She tipped her head to the side. "I knew that anyway. I don't need a history lesson from Fate, Death, or Time, thank you very much. Still, something is stealing souls, and I'm no closer to finding out what."

"Don't give up. It's here, somewhere. I can feel it," Gabriel said.

"Well, angel, if you can't get me out of here, what exactly can you do for me? You are about two days away from losing your last Soulkeeper for good and having no one to blame but yourself. Kirsa will kill me. And if I come back, she'll kill me again."

Gabriel's usually angelic glow darkened. "Moses wasn't allowed to give up and go back to Egypt, but he was able to split the Red Sea. You can ask me for help, but I can't save you from hardship."

Hope stood. The skin behind her knees was sticky with blood and felt stiff. She turned the problem over in her head. If she had any chance of solving this puzzle, she needed to free her body from Kirsa's daily torture and gain greater access to the people who ran the school. There had to be a way.

"If I can't leave, then I'm going to need your help to be effective. I'm going to need you to part the Red Sea," she said slowly, an idea coming to her.

Gabriel ruffled his feathers, straightening to his full height. An honored smile spread across his mouth. " I can do that. What do you have in mind?"

"Listen to me very carefully. This is going to take a miracle."

🦢 26 🦢

ENCHANTED

Finn stopped with his fork halfway to his mouth. Hope had entered the already full dining hall with a determined stride and a distracted expression. For some reason, she wouldn't make eye contact. He waved to her and she acknowledged him with a quick nod, but instead of continuing to the buffet, she stepped onto the platform at the head of the room and cleared her throat.

"What are you doing?" Ms. D asked. The other teachers stopped eating and glared at Hope.

"I am in the wrong troupe," Hope said.

Kirsa waved her hand. "Ridiculous. You heal faster than any of them. You are resilient."

"Students are not permitted to question their assignments." Ms. D's eyes darted to Ravenguard, who took a step from his place near the door.

Hope straightened, clasped one hand in the other, and without even a glance toward Ravenguard, began to sing. The purest sound Finn had ever heard cascaded from her mouth. He couldn't look away; she was enchanting. Ravenguard hesitated at the base of the platform.

The lights dimmed and a shower of green sparks exploded from Hope's heart. The fireworks broke apart, forming stars, a galaxy that swirled above the table. As her voice soared and swooped with equal mastery, the galaxy morphed into a glittering, wispy cloud that gathered around the antler chandelier. A piece of the cloud landed on the table in front of Finn's plate, then another. He held out his hand and a warm, fat drop slapped his palm.

Hope was making it rain... in the dining room.

The drops came faster, turning into a storm that transformed the dining hall and everything in it. The chairs became the bent branches of an enchanted forest, the table, a jagged crag of stone. A dragonfly buzzed past Finn's face, zooming toward Hope. Exotic plants bloomed massive, dish-sized flowers that gave off a heady scent.

Finn reached out to stroke a red orchid and his fingertips kissed soft, wet petals. As far as his senses were concerned, this was real. Wendy caught his eye and giggled in awe. Jenny twirled, wide-eyed and open-mouthed. Jayden and Mike murmured in wonder.

What language was Hope singing? He guessed Italian. It was definitely an opera piece. She was a solid, athletic girl, but the power originating from her dwarfed her physical presence. He couldn't explain it, but he could feel it. Pure emotion flooded through him, binding him to the rain, the green, the fresh smell of the forest.

The music built, Hope's voice soaring to a crescendo before her magnificent aria concluded. As her final note faded, her illusion came apart, the forest breaking into pieces that spun and dissolved into themselves. When the lights came back on again, Hope was herself once more. Human. Vulnerable.

No one made a sound. Every student, every teacher, stared at her, a unicorn in their midst, as if she held the secrets of the universe inside her lungs. Maybe she did. The simple memory of her voice caused Finn's eyes to mist.

Ms. D cleared her throat. "That was unexpected."

Juliette placed a gloved hand on the buttons of her peacock-blue dress. "You can't be suggesting…"

"You saw what she can do." Ms. D folded her hands on the table. "You will begin training her posthaste."

A collective gasp rose from the instructors. Kirsa's fist slammed on the table. "No! The next enchanter was supposed to be me. This one was to take *my* place. I've already been selected to apprentice with Juliette."

"Juliette did select you, and you have trained, unsuccessfully, for some time now. I'm beginning to believe Juliette selected you to make herself indispensable."

Juliette stood. "Sacrilege. You insult me."

Ms. D peered over her red bifocals at the enchanter. "The choice is made. Unless Kirsa can demonstrate equal mastery." She gestured toward the platform.

Kirsa pushed the table forward, rattling the dishes and spilling the drinks. She stood from her chair, which stayed exactly where it had been and marched to the platform, chasing Hope from her spot with a deadly stare. Clasping her hands, she took a deep breath and began to sing.

It was a pleasant tune—Kirsa had a believable operatic voice—but there was no magic. The dining hall remained a dining hall, and in the end, she stopped singing before the final note.

"I thought so," Ms. D proclaimed.

Kirsa's hands balled into fists, her face reddening with what Finn assumed was either anger or embarrassment. Maybe both. She ran from the room, knocking Ravenguard out of the way to get to the door.

With a deep sigh, Ms. D dragged her heavy chair to the table's new position.

"It's too soon," Juliette insisted.

"I've made my decision." Ms. D began to eat again.

Juliette pressed both hands into her stomach. "Please excuse me. I've lost my appetite." She sashayed from the room, back straight and chin high. Finn stared after her, horrified. Clearly something big had happened. New students never became magicians or enchanters. Ms. D had told them so the first day, and Theodor had confirmed as much. Hope must have had the predisposition for enchanting, just as Finn had a talent for aerial and magic.

"What are you all staring at?" Ms. D waved her hand. "Eat. Finish your meal. You too, Ms. Laudner."

Hope nodded and drifted to the buffet to load her plate. When she finally sat down, Mike patted her shoulder. "That was incredible! Damn, I wouldn't have guessed you had it in you."

Jayden laughed. "That took balls. I have a whole new respect for you."

But Finn had a different question. "How?"

"You're not the only one with tricks up your sleeve, Finn Wager." Hope gave him a knowing smile, like she could see right through him.

Finn balked. Did she know about the cards and his relationship with Theodor? The symbol in his arm did not burn. If she suspected anything, it was not his doing.

"Michael Carson," Ms. D called, causing them to pause their forks once more.

"Yes?" Mike frowned as he responded. Trouble was in the air, hovering like dust over the table.

"You will take Ms. Laudner's place in the resilience troupe."

Mike's entire body froze like he was caught in the headlight of a speeding train.

"What about me?" Jenny interrupted.

"As you have not been chosen for a troupe, I'm assigning you to the position of stage manager. You will be responsible for the behind-the-scenes operation of our show. Costumes, set design, and the like. Mrs. Wilhelm and staff will train you."

Jenny grinned, and Finn watched a flash of jealousy wash across Mike's face. Jenny's job was exciting and important. Resilience was an awful fate.

"I'm no good at resilience," Mike finally said.

Ms. D's cold eyes fixated on his face. "Then may I suggest you work harder at becoming good at it? Or do you need more intensive intervention?"

Mike's expression turned from shock to horror. Finn met his eyes but had no idea what to say. What could he say?

Hope placed a hand on Mike's arm, her expression suddenly worn. "I'm sorry."

Mike shrugged her off, pushed back his chair, and rushed from the room. The look he gave Ms. D as he left could have soldered iron. The one he gave to Hope was almost as deadly.

"Don't worry," Finn said to Hope. "He'll come around. He'll change faster now that he'll be doing it full-time." He hoped it was true.

The comment didn't seem to comfort her. She dropped her fork and chased after Mike.

"Change faster?" Jayden balled his napkin and tossed it across his plate. "Bullshit, Wager. You've been here too long if you think Mike should have to change at all. He was the best. The best of any of us. A truly good person. If you're more worried about Mike changing than the fact that your friend was just sentenced to weeks of torture, you need to reconsider your priorities."

The whispered words settled like a heavy weight over Finn's heart.

27

LOST THINGS

When Finn returned to his room, he was anxious to talk to Hope about the Mike situation and how she'd figured out she was an enchanter. She wasn't there. But something else was—his great-grandmother's antique Louis Vuitton trunk.

He plucked a folded white note from the lid.

YOU ARE IN GRAVE DANGER. BRING THE GIRL TO MURDER MOUNTAIN. *We have much to discuss and little time.*
-A friend

UNDER THE SIGNATURE WAS A DRAWING OF THE SYMBOL HOPE WORE around her neck.

"I'm not sure Michael is going to forgive me for today." Hope entered the room, wiping tears from under her eyes with both hands. "Oh! They found your trunk?"

Finn handed her the note.

"A friend?"

"Your guess is as good as mine."

"They marked their signature with the triquetra," she breathed.

"The symbol from your necklace. What does it mean?"

"It means this *friend* is someone we can trust. We should go."

"Trust a complete stranger who stole my trunk and waited until now to return it? Are you insane?" Finn narrowed his eyes at her. "Not to mention, this 'friend' wants us to meet on Murder Mountain of all places. Why don't we just wear T-shirts that say *abduct me* and chase after creepy white conversion vans with blacked-out windows?"

Hope gripped the paper like a drowning victim grips a buoy. "We have to trust someone. We have to take risks."

"Why?"

Hope floundered for the right word. "Did you see what happened today?"

"Yeah, when did you become an enchanter?"

"That's not what I mean. Juliette and Kirsa were irate. And after what happened with Amanda and Paul and what you saw with the clowns, it's clear this school is dangerous. Whoever this is knows what's going on. They might know how to stop it."

Finn took a deep breath and puffed out his cheeks. "I'm not sure *what* I saw with the clown. It might have been a dream for all we know."

"What? You said it stole my hair."

"And we found no evidence that anything I saw was real. Maybe it was a nightmare."

"Finn..."

"And it's not as bad as I thought it was here. There are good things."

"Like that, you can fly?" Hope said, an edge to her voice.

"And other things. I belong here. I'm really good at aerial."

"What if what you saw *was* real? What if Mike is in danger? He's not ready for resilience. Don't we owe it to ourselves to see what this is all about?"

Finn spread his hands and scoffed. "We're almost halfway through the program. I don't want to mess up my chances of getting out on time."

Hope plunked on her bed in frustration. "What about the side effects? Whatever it is about this island that gave you... us... these abilities, how do you know it won't also give us cancer? Drive us insane?"

"If that's the case, it's already done its damage." Finn ran his hand along the top of the trunk. "Sorry, but I'm not going anywhere. I won't stop you from going alone, but I won't help you either."

"I don't think I can do it without you."

"Then you can't do it."

With a huff, Hope retreated to the bathroom, slamming the door.

"Girls." Finn flipped the drawbolts on his trunk and chuckled at the stacks of carefully folded sweaters inside. His hand fell on his stash of ADHD medication and a flash of guilt cut through him. Hope had helped him when he needed it most. No. No. This was crazy. He would not throw away his chance at graduating from this place over a cryptic note.

He shoved the meds aside and raised a sweatshirt to his nose, inhaling the fresh scent of his father's laundry detergent. His heart sank. He hadn't thought much of his family since he'd been here, but homesickness came on with a vengeance. His thoughts went back to the day he left, to the last hug his father gave him.

I left a surprise for you in the trunk.

He'd almost forgotten what his father had whispered in his ear. Quickly, he removed the piles of clothing, but the phone wasn't there. Had the stranger taken it? After checking the stack thoroughly, he had an idea. He ran a finger along the edge of the tattered liner. The corner depressed slightly beneath his touch.

His great-grandmother had been about his age during the Vichy regime in France, World War II. Her parents, Finn's great-

great-grandparents, were Jewish and would eventually die in a concentration camp. They saved Great-Grandma Mimi by placing her in the care of a nun at a Catholic orphanage who they paid handsomely to swear she had been there since birth.

Great-Grandma Mimi eventually married a German man who became Finn's great-grandfather. She was famous for saying, "Survivors don't weep for the dead; they celebrate the living. There is no shame in survival."

Finn pressed down harder in the corner. A spring latch popped the section up, and he was able to dig his fingers under the edge. A false bottom. A secret compartment.

Inside was the most beautiful vision he'd ever seen. His phone! Unfortunately, when he tapped the screen, the battery was completely dead and the included charger was useless here. All the lamps were gas, and there were no outlets in the walls. Didn't matter anyway; according to Ms. D, there was no cell service on the island. Sorely disappointed, he tossed it back in the bottom of the trunk where it skimmed across the leather into the opposite side. *Click.*

A secret compartment opened on impact. Squinting, Finn leaned forward to investigate. Inside, an accordion of yellow paper poked from a small pocket. Finn pulled it out and unfolded the ancient page, the smell of old books filling his nostrils.

At the top of the paper, *Der Unhold* was scrawled in tight, neat cursive. Below it was a three-column list of names. About half of the names in the first column were crossed off, but Finn's eyes locked onto a name in the center of the third: *Wulfrid Ravenguard.*

❧ 28 ❧

QUESTIONS

"And yet another exhibit for the Bizarre Life of Finn Wager Museum," Finn murmured. He refolded the list and jammed it back into the secret compartment. The name on the list was a weird coincidence. How many Wulfrid Ravenguards had existed throughout history? He'd have to show it to his dad when he got home. He closed the trunk and crammed it under his bed.

Exhausted, he flopped onto his mattress. "Ah—Ow." A burning sensation developed in his side, below the interior pocket of his jacket. He dug for his cards. The joker smiled back at him, hands empty. Time for magic lessons.

He raced out the door and up to the library, where he found Theodor in an unusually contemplative state. Without a word, the magician tossed the card to teleport both of them to his office.

"I came when you called, but it's almost sunset. We don't have much time," Finn said.

"I know, Finn. Have a seat. This won't take long."

Finn slid into the student desk at the center of the room.

"What happened today with Hope Laudner was not supposed to happen," Theodor said.

"I got that sense from the way Kirsa and Juliette reacted. Why is it such a big deal?"

"At Revelations, talented students are asked to become teachers, teachers are sometimes asked to train as enchanters or magicians—like Juliette and me. Enchanters and magicians are sometimes asked to become the performance architect. The performance needs but one magician and one enchanter. Hope will train with Juliette, but Juliette has no position to move into. Ms. Duvall will remain as performance architect. That means when Hope's training is complete, Juliette must return to the mainland and find other means of existence."

"She'll lose her job."

"She'll lose her power." Theodor smoothed his mustache with his thumb and middle finger. "Orelon tells me you can fly."

"I did and it was incredible. I'm working on having more control."

"Your transformation has occurred faster than expected, as has Hope's. The two of you are breaking records. As you might suspect, this has created quite a stir with other members of the faculty."

"Because they don't want to lose their jobs or their power," Finn repeated.

"Now that you can fly, are you looking forward to the day you'll go back home to Beaverton and never fly again?"

Finn scratched the back of his head. "It only works here? I won't take it with me?"

"Oh, you'll keep it for a time. Weeks. A month if you are lucky. The longer you stay away, the more it will fade. No one has retained their power longer than a year away from the island."

"I see. So Juliette is upset because she'll lose a piece of who she is."

"Well put. Her voice has become an appendage, a crutch. But it is more than that. She will age... quickly."

Finn's mind drifted to the posters Hope had shown him in the library. "What exactly do you mean by that, Theodor?"

"I was born in 1904," he murmured.

Finn chuckled. "It sounded like you said 1904."

"I did." The magician's expression turned deadly serious. "Revelations Island suspends the aging process. When I leave here, I will die."

"Huh? No." The symbol on the inside of his arm began to burn and he scratched it furiously.

"You agreed to keep an open mind. I would not lie to you, Wager. I am over one hundred years old, and Juliette is in her late fifties."

Finn swallowed hard, the burn fading with his acceptance of Theodor's words.

"Juliette won't simply lose her power if Hope replaces her—she'll become old." Theodor sat down at his desk and rested his chin in the web of his hand. "She chose Kirsa as her apprentice knowing that the woman had no aptitude for the subject. She did this intentionally, to maintain her position."

"And now Hope is a threat to her." The revelation sent a chill up Finn's spine. "But that means, if you leave this island, you'll die."

"Yes."

"So, why are you mentoring me? You can't want me to take over your position."

Theodor nodded. "Did you read the book I gave you?"

"Most of it. Why?"

"Then you know that Victoria Duvall is also very old. She's my age, in fact."

The truth came to Finn in a rush. "You want to be the performance architect! That's why you are training me in secret. Ms. D can't know. You plan to force her out the way Hope is forcing Juliette out."

"You are a smart boy."

"But why? Don't you like being a magician?"

"Victoria hasn't been the same of late." He stood from his desk and turned to face the window. "We started at Revelations at the same time, you know. She was an enchanter. Before that, a member of aerial and then an instructor of pyro. I watched her light herself on fire once as part of a performance. It was beautiful. She defied natural law for the sake of her art. Victoria was a genius of the performance arts who mastered every Revelations troupe before she became performance architect."

Finn studied Theodor's profile for a moment. The man stared at the wall with the absent expression of one who had experienced great loss. He recognized it; he'd seen it before in his father's eyes when they'd talked of his mother. "You... you loved her."

Theodor looked at Finn in surprise. "Is it obvious?" He frowned. "She's changed. She aged when she took on her current role. That was to be expected. The architect is always of a certain age. But there was something else. Victoria changed after last spring's performance. She hardly speaks to me anymore. Spends all her time with Ravenguard and Applegate." He shook his head.

"What happened last spring?"

He tipped his head. "I wish I knew." He leaned against the window frame. "I fear for your safety, Finn. There may be retaliation for what happened today. It is my duty to teach you how to protect yourself."

"You mean from Juliette? Why would she want to hurt *me*?"

"You and your roommate have proven yourselves extraordinarily powerful. If you can't see why most of the staff would find that threatening, you haven't heard a word I've said."

"Are you saying I might have a target on my back because I can fly and have an enchanter as a roommate?"

Theodor glanced toward the darkening window. "It's late. You must go. I will call you tomorrow and we will begin our next lesson."

❧ 29 ❧

SECRETS

Hope paced her room, arms crossed and fingers tapping her bicep. What she'd pulled off tonight was nothing if not dangerous. Gabriel had given her the powers of an enchanter. They weren't hers to keep but loaned to her for the duration of her mission at Revelations, for the purpose of extending her reach inside the school. After seeing how Kirsa and Juliette reacted, she was sure she'd made the right choice, hit a nerve, and possibly exposed the enemy.

But she was also sure that Finn's experience with the clowns was another clue. There were no accidents when it came to God's purpose. Finn was her roommate for a reason, and the place he described certainly sounded like the workshop of the enemy. Whoever had left the note on Finn's trunk must know something, but how could she convince Finn to go? Not only was it risky going alone, but also the note suggested they were supposed to go together.

The door opened and Finn shuffled in, looking exhausted. "Where have you been?" she snapped.

"None of your business," he murmured. He made to move around her.

"I'm making it my business." She stopped him with a hand to the chest and felt a small rectangle in the interior pocket of his jacket. Quickly, she slipped her hand inside and retrieved a pack of playing cards.

"Hey! Give those back!" Finn grabbed for the cards, but Hope dodged out of his reach. She was faster, and he knew it. He plopped onto his bed with a groan. "Come on, Hope. Don't do this to me. I need those."

"Why? What are they?" She flipped one over, then another. "They look like ordinary playing cards, but the energy coming off them is incredible."

"Is it interfering with your reiki? Or maybe your enchanter powers?" Finn's lips pulled into a tight line.

"What's your point?"

"You're so full of shit, Hope. You didn't learn that aria overnight." He flopped flat on the bed. "Look, you have your secrets and I have mine. Let's leave it at that."

She turned the cards between her fingers and held one up to the fading light of the window. Still nothing. No clue to its secrets. Just ordinary playing cards. Playing cards. Where did Finn get playing cards at Revelations? Her eyes widened. "You've been training with the magician!"

Finn did not answer. He folded his hands across his stomach. "I'd like my cards back now."

"He's teaching you magic? But why hasn't he told Ms. D? And aren't you exhausted training with aerial *and* as an apprentice magician?"

"Hope, why do you have to be such a pain in the ass? I told you, I *can't* talk about this." He rubbed the inside of his arm until it turned red.

"You *can't* talk about it, can you?" she asked.

Finn groaned and curled on his side.

Hope took pity on him and let the subject die. For now. A moment later, she said, "I think I really pissed Juliette off today."

"You did. There's something I have to tell you." Finn rolled over to face her. "You were right about the posters we saw upstairs. The faculty here does not age. This place, this island, it's like magic. And normally, Revelations has a hierarchy, students become instructors, and instructors become enchanters or magicians—"

"And an enchanter or magician becomes the performance architect," Hope finished. She noticed Finn was careful never to mention Theodor as he relayed what he'd learned. The magician must have bound Finn to secrecy. The way he avoided the subject was anything but normal. "Sounds like I ruffled some peacock feathers." She sighed.

"Yeah, well, I'd watch my back if I were you."

"Thanks for warning me. I can see it was risky for you to help me."

Finn didn't say another word. She crossed to his side of the room and handed him his cards. He tucked them away again.

"Don't you see? This is why we should investigate who this friend is who left you the note."

Finn groaned. "No means no."

Hope placed her hands on her hips. "How about a peace offering? I will tell you part of my secret if you want to know."

He lifted his eyebrows. "Really? Sure."

"The reiki I did on you the first day, it worked, right?"

"Yeah. It was amazing. I haven't taken a single ADHD pill since I've been here, and I'm fine."

"My abilities don't end with reiki. I'm what you might call gifted."

Finn frowned and pushed himself up on his elbows. "Gifted how?"

"Before I ever came to this island, I was faster and stronger than most people." She tangled her fingers together. "I've been able to heal myself and do what I've done because I had those abilities from the start."

"You did?"

"I was sent here for a reason, Finn. And I'm beginning to think you were too."

He flopped onto his pillow and closed his eyes. "No offense, Hope, but I don't care why we're here. I just want to do whatever's necessary to not be here a day longer than I have to be."

30

BLACK SUITS

"Take out your deck," Theodor commanded. The magician seemed abnormally anxious to get started.

Finn retrieved his cards from the pocket inside his jacket. After the night before, he'd expected Theodor to call him back for another magic lesson, but the intense determination on his mentor's face was new to him. Why was this lesson different from any other?

"Select a card in a black suit."

Up until now, everything he'd learned and practiced had involved a red card. He'd wondered when Theodor would get around to teaching him about the black suits. He selected the two of spades and placed it on the desk, readying his black Sharpie between his fingers. "What spell is this?"

"First, you need to understand how the black cards differ from the red." Theodor paced in front of the chalkboard, toying with the cuffs of his shirt as if the topic made him uncomfortable. "So far, every spell you've learned can be undone. What is bound can be unbound. What is extinguished can be lit again. This type of magic is always in balance."

"And the black cards aren't?"

Theodor shook his head. "What I teach you today cannot be undone even if it is reversed. Consider, if you will, a nail pounded into a piece of wood. The nail itself can be removed, but the hole it creates remains. When I open a portal to bring you here, the portal closes behind us. To go back, I don't reopen the same portal as if it were a door temporarily closed. You can't undo a portal. Sending you back involves a new channel from point A to point B. Returning to the library does not make it as though you'd never left. Do you see? The spells I will teach you now come with a price. The portal from the library to here requires only a tiny price from an experienced magician such as myself, an amount of energy I can handle on the relatively rare occurrence of our meetings. But these spells are not in balance with nature, Finn, and their use, at least for you, must be both careful and rare."

"Understood," Finn said. He wasn't exactly sure he did understand, but he was anxious to get started.

Theodor reached for the chalk and drew three parallel lines with a swoop at the bottom that wrapped around and intersected the set. "This is the symbol for eviscerate. It will shred your victim to the extent of your intention. This spell can kill, Mr. Wager, or at the least, maim."

Finn copied the spell exactly and watched it sink into the card. When he breathed life into the symbol, it did not open and close like bind/unbind or ignite/extinguish. It rose off the card stock and sank inside without ever changing. "So the opposite isn't to heal?"

Theodor sighed. "No, Finn. Healing is performed with a red card that can be reversed. For example, a wound can be bound to close it up or unbound to open it again, but creating a wound requires a dark intention that cannot be reversed with the same card. It can only be countered with a good intention of equal strength."

"It can't be undone?"

"No." Pivoting, Theodor strode to the bookshelf, searching the stacks of objects haphazardly shoved between and on top of the books. "You need something to practice on," he murmured, more to himself than to Finn. "You need to understand exactly the kind of power you hold in your hands. Ah!" He returned with a small glass vase painted with yellow daisies and plunked it down on Finn's desk. "I've always hated this one." The magician gestured for Finn to give the card a try.

Without hesitation, Finn raised the two of spades. "Eviscerate." A tiny chip tumbled from the lip of the vase and bounced across the desk. "You're right. Unimaginable power," Finn said dryly.

"Intention, Finn. You must mean to destroy it. Think of something you hate, someone you'd like to tear apart."

Finn's eyes narrowed. At one time he might have thought about the bullies at school. He'd certainly felt like he owed them payback for some time. But Revelations had changed his perception of the incidents he used to mull over endlessly, making them appear distant and muted in his memory. The bullies here were far more threatening. He pictured the day Orelon kicked the stool out from under Wendy. Wendy, who was about the best thing to ever happen to this place. He raised his card again.

"Eviscerate!" The vase shattered, tiny slivers of glass exploding in a way that made Finn turn away and cover his eyes.

Theodor patted his shoulder. "Nice work. That's the way." He took out his own red card and circled it over the dust. "Construct," he said. The vase rebuilt itself.

"You fixed it," Finn said.

"Not exactly. If I reverse my spell, this vase will come apart in the exact same pieces it was in a second ago. In contrast, if you use eviscerate again, it will explode into different pieces, a new destruction, not a return to a state of brokenness. Do you understand the difference?"

"Oh," he said. "I think so."

"Do you want to try it on something living? I could conjure a rat for you."

Finn swallowed. "I don't want to kill anything."

"You might have to someday. Make no mistake, Finn, I teach this spell to you as a weapon. You need to know how to defend yourself."

"I'd rather not kill anything unless I have to."

Theodor frowned. "Very well. Try again, and this time, see if you can control it. Make it come apart to the halfway mark and no more."

Finn tried. Sometimes only an inch of the vase would shatter. Other times the entire thing would turn to dust. It took him thirty-seven times to cut the vase in half. Again and again, Finn practiced the spell to Theodor's specifications, until he could produce a hole in the center of the vase without breaking the rest of it.

By then, the magic had taken its toll. "I feel weird."

"You're tired. This kind of magic is extremely draining. You won't be able to use it for long without physical consequences. Let's take a break." Theodor retrieved a glass of water for Finn from the pitcher.

After drinking it greedily, Finn thought about Wendy, about the clown dipping its finger into her blood. He'd never asked Theodor about the clowns. Not only because the topic seemed to be taboo among the teachers but because his time with Theodor was short. There simply hadn't been much opportunity. But after everything else he'd learned about the school, he needed to know.

"Theodor, can I ask you something about Revelations?"

"Of course, Finn."

"Can you tell me about the clowns?" Finn flipped a card between his fingers. "What exactly are they, and what are they doing under the school?"

Theodor grimaced. "How do you know about the clowns?"

"I was there, in their laboratory."

By the look on Theodor's face, Finn might have told him he murdered kittens in his spare time.

"Tell me everything about how you came to be in that place, Mr. Wager. And I warn you, I will know if you leave out a single detail."

Finn was more than happy to oblige. He told him everything, from Wendy's blood, to Hope's hair, to his nighttime visit to the secret room.

"I need an explanation," Finn said. He stared across the desk at Theodor, praying the man would indulge his curiosity. "Please, I have to know."

"We don't talk about the clowns," Theodor whispered. "It's important you stay out of their way."

"But what are they doing under the school in that... hive? What are those things in the vats?"

Theodor sighed. For a long time, he stared at Finn, stroking the left side of his mustache with his finger. His eyes narrowed and his lips pulled into a tight line.

"I've already placed you at risk by teaching you magic." He shook his head.

Finn said, "I need to know. If you don't tell me, I'll keep looking until I figure it out."

"Don't threaten me," Theodor said through his teeth.

"I wasn't."

"Then you're dumber than I thought. Here's what I know. What you called an iceberg, the white object behind the glass, it's not ice."

"W-what is it?"

"A fallen star."

Finn gave a low chuckle. Theodor did not join in. "A star is a ball of gas," Finn said. "What I saw was as solid as you and me."

"What you saw was a small piece of a very old star. Old stars are more than burning gas, for your information. The entire Earth is made up of elements born in a star."

"Okay. So it's a star."

"The star was here before I came to this place and, as far as I know, the hive came with it. What you and I call clowns are amazing creatures who live in a symbiotic relationship with the star. They tend to the star, keep its energy contained and nurtured, and in return, the star gives them the radiation they need to survive and reproduce on this planet."

"Are you saying they're aliens?"

"To be honest, I don't know what they are or where exactly they came from. They don't speak and tend to keep to the shadows. But, as far as I know, the clowns are harmless, *if* you stay out of their way."

"What happens if you don't stay out of their way?"

"I've never seen it, but I've heard stories from Amuke that they've become agitated when provoked. It's why we warn all new students to leave them alone."

"But why are they collecting samples of blood and hair from the students?"

"That I don't know. They aren't human, Finn. I can't say any of us fully understand exactly what they are, but they are amazingly adaptable, can work in high-radiation environments for extended periods, and don't eat or sleep as far as we know. I've been here almost a century, and I've never witnessed any aggression on their part. We assume they get everything they need from the star, and by tending to the star, they provide this place with its unusual properties. They are what makes this island special."

"The star is why I can fly?"

"You can fly because you trained yourself to fly. The star simply eliminated your body's need to conform to gravity. If you were to train to fight, you would become a powerful fighter. Train in magic"—he held up a card between his fingers—"you will become a sorcerer. Different people have different predispositions. But *everyone* changes."

Finn drummed his fingers on the desk. "Why do you think Mike and Jenny didn't change as fast as the rest of us?"

Theodor straightened his bow tie. "We don't know why some

change faster than others. Over the years, we've had dozens of boys and girls your age pass through these walls. A certain number excel. Most get by long enough to go home. Others never change at all until Ravenguard and Applegate get a hold of them."

"That's what I'm afraid of."

Theodor gave a curt nod. "If there is anyone you should be afraid of, it's those two."

❧ 31 ❧

THE SHOW

"What's going on?" Finn asked Wendy. She was waiting for him outside the gazebo beaming like she might come out of her skin.

"Finn, there you are! Have you heard?"

"Heard what?"

Orelon emerged from the gazebo behind her. "Class will be held in the theater today. Ms. D has an announcement about the spring performance."

Wendy grabbed Finn's hand. "The show, Finn! Finally." Her feet lifted from the ground with her excitement, and she floated at the end of his arm like a balloon. After spending two weeks at an uncontrollable and unpredictable hover, she'd finally learned to fly last week. She pulled his hand to lower herself to his ear. "We'll finally find out if we can go home." Her lips pressed to the area right below his earlobe and his ears grew warm.

"Stop messing around, you two, and come on," Natalie said. She followed Orelon toward the school, her feet touching the ground every third step.

"Is it just us?" Finn asked. Wendy dropped to his side as he followed toward the school. The aerial troupe was bigger than

Orelon and Natalie, but Finn had never met the others. They kept to the shadows in the rafters. He didn't even know their names.

"The purpose of the spring performance is to showcase *student* accomplishments," Orelon said. "Your parents want to see how much you've changed." He held one side of the magnificent front doors for them, and Natalie led the way to the main theater.

Aerial's entrance distracted Jayden and Fuse, who were juggling fire on stage. Jayden laughed as he missed a catch and the flames tumbled down his abdomen only to be knocked back into position by his knee. The flames didn't hurt him anymore. His skin was as fireproof as asbestos. In fact, he'd taken to impressing Jenny by holding his hand over a candle at dinner or producing a small, dancing flame that extinguished when he slid it into her hand. It made Finn happy to know that Jayden had connected to pyro the way Finn had to aerial. He gave his friend a mock salute, which was returned with a smile and a flip of the middle finger. Typical Jayden.

Resilience was the next to arrive. Kirsa whipped the heavy door open hard enough for its collision with the wall to echo through the mostly empty theater. Even Orelon groaned at the obviously attention-seeking behavior. Amanda entered behind her, followed by Mike, who trailed by a significant distance.

Finn cringed when he saw his friend. While Amanda looked the same as always, Mike was shockingly beat up. Bloody stab wounds covered his arms and legs under his torn uniform. His face was a collage of purple bruises, as was what little skin was visible. He walked with a pronounced limp.

Clearly the last week of full-time practice had not made Mike stronger. What upset Finn most was Kirsa's smug grin. It was as if she took a certain joy in Mike's pain. She yelled at him to hurry as he hobbled toward the stage.

Finn toyed with the cards in his pocket and wondered if *eviscerate* would work on Kirsa or if her resilience made her truly indestructible. He dispelled the dark thought and turned his attention to the front of the theater.

Ms. D had arrived and was waving her arms to get their attention. When everyone had quieted down, she said, "Very good, very good. Where is Amuke? Where is menagerie?"

"I am here, Headmistress." Amuke jogged toward the stage, followed by Paul and three boys Finn did not recognize.

"Who are they?" Finn asked Wendy.

"I don't know. Other than Paul, I've never seen any of them before."

"They must be part of the troupe, like the others in aerial."

"Yes, but then why are they here? I thought the purpose of this performance was to showcase student talent," Wendy said.

"I don't know." Finn did a double take as Juliette and Hope entered the theater at the balcony level.

"Wow, that costume is incredible," Wendy said.

Hope's long auburn hair was twisted along the back of her head and tucked beneath a pointed hat adorned with peacock feathers. The dress she wore sloped over one shoulder and skimmed along her body to her hips where more peacock feathers gathered and plummeted to the hem of a floor-length skirt. Next to Juliette's high-necked, Victorian-era garb, Hope looked youthful and dangerously beautiful, a powerful elegance that brought a hush over the other troupes.

Ms. D clapped her hands to call everyone's attention to the front of the room. "I am delighted to have you all here. We have four weeks until our final performance. Four weeks until your parents and our guests will sit in these seats and expect to see the stunning results of your rehabilitation."

"Tell us!" someone yelled from menagerie.

"Patience. This is the first time for these students." Ms. D spread her hands. "It is tradition at Revelations for the performance architect, that's me, to announce the theme of the spring performance and approve the proposed acts of the troupe leaders.

Once your act is approved, your leader will help you perfect your performance over the next four weeks. Exceptional performers will be featured in Revelations promotional materials." She rubbed her hands together, glancing at each of the troupe leaders. "The theme of Revelations spring performance will be... Metamorphosis!"

Applause rose up from students and teachers alike.

Ms. D continued. "We will take our inspiration from the life-cycle of the butterfly, explore the changes manifesting within, and develop acts that draw the audience into your transformation. The preparation, the waiting, the painful act of transition, the loom of death, and then the explosion of new life. Bring me ideas!"

"I will open with a simple wooden box," Theodor said. When had he arrived? "I will toss in ordinary objects, a red ball, a yellow teddy bear, a green kite. Then I will levitate the box and ignite it above my head. Out of the fire, doves will emerge and fly over the audience—one red, one yellow, one green. The box will reduce, folding in on itself. With the snap of my fingers, the doves will return to the flames right when the entire thing crumbles to dust and three origami doves drop into my hands."

"Perfect, Theodor. Who is next?"

"Red silk cocoons," Orelon yelled. "My students will suspend from the ceiling, slowly unraveling themselves with a series of moves demonstrating strength and flexibility. They will perform multiple death-defying feats. And then, the boy"—Orelon pointed to Finn—"will scale the silk to the very top until he stands in the rigging above the stage. He'll dive headfirst toward certain death. At the last moment, he will pull up and fly over the audience, until he circles back and lands effortlessly on the stage."

Ms. D clapped her hands in delight. "I want to see the girl as a catalyst. Use her. Wendy must be the reason he flies. Jenny, dear, costume is everything on this one. We must design wings for this boy. Perhaps we could light him on fire! Yes, yes, his wings could burn away."

Fuse tossed up one pointed finger. "A phoenix! The flames will appear to completely consume him. Jayden will emerge from the inferno and perform the fire dance of the Seven Kingdoms."

"Excellent. You have me. The boy is not a bird but a phoenix. Jayden, you will rise from the ashes. Then... then... Amuke?"

"The troupe will start with a dance to display our athleticism. At the conclusion, Paul will call the baby tigers to the stage. He will run them through their paces, then transform them into adult tigers. The audience will delight in the animals' grace and discipline."

"Fabulous! You're sure the tigers will perform predictably?" Ms. D asked, raising an eyebrow.

"Unequivocally," Amuke said.

She pointed a finger at his head. "No blood on the audience."

"We will take precautions."

Finn frowned. Why would there be blood?

"That leaves resilience. Kirsa, what say you?"

The beefy woman surveyed her charges. "We will start with a glass water bowl in the belly of a giant oyster. The water will represent the transient nature of life, our students, the pearls. Amanda will dive from a platform into the bowl. Of course, the water will seem too shallow for her not to break her neck, but our audience will delight in her survival and explosive exit from its depths. Michael will follow and pull Amanda back into the water. Amanda will become angry at his antics. They will battle violently in the small pool of water. Then Amanda will flip out of the bowl and close the oyster's shell so that Michael is trapped inside. Michael will drown. After he is dead, she will regret her decision, lift him from the liquid, and with love's first kiss, bring him back to life."

Mike's gaze darted around the room, his face paling and his head shaking vigorously.

"Your student does not appear confident in his ability to perform your proposed act, Kirsa. Are you quite certain you can resurrect him?"

"He'll be ready," Kirsa said.

Ms. D bobbed her head.

"You're talking about drowning him in front of a live audience," Finn yelled. "Don't you think you should ask *him* if he's ready?"

Orelon nudged his side. "Watch yourself, Finn," he whispered in his ear.

Ms. D paused, a wicked smile bending her lips. "I am sure Ms. Hildburg will adequately prepare her charge, Mr. Wager. Your assistance in this matter is unneeded. I assure you, Michael will return to his parents unharmed. Oh, excuse me, his aunt. As I recall, his parents are no longer with us."

Finn gritted his teeth. It was a low blow to bring up Mike's home situation in mixed company.

"What if I can't do it?" Mike yelled, garnering sharp glances from around the room.

Ms. D narrowed her eyes on him. "Mr. Carson, if you believe you cannot... sink to the occasion, Ravenguard and Applegate would be happy to help you do so."

From her place above the theater, Hope met Finn's gaze and placed a finger over her lips. He refrained from saying anything more but crossed his arms over his chest in disgust. This wasn't right. Mike was in real trouble here.

When no one offered further protest, Ms. D said, "Very well. I approve your proposals. Be prepared to perform your act in four weeks' time. One show only. Metamorphosis will be our most brilliant work!"

Everyone broke, rushing to begin preparations and practice their new acts. "We should bring the silks back to the gazebo. Easier to practice there," Orelon said. He jogged toward the rear of the stage.

"Our act is going to rock," Wendy said, smiling.

"Yeah. We've got the best troupe," Finn said, but he wasn't thinking about his act. He was worried about Mike. He had to talk to Theodor. Was this Kirsa's revenge? Did she mean to hurt Mike as a way to get to Ms. D?

Mike folded in on himself as he followed Kirsa out of the theater. He wouldn't be ready in time. How could someone be ready to *drown*?

If Finn wanted to save his friend, he'd have to do something and fast.

⚅

"YOU HAVE TO HELP HIM," FINN SAID IMMEDIATELY UPON ENTERING Theodor's office that afternoon.

"I'm afraid there is nothing I can do. If I suggest to Victoria that Mike isn't ready, she'll insist on intervention by Ravenguard and Applegate. As you know, that is a highly risky alternative. Your friend may never fully recover psychologically from the process."

Finn balled his hands into fists in frustration. "What do they *do*? What happened to Amanda and Paul?"

"I can't say I know for sure, Finn. The two of them are very secretive about their work. They take the student to a building off school grounds, at the base of the mountain. When they come back, the student is forever changed. You must have noticed that the admissions counselors are the muscle around here. This island changes people, and Ravenguard and Applegate have been here a long time. The star has made them very good at what they do, and what they do is discipline. My advice is to stay as far away from the two of them as possible."

"Then can't you use magic to help Mike adapt?"

"My magic doesn't work that way. Mike is struggling because he doesn't belong in resilience. When Ms. D selected him, she was fitting a round peg in a square hole. Victoria knew that Mike would fail in Kirsa's troupe but intended to use him to punish Kirsa for questioning her judgment when she reassigned Hope. Victoria is dense if she hasn't figured out that Kirsa intends to sabotage the show in retaliation."

"But he could die! They're talking about drowning him." Finn grabbed the sides of his hair. "We have to do something."

"There's nothing I can do."

Finn lowered his voice. "You said you wanted to overthrow Ms. D. Now is the time. If you become performance architect, you can change the act and save Mike."

Theodor gave a sad laugh. "Even if I was strong enough to challenge her for her position on my own, I can't get close enough. Ravenguard and Applegate are never far from her side. If you were a fully trained magician, maybe we could do it together. But you are not. It's too soon. I'm not ready and neither are you."

"Then what can we do to help Mike?"

Theodor frowned. "I'm afraid, given the circumstances, Mike is going to have to help himself."

HOPE AND JULIETTE

Each day after breakfast, Hope followed Juliette back to her tower apartment for her enchanter training. She wondered how they would develop enough music to support all of the acts in Metamorphosis in only four weeks. Juliette didn't seem concerned, and Hope worried it was because she wanted Hope to fail.

As usual, before Juliette even reached the door, one of her servants opened it for her, as if the woman had been waiting there, standing at attention. Hope wasn't surprised. Juliette ruled her corner of Revelations with a tight fist and a sharp tongue.

Juliette's apartment was acutely Victorian, all gilded mirrors and feathered shades. There wasn't a patch of wall or table that hadn't been decorated in some way. An antique trinket rested on every bare surface. Juliette didn't give the opulence a second glance as she navigated the foyer and sitting room to pause at a window overlooking the gardens.

Hope wasn't certain if Juliette's perpetually stiff posture was due to the whalebone corset she insisted on wearing or the proverbial stick she acted like she had up her butt. The woman was awful. Critical. Petty.

And Hope's best bet for solving the mystery of the lost souls.

"You'll never be ready on time," Juliette said toward the glass.

"Tell me what I need to do and I'll do it."

Juliette pursed her lips and gazed down her nose at Hope. "When last we met, we addressed the topic of control. Today we continue that lesson. It is important that you be able to split your illusion between multiple listeners. You may find yourself with a need to have the guests on stage right see something entirely different from those on stage left."

"Why would we want part of the audience to see a different performance?"

With a look of annoyance, Juliette smoothed the side of her hair. "If you must know, accidents have been known to happen. At times it is simpler to disguise the error than correct or hide it. For example, if a performer breaks their leg by falling from a great height, those nearest the stage might hear the snap. You cannot undo the sound of the breaking bone. It would be better to show them the bone's magical healing as if it were part of the act. On the other hand, if possible, we always conceal the break. Splitting the illusion is necessary, if and when we must improvise."

Hope swallowed, her lips rolling together before she hazarded her next question. "It sounds like you have experience with this scenario. How often do students get hurt during the show? Do you *expect* someone to get hurt?"

Juliette's prim-and-proper demeanor morphed into something darker, something cruel, eyebrows peaking in mock surprise. "Are you asking about young Michael? What did you think would happen when he had to take your place so unexpectedly?"

The words struck like a snakebite, knocking Hope back a step. Was Juliette accusing her of being at fault for Mike's precarious position?

"As an enchanter, you see what no one else sees. Even the performance architect is blissfully ignorant of the reality on the stage behind her. An enchanter's voice is a cosmetic to cover every blemish. As my apprentice, you need to know that, yes, students get hurt—seriously injured. It's your job to make sure no one else knows it."

"How seriously injured? The brochure for Revelations said the school has never had a serious accident."

"Oh, don't concern yourself, dear. We haven't lost one yet." Her eyes darted toward the window and she lowered her voice. "They all end up exactly where they're supposed to be."

Hope's skin prickled, her gut tightening ominously as if she were in the presence of evil. Was Juliette human or demon? She focused her abilities, dropping her consciousness into the purest part of herself. Breathing deeply, she smelled perfume and powder and an undercurrent of malice, but not the arsenic-sweet stench she'd been taught was demon or fallen angel. She came out of her power sure that, although Juliette had a dark soul, she was human. Still, the disclosure that the enchanter had hidden serious accidents in the past worried Hope. Juliette had confirmed that Mike was in real danger.

"Howard? Gertrude?" Juliette called to her servants. "Please join us. Hope needs to practice on someone."

The two redheaded servants jogged into the room and took a seat on a teal camelback sofa.

"Enough talk. Produce a juggler for Gertrude and a dog for Howard. I must see both illusions. Do it now." Juliette lowered herself onto a firm chair near the sofa.

Hope straightened, clutched one hand in the other, and began to sing.

❧ 33 ❧

A NEW PLAN

"I need to talk to you," Hope said, charging into their room after class. Rain pelted the window, and the sky outside was a dark gray color.

Finn leaned over and turned on the lamp. "Talk."

Hope floundered for the right words. "Juliette implied today that she expects Mike to be seriously injured during the show. As enchanter, she plans for me to cover it up so the audience doesn't see it. She's done this before. The way she talks, it's part of our role."

"I think Juliette and Kirsa *want* a tragedy. Kirsa thought she'd be the next enchanter, and Juliette assumed it would be years before she'd be ousted from her position."

"If Mike dies in front of a live audience, it would be a way for both of them to get their revenge against Ms. D and the school. Revelations' first death," Hope said. An icy-cold ripple cut through her system. "And if they find a way to frame me for it, they'll both get what they want."

"Do you think they would do that?" Finn asked.

"I don't know if they'd be bold enough to go that far, but Juliette has been abrasive since the moment I joined her troupe. It's like she's setting me up to fail, Finn. The only consistent message I get from her is that I won't be ready in time for the performance. And did you see Kirsa's face? She said straight out that her intent was to drown Mike and resurrect him."

"We have to do something," Finn said.

Hope sighed. "We need help. We need a friend." It pained her to admit it, but she regretted more than ever not visiting the Immortals before coming to Revelations. She'd thought she could handle whatever came her way. She was wrong.

"You're talking about the note. You want to go to Murder Mountain."

"We have to go. Maybe this stranger can help, or at least get word to someone outside the school about what's going on here. Maybe they can stop the performance."

Finn toyed with the side of his shoe, quietly contemplative.

"Oh my gosh, Finn. You don't *want* the show to be stopped."

"I'm afraid for Mike. We have to help Mike. But the show must go on. The problem isn't Revelations, it's Kirsa."

"After what happened with Amanda and Paul and how badly Mike was beat up today, how could you believe this school isn't dangerous? A school with no academic classes, where children can't speak to their parents, and medication is lost and never replaced. A school with a hive under its floor and clowns that are doing God knows what in the basement. This place isn't a school —it's a work camp, a circus of child slaves performing for profit. Someone needs to put an end to it, Finn, permanently. Whatever they did to Paul and Amanda, it isn't right. Can't you see that this place is like a cult? Yes, they change you, but at what cost?" Hope stared at him incredulously. What had he become? Why was he buying into the bullshit?

Finn took a deep breath and puffed out his cheeks. "Before this island, the only thing keeping me from having my face rubbed in the dirt on a daily basis was Mike. He protected me. And my special ability, if you could call it that, was cruising under the radar. I was practically invisible. I was a geeky lightweight with a YouTube channel where I played stupid pranks on other people to make me feel better about myself. Just a scrawny kid with no mom and nothing going for him besides a rich dad."

"Finn..."

"No, listen. You, Hope, seem like the kind of girl who has always been the special little snowflake. Girls like you have always fit in and been popular. This is the first time I've been good at anything. It's the first time I've been accepted as part of a community. This place may be just a school to you, but it has been a sanctuary for me. A deadly one, yes, but an exciting one."

"First of all, being special isn't all it's cracked up to be. Do you think I wouldn't change places with you in a heartbeat?" She met his stare and held it. "They're asking Mike to die, Finn. Not fly. Not juggle fire. The act is for him to drown. Are you willing to sacrifice Mike so that you can feel important?"

"No, of course not." Finn scowled.

"Then why aren't you doing anything about it?"

There was a long pause while Finn seemed to turn the idea over in his head. "You're right," he said slowly. A pained sigh left his lips. "We have to do something. I'm responsible for Mike. I got him into this. I have to get him out."

"Trusting this stranger is the only way. You won't be sorry, Finn."

"Don't make promises you can't keep."

"We'll need a plan. It won't be easy to sneak out and back without anyone noticing."

"Nothing about this will be easy." Finn folded his arms across his stomach and stared at the ceiling.

"Tomorrow, after dinner, let's meet in the library. We need to find a map of the island. I think I saw one in the alcove where we found the performance posters."

❦ 34 ❦

MAP

Hope found the map of Revelations Island sketched on a roll of yellowed parchment within the tree alcove she and Finn had visited before. The map seemed too old to exist outside a glass museum case. She carefully unrolled it on a small table between the alcoves, pinning the corners with books to hold it in place.

"It looks like the shortest way to Murder Mountain is to go through the Crimson Forest; that's the one we can see outside our window."

"It's also where the menagerie animals live. I'm not sure I'd care to run into a pack of wolves or a bunch of tigers," Finn said. "Any way around it?"

"This river—it's called Fever River—winds around the coast and branches under the school where it eventually meets up with the Hispida Tributary."

"Under the school?" Finn perused the section of map near Hope's finger. It did, indeed, appear the river flowed beneath the school. He wondered if it was the source of the water bathing the fallen star.

"We could follow Fever upstream and backtrack along the side of the mountain. It's a longer journey, but it doesn't go through the forest."

Finn pointed to a dark triangle of land labeled only with a skull where Fever River met Murder Mountain. "And go through that? Not only do we not know what this is, the trip will be considerably longer. I'm not even sure we can do it in one night."

"I agree. We have to risk the woods."

"So, we need to prepare to fight." He thought of his cards, of the new eviscerate spell he'd been practicing.

She shook her head. "Amuke will notice if one of his animals is injured. We'll pass through as quietly as possible, try not to stir anything up. If we get attacked, you fly and I'll run."

"You can't outrun a tiger."

"I'm fast. I can't fly, but I can do other things."

"What kind of other things? You can't sing your way out of a tiger attack."

"Who says? I healed your ADHD, didn't I?"

"Are you going to stop a tiger with reiki?"

"Don't worry about me. I can take care of myself."

Finn dropped onto the window seat. "I think we should go out the window of our room."

"I agree. I can pull off a fall like that. It's not that high. You can close the window behind us."

"I might be able to carry you," he said.

"I can jump."

"It will be quieter if I help. Someone might hear you fall."

She nodded. "Are you sure you can lift me?"

"I'll practice tomorrow with Wendy."

She pulled out a napkin from dinner and began to sketch a crude version of the map on the back. "What's up with you and Wendy anyway?" she murmured.

"What do you mean?"

"I see the way you stare at each other. You're always together.

The touches. The smiles you only have for each other. Everyone's noticed."

He shrugged, his cheeks turning red. "We're... troupe mates."

"Hmmm."

Finn snorted. "We're planning an almost impossible mission through a malevolent wood to meet a stranger in a place called Murder Mountain and you want to talk about Wendy?"

She grinned. "Absolutely. Have you kissed her?"

"No." Finn leaned against the bookshelf. "Orelon is always looking over our shoulders. It's like he can sense when we're alone together."

"But you want to."

"Who wouldn't want to kiss Wendy? The braids and the freckles? She has a face that belongs on a box of cookies."

Hope laughed. "You are absolutely right. There isn't a person alive who wouldn't want to kiss Wendy. It's a moot point." Smirking, she finished her sketch and rerolled the map, returning it to its place on the shelf. "Come on. Let's get some sleep. We go tomorrow night."

35

THE CRIMSON FOREST

"Get on my back." Finn squatted for Hope to climb on.

"You practiced this with Wendy today?"

"Yeah, well, kind of."

"What do you mean, kind of?"

"She's smaller than you and can fly. It's apples to oranges."

Hope huffed. "Are you saying I'm heavier? Will you be able to carry me?"

Finn shrugged. "Climb on and we'll find out."

Hope did not go gentle onto his back. She grabbed his shoulders and hopped, bringing her weight down hard on his hips.

"Oomph." Finn groaned. "Practically weightless."

"It's a gift."

Finn opened the window and carefully climbed out on the ledge. It was awkward with Hope on his back. She was taller than he was and fit like an ill-proportioned backpack.

"Ow! Watch it." Hope shifted, rubbing her forehead. She must have hit it on the frame.

"Sorry." Crouching on the ledge with Hope clinging to him, he measured the distance to the ground. "Here goes nothing." Finn leaped, working against gravity. Although he willed himself to rise, his body stubbornly sank, gaining speed as he neared the ground, more like a slow fall than actual flight. He landed hard in a series of tripping steps that ended with his face in the grass. Hope stumbled off him, perturbed.

"That was much better than jumping," she whispered sarcastically.

He rolled his eyes, then flew back up to close the window. He was still in the air when the rapid bark of dogs began behind the school.

Hope looked up at him in horror.

Run, he mouthed. Without hesitation, Hope sprinted toward the Crimson Forest. Finn took off, flying across the side gardens above Hope's head. The hunting party galloped into view, giant black dogs barking and snarling, followed by a cavalry of horses. Applegate and Ravenguard, dressed in their red riding coats, were accompanied by two clowns, pale faced and black lipped, on steeds as dark as the lines around their eyes.

"The dogs have something," Finn heard Ravenguard say. "A runaway?"

"Let's find out." Applegate whistled for the hounds. At once, the beasts halted their yapping and gave her their full attention. "Hunt," she commanded. The dogs raced toward the trees.

Finn flew, faster than he'd ever flown before, careful to stay out of the hunting party's line of sight. Relieved when he reached the shelter of the woods, he landed in the upper branches of a massive oak tree.

"Psst." Hope waved at him from a tree a few yards away, her head poking out from a cloak of pine branches.

"How did you—?"

"I jumped," she whispered. "Come on." She waved him over.

Stealthily, he soared to her branch and nestled into the shadows, as the hunting party trotted in below him. Hope placed a finger over her lips. One look at Applegate's deadly expression and Finn decided silence may be golden, but he trusted magic. He gripped Hope's arm and tapped the three of diamonds to his knuckles.

"Extinguish," he whispered. Hope inhaled sharply as her pale skin blurred to something ghostlike.

Hoofbeats slowed under their tree. The hounds circled, whimpering. Finn stopped moving, stopped even breathing.

"They've lost the scent," Applegate said.

"Perhaps it was a rabbit or other prey. The hounds are notoriously distractible." Ravenguard patted his dappled gray steed.

"Hmmm." Applegate scanned the forest, her head moving robotically from left to right. Her eyes flashed luminescent green in the moonlight like some sort of animal. "One of the beasts may have snatched up whatever the hounds were tracking."

A clown dismounted and lowered its face to the dirt. One white-gloved finger cut a trail through the pine needles and inhaled deeply. Hope gripped Finn's hand as the thing tipped its head back and sniffed the air in their direction.

"It has something," Ravenguard murmured.

Silently, Hope plucked a pinecone from their tree and whipped it toward the school. The hunting party turned at the resulting *plunk* and rustle. Applegate narrowed her eyes, her horse's hooves stomping in place. It wasn't enough to draw them away.

The clown's eyes rolled toward its twin, nose sniffing the air again. It took a step toward the base of their pine tree. Finn covered his mouth and held his breath. Could it smell where Hope had stepped at the base of the tree? If it looked up...

With slow, even movements, Hope lifted her triquetra pendant from the base of her throat and whispered something under her breath. A strong breeze stirred in the heart of the woods and gained power, blowing through their sky-high perch. Finn clutched the pine's trunk as it bent and swayed.

A branch snapped nearby. The hunting party turned. There, between the trees, was a massive buck, horns tangled in the branches. The hounds lowered their heads and growled, ready to

G.P. CHING

attack. With a nod to Applegate, Ravenguard drew a crossbow
from the back of his saddle and leveled it. *Whoosh.* The arrow
barely missed the stag's head as the deer freed its antlers at the last
moment and sprinted deeper into the woods.

With an eruption of yapping, the dogs pursued the deer at a
full-out run, the admissions counselors kicking their horses into
gear behind them. Eventually, with one last look toward their
tree, the clowns mounted their horses and joined in the chase.

"Come on. The buck won't last forever," Hope said.

"Wait, what?"

"It's an illusion. It'll disappear in a few minutes."

"You made that thing?"

"Not me, per se. I asked someone to do it for me."

"What? Who?"

"We don't have much time." She leaped to the next tree and the
next. Finn tried to keep up, but Hope was fast, very fast. Was it
because she was an enchanter? Had the island changed her to this
in the same way it had allowed him to fly? She'd said she'd always
been fast, but no one was this fast. Not naturally.

Finn shoved aside the branches as he barreled through the
trees after her. The mass of shifting leaves and darkness blinded
him, and he ran right into Hope's back, almost knocking her from
the tree. She didn't have to explain why she'd stopped short.
Orange-and-black striped muscles tensed on the next branch. The
green eyes of a tiger glowed from the shadows, locked on to Hope.

"You ready to try coflying again?" she asked nervously.

"Uh…"

She hurled backward into his arms. The tiger pounced. Finn
caught Hope but still couldn't carry her weight. While he
succeeded in breaking her fall, they tumbled through the unforgiving branches until their bodies slapped the forest floor. She
was on her feet in a heartbeat and tugging at his arm. "Get up. Get
up! Run!"

The tiger landed beside Finn's head, teeth bared. Razor-sharp

242

claws swiped toward his face. No doubt he'd be shredded if it weren't for Hope. She caught the cat by the hide and flung it away with more force and strength than her body seemed capable of.

As the cat rebounded, so did Finn. He scrambled to his feet.

"Fly, Finn. Get out of here," Hope yelled. A disc of light formed around her fist, blinding, with a razor-sharp edge.

Without hesitation, Finn jumped into the air, giving Hope room to fight. The tiger roared and attacked, charging Hope straight on. Finn expected her to swing the weapon in her hand, but as the tiger got closer, her face changed.

"Oh no," she said. "Finn, help!"

The light withdrew into her fist. She jumped, catching Finn's hand. But as hard as he tried, he could not raise Hope higher into the air. The tiger grabbed her by the legs, sinking in claws and teeth. Hope's fingers slipped from his wrist to his hand. He rotated. Gripped her with his other hand. Too much weight. It was no use. With a scream, she slid to his knuckles, then to his fingertips. He'd never forget her expression as she hit the dirt. Not fear or helplessness. Straight-up acceptance—like she was forgiving him with that last catch of the eyes.

The tiger attacked, teeth flashing. Blood sprayed in a sick, sputtering fountain.

Finn had to do something. He searched the forest floor for anything to use as a weapon. A heavy stone lay along the path. He pried it from the dirt and lifted it above the tiger's head. Then he dropped. All his weight came down behind the stone and collided with the tiger's skull. There was a sickening *crunch*. The tiger seized and tipped off Hope. It landed on its side, and with one last spasm, stopped moving altogether.

Carefully, Finn dragged Hope a safe distance from the tiger's lifeless claws and pressed a hand to the gurgling wound at her neck. He'd never seen a person bleed this badly. Her jugular pulsed gallons of blood and her face took on a ghastly pallor. An attempted breath resulted in more blood spilling from between her lips. Her eyes glazed. She stopped breathing.

"Hope. Come on, Hope." He couldn't remember exactly how to do CPR, but he tried anyway. He breathed into her mouth, performed chest compressions. Nothing helped. The blood pooled behind her head. Her skin grew cold. No heartbeat. No breath.

Tears streamed down Finn's cheeks. He shifted in the bloody grit beside her body, pulling his knees into his chest. So much blood. His hands were slick with it. Somewhere deep within the woods, a cricket chirped. A bat fluttered above his head. He reached out a trembling hand to close Hope's eyes.

She was dead.

❧ 36 ❧

MURDER MOUNTAIN

Finn's experience with death was thankfully limited. Aside from his mother, he'd never been close to anyone who'd passed away. This was real. This hurt. Hope was more than a roommate; she was a friend, a coconspirator, someone who had his back. The loss felt like being torn in two, like losing a sister.

What should he do? His only option would be to contact Theodor. But surely this was an infraction far beyond even his protection. Minutes passed. He needed to make a decision.

He was mulling over his predicament when her body took on a soft glow. At first he thought it was his *extinguish* spell wearing off —which seemed odd considering he'd lost the effects twenty minutes ago. He leaned toward her body. A column of bright light blasted from Hope's chest, pure energy that made Finn blink his tears away and scramble to his feet. Yellow-red light like liquid fire formed over her heart, spreading through her torso and to her fingertips like a cosmic disease. Her eyelids flipped open, her body arched. Only her heels and the top of her head touched the ground as a long rasp of air entered her lungs.

"What the—" To Finn's amazement, the wound in Hope's neck

filled itself in, and her complexion went from pale white, to pink, to her regular alabaster. She was still bloody, but she was whole.

All at once, the light blinked out and Hope's body collapsed onto the dirt once more. She was panting, blinking into the darkness.

"What in the name of all that is holy just happened?" Finn stared at her as she rolled over and got to her feet.

She held up her hands. "I can explain."

"You were dead." He backed away, shaking his head.

"No, Finn. Wait. Hold on." She grabbed a hold of her own head and yanked. There was a crack from her cervical vertebrae. She tipped her head from side to side and rolled her shoulders. "I'm not a zombie or anything. It's okay."

Finn blanched. "A vampire?"

She shook her head. "I'm a Healer."

"A what?"

"A Healer. It's a type of Soulkeeper."

"What the hell is a Soulkeeper?"

"Soulkeepers are people with a genetic predisposition to fight evil. You know, Lucifer, fallen angels, demons, hellhounds, wicked curses—that type of thing."

"Er. Sure." He looked at her blankly.

"I'm the last one." She shrugged her shoulders. "I am the balance against the one fallen angel left on Earth. What I'm trying to say is, I can't die unless the world is completely rid of evil."

"You... can't... die?"

"Well, not exactly true. I *was* dead just now, but I was resurrected. I can't be *permanently* dead. It's a side effect of being a Healer." Her head undulated forward and her cheeks puffed out. Vomit spewed from her lips onto the dirt.

When the retching finally stopped, she rasped, "That's another side effect. When I heal myself or others, it makes me puke. That's the price that comes with my power." Her stomach heaved again. "The last Healer used to burn when she used her power. Almost burned herself to ash once. I suppose between throwing up or burning alive, I'll take throwing up." She heaved again, but this time nothing came out but air. "Not that I have a choice."

"You're not human."

"Human? Yes, of course I'm human, but I'm also a Soulkeeper."

"To fight evil…" Finn babbled. It still sounded made up.

"I work for God," she said.

"You work for God. Like you talk to him and stuff?"

"No, silly—"

"That's a relief because that sounded insane."

"I talk to his messenger, an angel named Gabriel. God is too busy."

Finn's lips parted. "I don't know what I should say here. That's the craziest thing anyone has ever said to me."

"I'm sure it's a lot to take in. I didn't mean for you to find out this way."

"It's just so unexpected. Like, number one, you're saying you know firsthand there is a God and that His existence isn't a bunch of baloney."

Hope wiped her face with the back of her arm. "Believe what you want to believe. What's true is true. What isn't, isn't." She shrugged. "Tell yourself a story. That's what most people do."

"What's that supposed to mean?"

"It means I'm not going to sell you more baloney."

Hands on his hips, Finn's gaze traveled over Hope's bloody shoulder to the tiger's body on the trail. "It's moving." He pointed at the contorting orange fur.

Hope shuffled to his side. "Oh crap. This was why I couldn't kill it, Finn. When it got close to me, I could tell…"

"Tell what?

"It had a soul." Bones snapped and muscles roiled under the tiger's fur. The back legs straightened, the abdomen hollowed out. When the process was finished, a human body lay in the dirt, a male with brown hair and a bloody gash in the back of his head.

Finn backed up a few steps feeling disoriented.

Hope said, "Aerial kids fly. Pyro kids burn. Resilience kids toughen. And menagerie kids... they shift. Amuke can change which animals are in the cage because they aren't animals at all."

Finn's gaze darted to Hope. He pointed a finger at the boy. "Did he change back because he's...?"

"Dead? No. He's alive."

"How do you know? Shouldn't we check his pulse or something?"

"I can hear his heart beating."

"You can hear—" Finn shook his head.

"We should get out of here. I'm sure the rest of the troupe can't be far behind, and when this guy wakes up, he's not going to be happy." Hope took off at a jog.

"Wait!" Finn ran after her, navigating the winding trail, always five steps behind. She was fast, exceptionally fast. Even flying he could barely keep up. She only stopped when they reached the base of the mountain and then, only because she had to.

A dense, impenetrable fog hovered where the path drove sharply upward. A swarm of black birds—he couldn't tell if they were ravens or crows in the darkness—circled above their heads, cawing and flapping above the thick, cloudy white.

"At least we know why it's called Murder Mountain." Hope took his hand and set foot on the trail, blindly leading the way.

"Why?"

"A group of crows is called a murder."

"Truly?"

"Yes. And it appears this mountain is infested with them." The slope was steep enough that Hope used her hands to feel her way along the path.

"Let me see if I can get above it." Finn coasted straight up. He broke the cloud of fog and aimed for a patch of trail farther up the mountain. "Follow my voice."

"Stay there," she called back. A few minutes later, she caught up to him.

"Should I do it again?"

She nodded. They climbed for the better part of an hour until the side of the mountain opened. Along the deep plateau that cut into the dirt and stone, a thick green pasture surrounded a lake of a blue color that seemed lit from within beneath the fog.

Hope stopped and pulled the napkin map from her back pocket. "Lake Azure."

"I thought this supposed friend said they'd find us on the mountain?" Finn rested his hands on his hips, completely exhausted.

"That's what the note said, but the stranger left it over a week ago." Hope scanned the foggy beach of the lake, her head stopping when her eyes caught on a humanoid figure watching them from the fog.

"Stay where you are. Don't move a muscle," a woman's voice said.

Finn bristled. He knew that voice. When the figure stepped into the moonlight, his reaction proved warranted. Ms. D's rheumy eyes stared at him from beneath wild gray hair.

"We just—" Finn started, digging through his mind for an excuse to be out of their room in the middle of the night. Hope didn't even bother.

Ms. D adjusted one of the layered shawls on her shoulders. "I know exactly why you are here, boy. I sent for you. I left you the note. I am the friend you came to meet."

✣ 37 ✣

DUPLICITY

Finn stared at Ms. D as if he could wring an explanation from her by will alone.

"It's not safe to talk here," she said. "Follow me."

She led them around the lake, toward the side of the mountain. Pausing on the gritty, pebbled bank, she raised her thumb and forefinger to her lips and whistled. Finn heard a splash come from the center of the lake but couldn't see the source due to the fog hanging over the water. Moments later, the winding body of a crocodile neared the bank.

Finn and Hope backed away as the reptile crawled onto shore, its eyes locking onto the two of them. Seemingly unconcerned, Ms. D waited patiently as a shiver ran the length of the crocodile's body. Its bones and muscles bunched and stretched under leathery skin. Curling on its side, the crocodile coiled its tail around its head, and when it unraveled again, the beast was no longer a crocodile.

"Paul!" Finn gasped.

The boy was naked, chest down in the stones. "Would you mind?"

Finn turned his back as did Hope.

"Okay."

When Finn turned back around, Paul had dressed and was sitting in a wheelchair. He hadn't noticed either clothes or chair before, but the thick fog made it difficult to see more than a few feet in any direction.

"I don't understand. I just saw you yesterday at school. What happened to your legs?" Hope asked.

By way of response, he gestured in the direction Ms. D moved and rolled his chair down the path after her. Finn nudged Hope's elbow, raising an eyebrow, but she simply shrugged. Nothing was said until they were safely within the confines of a cave in the side of the mountain. Paul parked his chair next to a small fire in the homey interior chamber.

"It is said this cave was built by the indigenous people of this island. It has excellent living conditions and certain magical properties," Ms. D said. "I've enhanced those properties to ensure our safety and privacy."

"What gives? Why lure us all the way out here? What couldn't you tell us at school?" Finn asked.

Ms. D crossed to a pitcher of water and poured it into a large porcelain basin. She set it down between Finn and Hope and handed them a small stack of towels. "For the blood," she said.

Finn had almost forgotten they were both covered in Hope's blood. He submerged his hands and rubbed them together under the water. Hope dipped a towel in and started cleaning up.

Adjusting her shawl, Ms. D sat down on an upholstered chair that had no business being in a cave. "The people at your school who look like Paul and me are not us. The Paul you know is not this Paul, and you and I have never met before."

Finn dropped the towel he was holding and darted a glance toward Hope, who was equally shocked. He looked back to Paul and Ms. D.

"Don't you remember seeing me on the edge of the wood, Finn?" Paul said, stroking a scar on his lip.

Finn opened his mouth to acknowledge the incident but couldn't find the words. The mere thought that the tortured thing he'd seen outside his window had actually been Paul filled him with a crushing guilt.

Paul's gaze traveled to the fire. "I don't blame you. There was nothing you could have done."

"You've been here since then?" Hope asked.

"Yes," Paul said softly, staring into the fire. "When there is an incident at the school, Ravenguard, Applegate, and those… things, hunt you like an animal. I'd be dead if Ms. D hadn't rescued me."

"So, is Amanda here too?" Hope asked.

Ms. D shook her head. "I tried to save her, but she wouldn't trust me. She ran in the opposite direction. We don't know what happened to her, but the clowns have replaced her just as they've replaced Paul and me."

Hope stopped washing. "What do you mean, replaced, exactly? Is it some sort of illusion?"

"The clowns are not human," Paul said.

Ms. D warmed her hands over the fire. "The only way I can explain about the clowns is to tell you the story of how I came to know of their true intentions. A year ago, during the last spring performance, there was an accident. A boy fell to his death right in front of me, close enough for me to hear the snap of his neck breaking. Once the curtain closed, the clowns moved in to clean up the body and the blood. That's when I discovered their chilling secret."

"What did you see?" Finn asked.

"I saw the boy standing among the clowns. The exact same boy, who I'd just watched break his neck, whose body was hoisted on the shoulders of the clowns. He stared at me from backstage in the way the clowns do, expressionless. And I realized that it was the boy, but it *wasn't*. There had been signs before this. Children punished by Ravenguard and Applegate experienced drastic personality changes, but we always thought it was due to the method of their punishment. That day, I learned the clowns were replacing students with doppelgängers. And after some further investigation, I now know they are clones, biologically equivalent to the students but inhabited by the creatures we call clowns."

Finn fidgeted, his chair suddenly uncomfortable, his skin contracting as goose bumps broke out across his arms. "They took Wendy's blood and your hair, Hope," he said. "That's what they were doing in the laboratory under the school. They were cloning you."

"You saw them?" Paul asked.

"I-I followed one of them after it took Hope's hair. They have a hive under the school with these... tubes. I thought the clones were dead bodies."

Hope grimaced. "But why? If they wanted us all dead, they could have done it on the first day. And why inhabit a bunch of teenagers?"

"The clowns are killing the students and replacing them, but that's not all they are doing. The hive is feeding on the souls of their victims," Ms. D said. "When the clown came for the boy who died, it reached inside his chest and extracted pure light. I watched the creature ingest it."

"Ate it? You're sure?" Hope asked.

"You never forget a thing like that," Ms. D said. "There's more to this, though, than simple nourishment. While I was still head-mistress, I was privy to how Ravenguard and Applegate decided whom to invite to Revelations. They wouldn't have told you this, but in my office are genealogy charts dating back hundreds of years. Everyone who is invited to Revelations is a descendant from one of those charts. I never understood why. Now I believe the clowns are replacing the students in the outside world."

Hope buried her face in her hands. Finn understood. It was a lot to process.

"But why just Paul and Amanda? Why not all of us?" Finn asked.

"We think that the longer you are here on this island, the easier the clowns find it to inhabit your body. Take Amanda for example. They replaced her on the first day, and it was weeks before she could appear human. Paul's clone took slightly less time. Still, they made sure to room them together. It takes months for a clone to develop into a passable human boy or girl, and the longer they can observe you, the longer they can sample your essence, the better the results. Over the years, hundreds of these clones have gone home with unsuspecting parents. Model citizens."

Finn's stomach clenched at her description. "Model citizens. That's how the stranger who started the fire in my school described himself. He framed me."

Hope rubbed small circles over her temples. "What in the hell are they?"

"I don't know what the clowns are, but they've been here for as long as Revelations has existed." Ms. D stroked her chin thoughtfully. "We used to think they were harmless, a beneficial organism."

"There's something I don't understand," Hope said, spreading her hands.

There were several things about this conversation Finn didn't understand, but he listened anyway.

"They told us that students become instructors, instructors become enchanters or magicians, and an enchanter or magician can become the performance architect. Why did the clowns replace you with a clone? Why didn't they promote Theodor or Juliette?"

Ms. D smiled a wicked, vengeful smile. "Because they can't. I have to die for Theodor or Juliette to take my place, and as you can see, I haven't cooperated."

❦ 38 ❧

RULES, PROVISOS

"You were the enchanter before Juliette," Hope said, remembering the poster in the library.

"I was. When the previous headmistress decided to move on, she trained me for the role and left the island. She died days later, and that is when I was transformed to this." She gestured toward her face. "You see, the island stops the aging process. If I was still an enchanter, I'd look as young as Juliette. They could have named someone else to the position, but the process of *becoming* the performance architect, of aging into the role, would never occur, and that, dear friends, would mean they would not inherit my power. My clone has it only because its body is an exact copy of mine."

"That's why you can't leave the island," Hope said. "You'll age and die."

Ms. D nodded. "Smart girl. They hunt for me every night, you know. Without magic, I'd be dead by now. Ravenguard and Applegate are expert huntsmen."

"You invited us here for a reason," Hope said. "What do you want? Why us?"

"We've been watching you. I've never seen two students adapt as quickly as you. With your help on the inside, Paul and I might be able to save the others. Without you, we're doomed."

Hope stood and paced before the fire, rubbing the palms of her hands together in slow circles. "This is bigger than Revelations," she said slowly. "And there's someone else whose help we need."

Ms. D squinted skeptically. "Who?"

Hope leveled her gaze on the fire and clutched her triquetra pendant. "Messenger, I call upon thee."

Instantly, the cave filled with light that coalesced into a dark-haired angel with piercing blue eyes and fluffy white wings. Gabriel turned in place, eyeing each of them before facing Hope. He filled the cave with a sunny glow.

"How can I help you, Daughter of Angels?"

Ms. D's eyes widened. "When I copied the symbol from your necklace onto my note, I had no idea it meant something more. I simply wanted both of you to come together. What are you, Hope Laudner, to command angels?"

Finn stuttered, "Sh-she's a Soulkeeper." As if that explained everything.

Hope reached out to steady Finn before he fell off his stool. "I know this must be overwhelming for all of you," Hope said, "but I can explain."

"Overwhelming? Overwhelmed was what I felt when I saw you die and come back to life," Finn said. "It would take twenty years for the light from 'overwhelmed' to reach my planet right now."

While the others stared at the angel in varying states of shock, Hope relayed to Gabriel what she'd learned about the clowns. "They're ingesting souls and taking over the lives of students. What do you think they are?"

Gabriel scratched the stubble on his jaw. "You say they've been here for a century?" he asked Ms. D.

"Y-yes. At least since 1934. Maybe longer." Her eyes raked over him, no doubt registering how unangel-like Gabriel's appearance was aside from the glow and the wings. At the moment, he was dressed in cargo pants and a waffle weave shirt.

"And there are the same number today as when you first arrived?" Gabriel asked her.

"I believe so. More, if anything."

"That means they reproduce. They replace the ones who become clones. They can't be watchers. Fallen angels do not reproduce."

"Some kind of demon?" Hope asked.

"It's possible." Gabriel paced. "Normally, demons cannot survive outside of Hell but they may be using the cloned bodies of the students as a kind of vessel, a human spacesuit."

"They can survive here because of the star," Finn said.

Everyone's attention refocused on him.

"The fallen star under the school. It's what gives this island its power," Finn said. "The clowns' hive is built around it. I saw it myself."

Gabriel paused, stroking his chin thoughtfully. He turned to Ms. D, his brow furrowed in thought. "Victoria, how is it you came to this place? Did you come here on your own, or were you invited?"

She shifted, her gaze settling on the fire. "Oh yes, we were invited, Theodor and I. But there is more to the story than that."

❧ 39 ☙

BERLIN 1934

Well past dusk, in the smoke-filled dressing room of the Kade Ko Kabbarett, Victoria Duvall adjusted the straps on her costume, a formfitting black leotard embellished with layers of lace from chest to thigh. It was conservative by Kabbarett standards. Over the last three years, as the German economy had come to a screeching halt, she'd watched her fellow singers and dancers cut and re-sew their costumes in designs meant to bare as much as could be bared. It wasn't vanity but hunger that drove the change. German soldiers were apt to tip a revealed shoulder over a talented voice.

Victoria wasn't interested in money or in eating. She was obsessed with the art. Her partnership with the magician from London, Theodor Florea, had allowed her to shatter the boundaries of dance and acrobatics. Their performance did not bare shoulders but stripped minds. They challenged all preconceived notions of what the human body could do. For thirty glorious minutes, she and Teddy became gods, capable of things most people would only dream of, thanks to smoke, mirror, and wire.

"Full house tonight." Teddy arrived silently, as always, standing in the open doorway to her dressing room as if he'd formed out of the smoke itself. "Nazis. Brownshirts and swastikas everywhere."

"Rumor is they've come to shut the place down." She twisted her long black hair behind her head and pinned it into place. The lipstick she reached for was garishly red.

"The cards say it is only a matter of time."

"The cards. The tarot cards? Why do you waste your time on children's games?"

He turned a shoulder to her, pouting as he hunched until the arch of his spine rolled into the wall. "I'll have you know, the cards have been quite accurate for me in the past. I have a talent for them. Every deck has its own personality."

"Bah." She hooked her arm over the back of her chair. "Generalities and intuition. A person could fit any truth within the confines of your readings."

"You should allow me to read for you. Perhaps you would feel differently."

She swiveled to face him, crossing her legs and trying not to notice the beginning of a run in her stockings. "We have a few moments. Read them now."

Theodor's crooked grin showed few teeth and had a purpose greater than coyness. It was a practiced smirk, perfect for hiding things in his cheeks during the show. He pulled his tarot deck from the pocket of his tuxedo jacket. The yellowing set was decorated with wings. Quaint. With one arm, he swept aside the hodgepodge of hairbrushes and makeup boxes on her vanity table, clearing a small space.

"Your past, Fräulein Duvall." He flipped a card. A woman sat on a throne with a staff in her hand. "The queen of wands. Always the center of attention yet you exist for the benefit of others. You've been fair and generous."

She rolled her eyes. "Who would argue with something like that?"

"Your present." He flipped another card. "The wheel of

fortune." He frowned. "This card represents forces and events at work in your life that you may not be aware of. Your best-laid plans have a strong chance of being disrupted, for good or evil intent."

With a sigh, she rested her head in a web of her fingers. "Obvious. We've just admitted our Kabbarett is likely to be shut down sooner than later."

"Your future, my lady." Grinning, Teddy flipped a third card. His face fell. The card depicted a tall building on fire, people throwing themselves from burning windows, bodies plummeting to their deaths.

"The tower," Victoria read. "What does it mean?"

But Teddy's face had paled. He stared at the card as if he could see through it.

"What? What's wrong?"

He placed his hand on hers and smiled. "Come away with me. Forget about the performance. We'll go now. Leave the country. There's a place in London that would take us on in a heartbeat."

"Don't be ridiculous. Fritz is going to introduce us any minute."

"It's not safe. This card... it warns us of impending tragedy. Something big is going to happen, Victoria. An unexpected change that will shake you to your core." He knelt in front of her. "Let's make it a good change. Marry me. We'll move to London and start our very own theater if you like."

She placed both hands on his cheeks and searched his eyes. "There will be time for all of that. But first, we have a job to do."

Ladies and gentlemen, I present to you, the act you've been waiting for, the man who walks the line between our world and the next, who controls the supernatural elements all around us. Please welcome the great and powerful Theodor!

"We're on." She took his hand and pulled him off his knee and toward the stage.

"Victoria... Victoria, the cards."

"After the show. It's time." They'd reached the curtain. She kissed him on the cheek before descending into the corridor under the trap door. There was a moment of silence and then applause as Theodor burst onto the stage, no doubt with his usual finesse. She took her mark. Teddy introduced the box of mysteries. The metal-on-metal sound of him inserting swords into the box was followed by his plea for the spirit world to send him a siren from the beyond.

Victoria opened the trap door and climbed partway into the box. The decorative prop was made to look extremely narrow and short, too small to hold a human being. Victoria folded her shoulders in and positioned her hips at a diagonal to fit through; her lower half was perched on a small platform below the stage.

Boom, the smoke bombs exploded to the collective gasp of the audience. She leaped through the false top, landing on the supported edges of the frame with both hands over her head. Shouts of amazement rose from the crowd.

While Teddy continued his performance—using sleight of hand to tug a bouquet of flowers from his sleeve, conjure a woman's necklace from her own ear, and produce a trio of doves from his top hat—Victoria began to sing. Her voice was operatic, big and hollow in a way that defied her reedy physique. A black velvet rope, barely visible behind the smoke, became her apparatus. She cinched her wrist inside a loop of it and pushed off from the box, gaining speed and momentum using long, split-legged leaps between the posts that held up the ceiling. Once the angle of her body reached forty-five degrees, she gripped the rope with both hands and used her shoulder muscles to lift her legs perpendicular to its length.

This move always brought a series of gasps from the crowd. Her bare arms were as corded with muscle as any man's, her abdominals a rippling washboard beneath her leotard. All the while, she sang as if the feat required no effort at all, and with one firm twist of her body, she was spinning. Around the room she went, alternating the position of her legs and free arm to slow or hasten her rotation. Until finally her song came to an end and she landed on top of the box again. By then, the room was silent, not a clink of a glass or the scrape of a fork on a plate. She had them.

Teddy looked up at her, nothing but love in his eyes. "Thank you, Siren. You may return to the spirit world." He gestured with his arms, and the smoke plumed again. She dropped through the box and trap door. Even from below, the applause was deafening.

Smiling, she danced all the way to her dressing room to wait for Teddy. She was going to say yes. What would London be like this time of year? Would the audience be as captivated by their performance?

But when she reached the door with her name on it, Fritz was waiting for her. The Kabbarett's owner gripped the doorframe as if the wall was the only thing holding him up.

"Victoria, you must come. The commandant says he will shoot Theodor if you do not come out at once."

"What are you talking about? We just finished the show. The soldiers were eating it up."

Fritz mopped his brow. "They've accused him of occultism. It's illegal now. Don't test these men, Victoria. They have dark hearts."

Victoria snatched her floral silk dressing robe from its hook and wrapped it around herself, cinching the waist. She dodged Fritz and ran for the front of the Kabbarett before he could say another word. The crowd was gone, all the tables empty. By the stripes and pins on his brown uniform, Victoria identified the commandant, waiting for her at a center table. He must be powerful. He'd cleared the room in less than three minutes, aside from a male and female soldier who guarded the door.

Beside him, Theodor sat stiff and sweating. There was a gun in the commandant's hand.

"You called for me," she said.

"Yes. I am a great fan of your work. Please join us."

She approached the table on legs that betrayed her fear and

ungracefully sank into a chair next to Theodor. The commandant's white-blond hair was distracting, as was his perfectly
straight nose and azure eyes. He looked like a living doll. Too
perfect to be real. Inhuman.

"What do you want?"

He smiled a set of straight white teeth. "I have a proposition
for you, Fräulein Duvall. I lead a highly classified division,
reporting directly to Himmler. Our charge is to further Republik
pursuits using archeology, the lost knowledge of ancient powers."

"I would not know anything about that," she said.

"Our latest expedition has uncovered a yet uncharted island
with conditions that show remarkable potential to enhance our
future German soldiers."

"What does that have to do with me?" Victoria steadied her
hands in her lap.

He stroked his chin with the back of his fingernails. "When
exposed to the environment on this island, strong boys became
stronger. Fast boys, faster. But anxious men go mad with para-
noia. Can you explain this?"

Victoria shook her head.

"Neither can we. Not yet. Which is why you are here. We
would like you to go to this new land and investigate its properties. We would like you to help develop a curriculum for an elite
group of boys from the Hitlerjugend. See what you can make
of them."

"I am not a soldier, Commandant."

"No. You are the woman who sings like a siren and flies as if
she were born with wings."

She snorted. "I cannot fly. It is a trick. I can show you how it
is done!"

"Perhaps with enough time in this new place, it will accentuate
what is already inside you."

She scrutinized him for a moment, every line of his chiseled
features. "You believe I might truly be able to fly?"

"Not just you, Fräulein. By training the boys to do what you do and more, we hope to develop an entire troupe of men with supernatural abilities."

She shook her head and scoffed. "What you are asking is impossible. There is a vast difference between a change of atmosphere's effect on a runner's speed and actually defying gravity. It cannot be done."

"Perhaps not, but your government is enlisting you to try." Those blue eyes bore into her, daring her to refuse him. He'd take pleasure in punishing her if she did. She could see it in the way he held himself, his smug grin.

"I have no choice then?"

"You can be taken to detention like most of those involved in the debauchery you displayed tonight." He motioned to the walls around him. "I'd hate to do that to you. Such lovely skin you have."

"I'm not a teacher. I won't know what to do with a group of boys," she cautioned.

"Do not fret. My cohorts, Applegate and Ravenguard, will accompany you and act as disciplinarians. You are only requested to demonstrate what you know."

"If I do this, Theodor must come with me. I cannot build the apparatus to train the boys properly without him."

The commandant's head bobbed his agreement. "Very well, Fräulein."

"Then yes. I agree to do it. We will pack and be ready to go within the hour." She eyed Theodor, hopeful to get him alone.

"No need. All will be provided for you." The blond man stood.

"But I—" Victoria pointed back at her dressing room, but the man called Ravenguard grabbed her around the upper arm and squeezed.

The woman guarding the door opened it with a click of her heels. "Thank you, Applegate." The commandant pointed his hand toward the dark street. "There is a car waiting for you. If you please."

❧ 40 ❧

RETURN

inn could hardly believe what he was hearing, although he didn't doubt for a moment it was true.

"I did not leave the school again until 1990." Ms. D folded her hands in her lap, ending her story with a nostalgic sigh. "I was able to leave because Juliette took over my role as enchanter but the original performance architect hadn't retired. It was the last time I was free."

"And did you leave the school on your own?" Gabriel asked.

"No. Ravenguard escorted me. We're on an island. There is only one way off, and that is on a Revelations bus. No one leaves without being escorted by either Ravenguard or Applegate."

"That's when you wrote the book," Finn said. "When you taught dance at the university."

"You've read my book?"

"Theodor gave it to me."

The muscles of her cheeks tightened in muted satisfaction. "Easy to believe in human evolution when you've seen it firsthand."

"So Ravenguard and Applegate have been here since then too?" Hope asked.

"Yes. Since the day Theodor and I came here, Applegate and Ravenguard have controlled who comes to this island and who goes. They've disciplined the students from the start. Only recently have I realized that it is they who have enabled the clowns to take over the lives of the students. Before that, I took for granted they were necessary to the successful operation of the school."

"Applegate and Ravenguard kill the students so that the clones can ingest their souls and replace them," Hope said darkly.

"They weren't hunting me down to throw me a party," Paul said.

Finn hugged himself, rubbing the outside of his upper arms.

After much pacing and contemplation, Gabriel flexed his wings. "What if the reason that Applegate and Ravenguard always escort anyone who comes or goes from this island is the same reason we did not notice the missing souls until now and the reason the demons can still exist here."

Hope shook her head.

"This isn't merely an island, Hope. It's a false Eden."

She analyzed the words. False. Eden. Memories of her lessons came back to her. Eden was a safe place where Soulkeepers trained. Getting there wasn't exactly easy. "Are you saying the reason there are demons here is we aren't... on Earth?" Hope tensed. Could it be true?

"Applegate and Ravenguard must escort everyone to and from this island because they travel by portal. This place isn't just an island, it's a place between places."

"That's why I couldn't transcend to the In-Between to talk to the Immortals," Hope said.

"Excuse me, but what the hell are you talking about?" Finn asked.

"Think of a football field," Hope said, turning toward him. "If Heaven is one goalpost and Hell is the other, Earth would be on the fifty-yard line. There used to be a place called Eden—"

"Like where Adam and Eve were from?"

"Exactly. It was of Earth, but not of Earth. Once it was closed off, only certain people could travel there, by portal. You couldn't find it on any map. Revelations is that kind of place. Not quite on the fifty-yard line. A place between places."

"We're not on Earth?" Finn said disbelievingly.

Hope shook her head. "Think of it as another dimension. A different... land. We're here, but we're not. It's why people don't age the same here."

Finn's mouth gaped.

"You know what you need to do, Hope," Gabriel said.

"Yeah, kill every last one of them." Hope pressed a hand into her stomach like the thought made her sick. "If these things have access to Earth, they could be doing Lucifer's bidding from Hell."

"Exactly," Gabriel said. "The one advantage we have is they don't seem to know who you are. Once they know you are a Soul-keeper, they'll scatter. You need a way to lure them to one place and end them before they can react."

Hope's eyes darted around the room. She had no idea how to attract the clowns to one location. How many were there to begin with?

"When the boy died, they came," Ms. D said softly. "There were at least twelve of them backstage, grouped around the clone."

"So, we need to fake a death?" Finn asked.

Hope shook her head. "We don't need to fake anything. We already know who is next. Juliette practically came right out and told me. Mike is going to die during his act. They plan to drown him."

Silence fell over the group.

"They'll come," Ms. D said. "And if you can take care of the clowns, I can save Michael."

"As enchanter, I'll be in a position to see everything that's going on in the theater," Hope said. "Since Finn can fly, he can relay messages between us. When I see that the clowns have collected to replace Mike, I'll strike. Meanwhile, Ms. D can move in and resuscitate him. "

"Are you strong enough to face them all?" Ms. D asked.

"She is," Gabriel said. "This is what she's been trained for, what she was born to do. As a Soulkeeper, she is the world's most effective demon slayer."

"Be warned, my clone has access to all of the abilities I possess, every skill taught at Revelations, including a mastery of magic and sorcery. You'll need me for more than saving Michael."

"I'll help," Paul said.

"No, Paul," Ms. D insisted. "I need you here. In case there's trouble, this will be our safe house. I want you to guard it the way only you can."

Paul gave her an understanding nod.

"I'm in. I'll help Hope," Finn said.

Gabriel shook his head. "You are kind and brave to offer, Finn, but without a weapon like Hope's, you'll be helpless against them."

"I'll use magic," Finn said.

"Magic?" Ms. D asked.

"He's been training with Theodor," Hope said.

Finn scratched the inside of his arm. He looked down at his toes and pressed his lips together.

One gray eyebrow arched toward Ms. D's wild curls. "He *would* swear you to secrecy. Training you breaks an old and respected theater tradition." She paused for a moment, studying him. "You should know there is a fine line between magic and sorcery. Magic is an exchange of elements. It is as simple as asking these atoms over here to do this other work over there. An even exchange of energy. Sorcery is much darker. It pulls energy from other worlds, creates and destroys it. All sorcery comes with a price."

"He told me," Finn said.

"But yet he continues to teach it," Ms. D said. "Teddy always had to walk the line. Never fully in the light."

"Or the dark," Finn said defensively. "He figured it out, you know? He suspected the Ms. D in the school was not you. That's why he was training me. He was planning a coup."

A smile spread her thin lips. "Of all people, he would know. We've been working together since 1931."

"Then should I tell him what's going on? He can help."

"Absolutely not," Gabriel said. "Sorcery in the presence of demons is too risky. If this man walks the line between light and dark as you say, you must not trust him, and you, Finn, must not resort to using what sorcery you've learned for any reason."

Finn scratched the back of his head. "Okay."

"So we're in agreement?" Hope asked. "We attack during the performance." The others nodded.

Gabriel turned his face toward the cave opening. "I must go. I am called." With a nod from Hope, he dissolved as quickly as he'd arrived.

Ms. D jumped out of her chair and shuffled toward the entrance to the cave. "Oh dear, the time. You must go back. We've dallied too long. If you are not dressed and at breakfast on time, there will be hell to pay."

Finn was afraid there was literal truth in that expression. Hope yanked him up by the elbow. He could hardly move. Not only was he physically exhausted from being up all night and climbing half a mountain, but he was mentally exhausted. Who could digest everything he'd heard that day? Hope was some sort of vigilante hero working for God. Soul-stealing clowns wanted him dead. Doppelgängers of past students roamed the world in positions of power. It was too much to take in.

"They'll never make it," Ms. D said to Paul.

"I'll take them." Paul rolled his wheelchair after Hope.

Ms. D placed a hand on Finn's shoulder. "Don't let us down, Finn. As strong as she is, she can't do this alone. Hope needs you."

All he could muster was a nod. He didn't know what else to say.

Outside the cave, the sky had already taken on the faint glow of the coming dawn.

"Give me a second, and I'll help you down the mountain," Paul said.

Finn arched an eyebrow.

"I was destined for menagerie. Funny the things we're afraid of. It turns out our fears are no more than reflections of what we see inside ourselves." Paul removed his shirt and flopped out of his chair. Finn pivoted away from the pop, stretch, and slurp of his transformation. Hope did too, but not until she'd nudged Finn, her eyes widening in disbelief.

Not three minutes later, a whinny came from behind them. Paul had transformed into a draft horse, its chestnut coat the same color as his hair. With three running steps, Hope sprinted toward him, planted her hands on the length of his back, and vaulted one leg over. She held out a hand to Finn. He snorted at the offered help and levitated into position. But if he'd rejected the hand on principle, he did not avoid her waist as Paul took off running down the mountain. The sheer speed and agility of the horse was a clear indication of Paul's magic, and they reached the thick fog at the base of the mountain in a fraction of the time it had taken them to climb.

"Thank you," Hope said, as they slid off Paul's back.

The horse bobbed its head and disappeared into the fog.

Finn cracked his neck, eyeing the brightening sky with apprehension. "Try to keep up," he said to her through a half smile. He took off in the direction of the school.

"Whatever." Hope sprinted after him, passing him in a heartbeat and navigating the dark forest like a native animal. Finn powered after her, half running, half flying.

His speed was such that when Hope tripped and face-planted in the dirt, Finn passed her by a good three feet before he was able to stop his momentum.

"What happened?" He extended his hand to help her.

She crouched to inspect the protrusion she'd encountered, her hands dusting along what looked like a root. Gradually, Finn made out a series of regular grooves in the pale arch. She dusted more vigorously, digging and yanking on what lay beneath. Her fingers caught on black leather.

"Is that...?" Finn didn't want to believe it.

"I think we found Amanda." The skeleton was face down, the spiked leather collar Finn remembered Amanda wearing still fastened around the cervical vertebrae. White bones, no smell. The corpse was picked clean by whatever scavengers lived in these woods.

"We've got to go, Hope. We've got to go now." Finn scanned the trees for any movement.

"What should we do? She deserves better than having her remains left here to be chewed on by animals."

Feeling sick, Finn tried to appeal to reason. "Once we do what we intend to do, we can come back for her."

Logic won the day. She nodded, launching herself toward the school again. The sun broke the horizon. With a grunt, Finn soared to the ledge to open their window. He planned to go back down to get her, but Hope landed beside him on the ledge.

"Jumped," she said.

Nodding, he closed the window behind them. "Ugh!" Finn grunted as Hope pulled his shirt and jacket over his head at super speed and kicked them under his bed.

"Wha-what?"

She disappeared into the bathroom.

He rounded the bed and selected a fresh uniform from his drawer. He was pulling on a clean pair of pants when the door-knob turned.

"Excuse me, I'm not dressed," Finn said to Applegate, who didn't pause for a second but invited herself in.

"You two are late for breakfast," she said unapologetically. She sniffed the air, her eyes narrowing.

Finn pulled a clean shirt from his drawer and pulled it on over his head. "We're late," he called toward the bathroom.

Hope jogged out in a fresh uniform, pulling her newly wet hair into a high ponytail. "Sorry, Ms. Applegate." Shoulder to shoulder, they raced past the admissions counselor and down to the dining room. Hope checked over her shoulder before reaching out to wipe a spit-moistened thumb across his cheek. *Blood,* she mouthed. He scrubbed his face with his sleeve without missing a step.

They crossed to the buffet, Applegate watching them from the stairs.

❦ 41 ❦
PRACTICE

If Applegate suspected anything, she didn't say a word. Finn continued to aerial class, as always, without further incident.

"Are you having trouble sleeping?" Wendy asked, sidling up to him in the garden.

"No. Why?" Finn asked.

She gestured under his eyes. "Matching luggage. Those dark bags under your eyes weren't there yesterday." Her freckled nose wrinkled. "Is everything okay?"

Finn was afraid he wouldn't be able to keep a secret from Wendy if she asked the right questions. He couldn't lie to her. One piercing look from her, and he'd fold like a tower of cards. He decided his best bet was to change the subject. "Uh, thinking about things." He scratched the back of his head. "You know, things from the past. What did you do to end up here anyway?"

She did a double take, staring at the side of his head as they walked toward the gazebo. "Is that what kept you up? Thinking about what you did? That first day Ms. D said you burned down a school."

Finn gave one curt nod.

"You certainly don't seem the type."

"It was an accident."

"I see. I'm here for stealing. I'm an accomplished thief actually." She picked at the corner of her thumbnail. "It's always been easier for me because I'm small."

"A thief?" Finn laughed. "*You* don't seem the type."

"You might be surprised." The corner of her mouth curled into a knowing grin. "I was a cashier at Coffeeworks. You know that place where you can get those super-expensive espresso drinks?"

"Yeah, I've been there."

"So, they have this thing called an Americano on the menu. Basically, for two dollars you get a twelve-ounce cup you fill yourself at a coffee station. Anyway, I'd ring up the coffee drinks but not the Americanos. Only when people paid cash. I'd pocket the two dollars."

"So how'd you get caught?"

"Missing cups. I stole two thousand dollars and they busted me for the missing cups."

Finn laughed. "So, you're here for stealing cups?"

"Ah, no. Fired, but not arrested. No, I'm here because I was walking out of a department store when someone bumped into me, and the alarms started going off. Turns out the person dropped expensive jewelry into my bag. The next thing I know, I'm sitting in a police station trying to explain why I have a stolen necklace in my purse. I was set up, but nobody believed me." She gave a small giggle. "I guess it was karma."

"What do your parents do?"

"They're not thieves, if that's what you're wondering."

Finn chuckled. "No. I wondered if you stole because you needed the money."

She rolled her eyes. "Sorry. Not Robin Hood. My dad is an appellate court judge and my mom is a semifamous novelist. I'm a delinquent. I deserve to be here."

Finn let that sink in for a few steps. "Me too. The fire may have been an accident, but I earned my place here. I did other things."

She bit her lip. "I get it. You know, I've taken what I wanted my entire life. Never got caught. Never even got questioned. Still, it's hard to accept that the thing they got me for, I didn't do. I mean, why would someone steal something only to ditch it in someone else's bag?"

A chill coursed through Finn's body. *Because you were chosen. Because your name is on a scroll in the headmistress's office.* "Weird," he said.

"I told my lawyer, and he got us access to the security tapes. You can't see the woman at all. It's like she was a ghost." Wendy chewed her lip pensively.

"I'm sorry to bring it up."

She shook her head. "Don't worry about it. It would have caught up with me sooner or later. At least, the way it went down, I ended up here."

Finn smiled and reached out to tuck a stray hair behind her ear. "I'm sorry you got in trouble, but I can't say I'm sorry we both ended up here."

She leaned in until her freckled nose was almost touching his. "I agree." He stared at her lips. Full. Petal pink. He should kiss her. He should kiss her now. He leaned in. Her eyes wrinkled at the corners, focused on his mouth.

"Wager! Matthews!" Orelon yelled. Breaking the spell, Wendy stepped back, giggling. Then she whirled, her brown braid flying over her shoulder, and ran for the gazebo.

✦ 42 ✦

THE MAGICIAN AND THE
ENCHANTER

When the joker warmed in Finn's pocket, he thought about ignoring it. Gabriel had told him not to trust Theodor. Although Finn didn't agree that the magician was dangerous, it was hard to argue with an honest-to-goodness, white-winged angel. But when Finn's arm started to itch, it became clear avoidance wasn't an option.

Theodor didn't say a word to him until they'd made the journey from the library to his office, where the magician took a seat behind his massive mahogany desk. Today, the surface of the desk was covered with a complex spread of tarot cards that Theodor perused for a moment before focusing on Finn. He did not look happy.

"You had quite the adventure last night, and it appears you have something to tell me."

He shrugged. "Like what?" To keep from meeting Theodor's gaze, he looked at the series of rune symbols scrolled like equations across the chalkboard. Difficult magic. The most complex spell Finn had ever seen.

"What happened last night?"

Finn remained silent.

"We had an agreement, Finn. Total trust. "

His arm began to burn again and he rubbed it anxiously. Hotter and hotter. Sweat broke out across his upper lip. "You were right about Ms. D," he blurted when he could stand no more.

"What about Victoria?" Finn blew out a relieved breath as the pain abated.

"That she's not herself. She is quite literally not herself. I met the real Victoria Duvall on Murder Mountain last night."

Theodor's face remained impassive, but he reached for the deck of cards within his jacket and tossed one at the door. "Mute," he said. Purple ice grew from the point of impact, up over the ceiling, across the floor, and around the perimeter. By the time Theodor caught the returning card, they were sealed inside a purple igloo. "Go ahead."

"I thought your office was already charmed for privacy."

"It was, but a magician can never be too careful."

Once Finn began to speak, he couldn't stop. Everything from finding Amanda's bones in the Crimson Forest, to Paul's survival, to Hope's resurrection and her angel Gabriel poured out of him in goose bump-inducing detail. Theodor listened intently, stroking his ever-tightening jaw with the back of his knuckles. His lips pursed when Finn finally ran out of words.

Theodor leaned back in his chair like he'd finished a heavy meal. "You were right to share this with me."

"They didn't want me to. Gabriel said sorcery in the presence of demons is too risky."

Theodor swept the cards off his desk and into a pile. "Don't worry, Finn. No one needs to know that you've told me. I won't get involved unless I need to."

"And you'll be careful if you do? You won't use sorcery."

"Victoria is wrong about me. I've never crossed the line. The power I have, I've developed carefully, and I wield it with the utmost responsibility."

Finn met his mentor's gaze and held it. "I thought so."

"YOU'RE NOT READY," JULIETTE SAID THROUGH DRAWN LIPS.

"I can do it. You saw me do it." Hope looked to the two servants sitting on the camelback sofa for backup. She'd successfully split her illusion so that Howard had seen a cat dancing, Gertrude had seen a fountain in a vast garden, and Juliette had been transported to a field where a white palomino charged at her through the wheat.

The servants didn't say anything at first, but under the weight of Hope's stare, Gertrude caved. "It felt as if I could touch the water, and the colors of the flowers were lovely."

Juliette huffed, waving her hand at the two servants. "You are dismissed." Gertrude and Howard scattered. "What do they know? I could clearly see the outline of the cat through the palomino in my vision."

"If that's true, what color was the cat?" Hope asked.

"Palomino colored. I told you, I saw an outline."

"Okay, what type of cat was it?"

"You want me to tell you the breed of the cat in your illusion?"

"Not the breed, just what it looked like. Did it have long ears or short? A snout or a pushed-in nose? What was the length of its hair?"

"Your behavior is pugnacious, Hope. I expected better from you."

"How is it pugnacious to want credit for doing what I did? I have done everything you've asked of me. I am ready to perform."

"We will perform together, and you will remain my mentee for another semester."

Not likely, Hope thought. She'd be relieved when she was home and Revelations was a distant memory.

"Honestly, by now I'd expect a little more from you. I've tolerated your aggression because of your natural talent for enchanting, but how much insubordination can a teacher tolerate?"

"Insubordination?" Hope cried, appalled.

"I've had enough of your outbursts. You are dismissed." Juliette pointed at the door.

"But shouldn't we practice—"

"Go!"

Hope shuffled out the door with a burgeoning sense of dread. The spring show was less than two weeks away. A practice cut short almost guaranteed they'd not be in sync for the performance. She was being set up to fail. But what to do about it? The plan was to overthrow Ms. D and close down the school. Did she truly care how she performed in this production? She had to admit she did. Hope wasn't the type to do anything halfway.

But more than that, she was sure Juliette had a reason for setting her up to fail. *Mike.* If Hope's intuition was right, Juliette would try to frame her for his death. *Just try it,* she thought as she exited the apartment. She was more than ready to take on Juliette.

☙❧

THE NIGHT BEFORE THE SHOW, FINN LAY AWAKE, STARING AT THE ceiling. "Are you sure you're ready?" he asked Hope.

"I was born for this," she said softly.

"I heard Gabriel say that before, but I don't really get it."

"What don't you get?"

"You were born with certain abilities. I get that. But because someone is good at math doesn't mean they will become a mathematician. It's just as likely they'll be a scientist or an accountant. What if they're good at math but they have the heart of an artist? What you're born with is biology. What you choose to be is vocation."

"Did you read that on a greeting card?"

"Inspirational poster."

"I get what you're saying. I do. But this is different. I'm the only one. The last Soulkeeper. I'm done fighting it. It's my responsibility and that's all there is to it. Besides, I can't watch you get demon-snatched. It would break my heart."

Finn smiled into the darkness. "I'm glad I mean that much to you."

She chuckled. "Plus, once I'm done with this, we'll all be able to get back to our normal lives. That's worth any amount of effort."

"I take it this isn't something you do every other Tuesday, then?"

"Nope. This is my first official mission. There's only one fallen angel left on the planet—the demon of greed—and he's more interested in amassing wealth than fighting me. This place represented an unusual and rare situation. Hopefully the last one for some time."

"Why did Gabriel call you Daughter of Angels?"

She took a deep breath and let it out slowly. "Because I am. My father was an angel named Gideon who fell in love with my mother, who was a fallen angel. They couldn't be together. Good can't be in the same place as evil, and fallen angels have evil in their skin. But they worked together and did God a favor, and in return, He made them human."

"They could finally be together. Sounds romantic."

"It was. They got married and my mom—her name was Abigail —became pregnant with me. But then the war between Heaven and Hell happened."

"When was this?"

"2012."

"Hmmm."

"You won't read about it in any history book. It was wiped from the memories of the human population. Lucifer and his fallen angels occupied Earth for a time and the Soulkeepers, including my parents, had to stop him. To make a long story short, I was born the day both my parents died at the hands of a fallen angel. My adoptive parents, Jacob and Malini, are former Soulkeepers who knew them well."

"I'm sorry about your real parents."

"It's not like I ever knew them," she said, but Finn could tell there was pain there, under the words.

"I never knew my mother either, but it still hurts not to have her. She died when I was born too." Silence stretched between them in the darkness. "That's pretty wild that you are, in fact, the daughter of angels and your real parents are why you are a Soulkeeper."

"Yeah. It's genetic. Only, the Soulkeeper gene can't be activated anymore—that's why I'm the last one. It has to do with fate and balance and natural law. There was also this agreement that ended the war." She yawned. "Probably more than you wanted to know."

"I wish I was you."

Hope laughed. "What about my story would make you want to be me?"

Finn scratched his ear and tried to put it into words. "You know who you are and what you're supposed to be. When I go home, I'm facing the choice between taking Spanish since I failed French last semester or maybe giving up on foreign language and becoming a plumber."

"I hate to break it to you, but I can think of several scenarios where a plumber would benefit from speaking Spanish."

"I think you just made my point. Everything about your life is important. You've had this talent handed to you without even trying. Not only am I not good at anything, but I have no idea what I *could* be good at if I put in the effort. My life is so... so... insignificant."

Hope didn't respond for a long time, long enough for Finn to be on the verge of falling asleep by the time she did. "You're a good friend, Finn. That's significant to me. I think you underestimate yourself. Maybe outside of Revelations you're not supposed to be the best at any one thing. That doesn't mean you don't have a purpose. You might be the person who helps other people be the best at what they do. All I know is, I'm thankful that you're my roommate. I couldn't do this without you."

Finn fell asleep thankful that Hope was his roommate too.

✻ 43 ✻

PREPARATIONS

The day of the show came faster than Finn ever expected. Was he ready for this? Not only did he have to give the performance of his life in front of his father, he needed to save Mike from certain death and help Hope stop the clowns from stealing anyone else's souls. For the seventieth time, he checked that his cards were safely tucked up his sleeve.

"Hold still. I have one more adjustment to make." Jenny fussed with a strip of fabric that hung from Finn's shoulder blade, splitting it with a pair of scissors. "Jump. Let me see how it moves."

Finn leaped into the air, arms extended, and dropped quickly to give her the full effect. Red, blue, and black feathers splayed outward with his movement. His costume, from the white strip of makeup that veed upward from the tip of his nose, to the feathers he wore over his hair, all the way down to his painted feet, was designed to make him look like a phoenix. Wendy, on the other hand, was dressed in black and orange silk, long and smooth, to resemble a monarch butterfly.

Jenny clapped. "You have wings, Finn. You look fabulous. You two will knock them out of their seats."

"Thanks, Jen."

"You're welcome." She started packing up her supplies, smiling to herself.

"You did an incredible job on these costumes. All of them. And I have no idea how you got the set done in time."

"It was Mrs. Wilhelm's crew. There are dozens of them living here, and they all seem to be related. She was born on the island."

"And they all wanted to be servants? No one leaves?" He was genuinely curious if Mrs. Wilhelm's crew could leave, even if they wanted to.

Jenny stared at him quizzically. "They're not servants, Finn. They're managers. Facility managers. It takes a ton of expertise to pull off what they do every day. It's not like there's a Walmart on every corner here. And the logistics of getting everything where it needs to be is nothing short of a daily miracle. Mrs. Wilhelm and her family have a gift. They're proud of what they do, and they should be."

Finn's stomach sank. He had an idea of what Jenny was getting at and as someone who spent his pathetic basketball team involvement on the bench, he understood in a personal way. "Hey, I'm sorry. I didn't mean it like that. You're right. What you do—what they do—is the most important part of the show. It makes everything else happen."

Jenny smiled. She lifted a hand to brush back her hair and Finn noticed a series of tight, straight scars on her wrist.

"What happened?" he asked, reaching for her.

She tugged her sleeve down. "Nothing. Old battle wounds." She laughed but wouldn't look him in the eye.

Finn let it drop.

"You're a good person, Finn Wager." She walked behind him and tugged the small pyro box that was fastened to his back. After a second, he heard the subtle cloth-on-cloth sound of steady stitching. "I don't believe for a minute you burned down that school."

"Thanks. I didn't." He smiled at her over his shoulder.

"Jayden told me."

"You never said what you did to end up here."

Her face fell. "I hurt someone. Almost killed them." She tied off her stitch and cut the thread. "I caused a car accident. Drinking and driving." She shook her head. "I must have fallen asleep."

"Must have?"

"I don't remember the accident. I don't remember anything." She tugged at the shoulders of his costume. "You're ready. Don't forget that this thing is only flame retardant for a maximum of three minutes, so unless you want to join the pyro troupe, get it done before then."

"Okay."

She stared at the floor to his right for a second, her hands on her hips. "You know what's strange?"

"Pretty much everything about this place." Finn snorted.

She laughed in agreement. "Besides that."

"Tell me."

"I'd done it before, drank and drove. I'm from rural Oklahoma. You can drive a hundred miles without seeing another car. I'm not saying it was right. I'm saying that I got away with it before—times I'd drank so much more. This time, I had one beer. One. I wasn't even buzzed. But the next thing I know I have a half ton of metal wrapped around me like a second skin. I hit the pastor's wife. The kindest woman I'd ever known. Put her in a coma for a month." Jenny's face went slack, emotionless, as if she held her guilt at an arm's length. "They tested my blood. I was under the legal limit for an adult. Minors don't have a legal limit. Besides, when the pastor's wife almost dies, someone has to pay. So here I am." She lifted a graceful eyebrow and tossed her platinum hair over her shoulder.

"Life sucks sometimes, you know?"

"Yeah. Only this didn't turn out so bad." Her bubblegum-pink lips bent into a grin. "I never did anything like this in Oklahoma. Something about this place makes me want to... create. I think it's making me a better person. Plus, there's Jayden." Her cheeks warmed to a blush.

Finn's eyebrows pinched together above his nose. "I think I know exactly what you mean."

She nodded her goodbyes and descended the metal scaffolding toward the stage where the pyro troupe had convened. How could he have ever thought she looked like Barbie? Jenny wasn't plastic. She was a survivor like he was.

The murmur of voices attracted his attention across the stage. Hope had arrived, wrapped in layers of teal and sapphire silk with a fan of peacock feathers behind her head. Her blue eyes seemed to glow from beneath falsely extended lashes. The amount of makeup she wore rendered her almost unrecognizable, but he crossed the catwalk to compliment her and put her at ease. She had a big night ahead of her.

"You look great."

"Thank you, Finn. How sweet you are."

"Are you ready for this?" Finn wasn't talking about the show.

Hope gave a toothy grin. "Of course. This is the night we've been training for. Finally, the performance, and then we can all go home."

She was acting weird. For one, he'd never known Hope to smile so much, and the way she sat was far too feminine. Hope was a girl who carried great reserves of coiled energy, like she might punch you in the throat as quickly as say hello to you. Today she seemed passive and submissive. He had an urge to smudge her lipstick.

"Have you thought about what I said?"

Her face went blank. *Blink. Blink.* Big, empty doe eyes. "About what?"

"About doing the best you can to make this show special for my parents."

"I'll make you sparkle."

He backed away along the scaffolding. "Do you want to meet my mom after the show?" he asked lightly.

"I'd love to," she said, the smile firmly in place. "I'll see you then."

A prickle danced across the back of his neck. He fought to keep it from his expression. "Cool."

Hope knew he didn't have a mother. They'd talked about it on multiple occasions, as recently as last night. Carefully, he swooped to the platform where Orelon and Wendy made final preparations. When he landed, his hands were shaking.

"What's wrong with you?" Wendy asked.

"Just nerves," he lied. But it wasn't nerves. He'd just met Hope's doppelgänger. He'd known something was up the minute she'd acted like she didn't know about their conversation. The clown had taken a piece of her hair. Why hadn't he considered this possibility? And if her clone was here, where was the real Hope? And what did that mean for their plan?

Orelon clapped his hands. "One more time before the big show."

⚜

FINN DIDN'T HAVE A SINGLE OPPORTUNITY TO SEARCH FOR THE REAL Hope. Orelon made him and Wendy practice all the way up to the performance. Worse, he had no way to contact the real Ms. D to tell her Hope was missing.

"Oh, I see my parents!" Wendy said. She pointed to the theater doors from the scaffolding above the closed red curtain.

Finn searched the faces entering the theater, and sure enough, there was his dad. His heart swelled. He hadn't thought about how much he'd missed his father until now, and with the danger all around him, he was tempted to fly to his side and beg to go home. But he couldn't. He'd promised to help. Mike's life depended on him.

His father and the other parents milled among a crowd of the wealthiest patrons he'd ever seen in one place. The email HORU had read to him about Revelations before he'd come here wasn't misleading. His father's business suit was downright plain beside the glitz and glamour of the rest of the audience. A sheik with gold embroidered robes entered with six attendants who tossed rose petals at his feet. An entourage of burly men carried an African princess, dressed in a gown made entirely of sapphires, into the theater on their shoulders. A geisha, wrapped in silk with a white face and red lips, followed an ordinary Japanese businessman to his seat. It wasn't difficult to imagine any of these people paying $10,000 per ticket.

The parents of the students were easy to find. They were the ones gawking at the other attendees and looking completely underdressed. Finn finally understood what HORU's research had suggested. This place didn't just attract the wealthy; it *made* people wealthy. The entire time the audience was here, the star was working its magic on them too, making them better at whatever it was they already did.

"Take your places," Orelon said. "We're about to begin."

Wendy walked along a narrow rack of stage lighting to the rigging where her red silk was fastened and sat down to watch the start of the show. Once Orelon descended to help Natalie double-check the set, Finn was finally alone. He flew to the platform near the scene curtain and pulled the joker from the sleeve of his costume.

"Theodor," he whispered over the card.

A draft ruffled his costume, and then the magician was there. He straightened his bow tie and tugged at his cuffs. "What is it, Finn? I'm opening the show. I don't have much time."

"They took Hope."

Theodor froze. "No."

"Yes. The person sitting in that box with Juliette is not her."

"Are you sure?"

"Positive. I don't think it's a coincidence that Ravenguard and Applegate are missing, either. What should we do?"

"You were right to bring this to me. I can help." Theodor rubbed the side of his face. "After your performance, lure the clowns to their hive."

"What? How?"

"I'll be waiting for you. I'll set a trap. Without Hope, you'll need help."

"You want me to act as bait?"

"Yes. Bring them to me. I'll end this."

"What about Hope? We have to find her!"

"I will. After my performance. Ravenguard and Applegate are secretive and infamously good at what they do. I can't make any promises, but I do promise to try."

Finn frowned. "They'll hunt her, Theodor. Follow the dogs."

The magician wrung his hands. "Don't give up, Finn. We move forward, with or without her. Agreed?"

This was not how it was supposed to be. Hope was the hero, not Finn. He couldn't do this without her. Still, he nodded his head. It came down to this: he'd rather die saving his friends than live knowing he hadn't.

Theodor's gaze drifted to the stage. "I must go. Lead the clowns back to the hive. I'll be there, and I'll be ready."

All he could manage was a nod, which was lost in darkness as the stage lights extinguished. It didn't matter. Theodor was already gone. Finn tucked the joker card back into his sleeve with the others.

Below him, a single spotlight clicked on and focused on the imposter Ms. D.

"Welcome, ladies and gentlemen." The clone's hair glowed silver against her sparkling purple suit. "I am Victoria Duvall, dreamer, imagineer, performance architect. Today, I bring you the finest in athletic talent in all the world. These students have trained for months to tell you this story, a tale of transformation. But I have a secret."

She reached into her pocket and produced a velvet bag. "The actors do not know that I have procured a measure of fairy dust with magic capable of rendering the ordinary extraordinary."

Wrinkled, spotted fingers dug into the drawstring and opened the mouth of the bag. Instantly, a shower of sparks sprayed toward the ceiling, fireworks that grew bigger and broader, expanding the size of the bag until it became too large for the imposter to hold. She dropped it onstage.

The audience gave a collective gasp.

"Prepare yourselves," the clone said from beside the geyser of sparks. "Tonight, the laws of nature are rendered powerless. Tonight, everything changes, including you. Tonight, the magic is real. Now, without further hesitation, let us all embark upon… Metamorphosis!"

She spread her arms, and the heavy red curtains parted to reveal a stunning display of color and light. The voice of an angel pierced the space from the balcony above.

The show had begun.

✵ 44 ✵

INFRACTION

Hope came awake in a dim cinderblock room that smelled of death. Her head throbbed and her arms ached. Based on the warm, wet heaviness in her hair, she was sure the first was due to a blow to the back of her head. The pain in her arms required no deductive reasoning. Her wrists were chained to the ceiling, her flesh raw where the manacles dug in. Although it hurt to stand, she managed to get her feet under her, but still couldn't lower her arms enough to relieve the pins and needles feeling in her hands or the ache in her joints.

What happened? She'd woken that morning and left the dining hall in order to meet Juliette and prepare for tonight's show. The memories bubbled up in incomplete, foggy segments: Ravenguard waiting inside Juliette's door. Juliette yelling, "Infraction." Her peacock-feather fan waving. An explosion of pain at the back of her skull.

Sweat ran down her cheek and she wiped it away with her shoulder. The heat in the small shed was stifling and the airflow from the two-inch slit near the roof, the building's only excuse for a window, was almost nonexistent. The moonlight coming in through that slit was barely enough for her to register her surroundings.

"Gabriel," she murmured. She shifted, trying to free her triquetra, tugging one bound hand toward her neck. On her tiptoes, she was able to run her fingertips along the base of her throat, feeling for her amulet in the dark. "No. No. No." Gone. Without it, she was still a Soulkeeper, but she couldn't call Gabriel for help. She squeezed her eyes closed against the dark and cursed under her breath.

A grating rattle echoed in the small space, like a chain slipping through a metal ring. The scrape and slap of metal on metal made her teeth hurt. The door slid open, moonlight streaming in around a dark silhouette.

"Help me," she said. She didn't know what else to say.

"There is no help for you. Not anymore. You've earned your punishment." Ravenguard's long, cool fingers clasped one of her wrists.

"What did I do?" she asked.

Ravenguard didn't answer. He unlocked one shackle and then the other. With her wrists pinned inside one hand, he lowered his lips to her bloodstained ear. "You get a five-minute head start. I suggest you run. I dare you to hide." His voice was saccharine and sulfuric acid, dripping with evil anticipation. "You can sing if you want to, but Applegate and I can see through enchanter magic. The sound will only help us find you faster. Personally, I prefer a harder target."

She struggled against him in the dark as something warm and wet stroked her ear. His tongue. He'd licked blood from the side of her face. Was he human or demon? She sensed human, but then why the taste for blood? A psychopath. A murderer.

His wicked laugh echoed in the small room. He released her wrists. "Run, little rabbit, run."

Hope did not hesitate. Although her body was racked with pain, and her arms throbbed with the return of blood, she bolted out the door, stumbling across uneven ground in the direction of the nearest cover, the edge of a forest. Something sharp poked through her leather slipper and she hopped once to pull it from the side of her foot. A splintered bone. She paused, throwing the bone down. The ground was white. Bones. Skulls. Carnage stretched at least twenty feet in every direction. She was standing on a mass grave.

Her breath came in pants as she paused to assess her surroundings. In front of her was the side of Murder Mountain and the edge of the Crimson Forest. That meant if she continued running in this direction, she'd circle back toward the school. She might be able to climb the mountain to Ms. D's cave. Paul was there. He'd help her. But with Ravenguard on her heels, the dogs having her scent? Chances were they'd find and kill both of them.

She pivoted and listened. Her Soulkeeper hearing focused in on the faint rush of water in the distance. *Fever River*, she thought. As she closed her eyes, she tried to picture the map of Revelations Island in her head. Didn't the river run under the school? Maybe she could use the water to hide her scent and guide her back to the theater where she could help Finn and the others.

"Four minutes, thirty seconds," came Ravenguard's voice from the shadow of the shed.

Hope considered her options and ran for the river.

❧ 45 ❧

THE SHOW MUST GO ON

Finn gripped the steel railing of the catwalk as Juliette's voice rang like a bell through the theater, and Hope's clone smiled prettily from the chair in front of her. Was the clone even able to sing? It couldn't have been in Hope's body for long. Finn had seen the real Hope that morning at breakfast. And although the clone could have existed before her disappearance, Finn had a feeling the duplicate was rushed. It wasn't singing for a reason.

Below, Theodor took the stage, executing his Metamorphosis act as precisely as he'd described it. The audience cheered as the multicolored doves swooped over their heads and the magician's cards danced in the lights around him. Kings and queens, spades and hearts, light and dark in a whirlwind around a man and a floating magic box. Finn marveled at the power. This was no illusion. Theodor's magic was as real as the man himself.

The doves ignited and the entire act collapsed in on itself, spark to flame, flame to ash, the birds, the cards, the man, disappearing at the crescendo of sound and light, sucked into a microscopic black hole. Three origami doves dropped from thin air onto an empty stage.

The audience exploded in applause.

The imposter Ms. D took the stage again, sweeping the paper birds into her hands. With a few apt words, she tossed the doves into the air where they transformed into a shower of glitter.

"And now, dear visitors, I challenge you with a performance designed to ignite the animal within!" She waved her red glove.

Menagerie took the stage, the entire troupe dressed in matching black shirts and tights. The boy from the woods whose head Finn had almost crushed when he thought he was a tiger was among them. Hope was right: he'd lived. Finn bristled. Was the boy the cause of the real Hope's absence? Did he remember her? Rat her out?

The troupe danced, their legs flying beneath them as they rode the rhythm of the music. They gathered in a tight group at the center of the stage and in the blink of an eye, transformed into tigers. The audience oohed and aahed at the illusion, never realizing that the bodies in front of them had changed into the animals in the most grisly way. Juliette made the shift appear seamless, smooth, painless.

As Paul ran his troupe through their paces, Finn counted clones. There was Ms. D, Hope, Amanda, Paul. And the clowns had already gathered near the side of the stage. They'd have a clone among them. Probably one that looked like Mike, ready to replace him once he died during the act. Finn swallowed the bile that rose in his throat.

The audience was on their feet again, hands clapping furiously. Menagerie took a bow before leaving the stage. Finn's act was next. He flew to his red silk, noticing that Wendy was already in her cocoon. Methodically, Finn began to wrap himself.

The clowns shifted, giving Finn a clear view of the person standing among them. A sick feeling gripped his torso like a vice. The face he saw was not Mike's. *Wendy. Mike isn't the next target. It's Wendy.* Finn's heart pounded.

The lights clicked off. It was time. With resolve, he finished folding himself into the red cocoon and waited for his cue. He wouldn't let them take her. Not while he was still breathing.

⚜

HOPE SPRINTED TOWARD THE SURGE OF RUSHING WATER. THE churn of the river was getting louder, which meant she was headed in the right direction. If she waded into the river, she might be able to mask her scent from the dogs while using the path of the water to guide her back to the school. With any luck, she'd arrive before the end of the performance. She wasn't sure how she'd kill the demon clowns without her triquetra, but she'd cross that bridge when she came to it.

As Hope saw it, she had a few things going for her. She was faster than any human, had heightened senses, and although her pendant was missing, it was entirely possible her angel would sense she was in trouble and help anyway. Most importantly, she was already healing. As her ears picked up the yap of dogs in the distance, she remembered that Applegate and Ravenguard had powers of their own. They'd come to the island as security personnel and disciplinarians. One hundred years later, they'd evolved into killing machines, hunters of anyone who broke the rules. Tonight she was their prey. She did not take the revelation lightly.

Hope broke from a grove of trees to traverse a stony beach and wade into the gray foam of the river. She shivered as the cold water gurgled over her calves. It was too dark to see to the bottom, but she learned quickly that the bank angled sharply deeper. Her right foot dropped, her leg plunging in up to her thigh, prompting her to shuffle closer to shore. She'd have to step carefully.

"This is miserable." She shook her head and looked up at the stars. "If you're listening, I could use some help about now. Are you listening? Or sitting on your throne in the clouds watching my legs freeze off like my life is your daily soap opera?" It wasn't the smartest thing to taunt God, but Hope couldn't help herself. She resented her situation and her lot in life more than ever. Wasn't it enough that she'd discovered the demons and agreed to risk her life to kill them? Why was it necessary for her to be captured and hunted as well?

Perhaps not having the option to be an atheist had ruined her for religion. When bad things happened, she didn't have the luxury of being able to blame it on a chaotic universe. No. She knew firsthand there was a God and that made everything worse. It meant that an omnipotent being understood that her legs were ice cubes from the knee down and that immortal Nazis were hunting her like an animal. And despite this knowledge, He chose to do nothing. There were names for people like that, and none of them were kind.

Her next step landed on a rotting log right under the surface. She stepped over its rough, spongy back and continued her journey. Two more steps and she heard the log slide into deep water behind her. Three more steps and she noticed a break in the current at her side.

"Oh no." She backed away as two reflective eyes locked onto her from under the surface. At once, she pivoted, lifting her knees high to sprint for the shore. The giant reptilian creature coiled and struck, sinking its teeth into the back of her legs and dragging her into the river's depths. No time to scream. She took one last hungry breath and was dragged into the river's depths.

⚙️

WRAPPED IN THE RED SILK, KNEES CURLED INTO HIS CHEST, FINN listened to the clicking of the opening curtain over his panicked breath. Wendy. The clowns must plan to sabotage the performance or they wouldn't be waiting with her replacement.

Juliette's voice rang out. The song she sang was written specifically for aerial's routine. The music started low like a rumbling thunderstorm on the horizon. Then the lights came on and her voice rose like the sunrise. It filtered into Finn's cocoon, casting a red glow over his skin, the color of blood.

The show must go on.

Head. Hip. Head. Hip. Finn unraveled from the center of the knot, somersaulting down the red silk at an angle that made his outstretched legs barely miss Wendy's. When he reached the end of the silk, he climbed back up, using only his arms, legs extended, toes pointed. He paused his ascent in the middle of the length of silk and rolled one wrist in the fabric. Then, he flew.

Flying against the bound silk created a different effect than swinging. Murmurs rose up from the audience as Finn and Wendy picked up speed, their costumes expanding to resemble the winged creatures they were supposed to be. Finn continued his routine, a phoenix fighting for the affections of a butterfly maiden. He gripped the silk with both hands, extended his body straight out into space, and let go, dropping like a rock.

A woman in the audience screamed.

Finn caught the very end of the silk and climbed back up. The woman's scream turned to an exclamation of wonder. Wendy's turn. She rolled an ankle and wrist in the silk, performing a split in midair before spinning in a way that defied simple physics. Faster and faster, Wendy shifted from a split, to a scorpion, to a pike, and straightened her legs to twirl horizontally in a way that could only be described as gravity defying.

Finn understood it was Juliette's voice that turned Wendy's ordinary costume into an organic second skin that sparkled and glinted gossamer in the lights. Although his brain reminded him of the trick, he was awestruck by the illusion. All he could see was the magic. Wendy *was* a monarch butterfly, delicate and beautiful. Finn stared, bewitched.

He was so lost in her beauty, he almost missed his cue. Almost. Just in time, he wrapped the silk around the back of his head and revolved without the aid of hands or feet. After several howls from the audience, he tumbled, catching himself with the roll of one ankle. Head down, arms spread wide, he revolved again. Wrist, ankle, one arm behind his back. He twirled and tumbled to the applause of the house.

Now was the time to act. If he was going to save Wendy, he needed to change the performance. Everyone expected them to execute the moves they'd practiced. But Finn had an idea. If he changed what happened next, the clowns would be at a disadvantage.

Halfway back up the silk, he flipped to the high wire, breaking from routine. Finn spread his bird wings and, without hesitation, tumbled along the wire—hands, feet, hands, feet—all the way to the other side. The audience clambered to their feet, clapping and whistling. He stopped, spread his arms, fingers upturned. He motioned for Wendy. Nothing huge. A tiny twitch of his fingers.

As he'd hoped, she followed his lead, breaking from routine to land beside him on the wire, her butterfly wings flapping. She flashed him a confused look before executing a series of pirouettes. Around and around. Enough to make him dizzy. When she came to a halt, every eye in the theater was locked on the two of them. She was close now. Within arm's reach. He took her hand. To the music, she spread her arms and went en pointe, her free leg bending along his side. She tipped forward until her free foot touched the back of her head. When she returned her foot to the wire, she pivoted and fell into Finn's arms.

"What are you doing?" she whispered.

"Improvising," he whispered back.

She nodded and kissed him right there in the spotlight. Her lips, soft and warm on his, produced a new kind of magic. The second of contact stretched on like a small eternity. And then he fell. They both did. Headfirst toward the stage.

She tugged his hand. "Fly, Finn. Fly!"

He came back into his head at the last second, arching his back and spreading his arms as hand in hand, they soared over the audience. His costume burst into flames. It was supposed to be a solo flight, but the audience seemed more than pleased with the conclusion. Wendy circled the theater with him, only releasing his hand when the flames engulfed his arm.

The people below them howled and pointed. They made a delicate landing on the stage. Finn and Wendy bowed as the song came to an end, smiling and waving at the onlookers. There was a moment when nothing existed but the applause and the lights.

And then an explosion of flames swallowed them both.

❧ 46 ❧

FEVER RIVER

Across the island, Hope struggled to free herself from the creature's jaws that held her under the river's icy depths. Her brain could not decide if the thing was a snake or a crocodile. At the moment, she might have called it a dragon. She stabbed its eyes with her fingers, dug her nails into its scaly flesh, and twisted against its slicing teeth. But even her Soulkeeper strength was no match for the beast.

Her head broke the surface long enough to grab a frantic sip of air before the beast pulled her back under. They were traveling fast, twisting and rolling with the current. There was a boulder up ahead. Would the thing smash her against it, soften her up before it swallowed her down? Not if she could help it. Thinking fast, she turned and kicked as hard as she could. Her foot connected with the neck of the beast, using the current and her weight to catch and turn its reptilian body. The back of its jaw collided with the jagged stone.

Sweet release! Hope swam for shore, away from the thing's slashing teeth. Her arms and legs burned with the effort.

"Oomph," she yelled, slamming into another boulder. Hard-won air billowed from her lungs. There were more stones where

G.P. CHING

that came from. She tumbled into rapids, the large rocks growing closer together. This was both a blessing and a curse. It might be harder for the creature to navigate, but she could be ripped apart trying to escape it.

Focusing, she called on her abilities, kicking off one stone to propel herself to the next. When her head bobbed above the surface, she gasped for breath. When the current dragged her under, she tried to use it to her advantage.

By the inconsistency of the current, she sensed the creature was behind her, still hunting her, although the boulders were too close for the massive beast to maneuver effectively. A red ribbon of her blood curled through the water beside her. She needed to rest and allow her wounds to heal.

With her last burst of adrenaline, she broke from the rapids and swam the remaining distance to shore. The stone bank might have been a feather bed for how eagerly she took to it, sputtering and numb. Without the cold rush of water, it quickly became clear she was hurt worse than she thought. Her left arm wasn't working right below the elbow, and half her face throbbed like a raw bruise. A gash in her leg gushed blood in time with her heartbeat.

Cursing, she glared at the stars above and waited for her body to heal.

"Such foul language." Applegate's face appeared above her own. When Hope gave a paltry attempt at escape, the woman's knees pinned her arms to the ground. Applegate whistled through her fingers. The hunting party must have heard her because dogs began to bark in the distance, and horses' hooves pounded in their direction.

"You are a challenge," Applegate said. "Fast as lightning and smart to take the river. Most students avoid it for the immediate shelter of the forest. No one ever expects the dragon." She laughed.

Removing her gloves, she gripped Hope's chin and squeezed.

"You're a monster," Hope rasped.

Applegate chuckled. "I'm whatever this place has made me." She slid her hand under the hem of her hunting jacket to her hip, where she pulled a dagger from its sheath. "Now…" As the admissions counselor leaned over Hope, silver flashed from her neck. Hope's triquetra. Hope struggled to reach for it. All it would take was her breath to hit the silver and her angel would come. But it was too late. The dagger plunged into Hope's heart and pain gripped her in a tight, breathless fist.

"You," Applegate said suddenly, face turning toward the woods. She yanked the dagger from Hope's chest and sprang to her feet, turning her weapon on the presence behind her.

Hope couldn't see what or who had come out of the woods, but an enormous reptilian head rose from the river at her feet. In a flash, cold teeth sank into her ankles and she shot from Applegate's side into the river's depths. This time she didn't struggle or thrash. By then, she was too damaged to put up a fight. She gave herself over to the darkness and left it to the higher power to sort out.

ॐ

FINN BRACED HIMSELF AS FIRE RAGED AROUND HIM AND WENDY. As soon as the pyrotechnics shielded them from view, Finn used his cards. "Extinguish!" He shed the smoldering outer layer of his costume and helped Wendy out of hers.

"Are you okay?"

"A few minor burns, but I think so," she said. "Thank goodness for my pyro lessons."

He ushered her from the stage in the opposite direction they'd rehearsed, as Juliette let out the first notes of the accompaniment for the pyro troupe's dance of the Seven Kingdoms. Jayden popped up through the trap door to walk directly through the swelling flames.

"Why are you going this way?" Wendy asked.

"Because I'm avoiding *them*." He pointed across the stage at the gathered clowns.

"What do they want?"

Some of the clowns broke off from the group, disappearing behind the stage curtain. With fewer of them together, Wendy's clone stood out like a sore thumb, as did another, a clone that looked exactly like Finn.

"What the hell?" she said at his side.

"The clowns are evil, Wendy. They want us dead."

She shook her head. "What? Why?"

"Do you trust me?" Finn asked.

"Yes. Finn, what's going on?"

"Fly up to that row of floodlights and stay there. Let's hope our clones can't fly."

"What are you going to do?"

"I'm going to fight. Now go."

"Be careful, Finn." Wendy kissed him on the cheek and took off toward the batten.

"Where is the real Hope?" Ms. D asked. She'd arrived silently, appearing in the space beside him like a ghostly manifestation.

"You noticed," he said sarcastically, gesturing toward the balcony box where the fake Hope pretended to sing. "Unfortunately, I have no idea where the real Hope is."

"If Theodor has taught you anything, now is the time to use it," she said.

Finn's eyes widened as the cloned Ms. D stepped up behind the real one. They were dressed identically. The only way Finn could tell them apart was by where each was standing.

"You should be dead," the clone said to Ms. D.

"I've never been good at doing what I'm supposed to do," Ms. D crouched, raising her hands defensively.

The two women circled each other, air vibrating with the magic building between them.

"Don't just stand there, boy," the real Ms. D said. "This one's mine. Yours is waiting." She'd barely gotten the words out when pure energy pulsed from the clone's hands and knocked her off her feet. She broke apart into a column of smoke and reappeared behind her clone. Her arm wrapped around the clone, choking it by the neck.

"Go," she yelled to him.

Finn soared to the catwalk and pulled his cards from his sleeve. A clown climbed toward him from stage right, but Finn's own clone flew straight at him. So much for hoping he couldn't fly.

Raising the card for *eviscerate*, Finn waited, trembling as the clone drew closer. With only one spell capable of inflicting damage, he couldn't afford to miss. The clone's familiarity, its movements, gave him the creeps. Could he do this? Kill his twin? His eyes darted to the two of spades. Dark magic.

"Crap," he said, lowering the card. He'd sworn he wouldn't use sorcery. The clone attacked, reaching for Finn's neck. There had to be another way. He sifted through his deck.

"Bind," Finn yelled, throwing the two of diamonds at the clone's feet. It stopped, unable to take another step. His lookalike flailed its arms helplessly toward Finn, who dodged out of the way, and caught the card as it boomeranged back toward him.

White-gloved hands gripped his neck from behind. Under the constricting pressure of the second clown's grip, Finn choked out, "Unbind." The thing's hands came apart, and Finn flew straight up and over its head. "Bind." He tossed the card at the second clown's feet. Success, but his luck was running out. His clone had successfully pried one foot from the metal floor. The spell was wearing off.

Finn flipped through his cards, tempted to use eviscerate but settling on another option. "Ignite!" he yelled and tossed the card. His clone burst into flame. The card caught the second clown on its way back, consuming it in fire as well. Its white face melted in the heat.

"Two for one! That's what I'm talking about," Finn yelled, catching the three of diamonds.

He may have spoken too soon. The clown opened its thin black lips, its mouth spreading into a gaping black hole that took over its face. A black, oily beast broke through its striped shirt and black suspenders, spreading wings made of liquid shadow. It shrieked in Finn's direction, loud enough for Juliette to have to sing louder to disguise it from the audience.

Finn's eyes darted to Wendy, who was watching in horror from the spotlight rigging. More clowns had gathered below him, watching his clone and the demon he'd ignited, bound and burning on the theater catwalk. The Wendy clone stared up at him with empty, calculating eyes.

"Theodor, I hope you have the trap ready because the bait is on its way," Finn murmured. He swallowed hard, then swooped over the clowns' heads, racing toward the back entrance and the stairwell to the hive. "Come on, you evil shitheads. Come and get it!"

※

VICTORIA DUVALL WAS NOT ABOUT TO LET HER CLONE GET THE BEST of her. As one who had held the position of performance architect, she had full control of all the benefits the title endowed. Her clone, on the other hand, may have developed the same skills but it didn't have nearly as much experience.

The clone clapped her mottled hands together and conjured a spiked club. Smart. A gun wouldn't work inside Revelations, and Victoria's resilience abilities would render a sword or blade almost useless. But skulls could be crushed with enough pressure and the right magic. Victoria bent backward, the club whistling over her belly button. With the speed and angle of the movement, her bowler hat toppled from her head.

The clone would expect her to right herself immediately. It wasn't natural for a woman more than a hundred years old to stay balanced on her tiptoes with her back parallel to the floor. But Victoria wasn't natural, and staying bent is exactly what she did.

Circling her forearm, she called on her pyro abilities and engulfed the clone in a column of fire. The demon may be fireproof, but the flames were enough of a distraction to give Victoria a split second of time. She used it to conjure a whip. *Snap.* The tip went out, wrapped around the club, and yanked it free of the clone's grip.

Victoria caught the weapon in her opposite hand. With a wave of the clone's hand, the flames receded, but Victoria was already on the offensive. She raised the club and swung, connecting with her clone's head. The skull collapsed, but it wasn't the end.

A massive, grotesque beast emerged from the clone's broken body, an oily creature with jointed arms and snapping jaws. It spread its dark wings and roared.

"Scary," she said coolly. "I'll give you that. Only, when you shed the protection of my body, you also shed my abilities." Victoria snapped her fingers and the demon froze. From the feet up, the dark, shadowy stuff the beast was made of hardened. Gas became liquid. Liquid became solid. Solid became brittle stone. Victoria punched the monster squarely in the chest. The demon shattered, a million tiny pieces flying around her in an explosion of oily black ice. The pieces landed on the stage where they sizzled and evaporated, leaving pockmarks in the wood.

With the back of her red glove, she wiped a bead of sweat from her brow. "Theodor would approve." She bent over to retrieve her bowler hat, repositioning it on her head.

"What the hell *was* that thing?" the pyro boy asked. He stepped around the smoking bit of floor to reach her.

Victoria didn't answer. She was distracted by the conclusion of Juliette's song. The imposter Hope had pretended to sing, but Victoria could not differentiate her voice. Clearly, the clone was rushed and not ready to perform. Or else Juliette was too vain to let her. Either way, the enchanter narrowed her eyes on Victoria from her balcony box. When she opened her mouth to sing again, her dagger-filled stare pinned Victoria's feet to the floor and sent a paralyzing wave through her body.

"I can't move," the boy beside her said.

"Give it a minute," Victoria whispered. "She won't be able to hold us once she starts in on the next act." So Juliette was in league with the demons. Victoria should have known. She never trusted the damn woman, not even when she was a resilience performer.

The spotlight clicked on again. Onstage, Mike and Amanda stood on a platform over a large crystal bowl designed to look like an open oyster. Mike dove in first, arching his back and slithering along the edge of the glass at a harsh and painful looking angle.

Resilience was about pain. It was about discipline. Victoria saw both in Mike's contorted spine and held breath. But Juliette's song smoothed his underwater image, making a graceful dance out of a demonstration of torture. Michael finally burst from the bowl to balance on his hands on the lip of the oyster. His pained gasps were drowned out by the music. Like a contortionist, his body bent until his legs jutted out over the back of his head.

Amanda was the next to dive in, the clone slithering around the bowl before splashing onto the opposite edge and executing a similar pose. Once they'd given the audience time to applaud, the two rocked back into the water, circling, splashing, churning up dark currents from below.

Victoria cleared her throat and tried to sing in retaliation, but Juliette shifted her gaze and redoubled her efforts. She'd grown stronger than Victoria remembered. The performance architect's voice petered out behind her useless lips.

Juliette's aria darkened and so did the act. In sweeping, artistic motions Amanda attacked Michael, wrapping her fingers around his throat and dragging him under. Water sprayed across the stage. The momentum increased, Mike tossing her from the bowl only to have Amanda flip higher and higher before returning to his arms. The audience was delighted. Only Victoria saw it for what it really was—a carefully disguised murder.

One more flip, and this time Amanda landed on the platform and pulled a lever. The upper shell of the oyster snapped closed, locking Michael under the water.

"She means to kill him," Victoria said to the boy.

"Who? Mike?" The boy beside her grew visibly agitated, struggling against his unmoving feet.

"What is your name?"

"You know my name, Ms. D." He patted his chest. "I'm Jayden."

She raised an eyebrow. "Jayden. I am afraid for your friend Michael. We have to help him."

"I still can't move," Jayden said.

The audience gave a collective gasp as Michael struggled against the lid of the oyster. A woman in the front row cried out his name. Juliette's voice soared, and Michael magically appeared next to Amanda. They grasped hands and raised them over their heads.

"He's still in the bowl," Victoria said.

"What?" Jayden's eyes darted from the bowl to the clone holding hands with Amanda.

"Jayden, do you still have your abilities?" Victoria rubbed her throat. She was still weak from her earlier battle and the force of Juliette's song.

"Yeah. I think so."

She smiled. It was like Juliette to underestimate the boy. "If you care for your friend, you will start Juliette's dress on fire. Now."

Jayden turned his confused expression on Juliette. The boy stared, unblinking long enough for Victoria to question his abilities. Then Juliette's peacock dress burst into flames. The imposter Hope attempted to beat the flames with their bare hands as Juliette struggled to continue to sing. Quickly, one of the crew closed the main curtain.

It was enough of a distraction to ease the grip on Victoria's vocal cords. She opened her mouth and sang, freeing her feet and clearing Juliette's illusion for those behind the curtain.

"Mike!" Jayden yelled, seeing for the first time that his friend was still inside the bowl. The real Mike flailed and pounded on the glass, drowning under the feet of the two clones that stood on the lid.

Jayden picked up the baton from his performance and charged the bowl, swinging at the glass. The strike bounced off the giant crystal oyster.

"Knock it off, Jayden." The Amanda clone jumped from the lid and popped him in the jaw. The boy took the pounding, wiped a spot of blood from his lip, and fired up his baton.

"Get Mike out of there," he commanded, pointing the flaming baton at Amanda's head.

Good boy, Victoria thought. She continued to sing but leaped to the top of the bowl and dove for the lever. Only, cloned Michael grabbed her wrist.

She kneed him in the gut, then dug her fingers into the skin at the back of his head and tore. There was a gurgling sound and the flesh gave way. A half-dozen long, segmented arms gripped Victoria with oily black fingers. She sang louder and the demon shivered, wings stretching as it struggled to break free of her illusion. She was planning her next move when a flaming sword pierced the demon's neck, sending its oily head tumbling. The headless body flopped from the platform, legs still kicking.

Jayden tossed the flaming sword above his head and caught it in his other hand. "Turns out, one of the Seven Kingdoms is badass."

Victoria pulled the lever and met his eyes. "As are you."

The cap rose, but Michael's head did not break the surface. Jayden jumped in and pulled his friend from the depths. "He's not breathing!"

Victoria hooked her hands under Michael's shoulders and

helped Jayden lift him onto the platform. The boy was blue. She started CPR, blowing into his mouth and compressing his chest in a steady rhythm, but Michael did not respond.

"No. No. No. Not again," Victoria said. "Don't you die." She needed help. She didn't have enough power left to revive him.

Her eyes caught on a small girl huddled on the rigging high above the stage. "You there. Where is Theodor? Can you see the magician?"

"I heard Finn say he was meeting him in the hive. What does that mean?"

"Never mind. Find Orelon. Ask him to load up the buses."

The girl flew.

"He's not breathing," Jayden said, looking from Michael to Victoria.

"Help the girl," she ordered. Then she gripped Michael tighter and dissolved in a column of purple smoke.

☙ 47 ❧

RESURRECTION

Hope's inhale was both loud and painful. She regained consciousness in a tunnel of bright blue light. Her body was floating in a hexagonal tube of warm water, and she assessed her surroundings with wild eyes and racing thoughts. Although she was still dressed in her torn uniform, both shoes were missing and her pants were shredded below the knee. Once her breathing evened out, she bent and straightened her fingers, flapped her feet, and cracked her neck. She'd definitely been dead again, which meant the growing queasiness in her stomach was going to become a problem.

She pressed her palms against the sides of the tube. Metal, like stainless steel. Her pointed toes touched stone. When she reached above her head, her fingers hit a waxy material. Wax she could deal with.

Flipping over, she got to her knees in the water, hunched in the tube. She recoiled her arm and punched. A fist-sized hole appeared in the wax, just as her stomach turned inside out. She cursed as the side effect of her resurrection blew through her lips. A wave of vomit hit the water and what was left of her uniform. She cursed and pulled her fist back again for another go. But someone else's fingers appeared in the hole she created, breaking off chunks and throwing them aside.

"Unbind." The wax melted away and Hope poured out of the tube along with the water and sick. She grunted when her body slapped the floor.

"Theodor." She stared up into the face of the magician before giving herself over to another round of vomiting.

"Scour," he said, tossing a card in her direction. In a blink of an eye, all the sick was gone, as was the water. The bloodstains from her uniform disappeared.

"Thank you," she said. "But I'm not finished."

He crossed the room in three long strides and returned with a garbage pail, shoving it under her chin.

"You were dead," he said.

"Yeah. Resurrecting is something I do."

"Your legs grew back."

"That's something I do too."

His eyes narrowed. "Finn sent me to look for you. By the time I found you, Applegate had done her damage. It was all I could do to evade her and pry you from the water dragon's jaws. Sorry about the tube. I needed to hide your body in case I had visitors."

Hope looked up into the man's impassive face. "Thank you for coming for me."

"Thank Finn. I wouldn't have known you were missing if he hadn't figured it out." He straightened his suit jacket. "As much as I'd like to prolong this chat, there's still work to be done." He rushed down a hall to her right.

Hope pushed to her feet and followed Theodor, the hall bending around an orb of glass that glowed bright blue. "Is that the star?"

"It is. Don't touch it. It's very hot." He stopped in a room that looked like a former laboratory, only all the equipment had been stacked against one wall. On the floor, in the cleared space, Theodor had drawn a symbol Hope had never seen before. It looked like a compass with arrows in eight directions, but he'd enclosed the entire thing in a triangle with circles capping each point.

"What is that?" Hope asked.

"Goat's blood."

"I mean the symbol."

"It amplifies the magic," he said quickly. "I'm sending these things back to where they came from. Only, I'm not exactly sure where that is. I've never been to Hell in order to picture it clearly. This magic is a spell for returning things. I've drawn it on top of a portal spell. It will analyze the creatures' constitution and open the portal based on what it finds. The circles at the points are anchors. You stand in one, Finn in the other. I'll be in the third. Everything else in this room will go straight to Hell." He dusted off his hands. "Wherever in the universe that happens to be."

Hope scoffed. "You're going to open a portal to Hell?" She hardly thought he was powerful enough, but even the thought was terrifying.

"Do you have a better idea?"

Automatically, her fingers probed the base of her neck for her triquetra. Applegate still had it. After a few moments, she answered, "No."

With a nod in her direction, he picked up a pail and added another layer of bright red goat's blood to the symbol. "Do you know where Hell is? If you do, it would make this easier."

"I've never been there personally, if that's what you're asking. This is dark magic. Are you sure it's safe to use in the presence of demons? All dark magic demands a price."

"Hmm," he murmured. "A price we will pay with the blood of our enemies." As Theodor placed the bucket against the wall, he removed his cards from his inner pocket, shuffling them in one hand—the top into the middle, the bottom over the top.

Hope looked toward the connecting corridor. "I hear foot-steps. Someone's coming."

"That would be Finn," Theodor said. "Come with me. Let's invite him in."

⚜

FINN RACED TOWARD THE END OF THE CORRIDOR WHERE HE remembered the entrance to the hive. "Open the door!" he yelled, praying that Theodor had successfully made it inside.

There was a rumble and the panel slid into the wall. Thank God.

"Back here, Finn!" Hope's voice. He turned the corner. What once was the clowns' laboratory was now the canvas for a giant symbol. The power radiating from the red pattern on the floor made his head throb.

"In the circle, Finn. The anchor!" Theodor motioned to the tip of the triangle.

A white-gloved hand clapped over Finn's mouth.

"Eviscerate," Theodor yelled.

The clown released Finn, its body shredding. Oily black goo sprayed across Finn's back, coating the shell of his ear in slick filth. He leaped into the circle Theodor had indicated. Instantly, purple light formed a ring of protection around him, a wall of energy that stopped the advancing demons, their white-gloved hands bouncing off the force around him. When he searched out Theodor, he and Hope had manned the similar circles at each point of the triangle, safe within their own wall of protection.

Theodor raised a card. King of spades. Dark magic. Finn held his breath. Gabriel had warned against using sorcery, but surely Theodor understood what he was doing. In all the time he'd trained with his mentor, he never once suspected that Theodor was impulsive or foolhardy. And Finn had relayed the angel's warning. The magician was aware of the risks. If he was using the king of spades, he had his reasons.

But the magician stopped short as a column of purple smoke

formed to Finn's right, between the symbol and the star. When the smoke cleared, Ms. D appeared, holding Mike in her arms. Mike, who sagged like a rag doll, like he was dead.

"He needs help," she yelled.

"The anchor will only hold three," Theodor said, turning his attention toward the advancing clowns.

"Help Mike," Finn yelled to Hope. "I'll hold them back."

Hope left the anchor and rushed to Mike's side.

Nothing could have prepared Finn for what he faced. He wasn't a fighter. He could fly and had his stack of cards, but that was it. But as the demons closed in, he reached down deep, inside his shaking, sick-feeling body, and found the courage to do what he had promised. The clowns couldn't walk through the protective barrier of the symbol, but they could walk around it. They tested the boundaries, one slipping around Finn. "Bind," he yelled flipping one card, then another through the purple barrier that surrounded him. "Ignite."

"Eviscerate." Theodor spun a card, leveraging Finn's work. It curved, around Finn, tearing the clown into tiny flaming bits. Barely enough to slow the herd behind it down. The magician selected the eight of diamonds from the center of his pack. "Cage," he yelled. Yellow shingles climbed around the entire group, locking them inside.

Finn cheered.

Until Hope's clone arrived. Still dressed in her peacock-colored gown, the imposter opened her mouth and began to sing before he or Theodor could react. The effect wasn't as powerful as Juliette's—Finn had been right about the clone being rushed—but the song was enough to transport Finn to the middle of a forest. He could still see the outline of reality through the weak illusion, but not well enough to trust himself to throw his next card.

Theodor had no such qualms. "Eviscerate," he shouted.

The forest tore in half, shredded leaves turning to black blood. The singing stopped. There was nothing left to sing. Nothing left of Hope's clone but oily strips of peacock-colored cloth. But the collisions of magic had unintended consequences. The yellow cage crumbled.

"Get back inside the anchor!" Theodor caught his card as white-gloved hands closed around Finn's throat and squeezed. When had he stepped out of it? It must have been when he was lost in the clone's illusion!

A pulse of magic from Ms. D knocked the clown off Finn, and he leaped back into the protective circle rubbing his throat.

"Theodor, look out!" Ms. D cried.

A blur of red and black came from behind the star and collided with Theodor, knocking him from his circle. Applegate! As a human, she was unaffected by the purple barrier. She straddled the magician's back, wrapping the crook of her arm around his neck. Theodor fumbled with his cards, but she was too quick. Her dagger landed, slicing into Theodor's flesh.

"No!" Finn threw the card he'd been avoiding all night. "Eviscerate!"

"Ahhh!" A bloody gash appeared in Applegate's arm but nothing more. She looked at Finn and laughed. "Is that supposed to stop me, Finn?"

Theodor crumbled at her feet, his blood spilling on the stone. But the magician wasn't dead yet. Finn watched him pull a card from his deck and flick it at Applegate's feet. She froze. Another card and the magician's body turned to mist. He was disappearing, transporting himself wherever he could get help.

"Ravenguard!" Applegate cried through her partially opened lips. Her eyes roved wild inside her immobilized face.

The second admissions counselor arrived from the same direction as Applegate and wasted no time stabbing his hunting knife into the magician's misty body. Theodor formed around the blade, his cards dropping from his hand as he thumped back into a solid state. The entire deck cascaded into the pool of blood surrounding Theodor. The entire deck except for the king of spades, which flipped from his fingers, arced across the symbol, and landed in Finn's hands.

Ms. D shoved Hope into a circle, then with a pulse of magic to keep Ravenguard at bay, dragged Mike into the last anchor. More clowns appeared from the direction Applegate and Ravenguard had come. At least eight more, including Paul and Wendy's clones. They were surrounded.

"Th-throw the card," Theodor gurgled.

"Victoria, go!" Hope yelled.

With one last glance at Theodor, Ms. D turned into a column of smoke and disappeared.

"Throw the card, Finn. Now," Hope commanded.

"I thought I wasn't supposed to use sorcery!"

"We don't have a choice. My triquetra is gone. I can't fight!"

The clowns scratched at the purple light around him as Theodor spasmed under Ravenguard's knife. The admission's counselors were twitching as the spells they were under wore off. Applegate could move her head, and Ravenguard succeeded in pulling his knife from Theodor's chest.

Finn wanted to help, but he'd never done this spell. Sure, he'd watched Theodor do it every time they met. He remembered his mentor saying "portate" before opening the portal between the library and his office. But he'd learned enough about magic to know that it wasn't only about saying the word; he'd have to concentrate his energy. What should he picture in his mind?

The purple light protecting them began to shimmer.

"Finn, now! Theodor is dying. The symbol won't last. Applegate will be free," Hope yelled.

"I don't know if I can do this. Where should I send them?" he yelled.

"The magic will decide. Theodor planned for this." She looked over her shoulder at Applegate, who had succeeded in sliding one foot toward them.

Finn had to do something. He didn't have a choice. He concentrated on the symbol, focusing his intent. "Portate!" he yelled and tossed the card at the center of the compass.

Unlike his previous spells, this time the card didn't come back. It sank through the stone where it seemed to have no effect. The purple light around Hope blinked like a lightbulb on the verge of fizzling out.

Then the compass began to spin, the stone melting into a swirling vortex. A black pit formed at the center of the symbol, bringing about a powerful suction that caused Hope's hair to blow forward toward the hole. Finn pressed his hands against the purple energy containing him as a laboratory table bounced from the wall into the abyss.

A clown was the portal's next victim, sending the others scrambling to find something to hold on to. Applegate, freed from Theodor's spell, grasped the railing of the star's enclosure and held on tight as his Theodor's body slid past her, his journey lubricated by his own blood, and tumbled into the vortex. Ravenguard sheathed his blade and grabbed on to the railing beside her. More equipment bent and crumpled before bouncing into the widening black hole at their feet. One clown and then another was torn from their bearings, having clung to equipment that gave way and was swept into the void. The remaining had gripped the railing beside the admissions counselors, who now dangled, parallel to the floor, their legs sucked toward the vortex.

All the weight, the sheer magical force, proved too much. The glass around the star cracked. The earth shook. Finn stumbled, holding himself up against the power of the anchor. If this went on much longer, he was afraid the entire school would be sucked into the depths of the portal, but he had no idea how to stop it.

Applegate slipped. Ravenguard caught her hand but grunted with the effort of holding her. And that's when Hope's triquetra flew out from under Applegate's shirt. It dangled horizontally toward Finn, as if it was avoiding the vortex. "Bind," he said, throwing his card at his own feet. Bound to the anchor, he bent forward at the waist and snatched the pendant. He yanked with all his might, but the chain wouldn't give.

With a crash, the glass around the star shattered. The clowns tumbled into the vortex, followed by Ravenguard. They circled in the darkness and disappeared, like spiders washed down the drain.

Only Applegate remained, dangling from the end of Hope's necklace.

Finn grunted with the effort of holding her, feeling like he might be torn in two by the force of the vortex.

"Finn, let it go," Hope yelled, tears streaming down her face.

Applegate struggled, her lips drawn back from her teeth. Arms flopping in the rushing wind, she snagged his hand and dug her nails into his skin. How could he be so stupid? With his free hand, he fumbled with his cards. "Unbind!" He tapped the pendant's chain. The triquetra came loose from Applegate's neck. Slowly, painfully, her nails tore from Finn's skin as her body slipped away, her scream echoing through the darkness.

Finn's upper body was yanked back into the anchor. He was bleeding, but he had Hope's triquetra.

The remainder of the glass shattered, and Finn raised his arms to shield his eyes from the light of the unconfined star. The brightness didn't last long. The star exploded. What a moment ago was blinding light turned to inky blackness. He lowered his arms.

"Finn?" Hope's voice trembled.

He rubbed his eyes and shook his head. Nothing made sense. He blinked again and again. Like a raft on a sea of darkness, the symbol, along with Hope, Finn, and Mike, who was still unconscious in the third circle, floated in space. Everything else was gone.

Mike shivered, pale and sweating. Finn was relieved he was alive but worried he might be in shock. His friend opened his eyes but did not move or speak.

"This can't be real. This isn't supposed to be how it works." Finn flipped through his cards, knowing there wasn't a spell in his deck that could fix this.

"How is it supposed to work?" Hope asked.

"Whoa!" Finn's stomach dropped. He blinked. When he opened his eyes again, they were back in the hive, the symbol back where it had been before. Their legs buckled with the impact of returning to reality. Finn was using his knee to help him regain his footing when Theodor's king of spades kicked out of the floor and returned to his hand.

"That's how it's supposed to work," he murmured. He glanced around the room, afraid to step out of the anchor.

Mike sat up and promptly vomited the contents of his stomach.

"It will be okay, Mike. Stay still," Hope said.

When nothing else moved, Finn looked around the empty hive and over at Hope. Tentatively, he gave her a smile, which turned into a laugh. "It worked. Hope, it worked!"

Hope's laugh echoed through the empty hive. "We did it! Oh Finn, we did it. It's over!" She raised her foot to step from the anchor when a column of purple smoke gave her pause.

Ms. D arrived, hands raised. "Don't move."

Hope returned her foot to her circle, smile fading.

"There is a presence in this room I haven't felt in a lifetime," Ms. D said. Her eyes widened as the floor began to quake and the bloody edges of the symbol boiled red.

"What's going on?" Finn asked.

"I don't know," Ms. D said. "But it's not good."

The boiling blood morphed into bugs, hundreds of insects—roaches, spiders, maggots—that swarmed to the center of the compass, the mass growing into a great bulbous sac of red and black that rippled and twisted. The bleached white of old bones bobbed in the mass, followed by muscle that attached itself to the bones within the churn of insects. Finn gagged.

At a grotesque pace, skin grew on muscle and hair sprouted from a barely fleshed out skull. By the time the infestation of insects returned from where they came, the thing at the center of the symbol looked like a human man, six feet tall, blond, blue-eyed, and wearing a brown military uniform with a swastika banded to the sleeve. Unnaturally straight, the man rose from the floor and cracked his neck. The entire room filled with the smell of sulfur.

Finn covered his nose and mouth with the inside of his arm. Mike tried to stand, but his eyes rolled back in his head. He stumbled out of his anchor and bumped into the hive wall, where he passed out again.

"Mike!" Finn yelled.

The blond man turned to face Ms. D. "Commandant," she breathed. She looked like she'd seen a ghost.

"Lucifer," Hope said in response, the name flying from her mouth like a curse. Her lips twisted in disgust.

The blond man rolled his neck, turning from Ms. D to face Hope. He chuckled wickedly. "The one and only." His voice was a hiss, a cup of water on a raging fire. He dug a finger inside his collar and loosened his top button.

"You can't be here. You're b-banned from Earth," Hope said. "Banished to Hell."

"Correction, I *was* banished, before *you* invited me back." He coupled his hands behind his back. "God gives you Eden; you eat the apple. God banishes me; you conjure me back. You human beings, you just can't live without me. What is it you people say? When one door closes, a window opens? You opened a window, Soulkeeper." The Devil's mouth twisted into a grin. "You must have missed me."

"I did not invite you," Hope said.

"Oh, but you did. Dark magic comes with a price, and you tempted Mr. Wager into dark magic."

She shook her head. "No."

"No? You didn't ask, no, demand that Finn use sorcery to save your life? He even reminded you that it wasn't allowed." Lucifer brushed a hand over his hair and smoothed his shirtsleeves. He stretched and rolled his joints as if still coming into himself.

"I... I didn't mean to!"

"And Eve was hungry when she ate the apple." He rubbed the corners of his eyes with his knuckles. "Boohoo. Awful how life forces us to make difficult choices, isn't it? Not only did you beg this boy to use sorcery, you offered me the blood sacrifice of his mentor."

"Theodor," Finn said.

"Theodor. Theodor who carried a trace of Hell in his blood from our previous meeting. It was his bright idea to build a spell that would return the demons to where they came. You knew they came from Hell, Soulkeeper. Who do you think built this place? The demons have been doing my work for centuries." He raised one foot and carefully stepped over the boundary of the symbol. "News flash: when you open a portal to Hell, it's arrogant to believe nothing from Hell will use it in the opposite direction. Theodor always struggled with pride, didn't he?"

"You cheated," Hope said. "What you did is against the rules!"

He narrowed his eyes and curled a lip. "Foolish child, evil doesn't play by the rules."

Ms. D groaned and grabbed her head.

"See how this works, Victoria? Sorcery has a price. When you take favors from the Devil, it costs you something. Fair is fair."

"What do you want?" Ms. D asked. "Take me. Leave these children alone."

Lucifer shook his head and charged Hope, grabbing her by the shoulders and shaking. "But it is these *children* I want," he spat. "You don't understand what this girl has done to me. Transformed a legion of fallen angels into useless puppets. Oh no. I will end the last Soulkeeper, and she'll have no one to blame but herself."

"Extinguish," Finn said, throwing a card at Lucifer's feet. The spell had no effect whatsoever.

Lucifer laughed wickedly and turned his full attention on Finn. "Did you mean for that to hurt me?"

"No. I meant for it to distract you. Hope!" Finn tossed the triquetra at her. She landed a foot on Lucifer's chest and flipped from his grasp, snatching the silver symbol from the air. She'd whispered into it before her feet hit the ground.

Gabriel formed between Hope and Lucifer, his wings stretching protectively.

"Vile creature. Be gone with you!" the angel bellowed at Lucifer, glowing as bright as the star that once burned behind him.

"You always were such a buzzkill, Gabriel. I hate to disappoint you, but I have a right to be here. She invited me. You can fight me, but don't expect backup." His eyes rolled toward the ceiling. "He won't help you here."

Gabriel turned his head to look at Hope behind him. "Run!"

❧ 48 ☙

BATTLE

Hope sprinted deeper into the hive as fast as her legs could carry her. Applegate and Ravenguard had come from this direction. There had to be a way out. But the faster she ran through the maze of honeycomb walls, the more she realized she was lost.

"Oh, you can run, you can even hide, but I will find you," the Devil said from somewhere in the dark labyrinth of wax behind her. "I can smell you. Humans have the most delicious smell when they're afraid. It's not quite as good as the smell of murder but better than greed. I love fear. I can tell from your scent you are filled with terror. Good. You should be."

The walls were different here, the tubes roughly hewn from the rock itself. As Hope searched for a place to hide, she soon discovered why. One of the wax-covered indentations still held a small twist of black. A baby demon, dead by the looks of it. She must be in their nursery. The thought made her shiver.

Heart pounding, she found the darkest corner she could and slid into one of the unused chambers in the wall, pulling her knees into her chest. She steadied her breathing and gripped her triquetra in her sweaty palm. Footsteps echoed through the section she was in but because of the tubes, she couldn't tell if they came from behind her or from inside the same room.

"I'm going to skin you alive," he said, his voice gritty and low. "I'm going to pry your eyeballs from your pretty little head. Maybe I'll wait for you to regenerate. Keep you as my plaything to torture over and over. I did that to your mother, you know, when she was mine."

He inhaled deeply through his nose. More footsteps. "Ah, that touched a nerve. Yes, I held Abigail in a cage for months while she was pregnant with you. I used to feed her maggots. Almost starved her to death. I tried to starve her, actually. I'm not sure how she survived. You shouldn't have. Not after what I put her through."

The footsteps grew closer, but all Hope could think about was her mother. She closed her eyes and pictured them, Abigail and Gideon, the photograph her adoptive parents had shown her of them. Abigail was beautiful and kind. Gideon was brave and loyal. Both Soulkeepers, tried and true.

"I remember the day your father, Gideon, died," Lucifer said smugly, his footsteps slowing. "One of my fallen angels broke him like a twig. I heard he suffered miserably. All to protect you. All to protect your whore of a mother. But she was as good as dead anyway." He laughed wickedly. "All for naught. How does it feel to carry the weight of your parents' deaths on your shoulders, Daughter of Angels?"

Hope gripped her triquetra tighter. It bit into the skin of her palm. She opened her hand and saw the impression the symbol left on her skin.

"When I'm done with you, you'll beg me to make you one of my own. You will gladly lead a new era of demons to stop the pain. Daughter of Angels... bah! You'll be Mother of Demons."

She gritted her teeth, anger steadying her trembling limbs. As she stared at the symbol of her calling in her palm, everything changed. Being the last Soulkeeper was no longer about a responsibility thrust upon her at birth. It was no longer a duty she must reluctantly fulfill. As she thought about her parents and Finn, all of the people she'd known and loved and the horrible fate they had endured and might still endure at Lucifer's hand, everything inside her coiled tighter, ready to strike.

She closed her hand around the triquetra, the disc of light forming with an audible hiss of energy. She was prepared to suffer and die to take Lucifer out. This was never about good vs. evil. This was personal. He'd made it personal.

Warmth spread across her heart and she opened herself up to it. With total humility, she accepted her accomplishments as well as her mistakes. She allowed the love of her friends and family to fill every corner of her being. She embraced her birthright.

Lucifer's footsteps stopped. His face appeared in the opening to her hiding place. "Gotcha."

With a warrior's cry that echoed from the tube, Hope punched forward, slicing his face with the ring of light from her triquetra. For a moment, his lower jaw dangled, his face cut almost in two by her assault. She did not let up. She slashed and sliced, cutting a deep gash in his thigh.

With a vile roar, a pulse of pure darkness blew her across the room. Her back slapped the far wall, forcing breath out of her body and extinguishing her disc of light. She landed on her feet and fired her power back up again.

Half of Lucifer's face dangled from his skull, a flap of lip torn from his teeth and one eye protruding unnaturally from its socket. "You surprise me. There's real faith in your weapon. More than usual for one so young. Too bad, it won't be enough."

He dug his fingers into his chest and tore, shedding the illusion of his broken human body. The real Lucifer stepped from the brown Nazi uniform, an enormous monster, at least eight feet tall, with horns and hooves and black eyes that promised Hope death and destruction. Massive leathery wings spread from his back, each with a hooked talon at the joint that rose above his shoulder.

Hope trembled, her bladder giving out. Urine trickled down her leg as tears formed in her eyes. She ignored it. Feet spreading into fighting stance, she grasped the triquetra with both hands, its razor-sharp arc of energy extending over her knuckles. Her chin lowered, and she looked at the Devil from under sunken eyebrows.

"Don't mess with me, child!" He circled one taloned hand over the other, conjuring a slick black darkness between his palms. "I've battled angels and nearly destroyed your God. What makes you think you have any hope of defeating me?"

"Because evil may not play by the rules," Hope said, "but good always wins."

He bared his teeth. "There's a first time for everything." Unleashing an unholy growl, he hurled the dark force in his hands in her direction.

A great umbrella of light spread from Hope's locked arms, colliding with the darkness in the space between them. Sparks flew. The walls shook. A chasm opened in the stone between their feet. She held her ground. When she thought the vibration from holding the triquetra would break the bones in her arms, she screamed. She screamed louder when her bones did break and the pain became almost unbearable. Tears streamed down her cheeks and blood poured from her nose, but she did not quit. She stood her ground, knowing the force of his power might grind her into dust.

All the while, she thought of her parents. They'd sacrificed themselves for her. Wasn't it the apple's way to not roll far from the tree? Now it was her turn to sacrifice herself. For the world. For her friends. For her family and the Soulkeepers who'd come before her.

The power flowing from the triquetra kicked back as if giving one final thrust before running dry. It threw her into the wall again, hard enough to rattle her teeth. She crumpled to the floor in a heap, her weapon returning to the confines of her pendant.

As she gasped and curled on her side, she saw that Lucifer was injured too, thrown against the opposite wall. The places she'd cut him were open again, his wounds unhealed, and his monstrous form looked smaller and darker than it had only moments ago. She'd hurt him. She was not the easy target he'd expected.

Still unable to breathe, she strained to lift her triquetra between them, propping her back against the wall and her shattered arms on her knees. The sharp light fired up again and glowed as strong as her resolve. She swallowed the lump that had formed in her throat.

With an awful hiss in her direction, Lucifer seethed, "This isn't over, Soulkeeper."

He twisted, melding into the shadows. He disappeared, leaving behind nothing but the smell of sulfur and a trail of black blood.

Hope lowered her hands and took a long, wheezing breath. "This may not be over, but neither am I."

✖ 49 ✖

AFTERMATH

When Hope was strong enough to hobble back to the room where she'd left the others, she collapsed as soon as she saw Gabriel. The angel caught her before she could hit the floor and she wept into his T-shirt. He smelled of citrus and vanilla, but it was his soft white wings that took her pain away. They enveloped her, infusing her with healing warmth. The pain that had racked her body moments before faded into nothing. Inside Gabriel's parental embrace, she could almost forget the people she'd failed, the truth that she'd played a part in opening a portal to Hell and giving the Devil a foothold into their world.

"Is he gone?" he whispered in her ear.

"Yes. I think so. I… injured him. I mean, he seemed injured. He poofed out of here."

Gabriel hugged her to his chest as if she were a child, a sigh of relief leaving his parted lips. "If I know Lucifer, he'll take time to regroup. He won't want to risk what he's gained. Coming back like he did… there will be consequences. His power is not as strong here as it was in Hell."

Hope met his gaze. "I didn't mean to bring him back. I'm sorry. I'm so sorry."

"Lucifer laid this trap before you were born, Hope. These demons, this school… it has been here for ages. The scrolls upstairs in the headmistress's office, the genealogy charts… Do you know why they exist?"

She shook her head.

"They were targeting Soulkeepers. By rounding up descendants of known Soulkeepers, Lucifer intended to replace people with the potential to become Soulkeepers before they could come of age. He started this place well before he lost the challenge that confined him to Hell, and it has continued ever since."

"I should have known. I should have predicted this."

"He created this place in a way that ensured you couldn't. It's as protected and isolated as Eden. There's no way you could have discovered its truth without coming here."

A hand gripped her shoulder and Gabriel's wings opened. "It wasn't your fault, Hope. It was mine." Ms. D placed a hand over her heart. "Theodor and I were part of the group who started this school under the direction of the commandant a lifetime ago. We had no idea we were doing the Devil's work. I didn't want to know. I wanted to take my art to new heights. Theodor wanted his magic to be real. We both wanted to escape the war. Revelations was our Shangri-La. We knew it wasn't natural what was happening here. We just didn't want to admit the source of our greatest joy could be something evil. And after the war was over, we built this place into something more. We turned it into a commercial success because we refused to live any other life."

"There's a reason we call Lucifer the lord of illusions, Victoria," Gabriel said. "You can't blame yourself for doing the thing he forced you to do."

"No, but I can blame myself for believing the lie, for perpetuating *this*, all these years."

Sobs came from the corner of the room. Finn was kneeling on

the floor near the wall, his hands sifting through a pile of cards. Hope wondered how the cards were still there, why they hadn't been sucked into the void with Theodor. Perhaps they'd been kicked out the way the king of spades had been.

"He's gone," Finn said.

"Theodor knew the risks," Ms. D said, her own voice catching with the loss. "He is a true hero, despite what Lucifer would have you believe. He would have never used a spell to open a portal to Hell if he understood the consequences." She wiped away a stray tear.

Mike stirred in the corner of the room, groaning and clutching his head.

"Are you okay?" Hope asked. She was prepared to heal him again, even in her weakened state, and broke from Gabriel's arms to go to Mike's side.

"Were you kicked in the head?" Mike snapped, pulling away from her. "I am definitely not okay." He shivered although the room wasn't cold. In fact, the fragments of the star that festered around what remained of the hive had raised the temperature to the point of discomfort. "I just want to go home."

"The buses are loaded," Ms. D said softly. "All of our guests had a wonderful time and are currently resting peacefully, waiting for their return trip home."

"You drugged them." Hope raised one eyebrow.

"A simple, temporary method to get them through the portal, but it *is* time to go. Gather your things, Michael. I'll take you home." She helped Mike to his feet. Finn gathered Theodor's cards and allowed Ms. D to lead him from the hive.

"Before I go," Gabriel said to Hope, "congratulations on completing your first mission. You solved the mystery of the lost souls and ended a century of demon terror. You are a worthy Soulkeeper, Hope. I am humbled in your presence." He bowed formally.

Hope glanced at Gabriel, placing her hand over the triquetra at the base of her throat. "Why do I think this isn't goodbye?"

"Because it's not. Lucifer is back. He's freed from Hell. We'll need to put him back where he belongs."

"So my life, it won't go back to normal?"

"What's normal?" he answered through tight lips.

"What will I need to do?"

"May I suggest you visit the Immortals and ask for help?"

She licked her lips and nodded. "Okay, Gabriel. You win. I will. I promise." She needed to become much better at being a Healer and the last Soulkeeper. Humanity was counting on her. And only she could clean up the mess she'd made.

❧ 50 ❧

HOME

H ours later, Finn helped his groggy father through the front door of their house, half carrying him to the couch. He eased his dad onto the cushions and removed his dress shoes.

"Thanks. I don't know what's wrong with me. I can't keep my eyes open."

"It's okay," Finn said. "It's late."

His father nodded and closed his eyes again. Finn spread the tartan plaid blanket they kept in a chest in the corner of the room over his father. When he tried to pull away, to retreat to his room, his dad caught his wrist, rousing once more. "You were really something tonight, Finn. A star. A superhero. It looked like you could actually fly." His father's sleepy eyes widened slightly.

Finn dug his toes into the carpet. "Smoke and mirrors," he said. "It was a lot of hard work, but I got good at it after a while."

"No kidding. You look like they pumped you full of steroids." His dad squeezed his bicep.

"Dad..." Finn shook his head and laughed.

"Seriously, son. All I ever wanted was for you to find your passion. I wanted you to plan what you needed to do to get what you wanted from life and then do it, even if it was hard. I know this semester wasn't easy, but you did it. You made it through. No one can ever take that away from you."

Finn thought about his months at Revelations and nodded his head. His eyes stung with unshed tears. He'd run the race, for whatever good and bad came of it. He hadn't quit. He'd survived. And he'd been part of something big, something important.

"You were right about what you said. It did change me. More than I thought it would. I think... I think I want to try to be good at something, like work harder in school and, you know, make my life count."

His father sat up, wrapping his big hands around Finn's shoulders. "I am so proud of you, Finn. I wish your mother were here to see the man you've become."

Without hesitation, Finn threw his arms around his father's neck and squeezed. He was home, finally home.

૭⊱૭

FINN SAT CROSS-LEGGED ON THE FLOOR NEXT TO HIS BED, TRYING not to stare at Wyatt, whose round, cocoa-colored cheeks and bright white smile were the most beautiful thing he'd seen in a long time. Wyatt, of all his friends, hadn't been exposed to the toxic environment of Revelations. He didn't carry the residue he and others failed to wash off, no matter how much scrubbing or how many hot showers. Finn had been exposed to evil. It made him misty with happiness that Wyatt had not.

"What was that school like, anyway?" Wyatt asked innocently. They were playing Space Sniper, Wyatt sitting within a window-shaped square of unappreciated sunshine.

"Hard. Painful sometimes. There were a ton of physical challenges, sometimes mental ones. But, I don't know, it grew on you after a while."

"Mike and Jay won't even talk about it. Mike acts like he's

having a fit or something and tells me to shut up. Jayden acts like it was one big joke."

"Mike had it the worst."

"Why? A teacher there have it in for him or something?" Wyatt frowned.

"Something like that."

"You must be glad to be home." Wyatt banged on his controller as a squadron of enemy fighters attacked.

Finn missed a shot and his character got hit in the head by a drone and died. He pressed the pause button.

"Would you like to play again, Finn?" HORU asked, her cat ears twitching.

"Not right now."

"It's good to have you home." She wagged her hologram tail.

"Thanks, HORU. I'm going to talk to Wyatt now." She nodded and powered herself down.

He removed his headset and turned toward Wyatt. "Some days at Revelations seemed like torture."

Wyatt nodded. "No wonder Mike doesn't want to talk about it."

Finn picked at the side of his nail. "But the weird thing is, at times I miss it."

His friend's face sobered. "Why?"

"Everything was simpler. I woke up every day knowing exactly what I had to do. I didn't have to deal with grades or sitting on the bench every game. I was good at my act. Really good." He thought of Wendy, but he didn't mention her. He didn't see the point.

"You gained like a hundred pounds of muscle in that place. One thing's for sure, no one is going to mess with you anymore."

"If you worked out all day for four months and ate the crappy food they made for us, you'd look like this too."

"No, thanks." Wyatt laughed. "But you say you liked it?"

He nodded. "I guess I did. Some of it. Weird, huh?"

The doorbell rang, interrupting them. A muffled sound came

through the floor below, and his father yelled up the stairs for Finn.

"Go ahead and play without me. I'll be right back," he said to Wyatt.

Wyatt put his headset back on and started talking to HORU. Finn jogged down the steps, wondering if Mike and Jay had decided to come over after all.

"Your friend from school is here to see you," his dad said. He pointed toward the foyer and disappeared in the direction of his office. Finn rounded the corner expecting to see Mike or Jayden. Instead, Hope Laudner stood awkwardly near the front door.

"Hope?" He looked at her in confusion. "What are you doing here?"

Her auburn ponytail swung as she tipped her head and smiled. "Can't an old friend pop by for a visit?"

He pulled her into a quick hug. "You popped by from Illinois for a visit? You live, like, seven hundred miles away. Did you drive here by yourself?"

"No. I haven't even had a chance to get my license yet." She tapped the top of her shoe behind the heel of her opposite foot. "My parents brought me. Official business."

"Official business deserves a drink. Come on." He led her into the kitchen and sat her down at the table. "Coke? Lemonade?"

"Ice water would be great."

"So what's this official business?" He started filling a glass from the fridge door.

"How would you feel about helping me with that problem we dug up at Revelations?"

He dropped the glass. It didn't break, but the water spilled in front of the fridge. Quickly, he grabbed a kitchen towel and set the half-full glass on the table between them while he mopped up the spill.

"I thought you and your, um, angel would have handled that by now."

She snorted. "You underestimate the Devil. I haven't been able to find him, let alone figure out how to stop whatever he's up to. Lucifer is a lot like a termite colony: he does the most damage when you don't know he's there. If he were walking down Main Street, horns blazing, he'd be a lot easier to deal with. No. First, we'll have to flush him and his followers out, then find a way to vanquish him again."

"Sounds like you've got your work cut out for you."

"That's just it. I do this thing now where I ask for help when I need it. I need it, Finn."

"What are you saying?"

"I want to reinstate the Soulkeepers. I told you about them. People charged with protecting human souls."

"I thought you were the last one."

"I am. Was. It's complicated. We upset the balance of things. The natural law requires balance between light and darkness, and darkness just experienced a huge victory. Which means the Big Good is taking my handcuffs off."

"But didn't you say that all the Soulkeepers had an inherited gene? They were predestined or something?"

"Yes. And you have it."

He shook his head. "No, I don't."

"Your great-grandmother Mimi's trunk was my first clue. Gabriel did a little research. She was part of a group of Soulkeepers who fought the Nazis during World War II. The Nazi regime was fueled by dark magic, demon magic. You are a descendant of a Soulkeeper, Finn. It's why you were able to adapt so quickly to the mutation of Revelations Island. It's why you were invited to Revelations Island in the first place."

"I don't understand."

"Ravenguard and Applegate were targeting Soulkeeper potentials. The charts in the headmistress's office contained your genealogic history. They invited you to Revelations to kill you. It's why Mike was so slow to change. He never had the gene. He was only invited because of you."

Finn felt off balance. "Ravenguard said he didn't have the potential, but I refused to go if they didn't take him too."

She nodded. "Lucifer started the school during WWII, when he still had access to Earth and Soulkeepers were still a real threat. They've been running on autopilot ever since. They didn't care if Mike died or not as long as you did too."

"Nice thought." Finn leaned against the counter, throwing the wet towel into the sink. "I thought you said that you didn't change on the island. *Couldn't change* were your exact words."

"I'm different. A Soulkeeper since birth, not a potential. If you'd already come into your power, you wouldn't have had the same results."

Finn took a long drink from the glass he'd poured for Hope. "We're lucky to be alive."

"I need your help, Finn. I can't do this alone."

"You want me to help you bring down the Devil?" He scoffed.

"You and the others. Anyone who still has abilities. Even Mike, if he's willing to help."

"I start at Beaverton in the fall."

Hope brushed her eyebrow with her knuckle. "Ms. D has promised to reopen the school and make the island safe for us. A place to train."

"You want me to come back to Revelations?"

"I know there are a lot of details to work out. We're considering a weekend-only program. We'll have to convince your father. All I need from you today is a yes."

Her stare was so intense it made him squirm. Did he want this? Lucifer was terrifying. He'd be signing up for something unbelievable, to be part of a select group of spiritual heroes. God and angels, the Devil and demons. Other dimensions. It sounded as ridiculous as a boy who could fly. He turned his back to her, resting his palms on the edge of the sink and looking out the window over the manor's front lawn.

"Can you still do it?" Hope asked softly.

He rose several inches off the floor, his fingertips leaving the counter. Hovering, he glanced at her over his shoulder, then lowered to the tile floor again. "The magic too, for what it's worth. I stay away from the dark cards though."

"Do more than stay away from them. Destroy them. Lucifer can use dark magic to track you."

Finn shrugged. "My cards are locked away, along with Theodor's."

"Are you curious about Wendy? She's on my list too. Something tells me she'd be apt to say yes if you did."

"That's playing dirty." He approached the table and looked her in the eye. "This is my life we're talking about."

Her smile spread slowly. "A life you said you wanted to be more significant. What could be more significant than this? You could be instrumental in saving the world."

"Have you asked anyone else yet?"

"I'm starting with you. You know damn well that if you say yes, others will too. They look up to you."

"Finn Wager, world-saver. It has a certain ring to it."

"Finn Wager, Soulkeeper."

"Is there a uniform?"

"No capes, I promise."

"I could totally pull off a cape. It's the leotard I'm not crazy about."

He met her eyes and took a long, deep breath.

"I need you, Finn. Please. We started this together. Let's finish it. You'll be a part of something bigger than any of us. An ancient society sworn to protect the innocent. You'll be a Soulkeeper like your great-grandmother."

The corner of his mouth pulled up. "You promise it won't be boring?"

"I promise."

He sighed and offered his hand. "When opportunity knocks…"

Relief softened her shoulders and she pumped his arm. "You're in?"

"I knew from the first day I met you at Revelations you were into me. Just couldn't let me walk out of your life, could you?"

"Shut up, or I'll kick your ass and tell Wendy you wet the bed."

"Ouch."

She sighed deeply. "Seriously, I need a firm yes or no."

A big part of Finn wanted to say no, but another part of him was sure he'd hate himself if he did. "Yes, I'll help you."

She tugged his arm and pulled him into a hug. "Thank you. Thank you. Thank you." Her voice cracked.

He rubbed her back. "It's going to be okay."

She pulled back and laughed as she headed for the door. "Honestly? Probably not. But I promise, Finn, it *will* be worth it."

☙❧

Thank you for reading. If you loved **Wager's Price**, please leave a review. Reviews are gold to authors and are always appreciated. Visit www.gpching.com to learn about G.P.'s other books and sign up for her newsletter to be notified of new releases, including Hope's Promise, Soulkeepers Reborn, Book 2.

ABOUT THE AUTHOR

G.P. Ching is a USA Today bestselling author of science fiction and fantasy novels for young adults and not-so-young adults. She bakes wicked cookies, is commonly believed to be raised by wolves, and thinks both the ocean and the North Woods hold magical healing powers. G.P.'s idea of the perfect day involves several cups of coffee and a heavy dose of nature. She splits her time between central Illinois and Hilton Head Island with her husband, two children, and a Brittany spaniel named Jack, who is always ready for the next adventure.

Sign up for G.P.'s newsletter!

- Never miss a new release
- Get access to exclusive content
- Select offers and giveaways

www.gpching.com
genevieve@gpching.com

ACKNOWLEDGMENTS

The first time I wrote Wager's Price, I was going through a hard time personally. A death of a young family member was followed almost immediately by a cancer scare and then a diagnosis of leukemia in another. At the same time, I was sending my oldest off to college with all that entails.

Although I was happy with Wager's Price when I published it the first time, people close to me could tell I was going through a hard time when I wrote it. And when I read it again, I could hear the difference. Without my knowledge or consent, life had slipped into my writer's voice. So I waited, and as my family member recovered, so did I. I dealt with the demons under my bed so that I could deal with the demons under the school. And now Wager's Price is ready and Hope's Promise is well underway.

Thank you to my tribe, authors Tara Cromer, Suzan Tisdale, and Laurie Larsen, for giving me the courage to rewrite this story and tell it as I'd always intended.

Thank you to editor Nicki Busch, who understands my voice and my themes and was able to give this work her attention. Your encouragement was an uplifting force in my journey.

And finally, thank you to Amy Conley and Debbie Eyre for beta reading Wager's Price. Your enthusiasm for the story gave me the confidence to set it free on the world again.

THE SOULKEEPERS

The Soulkeepers Book 1

Please enjoy this excerpt of the first book in G.P. Ching's best-selling Soulkeepers Series, The Soulkeepers.

THE BOY WHO DIED

Death lived up to Jacob's expectations.

The day he died was sunny, as it was most days on the island of Oahu where he lived. Only a few miles away, bikini-clad tourists stretched out on the sand of Waikiki beach. While they toasted themselves golden brown, Jacob lay on a steel surgical table, broken and bleeding. He'd heard that when a person died they saw a tunnel that ended in a bright light. If the person moved toward the light, God or some already deceased loved one like a great-grandmother would meet them on the other side. Jacob didn't believe it. He'd accepted that everything would end in black nothingness and, for him, it did. What he didn't expect was that the end was just the beginning.

The light returned. His eyes fluttered open against bright white and a face emerged from the radiance, materializing from the void. A rumbling voice called him by name. "Jacob. Jacob, can you hear me?" Behind the voice was the *clink-clank* of metal hitting metal and a smell like a copper penny soaked in Clorox.

"I think he's coming 'round," the voice said from behind a green surgical mask. Soulful brown eyes came into focus. Spikes of pain stabbed through Jacob's head and chest and he realized the man in scrubs was shaking him. He wanted to tell the man to stop, but a plastic dome pressed over his face. As he fought against the plastic, the tubes connected to his arm slapped against the metal pole near the gurney.

"Relax, my man," the face said, pressing Jacob's arms to his sides. "The mask has to stay on. It's oxygen and you need it."

In his confused state, Jacob couldn't understand who the green man was. All he knew was pressure and pain, like he'd been torn apart and put back together.

"Jacob, take a deep breath. Come on, kid, breathe."

Of its own volition, the air went in. The air went out. The pain made the air rattle in his mouth.

"That's it. A few more like that, Jacob. Slow and deep. Can you understand me?" the green man asked.

"Yes," Jacob tried to say, but his voice was nothing but a rough whisper, muffled by the oxygen mask.

"Are you in pain?"

He tried to say yes again but the word dissolved in his throat. He nodded slightly, too, in case the green man hadn't heard.

"Okay, just relax. I'm going to give you some morphine." The green man held up a syringe with some clear liquid in it, and then locked it onto the tube in Jacob's arm. He pressed the plunger and Jacob felt a cold ribbon twist into his vein. The pain ebbed. The light dimmed. On the ceiling there were tiles, foam squares in a steel grid that he guessed hid the wires and pipes up there. He counted the squares as he floated away, thinking of the wires and pipes under his own skin carrying the green man's juice to all his fingers and toes.

When the darkness swallowed him again, all the thinking his exhausted, numbed-out, maybe-damaged brain could produce was a vague feeling that he'd forgotten something. The missing thought was an irritation at the back of his skull. The more he concentrated on it, the more the memory slipped from his grasp, an oily shoelace through languid fingers.

2

THE UNCLE WHO WASN'T

The sound of footsteps woke Jacob in his hospital bed. He was annoyed that the nurses kept waking him up. All he wanted to do was sleep, but as it turned out hospitals were not a good place to rest.

Without opening his eyes, he said, "I'm not hungry and I don't need another pain pill."

A gruff voice answered him from the side of the bed. "That's good because I don't have either of those things."

Jacob's lids flipped open. A stranger sat in the uncomfortable-looking chair next to his hospital bed, the pads of his fingers pressed together under his chin.

"Who are you?" Jacob asked.

"I'm your Uncle John. John Laudner," the man said. He leaned forward and extended a calloused palm.

Jacob did not take the man's hand. "You've made a mistake. I don't have an uncle and my last name isn't Laudner. It's Lau."

The man pursed his lips, his green eyes shifting to the hospital floor. He sat back in his chair, opening his mouth as if to say something and then closing it again. At last he lowered his hands, linking them at his waist. "There's no easy way to tell you this,

Jacob. I am your uncle. I am the brother of Charles Lau, formerly known as Charlie Laudner. Your father changed his name before you were born."

Jacob licked his parched lips and reached for the cup of water the nurse had left him. He sucked greedily on the straw before speaking. "I've never even heard of you."

"It's a long story. You lived far away. After your father died, well, it never seemed like the right time to introduce myself."

"So why are you here now?"

"Jacob, do you remember anything about the accident?"

Jacob closed his eyes. The truth was, his brain did have an explanation for what had happened, but it was ludicrous. The memory was so far-fetched he could only believe his imagination had stitched it together to fill in the gaps. "No. I told the doctors, the last thing I remember was fighting with my mom that morning in our apartment. I don't even remember getting into the car with her."

"She's missing, Jacob."

"Missing?" he said, sitting up in bed despite the pain. "But she must've been in the car with me. How could they have rescued me and not her?"

"You were inside the car when they found it. She wasn't."

"But that doesn't make any sense."

"Your blood was on the inside of the car, Jacob. Hers was on the outside."

She'd had a gun. She'd been standing next to the door. He shook his head, ignoring the thought. It was a false memory, brought on by emotional and physical trauma. What had the doctor called it? Auditory and visual hallucinations: the brain's way of making sense of the damage it incurred when his skull collided with the windshield.

"How is that possible?"

"They think, maybe, you were driving."

"I don't have a driver's license."

John stood up and approached the bed. He unsnapped the arm of the hospital gown Jacob was wearing, pulling it down slightly. Then he tipped up the hideaway mirror on the overbed table. The bruise that arced across Jacob's chest looked like the top half of a large circle ... or a steering wheel. He traced the edge with his finger, a rainbow of purple-hued skin. A chill ran up his spine.

"Did I hit her?"

John returned the thin fabric to its place. "The police don't think so, Jacob. Her blood was on the passenger side door, not the hood of the car. You were found in a heavily wooded area of Manoa Falls. It's only a few miles from your apartment. They think, after the accident, your mom got out of the car to get help."

You'd followed her there. You'd had a fight and you wanted to apologize.

"I don't remember," Jacob said, but a more truthful answer would have been that the memory he had couldn't be real. It was nonsense.

"It's normal that you don't. The doc says people often block out extreme circumstances. It's your brain's way of protecting you from reliving the trauma."

"And then what? Where did she go?"

John's face contorted. His voice strained with emotion when he answered. "There have been abductions in the area. Nine women went missing in the last year; six were found dead. Murdered. There were signs of a struggle where they found you."

Jacob's blood froze in his veins. "Are you saying, my mom might have been abducted, or worse, killed?"

"They don't know for sure. I'm sorry, Jacob."

A tear escaped down his cheek and he wiped it away with his bare hand. It had been a long time since he'd allowed himself to cry. He wasn't about to start now. He'd survived by following two very important rules: don't feel anything and don't expect anything from anyone. To distract himself, he concentrated on the specifics of what happened. Why in the world would he have driven his mother's car?

The creature was coming for you. Your mom tried to fight it. He ignored the rogue thought. "What did I hit, anyway?"

John repositioned himself in his chair and folded his arms across his chest. "Nobody knows, Jacob. The front of the car is damaged like you hit a tree or something but they found the Toyota in the middle of the road. There wasn't anything in front of the car. They were hoping you could remember because no one has any idea what could've happened. They thought maybe the damage occurred earlier and then you drove to the scene ... but the car isn't operational and your wounds were fresh when they found you. "

"What happens now? Are they going to search for her?"

"Yes. There's already a group combing through Manoa Falls."

"I want to help." Only the irritating tug of Jacob's IV kept him from bounding out of bed.

"There's nothing you can do, Jacob. The doctor says you'll be in here for another week and then..."

"And then what?"

"The social worker says you need to come home with me."

"With you? I don't even know you."

"I am your nearest kin."

"Where do you even live?"

"Paris."

"Paris ... France?"

"No, a different Paris. Paris, Illinois. You have an Aunt Carolyn and a cousin, Katrina. They're waiting for us at home."

Home. The word annoyed Jacob. When he heard the word home, he thought of his apartment and the house he'd lived in before his dad died. He thought of how the smell of his favorite adobo chicken would fill the kitchen when his mom made it. He saw the faces of his mother and his father, bound to one another in some almost magical way. Home meant a sanctuary, as common and taken for granted as the sun rising in the morning. Wherever John was taking Jacob, it sure as hell wasn't home.

A wave of exhaustion overcame him. He took a deep breath and let it out slowly. "Do I have a choice about this?" he croaked.

There was a long stretch of silence. "No," the man said. The word was a guillotine.

It's for the best. You're not safe here.

Jacob closed his eyes. If he squeezed them shut tight enough, maybe his supposed uncle and the rest of the world would go away. A numb calm crept over him as he gave himself over to the future, unable to fight what would be, unable to care anymore. It crossed his mind that another person might pray in a situation like this, but Jacob didn't. Who would he pray to? If there was one thing his fifteen years of life had taught him, it was that there was nothing above him but sky. To believe in God would mean believing that He had allowed the tragedy that was Jacob's life in the first place. He didn't want to know a God who made a war then killed off people's fathers in it. No, Jacob was sure he was alone in this. Alone with an uncle he'd never even met.

⚜

THANK YOU FOR READING THIS EXCERPT OF THE SOULKEEPERS. Continue the story by downloading The Soulkeepers, Book 1 at the retailer of your choice. Or visit www.gpching.com to learn more.

Made in the USA
Lexington, KY
14 September 2018